Trial by Tournament: Champion of Valor
Book 2

Eric Balch

Copyright © 2022 Eric Balch
All rights reserved.

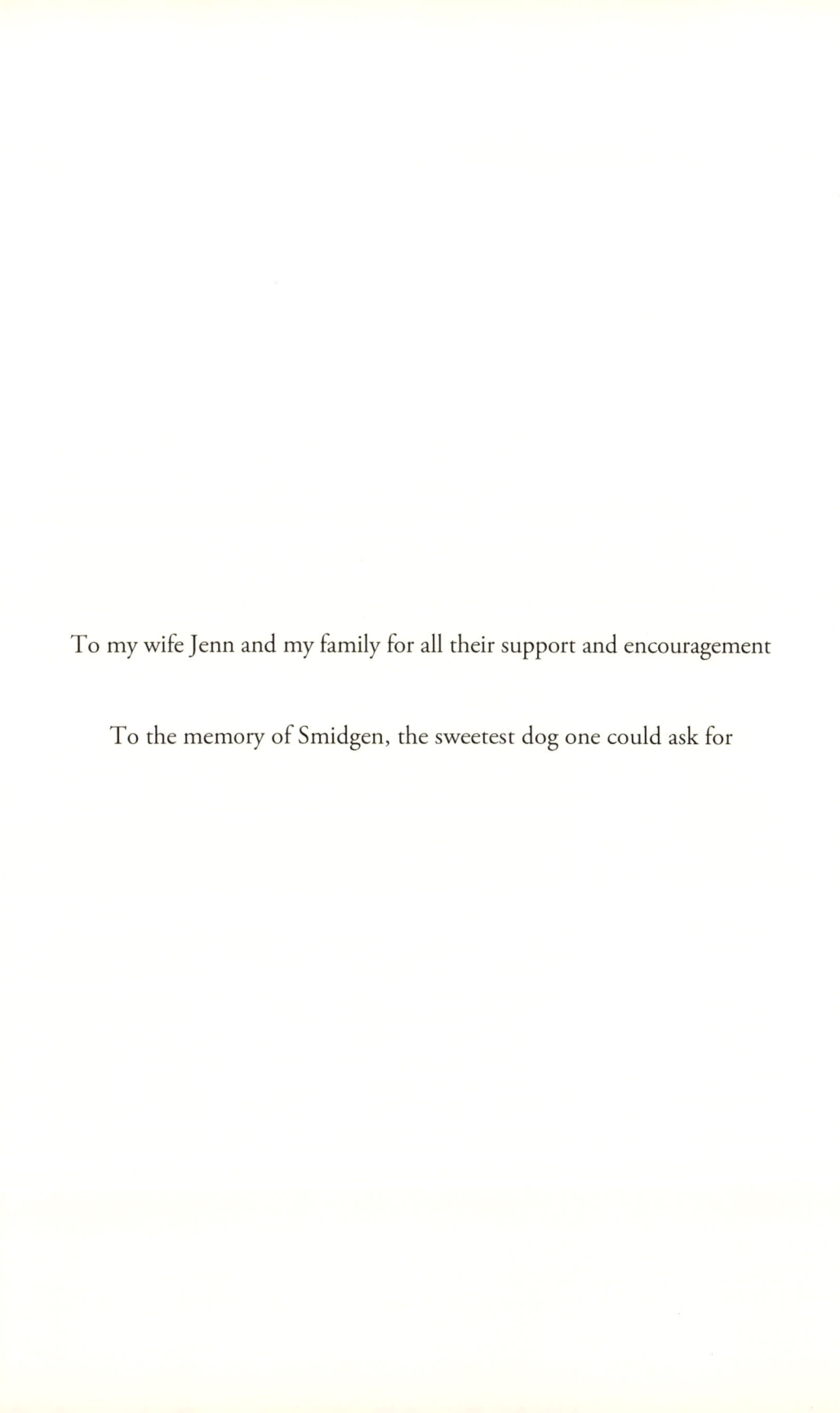

To my wife Jenn and my family for all their support and encouragement

To the memory of Smidgen, the sweetest dog one could ask for

Chapter 1

Pelagius sits upon the edge of his bed, deep in thought as he listens to the sound of pouring rain outside. A blast of thunder startles him from his stupor and draws his attention to the hushed activity in the room. Looking around, he sees Alithyra and Ralkgek standing over an unconscious Thakszut.

Kevnan sits in a chair nearby, his eyes fixed on the motionless fiendling. Iriemorel lies on his bed and appears to still be asleep at first glance, but on closer inspection, Pelagius can see he is awake. Aldtaw sleeps soundly; loud snoring vibrates the flaps around his jowls.

Reaching for the cane that Shukrat supplied for him, Pelagius slowly rises from his bed and hobbles to the others. "Good morning. How is everyone feeling?"

The others give him an incredulous look. Kevnan gestures to Alithyra's missing arm and the sewn-up wounds on his chest.

"Sorry I asked. Where's Shukrat?"

Ralkgek rolls his sightless eyes and wraps a strip of cloth around them. "I don't know how you slept through the bustle when the rest of us woke up. Shukrat left a few hours ago. He said that he was heading to the next village to acquire the services of one of their priests."

Alithyra glances at the door. "I hope he gets back soon." She turns her attention back to Thakszut and emits a dog-like whine. "Thakszut is fading fast."

As Pelagius limps to the fiendling's bed, Thakszut seemingly awakens. Although Thakszut's eyes glance around, his blank, glazed expression hints that he isn't fully conscious. His breathing becomes heavily labored.

"What are we going to do?" asks Alithyra.

Pelagius opens his mouth to say something when a portal manifests in the middle of the room. Shukrat steps through, followed by a male cecropsan in fiery red robes with the symbol of a burning hammer hovering over an anvil on his chest. Shukrat gestures to the priest. "Everyone, this is Serpensic, priest of the temple of Ferrak, God of Fire and the Forge."

"I thought you said the temples were warded against transportation magic," says Pelagius.

Shukrat waves in the direction of the portal, closing it. "They are, but the wards only prevent entering via transportation magic, not against leaving."

Serpensic slides forward. "A pleasure. Shukrat has already briefed me on the situation. I shall get started right away."

"Quickly," says Pelagius.

Serpensic approaches Thakszut first. He places a hand on the wounded fiendling and mutters a brief prayer. Serpensic's hand flares as though surrounded by fire and he reaches for Thakszut. Before Serpensic makes contact, Thakszut emits a choked breath and slowly exhales as his eyes darken. Serpensic stops, pulling his hand back as the energy dissipates, and slowly turns to the others. He places a finger to Thakzut's throat.

"I'm sorry," says Serpensic sorrowfully. "I am too late to save him."

Tears form in Alithyra's eyes, and she emits a dog-like whimper. "No. He can't be completely gone yet."

"Can't you heal his wounds and restart his heart?" asks Kevnan.

Serpensic shakes his head. "Resurrection is beyond me."

"I think he meant resuscitation rather than resurrection," says Pelagius.

Serpensic turns to Pelagius, lifts a finger as he opens his mouth to respond, but stops before he says anything. He raises his eyebrows and ponders the idea. "That is a possibility. The soul lingers for a few minutes after the heart stops, and there is a technique I learned from a priest of Agaila that I have witnessed revive the recently dead. It is not always effective. Even if healed, it will not work if the injuries that killed him were severe enough."

"Please try," says Pelagius.

"Very well." Serpensic places his hand on Thakszut and resumes his entreaty, praying until yellowish-red energy, flickering like fire, surrounds his body. The energy flows down his arm and engulfs Thakszut, glowing for several minutes before fading away.

Serpensic turns to the others. "Now this may seem a bit strange, but bear with me." Serpensic returns his attention to Thakszut, removes the brace from the fiendling's neck, and tilts his head back slightly. He opens Thakszut's mouth, inhales, presses his mouth against Thakszut's, and breathes air into his lungs.

He repeats the process a few times. He gently places his fingers over Thakszut's chest and pushes down. After a few presses, he sets his ear on Thakszut's chest. Hearing nothing, he repeats the entire process twice. Seeing no results, he begins a brief prayer. A small amount of electricity crackles at his fingertips.

Noticing the others have gathered around him, Serpensic waves them away. "Everybody, stand back for this. Anybody touching him or standing too close could be harmed."

Serpensic places his fingers over Thakszut's heart and discharges the electricity. He causes Thakszut's body to jolt, but without results. He tries again; still nothing. He prays once more, increasing the power in his fingertips. He again presses his fingers to Thakszut's chest and discharges the power. The electric jolt causes Thakszut's body to practically jump off the bed. Thakszut inhales deeply and coughs before falling unconscious.

Pelagius approaches and bends down to check on Thakszut. He gently shakes the fiendling but gets no response. Pelagius gives Serpensic a concerned glance. "Is he all right?"

Serpensic places his hand on Thakszut's chest and concentrates. "He is in no danger of dying, but he has fallen into a deep slumber. Some call it a false death. I do not know if he can or will wake from it, and none of my powers can bring him out."

Serpensic goes around to the others and repeats the healing process, saving Iriemorel for last. He approaches Alithyra and looks her over. "I can heal your wounds, but I'm afraid that I cannot replace your arm."

"Isn't regeneration a priestly ability?" asks Alithyra.

"Yes," says Serpensic. "However, it is an advanced ability far beyond the scope of normal healing. Only a greater priest or higher can safely regenerate a lost limb."

"I understand," says Alithyra.

"If you have it with you, I can reattach it as part of the healing process," says Serpensic.

Alithyra blushes. "I'm afraid I left it where it fell. We were in a bit of a hurry to leave."

"I see," says Serpensic. "Well, at the very least, I can still heal you."

Serpensic heals Alithyra's wounds and moves on to Iriemorel. As he places his hands on the dwarf's chest, he stops.

"What's wrong?" asks Pelagius.

"It would seem that today is just not a good day for either of us," says Serpensic. "Like the fiendling, I will not be able to heal this one completely."

"What do you mean?" asks Alithyra. "Are we too late to save him too?"

Serpensic shakes his head. "No, I can heal his injuries, but the damage is far more extensive than can be repaired by someone of my power. His spine has been completely shattered in five places. The dwarf has suffered semi-death of the body. Since the injury is similar, Thakszut has likely entered such a state too."

A shocked silence falls over the room.

"You can't heal his spine?" asks Kevnan.

"The spine I can fix," says Serpensic. "That's not the problem."

"What is the problem?" says Pelagius.

"Reversing semi-death is similar in practice to resurrection, and only the Archpriest can raise the dead without consequences," says Serpensic. "For all other priests, it is possible to perform a resurrection, but at the cost of one's own life. At my current power, I can reverse his paralysis, but I would suffer from mobility loss and lack of feeling in my body myself. That is not a price that I am willing to pay. I'm sorry."

Pelagius groans in frustration. "I should have known that would be the case. Will you at least heal his injuries?"

"Of course," says Serpensic. "Upon sensing the severity of his injuries, I just thought it best to inform you as to what I could and couldn't do."

Serpensic turns back to Iriemorel and performs the healing ritual, mending the broken and shattered bones in his body. He turns to Shukrat. "It is done. I must now take my leave."

Shukrat hands him a small bag of coins and opens a portal. "This will put you right outside the village."

"Thank you," says Serpensic. "Good day, my friends."

Serpensic steps through and the portal closes behind him.

Iriemorel emits a heavy sigh. "So that's it, then. My warrior days are behind me."

Pelagius lowers his head, then glances at Shukrat. "There is nothing we can do? Nobody who can help?"

Shukrat thinks for a moment. "There is one who may be willing: Grimadert the Healing Blade."

Pelagius raises an eyebrow. "Healing Blade? That sounds like a sorcerer's title."

Alithyra shudders. Her hair stands on end. "And an ominous one at that. How does one heal with a blade?"

Shukrat sits in a nearby chair. "He is a sorcerer, so he is no magical healer. However, he is also an apothecary, an herbalist, and an alchemist, and is quite skilled in mundane medicine."

Pelagius moves toward Shukrat. "And he would be willing to help?"

"Perhaps," says Shukrat. "For the right price. He does not usually offer his services for free."

"Any price would be worth restoring Iriemorel to health," says Pelagius. "Please, send for him."

Shukrat stands. "Very well. I have not been to his fortress, so I will send him a message rather than attempt magical transport." Shukrat sits at a desk and unrolls a piece of blank parchment. Dipping a quill in an ink bottle, he then writes a message. Upon completion, he rolls the parchment into a scroll, securing it with a ribbon. He lights a red candle and allows the wax to drip on the scroll's crease. He retrieves a small ring from a drawer in his desk and presses it into the cooling wax, leaving an insignia when removed. He walks over to an open window and emits a loud whistle.

A large red-tailed hawk answers the call, landing on the windowsill. Shukrat ties the scroll to its leg and whispers something to it. The hawk flies off.

Shukrat walks back to the others and takes a seat. "It is done. If he decides to answer, he will be here sometime tonight."

"Thank you," says Pelagius.

Alithyra touches her shoulder and rubs the stump. "Would he be able to do anything for me?"

Shukrat grins and shakes his head. "For you, his assistance is not necessary. I know an excellent ironsmith who can craft a very high-quality prosthesis for you. With the right adjustments, I may be able to magically attune it to your body so you can move and control it as though it were truly part of you."

"Thank you, Shukrat," says Alithyra.

"As for our potential guest, just a fair warning," says Shukrat. "Grimadert has a reputation for being slightly eccentric."

"How eccentric?" asks Iriemorel nervously.

Ralkgek shudders. "Let's just say that he's sometimes a little too eager to take on a challenge. And then, there's his smile."

"What about it?" asks Kevnan.

"I can't explain it," says Ralkgek. "There's just something off about that grin. It's a smile you will never forget."

"But enough about him for now," says Shukrat. "Once the rain stops, we must see that Adotiln receives a proper burial."

CHAPTER 2

A heavily armored, brown-haired minotaur cloaked in a purple cape walks down a stone hallway. As he rounds a corner, a busurin in similar dress greets him with a salute. The minotaur salutes back. "At ease. What did you need, guardsman?"

"There is someone outside who wishes to speak with you, Captain Mughan," says the guard. "He claims it's urgent."

"Did he say what he wants?"

"No, sir. Just that he would only speak with you or the king."

"Very well. Take me to him, and I'll decide if what he has to say is worthy of the king's time."

Mughan follows the guard down the hall to a large, wooden door. On the other side, they emerge into a large courtyard drenched by the pouring rain. Mughan looks around. "Where is he?"

The guard points to a dark alcove. "In there, sir. He does not wish to be seen."

Mughan raises an eyebrow. "Stand by."

The captain approaches the dark alcove. "Anybody there?"

The shadows shift and a large, imposing figure appears in the opening, but remains hidden. "Are you Captain Mughan?"

"I am. What is it that you want?"

"I wish for you to bring the king here. I have urgent news for him."

Mughan snorts. "I will be the judge of that."

"I'm afraid I must insist, sir. He must hear what I have to say."

"You try my patience, stranger. The only way to see the king at this late hour is to convince me or his advisors that you are worthy of his time. Now tell me what you have to say before I gore you and throw you out of the castle."

"You're welcome to try, captain. I doubt you could budge me, but I did not come here to fight."

Mughan glares at the mysterious figure in the shadows. "Then give me your report or get out."

The stranger grunts. "Very well. I bring grave news from Devil's Den regarding the fate of Marquis Babu."

Chapter 3

Glakchog and Shudgluv enter the barracks. Glakchog plops down on a chair, picks up a smooth stone, and uses it to sharpen one of his hookswords. Shudgluv sits on the edge of a bed, holding his chin in his hand and staring ahead with a furrowed brow.

Glakchog glances at him, dragging a stone across his blade. "I know what you're thinking. It's inconceivable that they managed to sneak around an entire army and a dragon. If not for Charndergh's incompetence, Babu would still be alive."

Shudgluv glares at him with disgust. "I don't care about that. It's just that I can't believe the boss did that to Eeshlith."

"She questioned him and disobeyed an order. For soldiers, there is always a penalty for insubordination."

"What he did seems harsh for such a minor offense."

Glakchog stops sharpening. "Eeshlith's punishment was simply an example and a reminder of who the commanding officer is."

"We're not in the military anymore, Glakchog. We're just attack dogs. Nothing more."

Glakchog rises angrily. "It may not be a traditional military, but we are still soldiers. Mind your tongue. I will not tolerate such talk from you."

Shudgluv stands, towering over the busurin. "What are you going to do? Kill me?"

Glakchog nods. "Without a second thought, if I had to. That's how a perfect soldier does it. No questions asked. An order is an order. Never oppose your commanding officer."

"You mean like how you stood behind the Green-Eyed Man when the Blood Guard came for him? How is that not disobeying your superiors?"

Rage fills Glakchog's eyes. "That was a mistake. I had a moment of weakness that should never have happened. If I was a good soldier back then, I would have helped the Blood Guard capture him. Instead, I ended up in a Battallian prison."

Shudgluv and Glakchog stare each other down, each one practically daring the other to make the first move.

Shudgluv grunts. "So, you would have taken the cowardly way out."

"There would have been nothing cowardly about it. It would have been the honorable thing to do. If we had simply turned him in instead of defending him, Alasdar wouldn't be the monster he is now and none of us would have ever gone to prison. It was a decision that destroyed our careers and our lives."

"I still say, standing up for him was the right thing to do at the time."

"Then you are a poor excuse for a soldier and always have been."

Anger fills Shudgluv's eyes and it becomes clear that he is barely in control of his rage. He glares at Glakchog, breathing heavily. Shudgluv grabs his weapons, prompting Glakchog to form a defensive stance. Instead of attacking, Shudgluv stomps toward the door. Shudgluv opens the door and the Green-Eyed Man stands on the other side, his hand extended as though he is about to grasp the knob.

The Green-Eyed Man crosses his arms and glares at Shudgluv. "Where do you think you're going, Shudgluv?"

Shudgluv emits a low grumble. "I was just going to wander around the fortress and clear my head. Is that a problem, sir?" He says "sir" with such disdain that the Green-Eyed Man glares at him with both surprise and anger.

"Mind your tongue, Shudgluv," says the Green-Eyed Man.

Shudgluv looms over the Green-Eyed Man. "Or what?"

The Green-Eyed Man stares down the troll and places a hand on his sword. "Back off right now. You know you can't win a fight with me."

"Oh, I could win a fight. You're not unbeatable."

Glakchog smirks as he watches the standoff. "Not unbeatable, Shudgluv. Just unkillable."

"Think very carefully about your next move, Shudgluv," says the Green-Eyed Man. "Are you sure you want to go down this path?"

Shudgluv stands his ground for a few moments, but reluctantly steps back.

The Green-Eyed Man nods approvingly. "That's better. Obviously, this act of insubordination can't go unpunished, but I'll have to deal with that later. We have some business to attend to. Alasdar wants to see all of us right away."

Shudgluv and Glakchog glance nervously at each other.

"What could he want?" asks Shudgluv.

The Green-Eyed Man shrugs. "We'll find out when we get there. Come on."

The Green-Eyed Man turns and heads down the hall. Glakchog follows immediately, but Shudgluv hesitates for a moment before joining them.

Chapter 4

Multiple red-eyed ravens surround Alasdar as he sits on Babu's old throne. Several minions attend to his wishes. After a few moments, the door opens, and Commander Charndergh enters. Close behind him is an umbra warrior slightly different from the others. He is somewhat larger, wears spiked armor, and carries a large greatsword on his back.

Charndergh bows, prompting the umbra warrior to do the same. "You wanted to see us, sir?"

Alasdar waves his hands, attempting to shoo away the ravens. "Yes, Commander. I see you brought Lieutenant Yilrig with you. Excellent. You may both rise."

Charndergh and Yilrig stand.

Alasdar grins as he observes them. "As you know, we are shoring up our defenses in case Pelagius decides to attack again. Do we have enough souls to create the number of umbra warriors sufficient for my needs?"

Charndergh nods. "Babu had thousands of souls stored for just such purposes. If you just combine two souls into one being, we should have plenty of umbra warriors to spare."

"Well, have some of your troops start the process. I want my army within a few months."

Charndergh raises an eyebrow. "An army, sir? Seems a bit excessive for extra defense."

Alasdar laughs and waves dismissively. "I have other plans in addition to the extra defenses, but that will be revealed in time. You have your orders."

"It will be done, sir," says Charndergh.

"Excellent, Commander." Alasdar pauses and ponders the situation. He shakes his head. "Actually, make that general."

Trial by Tournament: Champion of Valor

"Thank you, sir," says Charndergh. "Will there be anything else?"

Alasdar looks over at Yilrig. "In order for him to continue serving directly under you, I am promoting Yilrig to the rank of commander."

"We are grateful, sir," says Yilrig in multiple, simultaneous, echoey voices.

"That will be all," says Alasdar. "Proceed with the plan."

Charndergh and Yilrig bow and then turn to leave the room. As they exit, the Green-Eyed Man enters, followed by Glakchog and Shudgluv.

"You wanted to see us?" asks the Green-Eyed Man.

"Yes," says Alasdar. "There are going to be a few changes. First, due to your failure, you are no longer in charge of eliminating Pelagius. He is of little consequence, and avenging Babu is not part of my plan."

The Green-Eyed Man's mouth falls open in surprise. He raises his arms, then allows them to fall back to his sides. "So, what am I supposed to do? With Babu gone, there's no point in going out on soul hunt."

Alasdar laughs. "Oh, there will still be plenty of soul hunting. You will assist Garu in collecting more souls for the creation of umbra warriors. After that is done, I will decide what to do with you next."

"How many do we need?" asks the Green-Eyed Man.

"I need enough souls for at least another three thousand umbra warriors," says Alasdar. "Preferably more."

The Green-Eyed Man stares blankly at Alasdar, blinking his eyes as he processes the assignment. "That's not possible. There are only three of us. The only way to gather that many souls would be to raid a large city, perhaps even the capital of a kingdom, and we would need more soul hunters for that. Not to mention the fact that we would draw too much attention to ourselves. It cannot be done."

"Then gather as many souls as possible," says Alasdar. "I will put someone else in charge of recruiting other creatures for our cause."

"What cause would that be?" asks the Green-Eyed Man.

"That shall be revealed in time," says Alasdar. "At the moment, you do not need to know."

"Very well," says the Green-Eyed Man. "We will gather some umbra warriors and depart."

Alasdar holds up his hand. "Not so fast. There is more. Glakchog and Shudgluv are no longer under your command."

13

The Green-Eyed Man's jaw hangs open in shock. "What? They've been under my command for as long as I've been here."

"Well, I'm changing that," says Alasdar. "Is that a problem?"

"No, sir," says the Green-Eyed Man disdainfully.

Alasdar looks at Glakchog. "Step forward."

Glakchog approaches and bows.

"I hereby grant you the rank of captain. Not counting the soul hunters, you are second only to General Charndergh and Commander Yilrig."

Glakchog's eyes grow wide and he flashes a broad grin. "That is a tremendous honor, sir. What is my first assignment?"

"It's a long term one," says Alasdar. "You will be in charge of training new recruits, whether new umbra warriors or other creatures."

"I will not disappoint you, sir," says Glakchog.

"You are dismissed," says Alasdar. "Report to General Charndergh for further instructions."

Glakchog rises and turns to leave, but Shudgluv grabs him by the arm. The troll grins mischievously. "I dare you to tell Charndergh how his incompetence cost Babu's life. It would be quite entertaining to see how he reacts to the criticism."

Glakchog breaks out in a cold sweat and audibly gulps. "I think not. I overstepped my bounds then. I will not do that again."

Shudgluv chuckles. "Maybe I'll tell him then."

"You will do no such thing. If I have to face his wrath, I'll be sure that you will go down with me."

Shudgluv releases his grip and Glakchog leaves the room. Alasdar looks over at Shudgluv and ignores the conversation that took place. "We are now short a jailer. You are the dungeon master. Report to the dungeon for further orders."

"You want me to stand guard over Eeshlith?" asks Shudgluv.

"Exactly," says Alasdar. "Such sweet irony, don't you think? Dismissed."

Shudgluv glances at the Green-Eyed Man. "I'd say it looks like my act of insubordination is going unpunished after all, but I think Alasdar beat you to it without realizing it."

"Perhaps. We'll see, Shudgluv."

Shudgluv leaves the room, grumbling.

Alasdar turns back to the Green-Eyed Man. "Before you go, I have one other task for you. Gather up the remains of the defenders who fell during the last assault. I think I may be able to find a use for them."

"How?"

"I'm calling in a favor from an old acquaintance. I assume you know of whom I speak?"

The Green-Eyed Man gulps nervously. "You don't mean *him*, do you?"

"Of course. His form of assistance will catch our enemies off guard. That is why I am calling in this favor. Once you have gathered all the remains, have them sent to his laboratory. I'm interested in seeing what he can do."

Horrified and disturbed, the Green-Eyed Man exits the throne room, leaving Alasdar to continue plotting.

Chapter 5

As afternoon shifts to evening, the sky finally clears. A loud knock on the door catches everyone's attention. Shukrat answers the call. A wizened old gnome stands outside, a wild look in his eyes. His hair sticks out in multiple directions as if he has been electrocuted, and his shaggy beard is wild and uneven. Thick goggles with clearly extendable lenses sit on his forehead. A pair of identical busurin flank him.

The gnome emits a deranged giggle. "Did someone call for a doctor?"

"Yes," says Shukrat. "Grimadert, I presume?"

"Correct and these are my assistants, Rogi and Giro. May I come in, or shall we stand in the doorway?"

"By all means, please come in," says Shukrat.

Shukrat shows the three newcomers to the guest quarters. Seeing them enter, Pelagius, Kevnan, and Alithyra move to greet him, but Ralkgek moves to the farthest part of the room, clearly uncomfortable in Grimadert's presence. Aldtaw eyes Grimadert suspiciously.

"Everyone, this is Grimadert the Healing Blade," says Shukrat.

Pelagius bends down and extends his hand. "Pleasure to make your acquaintance."

Grimadert grasps Pelagius's hand and shakes it. "Likewise, I'm sure." Grimadert looks around the room. "Now, which one is the experime ..." Grimadert cuts himself off and stifles a chuckle. "I mean, which one is my patient?" The gnome flashes a smile far too wide.

Pelagius, Kevnan, and Alithyra look at each other with confused concern at this bizarre slip.

"Right this way," says Shukrat. "Your patient is the dwarf."

Grimadert follows him to Iriemorel, who watches the newcomer nervously. Grimadert examines him, giggling to himself on occasion.

"Your upper body seems to be fine. Now tell me if this hurts." Grimadert draws a dagger and stabs Iriemorel in the leg. Pelagius and the others step forward with concern, but Iriemorel does not react at all.

"I feel nothing," says Iriemorel.

Grimadert produces a needle and thread and stitches up the wound. "Semi-death of the body. Just as you mentioned. He lives, but much of his body thinks itself to be dead."

Pelagius inspects Iriemorel's leg. "Was that necessary?"

Grimadert nods. "Oh, quite necessary. I needed to see just how bad his semi-death actually is. If he could feel pain beneath the flesh, then it would be temporary. This seems to be of the permanent variety."

"Can you help him?" asks Alithyra.

"I believe I can," says Grimadert, with a slight giggle. "Not here though. I shall have to take him to my laboratory, where I will be equipped to perform the procedure."

Iriemorel gulps. "What kind of procedure?"

Grimadert's eyes light up and he flashes a grin of barely concealed derangement. "It's difficult to describe as it is quite experimental. I think if I can build a hollow golem body and fuse your nervous system with the legs, you should be able to walk again."

"Is it dangerous?" asks Pelagius.

Grimadert laughs. "Dangerous?" Grimadert looks over at the others in the room, howling with hysterical laughter. "He asks if it is dangerous." Grimadert stops laughing and smiles. "Oh, extremely. It has never been done before and may not work. I cannot even guarantee that he will survive the procedure. I could remove his brain and place it in a golem body, but that has never been fully successful. Those who have undergone that particular procedure tend to go quite mad. This new procedure is less likely to affect the mind quite so severely."

Pelagius stands silently, eyes wide. "So, um …" He takes a moment to compose himself and considers what he wants to say. "You're going to do that, no matter what?"

"Only if he agrees to it," says Grimadert. "I need his consent to proceed."

Pelagius turns to Iriemorel. "It's your choice."

Iriemorel sighs. "I think I'd rather risk it than retire. I'll do it."

"Excellent!" exclaims Grimadert, though a bit too enthusiastically. "With your permission, we can take you now and get started right away."

"Very well," says Iriemorel. "I'd like to be back on my feet as soon as possible."

"Then we shall be off," says Grimadert. "No time to lose. There's another storm coming from beyond the mountains, so we must make it back to the laboratory as soon as possible. Load him up, boys."

Rogi and Giro leave and reenter with a makeshift stretcher. They move Iriemorel onto it and carry him outside. Grimadert begins to follow but stops when he sees Thakszut lying comatose in a bed. "I'll take the fiendling along too. I may be able to do something for him as well."

"What can you do?" asks Pelagius. "The same procedure as for Iriemorel?"

"What is his full condition?" asks Grimadert.

"He has slipped into a deep slumber," says Shukrat. "And likely semi-death due to a broken neck."

"Another experimental procedure then," says Grimadert. "The golem shell most likely won't work on full-body semi-death, and he's too small to safely encase anyway."

Pelagius furls his brow and lowers his head. He looks up and glances between Grimadert and Thakszut. He sighs. "Very well. Take him and do what you can."

Rogi and Giro return to see what is taking Grimadert so long. Grimadert points at Thakszut and grins. "Grab the fiendling. We have another patient."

The twins comply and carry Thakszut outside. Grimadert eyes the sack on the table and opens it to peek inside. "Not much left of this one, I see."

Pelagius's eyes tear up and he shakes his head. "I'm afraid not. There's nothing you can do for her."

"Nothing, you say?" asks Grimadert. "Sounds like a challenge to me. I'll take the sack with me too. Perhaps I can rebuild her. I could possibly retrieve her soul before it moves on and rebind it to her repaired body."

"That is not possible," says Ralkgek. "Resurrection is the domain of divine magic and only the Archpriest can do it."

Grimadert grins, raises his hand, and wags a finger back and forth. "Not resurrection. Revivification. If I can find her soul, I may be able to bind it to an artificial heart, which may bring her back to life when implanted in her new body. I have no guarantee that it will work, but if you want your friend back, I can try."

Without waiting for a response, Grimadert picks up the sack, walks away, and exits the door. Pelagius and the others follow him through the doorway and watch the busurin twins load Thakszut into their wagon next to a surprised Iriemorel. A pair of horse-shaped metal golems pull the wagon.

Giro gets into the back with Iriemorel. Grimadert hands the sack to Rogi, who places it within the wagon. Rogi helps Grimadert into the driver's seat. Before they can depart, Pelagius steps in front of their path.

"I'm afraid that I can't let you take her," says Pelagius. "She died heroically, and there is no way to revive her. Please just let her rest."

Grimadert scowls and thinks for a moment. He looks over at Pelagius and grins. "Very well. What a waste." Grimadert retrieves the sack from inside the wagon and hands it to Pelagius. He turns his attention to the rest of the group. "Farewell, my friends. The next time you see your companions, they'll be as good as new. Or dead, depending on how this goes."

Grimadert laughs and urges on his horse golems, which take off at remarkable speed. Ralkgek approaches Pelagius. "See what I mean? There's something off about him."

"Shukrat, are you sure we can trust him?" asks Pelagius. "He seems a bit mad."

"Grimadert may be a little eccentric, but he has an excellent reputation," says Shukrat. "I'd stake my life on his trustworthiness. Now we must lay Adotiln to rest."

They assemble a small funeral pyre and place the sack containing Adotiln's head in the center. They gather around her and silently mourn her heroic sacrifice. Thunder booms in the distance and dark clouds loom over the mountains in the west, so they decide they had best light the pyre while they can. Shukrat conjures a small fireball and places it on top of the pyre, igniting it immediately. A strike of lightning follows a blast of distant thunder, hastening the need to end the funeral. With the fire controlled, they depart and enter Shukrat's house. As the door closes, the fire burns away the sack, revealing and igniting a small coconut.

Chapter 6

As night falls, a storm gathers over the mountains. Heavy rain falls as the clouds move in. Lightning flashes ever more frequently, and the thunder grows increasingly louder. A bolt of lightning strikes the ground, scattering a group of red-eyed ravens. The dirt shifts as though something is pushing up from below. A desiccated, rotting hand with exposed bones erupts through the wet soil. The mud explodes as an emaciated figure forces its way out of the ground. Scraggly hair sloughs off in clumps and two green orbs burn like fire where the eyeballs should be.

The creature steps out of its grave and surveys the area. He glances over his own body and raises his hand for a closer look. The remaining dried skin and muscle sag as the green orbs grow dimmer. His face contorts with rage, his eyes flare up, he raises his head to the sky and emits an inhuman shriek. A group of cloaked strangers emerge from the shadows and approach this pitiful thing.

"What do you want?" asks the creature, in a gasping, gravelly voice.

"Our master wishes to see you," replies one of the strangers.

"What would he want with me?" asks the creature.

"He wasn't clear on the details."

"Forget it. I'm not interested in your mysterious offer."

"He says he can help you."

"Leave me alone." The creature turns and begins wandering off in the direction of Bratenro. The lead stranger follows him. "Kragus, wait."

Kragus stops and turns back to his unwelcome visitor. "How do you know me?"

"My master instructed me to watch your grave. We've been expecting you to emerge. We have a proposition for you."

Kragus shakes his head. "Not interested. I told you to leave me alone."

"Where are you going to go?"

Kragus' dried and desiccated face sags and his shoulders slump. "Nowhere in particular. Anywhere but here."

"Looking like that, you can't blend in. The only place a necromort such as yourself would be welcome is the Necrotian Empire, and we're nowhere near their borders. My master can offer you sanctuary while you regain your strength."

Kragus thinks for a moment. "Fine. You've made your point. Seeing as I have nothing left to lose, I'll go with you to see what your master wants."

"Excellent," says the stranger. "Follow me."

The stranger opens a portal and steps in, followed by the rest of his group. Kragus hesitates for a moment before stepping through as well.

Chapter 7

Kragus sits on a rotten wooden bench in a small, filthy room. Multiple rats scurry across the floor. Extending his arms upward, he stares at his bony hands and his face sags. The door opens and Tohirata steps through.

"I apologize for making you wait," says Tohirata. "We thought it would be best for you to have some time to adjust to your new state. Have you gotten any of your strength back?"

Kragus continues to stare at his own hand. "A little, but not very much." Kragus looks over at Tohirata and narrows his eye sockets. "An ogre? No, you're too well spoken and seem too intelligent. You're a yamauba. Are you the lord of this castle?"

Tohirata shakes his head. "No. I'm second-in-command here."

"I was told that your master wanted to see me," says Kragus impatiently. "When do I have an audience with him?"

"Right now," says Tohirata. "Follow me. I'll take you to my master."

Kragus rises and follows Tohirata down several filthy hallways.

"This place is disgusting," says Kragus.

Tohirata chuckles. "My master likes it this way."

Tohirata leads Kragus to a large, rotten wooden door. He opens it and steps through, leading Kragus into the throne room. About halfway into the room, Tohirata bows to the mysterious figure shrouded in darkness on his throne.

"I have brought him as per your request, My Lord," says Tohirata.

"Excellent," says Scirrhus. "You may rise."

Scirrhus leans forward into the light, revealing his expressionless face and his unblinking bloodshot, yellow eyes. Kragus looks upon the obviously diseased shell of a body with disgust.

"Welcome, Kragus. I am Scirrhus, lord of this castle."

"What is it you want?" asks Kragus.

"An alliance," says Scirrhus. "Death and disease often go hand in hand."

Kragus glances around and notices the massive amount of red-eyed ravens perched around the room. "So, you're a carcinomancer and these are your spies?"

"Indeed," replies Scirrhus.

"What's in this alliance for me?" asks Kragus.

"I can help you get revenge against Pelagius," says Scirrhus. "Assuming you still want revenge."

Kragus' burning eyes flare a bright sickly green. "Of course I still want my revenge. Pelagius is responsible for my current state. However, I am still too weak to go up against him."

"Perhaps we can provide some assistance then," says Scirrhus.

"What kind of assistance?" asks Kragus. "Are you offering to take my revenge for me? I want him dead as soon as possible."

Scirrhus stares at Kragus, his expression never changing and his eyes unblinking. "Surely a necromort such as yourself has the patience to wait. After all, you have all the time in the world."

"Perhaps you're right," says Kragus, irritated. "What do you get out of this?"

"Nothing for you to be concerned with," says Scirrhus. "Let's just say that our alliance will help further my goals. The next step of my plan will take place when you have regained your strength. Until then, we shall simply observe."

Kragus looks over Scirrhus suspiciously. "Very well. I will agree to an alliance for now."

Chapter 8

Grimadert's carriage pulls up to a grim-looking castle of black stone. The structure sits right at the border of Diablos and Industria. While not as grandiose as Devil's Den, it is still imposing and intimidating, with gargoyles interspersed among the ramparts. Its towers are pointy and spiky, with several ravens perched along the walls. Out of several towers, tubes extending from the roof spew steam and smoke, creating a nearly constant cloud overhead. Large gears and sprockets of varying sizes cover the massive entry gate.

Grimadert hops down from the cart and approaches the enormous door. He pulls a lever, and the gears turn noisily. As they grind to a halt, the door pops forward and loudly rises into a slot in the wall. Grimadert climbs back into the cart and drives the wagon through the open doorway, which slams down and slides back into its closed position as soon as they pass through. As Rogi and Giro unload the cart, several large golems approach the carriage and take supplies to storage.

Grimadert turns to his assistants. "Rogi, take the dwarf to the lab. We must begin as soon as possible."

"Yes, Master," says Rogi.

Rogi hoists Iriemorel over his shoulders and disappears down a hallway. As Giro carries Thakszut off the cart, Grimadert discreetly pulls a sack from inside the wagon and hands it to him.

"Take these to the preservation room," says Grimadert. "We can't have the head rotting before we can begin on it. Keeping the fiendling in stasis will prevent him from suddenly dying."

"Right away, Master," says Giro.

Giro carries his load down a nearby corridor. As Grimadert turns to join Iriemorel in the lab, several gears above the doorway turn, pulling back a large log. As soon as the crank stops, the log releases. It swings forward and smashes into a massive bell above the door, making a clamorous ringing noise. Grimadert returns to the door and pulls the lever to open it. Outside stands a purple-skinned daemon and ten humans, accompanying several horses pulling large wheeled crates.

"I have a delivery for Grimadert," says the daemon.

Grimadert flashes a wide grin. "Ah, excellent. Wheel them in. My servants can handle the rest."

The delivery team brings the crates inside and swiftly departs. Rogi and Giro return to see what is taking Grimadert so long.

Grimadert turns to his assistants, smiling with excitement. "Boys, we have a delivery. Get a few golems and take these, uh, spare parts to the preservation room."

As the twins go off to gather helpers, Grimadert looks up at the red-eyed ravens observing him. "Are you watching me or are you observing my patients? Either way, enjoy the show."

Grimadert laughs madly, leaves the area, and heads toward the lab. His laboratory is a very large room filled with all kinds of equipment. Several tubes and bottles made of glass sit on various tables and a wide selection of wicked-looking surgical tools rest on a shelf. Lining the walls are bizarre devices made of levers, cranks, and gears, one of which includes a pair of large metal spirals spaced two feet across from each other.

A big pile of wood and coal sits next to a massive forge sitting in a pool of water. Over this pool is a network of metal tubes catching the rising steam, which travels through the tunnels and turns other various devices of unknown purposes. More ravens perch in the rafters. In the center of the room, a naked Iriemorel lies on a large table, with Rogi and Giro tightening straps to fasten him down. The dwarf nervously glances at Grimadert as he approaches.

"Is this really necessary?" asks Iriemorel.

"Very much so," says Grimadert. "I'll need access to your flesh for the procedure. It will allow me for a better fit for the pieces once they are constructed."

Grimadert goes to a corner piled high with raw materials, including several types of metal, stone, clay, wood, and other less discernible items. He searches through the supplies.

"Stone would be appropriate," says Grimadert. "A bit bulky and too slow though. Clay is too squishy, and wood is too flammable."

A deranged grin flashes across Grimadert's face as he turns to Iriemorel. "I'm thinking iron. How does that sound for your new legs?"

Iriemorel shrugs. "You're the expert. I'll go along with whatever you think is best."

Grimadert laughs and claps his hands. "Iron it is, then. I'll have Rogi and Giro get started on hauling out the raw materials. In the meantime, I've got a bit of soul searching to do. Try to make yourself comfortable."

Grimadert leaves the laboratory and heads to another area of the castle. As the twins return and pull large blocks of iron from the shelves, Iriemorel wonders if he has made a horrible mistake.

Chapter 9

Grimadert sits on a cot in a bare chamber. He holds a small red gem in one hand and a vial filled with black liquid in the other. He closes his eyes and breathes rhythmically as he concentrates. After a few minutes, he opens his eyes and raises the vial, focusing his gaze on it. "To Amyrus, outside Salernis Castle. I seek the halfling known as Adotiln."

A pulsating purple aura surrounds the black fluid. Tightly grasping the gem, Grimadert pops the seal on the vial and drinks its contents. He closes his eyes and lies down on the cot as a blinking purple glow surrounds his body and flashes until a spectral image of Grimadert ejects from the gnome's body. Grimadert glances around, ignoring his own form on the mat below. He shakes his head as though trying to clear it. "Astral projection is always so disorienting. Now to find my way to the land of the dead."

Grimadert floats through the wall and flies across the horizon, the landscape below him becoming hazier and less discernible the farther he travels. After traveling for an indeterminable amount of time, he stops and looks around. A greenish-black portal opens on the side of a nearby cliff. "That must be the way. It's never in the same place."

Grimadert enters the vortex and emerges in a dark, forbidding meadow. In front of him towers a gothic castle constructed of black basalt. Grimadert grins. "The Underworld always looks so bleak at first glance. Now to find my target."

Grimadert approaches the castle until he is nearly upon its wall. He follows the wall to the front gate, in front of which is a line of uncountable souls waiting to enter. Most of the spectral figures don't seem to notice him, but a few at the entryway shoot him an irritated look, as though they think he is trying to take their spot. Grimadert floats to the front of the line where a hooded figure thwarts his advance. The figure turns to Grimadert and raises its hand. "Halt. All new souls to the back of the line. You must wait your turn for judgment like all the others."

Grimadert giggles. "I'm just visiting. A halfling named Adotiln wouldn't happen to have passed through the gate yet, by any chance?"

The cloaked figure produces a scroll and looks through it. "Nobody by that name has passed through the gates as of yet. They are probably farther back in the line."

"Much appreciated, kind sir."

Grimadert slowly flies along the line, observing each soul. He stops at some to get a better look at the face due to a few appearing fuzzy. The majority of them do not acknowledge his presence, but a few glance in his direction when he comes closer. After an indeterminable amount of time, he finds the soul of a halfling who appears to meet Adotiln's description. Her ghostly image stands in the line, staring straight ahead. Grimadert approaches the potential match. "Excuse me, miss. Are you Adotiln?"

The spectral form shifts and looks in his direction. "Yes. And you are?"

"Just a friend visiting. I have something for you."

Adotiln shakes her head. "I'm not allowed to take anything with me."

"You won't have to, my dear. I just wish to show you something."

Adotiln sighs in annoyance. She turns to face him. "What is it?"

Grimadert opens his palm and shows her the now glowing red gem. "I would like you to take a closer look and see if you can identify it."

"I have little knowledge of gems. Perhaps you seek someone else."

"No. I believe you will know what it is. Please take it."

The line moves forward a few steps, forcing Grimadert and Adotiln to shift with it. Adotiln eyes the gnome wearily and reluctantly reaches out her hand. "Fine. Let me see it."

Grimadert smiles and drops the object into her palm. Adotiln raises it up to get a better look. "I still have no idea what this is."

Grimadert giggles maniacally. "It's a soul gem, my dear."

Adotiln gasps. Her eyes grow wide as her hand closes involuntarily around the jewel. The glow from the gem surrounds her and pulsates rapidly. She tries to throw the item away, but her fist remains clenched around it. Her already ghostly hand turns to mist and the gem draws it in. Her arm soon follows, and Adotiln screams as she dissolves. Her cries echo through the field as her smoky form vanishes into the gem.

Grimadert catches it before it hits the ground. "Mission accomplished. Now to return to my body."

Grimadert floats to the ground and stamps his foot. An unseen force abruptly yanks his spectral form backward. Grimadert flies back through the portal and slams into his own body. His eyes snap open and he sits up. He opens his palm and grins madly as he beholds the faintly glowing gem.

CHAPTER 10

Several days later, a hard knocking shakes Shukrat's door. Shukrat looks up from a scroll he had been studying. "Now who could that be?"

The aging goblin leaves his charges to answer the door. Captain Mughan stands outside, a massive warhammer strapped to his back. Behind him stand at least ten armed and armored soldiers of various species.

"Are you Shukrat?" asks Mughan.

"I am," says Shukrat. "May I ask your name?"

"I am Mughan, Captain of the Guard of Castle Demonicus. I demand entry to the premises."

"Of course, captain," says Shukrat. "I would never refuse the king's personal guard. Please, come in."

Shukrat steps out of the way. Mughan ducks under the door frame to enter, and his horns bounce off the sides. He turns his head and steps through the doorway.

"You need a larger door," says Mughan.

Shukrat rolls his eyes. "Apologies, captain. I don't get many large, horned guests."

Mughan walks farther into the house and his guard squad follows behind. They enter the newly created hospital wing and survey the area. Pelagius, Kevnan, Ralkgek, and Alithyra sit on chairs and stools at a nearby table, playing cards. Aldtaw, who seems to have aged a few years, sits up on the bed he had been resting on.

Mughan approaches Pelagius. "You there. I presume that you are Pelagius?"

Pelagius sets his card hand face down on the table. "I am. Is there anything I can do to help you?"

Mughan draws his warhammer. "You can come peacefully. I am placing you and your friends under arrest for the murder of Marquis Babu and several of his staff."

An expression of shock crosses Pelagius's face. "Murder?"

"The exact charge is assassination," says Mughan. "You stand accused of taking the life of a member of the king's court, a serious crime that cannot go unpunished."

Pelagius looks at his friends. "Very well. I take full responsibility. I simply ask that the others be left out of this matter."

Mughan snorts. "I'm afraid that is out of the question. They are accused of assisting in the assassination. If that is correct, they are equally as guilty."

Two guards step forward and clasp a set of manacles around Pelagius's hands. A few of the others do the same with Kevnan. Due to Alithrya's missing arm, it takes them a few tries to properly restrain her, but they eventually jury rig the shackles to work on a one-armed prisoner.

One of the guards approaches Aldtaw. "Stand up, canin. You need to come along as well."

"That will not be necessary," says Pelagius. "He was not involved in our assault."

Mughan glares at Pelagius and squints. "Then why is he here?"

"He was a prisoner of the Green-Eyed Man. We rescued him from certain death."

Mughan looks over at Aldtaw. "A likely story. Fine. He will not be arrested, but we must take him in for questioning."

Mughan approaches Ralkgek as two of the other guards clasp him in anti-mage irons. "You face a charge of treason for your involvement, Ralkgek."

"Babu destroyed my livelihood," says Ralkgek. "I simply exercised my right to pursue justice."

"We'll see if the king sees it that way." Mughan looks at Shukrat. "You've been harboring these assassins. I should arrest you as well."

"Shukrat had nothing to do with Babu's death," says Pelagius. "He thought we were simple travelers passing through."

"I see," says Mughan. "There were others listed among those who attacked Devil's Den. Where are they?"

"They did not survive," says Pelagius. "The dwarf's body was sent home to be laid to rest by his kin and the fiendling has been cremated. The halfling met a rather gruesome end that I would prefer not to describe."

"Pity," says Mughan. "Then I suggest we move out. Diablos is a big kingdom. The journey to Castle Demonicus will take a few days."

Mughan and the guards lead Pelagius, Kevnan, Ralkgek, and Alithyra outside and load them onto an enclosed cart with metal bars while Aldtaw rides with the driver. They make their way south toward the castle of King Demonicus. A stunned Shukrat watches helplessly as they disappear into the distance.

"This situation just got significantly more complicated," says Shukrat.

Chapter 11

Mughan hauls Pelagius and the others down a long, well-lit hallway lined with suits of armor. He approaches a set of massive, wooden double doors flanked by a pair of human guards, who salute him and open the doors. Inside is an enormous room, well-lit and decorated throughout with reds and golds. A long purple rug stretches from the doorway to the end of the room. Several balconies line the walls at three higher levels. Along the walls of the first floor, and filling the balconies, are individuals of varying species, humanoid and demonic alike.

At the end of the rug and up a small flight of steps is an opulent throne, in which sits an imposing figure. His basic body structure is roughly humanoid, but he is a little over ten feet tall with dark-gray skin, orange eyes, two pairs of jagged horns curving upward from his hairline, long white hair, claw-like fingernails, a tail with bony protrusions toward the end, and hooves for feet. He wears an outfit of golden-colored silk, a large purple cape, and a lavish crown inlaid with gold, purple, and red.

Alithyra leans toward Kevnan. "What manner of creature is that?" she murmurs in Kevnan's ear, so as to not catch the creature's attention.

"That is a Varklos," whispers Kevnan. "A species of demonkin."

"Be quiet and show some respect," says Ralkgek. "This happens to be the king of Diablos."

Standing next to the throne is a red-skinned daemon with a pair of horns on his head. The daemon unfurls a scroll and takes a few steps forward. As the figure on the throne stands, everyone else in the room bows, including the guards who force Pelagius and the others down into the same position.

"Presenting His Royal Majesty, King Demonicus IX," says the daemon.

Demonicus sits on his throne. "Thank you, Barbox. The Court may rise." The king's deep, gravelly voice echoes through the room.

The room returns to their standing positions as Barbox takes another step forward.

"Pelagius of Waskan?" inquires Barbox.

Mughan shoves Pelagius forward. Pelagius stumbles a few feet and takes a moment to regain his balance. He looks at Barbox. "Yes, sir."

"Ah, excellent," says Barbox. "Crusader Pelagius of Waskan, you and your companions are hereby charged with conspiring against the royal court of Diablos, entering the kingdom with malicious intent, and assassinating Marquis Babu. How do you plead?"

"Not guilty, sir," says Pelagius.

The crowd erupts into a frenzy of jeers and muttering. Barbox raises his hand. "Silence! Pelagius, we have several witnesses from Devil's Den who claim that you have slain Marquis Babu. Is this a lie?"

"It is no lie," says Pelagius.

"You admit guilt, yet claim innocence," says Barbox, puzzled. "Explain how you are not guilty if you did the deed."

"Sir, we did not conspire against the court, nor was there malicious intent," says Pelagius. "We simply took it upon ourselves to rid the world of a great evil that has plagued the kingdoms for too long."

"A great evil?" asks Barbox. "Babu was a norodrian. Reprehensible as it is, they must consume souls to survive as you and I must consume food. Is his very existence so objectionable that you must murder an unsuspecting demonkin?"

"I am aware of their need for sustenance," says Pelagius. "I also know that your laws allow for them and their soul hunters to operate only in a specific designated area, and that they are only allowed to harvest enough souls to stay alive. Babu has been violating both these laws for a very long time. His soul hunters, especially the Green-Eyed Man, have been attacking settlements in other kingdoms for decades, if not centuries. They have also been harvesting far more souls than is necessary for survival. Those that he does not consume, he stores for later or fuses together to form umbra warriors."

A shocked silence falls over the crowd, interspersed with hushed mutterings. Demonicus leans forward with intrigue.

"These are very serious accusations," says Barbox. "Why did you not come forward and inform the king of these alleged crimes? Why sneak into Devil's Den and assassinate Babu, who I was informed was unaware of the plot against his life?"

"We were unaware that Babu was a member of the royal court," says Pelagius. "For all we knew, someone in power was aware of his activities and was turning a blind eye."

"Outrageous!" shouts Barbox. "I will not tolerate such slander in the Court. Guards, take them away!"

The guards move to haul them out, but Demonicus raises his hand. "No. They will stay for now. Calm yourself, Barbox. This trial is not over."

Barbox bows. "Forgive me, Your Majesty." He returns his attention to the prisoners. "Continue, Pelagius."

"Your sources are also incorrect or lying," says Pelagius. "Babu was fully aware of our quest. He was ready and waiting for us when we arrived."

"If Babu knew of a plot against his life, he would have informed the court," says Barbox. "Any member of the nobility would have sought extra protection."

"Babu was arrogant and believed that he could repel us himself," says Pelagius. "To his credit, he very nearly succeeded."

Barbox shakes his head. "I doubt your words. What proof do you offer to back up your claims of his crimes? Nobody has ever come forward with these accusations before."

"It is very difficult for the northern kingdoms to come to Diablos thanks to the Battallian embargo," says Pelagius.

"True," says Barbox.

"As for evidence or proof, I have only my word," says Pelagius. "And the story of my journey."

Barbox sits in a chair next to the throne. "By all means, do tell. I'm sure we are all quite curious."

Pelagius proceeds to tell his tale, starting with encounters with the Green-Eyed Man several years prior as well as accounts of the Green-Eyed Man's attacks he has learned from others. After going over the brief history of the soul hunters' previous raids, he tells the story of that night in Inolutet. He relates the tale of the entire journey, with the others confirming various details and adding their own experiences that Pelagius did not witness. He does leave out Shukrat's knowledge of their quest, only informing the court that he allowed them to stay at his home for a few nights. The audience emits a collective gasp when he tells of Adotiln's fate. The room goes silent as he finishes his tale.

"Interesting sequence of events," says Barbox. "That does not excuse the fact that Devil's Den now has no lord or anybody to keep watch over the border. Babu had no successors, and choosing someone from the other nobles to take his place is going to be an arduous task."

"A soulborn named Alasdar has claimed lordship of Devil's Den," says Pelagius.

"This Alasdar has no right to make such a claim," says Demonicus. "This will have to be rectified."

"Is there anything else?" asks Barbox.

"That is all I have to offer," says Pelagius.

"What is your ruling, Your Majesty?" asks Barbox.

Demonicus sits back on his throne and thinks for a moment. "This trial is inconclusive. These accusations against Babu must be investigated. I shall send a messenger and a few guards to Devil's Den to look into the matter and relieve Alasdar of his unlawful claim. I shall also contact my allies outside of Diablos to inquire about these other attacks. Once all the reports have been returned and thoroughly investigated, I will make my decision. In the meantime, Pelagius and his companions are still accused of murder and will remain prisoners. Lock them in the dungeon until we can clear up this mess."

"The king has spoken," says Barbox. "Pelagius and company are dismissed."

The guards gather the prisoners and lead them from the room.

"Mughan, Ralkgek shall stay," says Demonicus. "He is having his own separate trial."

Chapter 12

Pelagius sits on a cot in a small cell. He shares the enclosure with Kevnan, who stands by the bars. Alithyra is directly across from them in her own cell, and Aldtaw is in the one next to her.

"Thrown into prison twice in one year," says Kevnan. "I don't know about you, but that's a new record for me."

Pelagius chuckles. "I agree. I certainly wasn't expecting to be put on trial for ridding the world of Babu."

"That trial did not go well," says Alithyra.

"It could have been worse," says Pelagius. "They could have called for our immediate execution. Fortunately, King Demonicus is amiable and willing to listen."

Kevnan steps away from the bars and plops down on the unoccupied cot across the cell from Pelagius. "How long do you think we'll be in here?"

Pelagius shrugs. "It could be a while. Possibly months or years. It depends on how long it takes the king to gather his information."

"However long it is for you, it will be the blink of an eye for me," says Aldtaw. "I always knew I'd die in a dungeon. I just didn't expect it to be a different dungeon."

"None of us are going to die here," says Pelagius. "I'm sure that King Demonicus will rule in favor of us once he determines the truth."

Aldtaw peeks through the bars, looking tired and decrepit. "I think I probably will. The spell that the Green-Eyed Man used to keep me from aging has been broken. I'm growing older every day. Sixty years are catching up with me. At the rate I'm going, I estimate that I only have a few months to live."

"How quickly are you aging?" asks Kevnan.

"It's difficult to say," says Aldtaw. "I estimate it to be roughly one year every two days. I could be wrong. It may be slightly slower."

"I'm sorry, Aldtaw," says Alithyra. "I really thought that I was rescuing you."

Aldtaw smiles. "You did, Alithyra. My life for the past sixty years has been torturous. Getting out of there is the best thing that's ever happened to me. At least I get to live out the rest of my life away from the Green-Eyed Man's clutches."

The door at the end of the hall opens and Ralkgek enters, followed by Mughan. The captain of the guard opens Aldtaw's cell and shoves the spice merchant in, shutting and locking it behind him.

"You got lucky, traitor," says Mughan.

The minotaur captain leaves, slamming the door behind him. Pelagius approaches the bars and looks over at Ralkgek.

"So, I assume your trial went well?" asks Pelagius.

"Depends on your point of view," says Ralkgek. "King Demonicus came to the same conclusion with me as he did for you."

Alithyra presses her face to the bars, her long nose sticking through, and glares at Ralkgek as best she can. "You're from Diablos originally. Why didn't you tell us that Babu was a member of the royal court when you first learned of our quest?"

Ralkgek shrugs and rolls his clouded eyes. "I thought you knew. It's not exactly a secret. Besides, after he ruined my livelihood, I was within my rights to seek justice. Granted, that usually involves challenging the offender to a duel."

"I suppose it doesn't really matter now," says Pelagius. "The deed is done. Now we just need to get through this new dilemma."

Kevnan lies down on his cot. "I hope Iriemorel is having a better time than we are."

Chapter 13

Grimadert walks through a green glowing archway into a massive chamber, followed by Giro. Bodies and body parts line the walls and lie on tables throughout the entire room. Although wounds of varying severity cover many, all are perfectly preserved as if death happened only moments ago. In the center of the room are the crates that were just delivered. Grimadert pulls up a small ladder and approaches the golems guarding the boxes.

"I've come to inspect my new spare parts," says Grimadert. "Stand aside."

The golems slide out of his way and Grimadert places his ladder among the crates. He hands Giro an ink quill and some parchment.

"I'm going to need notes for later," says Grimadert. "Write down everything I say while I am inspecting the crates."

Grimadert climbs up his ladder and opens a crate, peering in. "Hmm. Lots of oni parts. Cut up postmortem for transport from the looks of it. Most of the body is severely burned."

Grimadert looks into another box. "A blackened morag skull and a large pile of ashes. Not sure what I can do with that, but I'll think of something."

He moves on to the next one. "Onocentaur with a hole through the torso. Spine's been severed. Donkey half will be useless. These next crates seem to contain the corpses of three different creatures. Varying degrees of usefulness, judging by the wounds."

Grimadert moves on to the last crate and peers inside. "Oh, halfling pieces. Let's see. The limbs look usable. The torso and internal organs are too badly damaged to be of any use. I'll need another halfling body or two to fill in the gaps. Better than just a head, at least."

Grimadert walks over to Thakszut and magically examines his body. "This one will be difficult. Signs of small electric shocks to the chest after healing. Intriguing. To what purpose, I wonder? All signs indicate that the neck was severely broken, practically severed. Body will be useless. Only the brain, blood, and possibly the heart will be salvageable. I'll need to completely reconstruct this one."

Grimadert closes all the boxes and motions to the golems, who clamber back into their original positions. He and Giro enter the laboratory and join Rogi, who is busy picking out large chunks of iron and melting them down in the forge.

"Excellent work," says Grimadert. "Rogi, go get the dwarf-sized golem mold and get it into position."

Rogi goes off into another room and returns pushing a large metal box with a dwarf-shaped indentation in the center. He places it under the end of what appears to be a drainage pipe. Grimadert pulls a lever and several nearby gears noisily crank, pulling back a section of the forge. The molten iron flows through a tube, out the pipe and fills in the dwarf-shaped hole.

"Excellent," says Grimadert. "Once this cools, we can start hollowing it out and use it to do a fitting on our friend on the table. I doubt that this will fit the first time. We'll probably have to try different sizes to get it right. Once we get the sizing down, the real experiment can begin."

Chapter 14

A convoy of four people approaches the raven-covered gates of Devil's Den. Three of these people are humans, dressed in armor bearing the insignia of King Demonicus' personal guard. The fourth is an onocentaur.

As they walk up to the main gate, a gaki peers out of the flanking guard tower and tries to shoo away several birds. "Who goes there? State your business."

The onocentaur glances up at the guard. "I am Darderos, the king's personal messenger. We wish to speak to the ones in charge."

The gaki snatches a raven out of the air and pops it in his mouth, chewing noisily. "One moment. I'll send word."

After a few minutes, the gates open and General Charndergh and Commander Yilrig greet the convoy.

"Welcome gentlemen," says Charndergh. "Pardon his manners, but he must eat. Nobody needs a ravenous, feral gaki on the loose. How may I be of assistance to you today?"

"We come to investigate claims of unlawful activities," replies Darderos, taken aback. "We would like to speak to a few of the denizens of this fortress and to Alasdar."

"I see," says Charndergh. "Well, I cannot refuse a representative of the king. Feel free to interview my forces and as many of the civilians as you like. Commander Yilrig will accompany you so you do not get lost. When you are ready, Yilrig and I will take you to the throne room."

"Thank you, sir," says Darderos. "We will try not to disrupt the daily activities."

Charndergh walks away and the convoy steps through the gates, which slam shut behind them.

Darderos turns to Yilrig. "Do you mind if I ask a few questions, Commander?"

"What would you like to know?" asks Yilrig. "We will answer to the best of our abilities."

"We are aware that Marquis Babu was recently assassinated," says Darderos. "Was he aware of the plot against his life?"

"Fully aware," says Yilrig.

"Did he take any precautions?"

"Of course."

Darderos sighs. "Care to elaborate?"

"How would you like us to elaborate?"

"Exactly what preparations did he order?" asks Darderos.

"After he received word from the Green-Eyed Man, he doubled the guard and placed us on high alert. Then, he set up the divider defenses and placed a warrior chosen by Gulvgrum at each location."

"I see," says Darderos. "That does contradict the initial report."

Yilrig shrugs. "Perhaps the original contact was misinformed."

"Before the events that led to Babu's assassination, was he following the rules of where to gather souls and how many he could take?" asks Darderos. "Or was he, as recent accusations suggest, sending his soul hunters out beyond his territory and harvesting more souls than necessary?"

"He felt that the confines of his territory were too restrictive," says Yilrig. "Therefore, he would send his soul hunters to other kingdoms to gather souls."

"What of the numbers?" asks the messenger. "Did he have them gather only what was necessary to survive or did they harvest more?"

"Far more than was needed to simply survive," says Yilrig.

Darderos glances at his guards and turns back to Yilrig. "How many more? What does he do with these extra souls?"

"A few thousand. We are unaware of the exact numbers. He would keep them in storage until needed. Some he would devour, but many in his surplus have been used to create umbra warriors to supplement the ranks of the guards. We are the product of such a merging of souls."

Darderos gives a worried glance to his companions.

"Thank you," says Darderos. "You have been most helpful. So, are you a typical umbra warrior?"

"No, we are not," says Yilrig.

"What are you then? How long have you served Babu?"

"We are over one hundred years old, long-lived for one of us. As such, we have evolved into an umbra warlord. Unlike normal mindless umbra warriors, we have obtained self-awareness."

"Is there anything else you can share with us?"

"We are unaware of what else you want. Perhaps you would prefer to ask some of the other denizens."

The convoy goes around the courtyard and into a few of the buildings. Darderos asks the same questions to each individual he encounters and receives roughly the same answers. As they enter the barracks courtyard, they spot Glakchog going through combat exercises with a group of umbra warriors. Several other warriors and soldiers of various species are also partaking in various training exercises all across the yard.

Darderos approaches Glakchog. "Pardon me, sir."

Glakchog wheels around and glares at him. "I'm a bit busy here. What do you want?"

"I'm the king's personal messenger. I'd like to ask you a few questions."

Glakchog's eyes grow wide as he realizes his mistake. "Forgive me, sir. I didn't realize. Troops, take a five-minute break. What would you like to know?"

Darderos asks Glakchog the same questions as before, which he answers truthfully.

"What was your part in all this?" asks Darderos.

"I was assisting the Green-Eyed Man in recruiting helpers to help stop Pelagius," says Glakchog. "The Green-Eyed Man then assigned me and two others to ambush them in the mountains if they were to retreat from Diablos."

"So Babu was more proactive rather than simply building up his defenses?" asks Darderos.

"Of course," says Glakchog. "He ordered the Green-Eyed Man to make sure that they never entered Diablos alive. After several failed attempts, the Green-Eyed Man set up a defense force within Diablos as a last resort before the fortress. I don't know exactly what happened, but clearly he failed."

"Why was the king's court not informed of this plot?" asks Darderos. "If Babu knew they were coming, why would he not ask the king for assistance?"

Glakchog shrugs. "Maybe he felt it was a personal matter. I honestly can't say."

"And this Alasdar," says Darderos "He just stood by while it happened and then claimed Devil's Den as his own after Babu's death?"

"It would seem to be like that, yes," says Glakchog.

"Thank you," says Darderos. "You've been quite helpful."

The convoy leaves the barracks and heads back to the main courtyard. Spotting General Charndergh, they approach him.

"We would like to speak with Alasdar now," says Darderos.

"Very well," says Charndergh. "Follow me."

Charndergh enters a door and leads the convoy down a long hallway. Charndergh pushes open the massive doors leading to the throne room and leads the convoy inside. Alasdar sits on the throne, clearly unhappy at the interruption.

"General, what is the meaning of this?" asks Alasdar.

"General?" inquires Darderos.

"My Lord, this is the king's personal messenger," says Chardergh. "He wishes to speak with you."

"Very well," says Alasdar. "What is it that you wish to know?"

Darderos proceeds to ask him the same questions that he has been asking everyone else. Alasdar grins and answers him with absolute honesty.

"I see," says Darderos. "This news is most disturbing."

"Does it really matter?" asks Alasdar. "Babu is dead. Those facts do not change that."

"What of his soul hunters?" asks Darderos. "Since their master has passed on, are you releasing them from their contracts?"

Alasdar laughs. "Of course not. They're far too useful. I'm sending them out to collect more to add to the surplus, which I plan on using to create more umbra warriors."

"Harvesting souls for purposes other than sustenance is illegal," says Darderos. "The king will not allow it."

"That never stopped Babu," says Alasdar. "Since he's dead, I see no reason not to pick up where he left off."

"Speaking of his death, Babu had no heir," says Darderos. "Why did you claim lordship of Devil's Den?"

"Babu intercepted my soul after I died and created me as I am now," says Alasdar. "In a way, you could call him my father. Therefore, I have declared myself his heir."

Darderos shakes his head. "The king does not see it that way."

"Perhaps not," says Alasdar. "It doesn't really matter to me."

Darderos stomps one hoof and steps toward Alasdar. "Mind your tongue. You are treading on treasonous ground."

"Is that a fact?" says Alasdar. "Devil's Den belongs to me. That is all there is to it."

"The king has declared that you have no right to the lordship of Devil's Den," says Darderos. "I am ordered to tell you that you are relieved of your claim."

Alasdar crosses his arms and flashes an arrogant grin. "The king is welcome to try and take my claim if he wishes. My new army is loyal to me and me alone. I'm not so sure that the king will be willing to risk a civil war just to take from me what is rightfully mine."

"Is that your answer then?" asks Darderos.

Alasdar grins. "It is."

Darderos sighs. "Then I shall take my leave. The king will hear of this treachery."

Alasdar motions to Charndergh, who slams the doors shut. Several other creatures emerge from behind the throne and surround the convoy. Taking a glaive; a seven-foot-long pole with a two-foot long blade on the end; off the wall, Charndergh steps forward. With one rapid sweep of his weapon, he decapitates all three members of Darderos's honor guard. A few of the other creatures surround Darderos and shackle him.

Alasdar steps off the throne. "Oh, the king will get your message, but it will be very late. Guards, lock him in the dungeon. General, if anybody comes asking about the messenger, tell them he has already left and should have arrived at the king's castle."

The guards haul away Darderos, who curses and screams as they drag him down the hallway. Alasdar grins malevolently, turning his attention back to Charndergh.

"General, intensify the troops' training," says Alasdar. "As soon as the Grand Tourney is over, I want them to be ready for war."

Chapter 15

Several weeks later, the Green-Eyed Man, having returned from a soul hunt, enters the dungeon and approaches Shudgluv.

"How is our prisoner, Shudgluv?" asks the Green-Eyed Man.

"Which one?" asks Shudgluv glumly.

The Green-Eyed Man stares at Shudgluv, processing the question. "What do you mean, which one? Eeshlith, of course. Last I checked, she was our only prisoner."

Shudgluv gestures toward the cells. "We have two prisoners now. Things have been interesting here in the past few weeks."

The Green-Eyed Man passes Shudgluv and walks into the cell block. Eeshlith sits on her cot, eating some unidentifiable gruel from a bowl. Noticing his approach, she glares angrily at the Green-Eyed Man.

The Green-Eyed Man scowls as he meets her gaze. "You put yourself in here, Eeshlith. Do not blame me for your insubordination."

Eeshlith turns her back to him, refusing to retort. The Green-Eyed Man shrugs and turns his attention to the next cell. Darderos stands by the door, his hands wrapped around the bars and his face pressed between two of them.

The Green-Eyed Man eyes him quizzically. "Shudgluv, who is this? I've never seen him before."

"Get ready for a shock, boss," says Shudgluv. "He's the king's personal messenger."

The Green-Eyed Man's eyes grow so wide that they look ready to pop out. He quickly spins to look at Shudgluv. "What? Why is he imprisoned here?"

Shudgluv explains the events of the previous days to the best of his ability.

"You think that's what happened?" asks the Green-Eyed Man.

Shudgluv raises his arms in an exaggerated shrug. "I was down here the whole time. I only know what I heard from Glakchog. He's just as surprised as you."

Darderos watches the two as they continue their conversation. "You must be the Green-Eyed Man. Shudgluv and Eeshlith have been very gracious in answering my questions, confirming much of the information I got from other denizens here. They have told me much about you."

"What did they tell you?" asks the Green-Eyed Man nervously.

"They told me of your illegal soul hunting activities, and their part in helping you," says Darderos. "Sixty years' worth of hunting outside Babu's designated area is very serious. Strangely, they wouldn't tell me anything about you before you became a soul hunter, nor would they mention your real name."

A look of relief crosses the Green-Eyed Man's face. "Very wise. My name and history are secrets that shall be lost to time. If they had told you, I would have had to kill all three of you right now."

"That would be unwise," says Eeshlith. "According to Glakchog, Alasdar has plans for him."

"What plans?" asks the Green-Eyed Man.

"Nobody knows," says Shudgluv. "He won't share them with anybody except for General Charndergh."

"So, Green, what is your take on this treasonous act?" asks Darderos.

"Honestly, I'm shocked. I must have a word with Alasdar." The Green-Eyed Man turns and leaves the dungeon, heading for Alasdar's throne room.

Entering the chamber, the Green-Eyed Man notices that Hazgor and Garu are already there, both of whom seem just as surprised. The Green-Eyed Man approaches the throne. "Alasdar, what is going on? Why is King Demonicus' personal messenger imprisoned in our dungeon?"

"I was just asking the same question," says Garu. "We'll all be guilty of treason if the king discovers this."

Alasdar grins. "Calm yourselves. This is now part of my plan, thanks to Hazgor's idea to go behind my back and find another way to deal with Pelagius."

"How so?" asks Hazgor.

The Green-Eyed Man looks over at Hazgor. "Would you care to share the details of your strategy, Hazgor?"

"I simply anonymously reported the assassination of Marquis Babu by Pelagius's hand to the royal court," says Hazgor. "By doing so, I ensured that Pelagius and his companions were to be placed under arrest for the murder of a member of the court. Their trial is ongoing as we speak. If all goes according to plan, Pelagius and his friends will be found guilty and executed, thus eliminating them as a threat."

The Green-Eyed Man nods. "Impressive. Very clever. What does this have to do with the messenger?"

"It would seem that King Demonicus was more willing to listen to Pelagius's side of the story than I anticipated," says Hazgor.

Alasdar nods. "Yes, and while it does complicate things, I anticipated Hazgor's disobedience and planned accordingly. I knew that Pelagius would tell him of Babu's crimes and that he would send someone to investigate. I instructed everyone to give any investigator their full cooperation."

The three soul hunters glance at each other nervously.

"Why?" asks Garu. "That would seem to completely undermine Hazgor's plan."

"Hazgor attempted to undermine me, so I was forced to take these events into account," says Alasdar. "Even if the messenger hadn't learned too much to immediately report back, it would still not change the fact that Pelagius did, in fact, assassinate Babu."

"But it besmirches Babu's legacy with the court," says the Green-Eyed Man. "Having knowledge of his illegal activities would put doubt in Pelagius's guilt. Not to mention ousting us for our role."

"Babu's legacy is no concern to me," says Alasdar.

"Why was the messenger thrown in the dungeon?" asks Garu.

"The king has decided that I have no claim to Devil's Den," says Alasdar. "The messenger told me that I have been ordered to step down. I refused and told him that Demonicus is welcome to try and take it from me."

The soul hunters take a step back in shock.

"So, all this time, you've been building an army to spark a rebellion?" asks the Green-Eyed Man.

Alasdar grins malevolently and laughs. "Not a rebellion. A revolution. The title of marquis is just a fancy term for border guard. I seek the throne itself."

"You actually told the messenger this?" asks Garu.

"Not in those exact words, but he got the idea," says Alasdar. "I couldn't have him return with that news, so I locked him away. King Demonicus will receive his report when the time is right."

The soul hunters converse among themselves, clearly unsure of what to do.

"When do you plan to strike?" asks Garu.

"Soon, but not yet," says Alasdar. "The army is not complete and there is more training to be done. I would also like oaths of fealty from the nearby villages, whether voluntary or conscripted. Speaking of oaths, bow to me."

The soul hunters hesitate as they process this new information. Anger crosses Alasdar's face. His skin roils and slightly cracks as he rises to his feet.

"Bow to me!" shouts Alasdar in a deep demonic voice.

The blood drains from the soul hunters' faces and they rapidly drop in a bow. Alasdar's flesh returns to normal as he returns to a sitting position.

"You all swore oaths of loyalty to Devil's Den when Babu recruited you," says Alasdar. "You are to renew that vow to me."

The three soul hunters summon their urns and set them on the floor, placing a single hand on each one. "I solemnly swear my life and service to the lord of Devil's Den. My soul is yours to command, my life yours to give or extinguish. My very existence belongs to the lord of Devil's Den. My loyalty is to him and him alone. I swear this oath on pain of oblivion."

Alasdar smiles evilly. "Excellent. You may rise."

The soul hunters dismiss their urns and rise to their feet.

"What shall we do now, My Lord?" asks Garu.

"I want you three to travel to the nearest settlements and secure their oaths of fealty," says Alasdar.

"How far out should we travel?" asks the Green-Eyed Man.

"For now, don't go beyond the swamp," says Alasdar. "The hamlets and villages in the immediate area are small and remote enough to not be noticed for a while. We don't want to play our hand too soon."

"What if they refuse and remain loyal to the crown?" asks Garu.

"Those shall be made an example of," says Alasdar. "If they refuse, destroy them and harvest their souls."

CHAPTER 16

During Alasdar's meeting with the soul hunters, Glakchog listens through the door. Brelgvu stands nearby, intrigued by what they are hearing inside. As the meeting draws to a close, Brelgvu motions to Glakchog and disappears down a hallway. Glakchog follows until they reach a currently unused room.

Glakchog grunts and slams his fist against the wall. "So that's why he is having me train new recruits and umbra warriors. This is not good."

Brelgvu looks at him quizzically. "Why not? Are you questioning the decisions of your superior?"

"I would never question my superior," says Glakchog. "You taught me that. However, the king is superior to the marquis and all other members of the nobility. What Alasdar speaks of is treason."

"So, you are torn between serving your master and serving your master's master, correct?" asks Brelgvu.

"Yes," says Glakchog. "As a soldier, it is my duty to serve, but can a perfect soldier follow a superior who is betraying his own commander?"

Brelvgu thinks for a moment, clearly puzzled by the situation as well. "What do you plan to do?"

"I don't know," says Glakchog. "It may be my duty to report this to the king, but Alasdar is the one I am currently serving under. What is your advice, Brelgvu? What would the perfect soldier do?"

A wicked grin crosses the imp's face. He places his hand reassuringly on Glakchog's shoulder. "The perfect soldier would stick with his commander. You swore an oath to serve the lord of Devil's Den, did you not?"

"I did, but Babu was loyal to the throne. By serving him, I was serving the king. Alasdar is betraying the king."

"Ah, but that is the answer. You swore an oath to the lord of Devil's Den, not Babu specifically. Additionally, you never swore your service to the king. Your only obligation is to the lord of Devil's Den, which is currently Alasdar. The perfect soldier always keeps their oath to their lord, no matter what decision their lord makes. Do you understand?"

Glakchog sighs. "I believe so, but it still doesn't seem right to commit such treachery."

Brelgvu scoffs. "Since when do you worry about whether or not something is right? The perfect soldier would never concern himself with such trivialities. Perhaps you are not the candidate I was seeking after all."

Brelgvu turns to leave, but Glakchog grabs him by the shoulder and drops to his knees. "No. I am the one you seek. I am the one who has what it takes to become the perfect soldier."

Brelgvu grins malevolently as he keeps his back turned to Glakchog.

"After your expression of doubt for your superior, I'm not so sure," says Brelgvu, feigning disappointment. "How can I be sure that you truly are the one destined to be the perfect soldier?"

"I'll prove it to you," says Glakchog. "I will stick with Alasdar in his ambitions to rule the kingdom."

His back still turned, Brelgvu's grin stretches into a vicious smile. He brushes Glakchog's hand off his shoulder. "You've had so many chances, but you keep doubting the decisions of your superiors. Words mean nothing if you cannot commit to their meaning. Are you willing to do whatever it takes to prove your worth?"

"Yes," says Glakchog. "I will do anything to become the perfect soldier."

"Anything?" asks Brelgvu. "Are you willing to die to prove that you are the right choice?"

"I swear to you, Brelgvu," says Glakchog. "On pain of death, I will become the perfect soldier."

Brelgvu laughs and turns to face Glakchog. "Excellent, my friend. Perhaps you are the one I seek. However, this is your last chance. No more doubts. No more questioning your commanders. From here on out, you either embody the perfection you seek, or you give up on this dream. Do you understand?"

"Yes, sir," says Glakchog. "I understand perfectly."

Brelgvu reaches up and drapes his arm around Glakchog's shoulders. "I truly am the only one who really understands what you're going through. Nobody else can help you in achieving your goal. I am your only real friend."

"That you are, Brelgvu," says Glakchog.

"Now go," says Brelgvu. "If you're away from the courtyard much longer, your trainees will wonder where you went. I also doubt that Alasdar would be pleased to learn of your eavesdropping."

Glakchog stands and rushes back down the hall, heading for the barracks. A nearby red-eyed raven catches Brelgvu's attention as it shifts its position.

"I see that the diseased one is watching. Excellent." Brelgvu smiles evilly and disappears into the shadows.

Chapter 17

Pelagius and the others rest in their cells. Aldtaw, who seems to have aged several more years in the past few weeks, snoozes on his cot and Kevnan snacks on a chicken leg left over from a recent meal. The dungeon door opens and Mughan enters.

"Pelagius, you and your friends have visitors," says Mughan.

"Who?" asks Pelagius, surprised.

Mughan steps out of the door and in walks Shukrat, followed by a dwarf carrying an object wrapped in a blanket.

"Shukrat?" says Pelagius. "Why are you here?"

"I've been trying to visit for weeks," says Shukrat. "But it took a while to see King Demonicus to obtain permission. I'm doing my best to try and get you out of this mess."

Shukrat and his companion approach Alithyra's cell, which Mughan unlocks. He shuts the door as soon as they enter.

"Thank you, Captain," says Shukrat. "You may leave us. I'll call you when we're done or if we need you."

Mughan nods and leaves the dungeon, shutting the door behind him. Shukrat turns back to Alithyra.

"I was able to convince the king to allow my friend to fit you for a prosthetic arm," says Shukrat.

"Thank you, Shukrat," says Alithyra.

The dwarf sets his parcel on the cot and unwraps it, revealing a metal arm composed of iron and steel. The elbow has joints so that it can move, and several levers cover its surface. The dwarf slips a harness over Alithyra's good shoulder and tightens the straps so that a large metal circle with a hole in the middle covers her stump. He fastens several more straps to keep it secure.

"This harness is just temporary," says the dwarf. "Once we get you out of this dungeon, I can provide one that will be significantly easier for you to get in and out of on your own while still being just as secure."

The dwarf picks up the arm and inserts it into the slot. He pulls a few levers, clamping it in place and secures it with a few locks.

"Now, I need to show you how to work it," says the dwarf. "For now, it must be mundane, but later Shukrat can enchant it so that you can control it as though it were your real arm."

The dwarf grasps the upper and lower portions of the arm, then bends the elbow so that the forearm is parallel to the floor.

"This device is quite complex," says the dwarf. "Its inner workings are filled with various cranks, pulleys, gears, springs, and levers of many sorts. Pull this lever on the wrist."

Alithyra pulls on a small lever on the side of the wrist. As she pulls it, the fingers curl as though grasping something until they ball into a fist. The lever clicks as she pulls it all the way back.

"This way you can keep a tight grasp on something," says the dwarf. "With the fingers locked in place, you can hold a sword in battle or even grip a bow."

The dwarf takes her through a small amount of training, pulling a few levers here and there to demonstrate the arm's capabilities. Each lever has a different function, allowing the prosthetic to operate like a real arm in almost every aspect.

"I even worked a bit of infernal steel and war-iron into it, so it's very durable," says the dwarf with a grin. "You can even use it to block attacks by swords and axes, although I wouldn't recommend trying that until you can magically control it."

"Where did you get war-iron?" asks Kevnan.

"I'm actually originally from Battallia," says the dwarf. "I've traveled the continent, though, and, despite my kingdom's stance, I personally enjoy Diablos. I brought some war-iron with me on my travels, unknown to my government, and have been experimenting with combining war-iron and infernal steel. This is my finest creation yet."

Alithyra grasps the arm and bends it upward to look at it. "Thank you, sir. This means a lot to me. Hopefully, I'll be able to put it to use."

The entry door opens and Mughan returns.

"I didn't call for you," says Shukrat.

"I know," says Mughan. "The king has called for them. He has gone over all the reports, minus the one from the missing messenger, and is ready to make his decision."

Shukrat glances at the others, who nervously look at each other. Mughan and a few other guards open the cells and escort the prisoners to the main hall; where the king will decide their fates.

Chapter 18

The guards lead Pelagius and the others into the great hall to resume their trial. Everything is as it was before, complete with onlookers filling the balconies. As they come to a stop, Barbox steps forward.

"Presenting His Royal Majesty, King Demonicus IX," says Barbox.

King Demonicus rises from his throne as the entire gathering bows. He motions for them to rise, then sits. "Proceed, Barbox."

Barbox nods and turns to the audience. "We all know why we are here. Pelagius and company have been accused of the assassination of Marquis Babu. Despite admitting to the crime, he has claimed innocence and presented evidence that Babu has been committing unlawful acts unknown to the court. Do you stand by these claims, Pelagius?"

"I stand by them, sir."

"Understood," says Barbox. "All reports from the king's friends and allies outside of Diablos have been returned. All seem to corroborate your story. We have yet to hear from Darderos, the messenger who was sent to Devil's Den. The claims of its denizens are that he has already come and gone."

Demonicus furrows his brow. "We suspect that Alasdar or one of his subordinates is responsible for his disappearance, but we have no proof and nothing to act on in that regard. Troubling as it is, we must continue without his report."

The members of the crowd mutter amongst themselves, debating the information just provided. Pelagius glances nervously at his companions.

"The reports support Pelagius's claim," says Barbox. "The evidence that Babu was illegally harvesting souls beyond his territory, and well over the legal limit, is overwhelming. It is clear that Marquis Babu is guilty of the crimes he has been accused of. As such, it is clear that what was done needed to be done."

A look of relief crosses Pelagius's face, but a glare from Barbox quickly erases it.

"However, that does not change the fact that Pelagius and company conspired to assassinate a member of the royal court," says Barbox. "Not only did they conspire to do so, they carried out the assassination. If they had come to King Demonicus and explained the situation, the investigation would have uncovered this evidence, and Babu would have been brought to justice legally. Instead, they chose to murder the marquis. After considering all the known facts and evidence, King Demonicus has come to a decision."

Demonicus leans forward on his throne, resting his head on the tops of his hands. "Of a sort." He gestures toward Aldtaw. "As Aldtaw was not involved in the assault, he is cleared of whatever charges were brought against him. Guards, release him."

The guards unshackle the aging Aldtaw, and he shuffles to the side.

Demonicus turns his attention back to Pelagius. "Due to the evidence against Babu, it is unclear if Pelagius and company can truly be declared guilty. Clearly Babu deserved what happened, but the justice dealt was illegal. Therefore, this trial shall be decided in another manner."

The crowd erupts in a frenzy of confusion. Pelagius shoots a puzzled glance at Shukrat, who simply shrugs.

"In a few weeks' time, the Grand Tourney begins," says Demonicus. "Pelagius, you, Kevnan, and Alithyra shall enter the tournament. Should you make it past the qualifiers and into the final thirty-two, you and your companions may be cleared. In the finals of the tournament, for every combat round you win, one of your companions will be cleared of all charges."

"As for you, Pelagius," says Demonicus, "if you win the entire tournament, all charges against you shall be dropped. If at any time you lose, you and any companions who have not been cleared will be found guilty."

"What if one of us wins?" asks Kevnan.

"If you or Alithyra win, you will clear your own names only," says Demonicus. "If Pelagius manages to clear one of you before then, you may choose one other companion aside from Pelagius to absolve. Since he was the mastermind, Pelagius can only clear his name himself."

Pelagius bows. "That is a very fair ruling. Thank you, Your Majesty."

"To make it truly fair, you shall be allowed to train for the tournament," says Barbox. "While you are all still prisoners, you and your companions will be moved from the dungeon and placed in the guest quarters. You will all be kept under constant surveillance, of course, and your room shall remain locked whenever you are in it. You will be provided with weapons and armor for the training and the tournament itself. Alithyra, if Shukrat can enchant your prosthetic, he will be allowed to do so."

"That is the ruling," says Demonicus. "Win the tournament and you are free. Lose and you will face justice for your crimes. You may begin your training in the morning. Good luck at the Grand Tourney, Pelagius."

Demonicus dismisses the court and the crowd files out. The guards escort the prisoners to their new quarters, locking them in for the night.

Chapter 19

Pelagius and the others enter a luxurious wing near the center of the castle. Torches illuminate the entire area and opulent paintings line the walls. Several cushy chairs surround a table in the center of the room and several other doors lead to individual bedrooms. Pelagius looks around and notes that the door they came through is the only way in and out of this area.

"These are to be your quarters for the next few weeks," says Mughan. "You may gather and converse in the common area at your leisure. You have your choice of bed chambers, and you may enter and exit those chambers as you desire. However, while you are all here, this main door will remain locked. Guards will be stationed outside the door, and will respond immediately if you cause any trouble."

Mughan exits, shuts the door, and locks it behind him. Pelagius and the others sit at the table in deep thought about these recent events.

"So, the trial continues," says Ralkgek. "Honestly, I was hoping for a ruling just to get it over with."

"At least we have a chance," says Pelagius.

"It's a very slim chance," says Kevnan. "Winning the entire tournament is a tall order."

"For now, I'm focused on qualifying," says Pelagius. "After that, I'm more concerned with getting the rest of you cleared, but if I can win the whole thing, that in itself is worth the trouble."

"Is King Demonicus making one of us Diablos' representative in the tournament?" asks Alithyra.

Pelagius laughs. "No, I'm sure that Diablos' kingdom representative has already been chosen. We'll just be three more among the independent entrants. It will be interesting to see who else is competing."

The main door unlocks, opens, and Aldtaw hobbles in. The door immediately shuts behind him and re-locks. The aging canin takes a seat among the others.

"Why are you here?" asks Ralkgek. "You were cleared of whatever it was they accused you of."

"It's not like I have anywhere else to go," says Aldtaw. "At least here, I'm safe from being recaptured by the Green-Eyed Man."

"With everything that's been happening, I completely forgot to ask," says Kevnan. "You know his real name, don't you?"

The others look at Aldtaw with curious intent. Aldtaw sighs. "I did once. Unfortunately, while I wouldn't say that I'm going senile yet, my mind is aging faster than my body. I've begun to forget things, and I'm sorry to say that his name is among them."

"How much longer do you have?" asks Pelagius.

Aldtaw shrugs and sighs wearily. "It's difficult to say. Probably a few more months. At least I won't have to spend my last days in a dungeon. And I'll get to attend the Grand Tourney. Even before my imprisonment, I'd never been able to do that."

"Still, you deserve better than this," says Kevnan. "If we can find a way to reverse your aging and allow you to live the full life that was stolen from you, we will."

Aldtaw grins. "Thank you, Kevnan. There may be a way, but it's not something that I know of. If it were possible to live out my life normally, I would gladly take the opportunity to do so. But enough about my fate. You need to focus on the Grand Tourney."

"Indeed, we do," says Pelagius. "Let's get some rest. Tomorrow, the next journey begins."

Chapter 20

Shudgluv enters the dungeon and slams the door hard enough to nearly shatter its hinges. He furiously paces up and down the cell block as Eeshlith and Darderos watch him with looks of concern.

"I can't believe this," says Shudgluv. "Of all the most moronic plans possible, how could he actually be going through with this?"

"Shudgluv, what's wrong?" asks Eeshlith. "What did you hear?"

"You're not going to believe this," says Shudgluv. "Alasdar is planning something truly horrendous, and the Green-Eyed Man is going to help him."

"Calm down," says Eeshlith. "Take it easy, and tell me what you found out."

Shudgluv stops pacing and takes a few deep breaths. He explains the details of Alasdar's meeting with the soul hunters, having just learned of it from the Green-Eyed Man. As he finishes, Eeshlith stumbles backward and sits on her bed in shock. Darderos curses in multiple languages as he slams his fists against the wall of his cell and donkey kicks his bed.

"This can't be real," says Eeshlith, stunned. "Alasdar has never shown any interest in ruling a kingdom."

"He always was the most ambitious of us, even in his first life," says Shudgluv. "The soulborn transformation must have brought that ambition to the forefront."

"He must have been planning this for years," says Eeshlith. "He was waiting for someone to kill Babu. That's why he didn't help with the defenses."

"But why?" asks Shudgluv. "He's powerful enough to have been able to destroy Babu himself. Why wait for someone else to do it?"

Eeshlith shrugs. Finally calming down, Darderos steps up to the bars. "Because he probably didn't think anybody would willfully follow him if he did it himself, especially the soul hunters. He wanted them for his own purposes, but they were oath bound to Babu. If he had killed the Marquis himself, the soul hunters would never have willingly followed him."

"That does make sense," says Eeshlith.

Shudgluv slams his fists into the wall. "That's it. I'm done here. I will not stand by while Alasdar and the boss commit such a blatant act of treason. I'm leaving and I'm going to break you two out."

Shudgluv approaches Eeshlith's cell and reaches for the keys on his belt, but Eeshlith grabs his hand and stops him.

"No," says Eeshlith. "Not yet."

"Are you still going to try to appeal to the boss' remaining humanity?" asks Shudgluv. "Even after he put you here?"

Eeshlith shakes her head. "I'm still alive, so there is still a chance I can reach him, but that's not the reason I stopped you."

"Then why did you prevent me from freeing you?" asks Shudgluv.

"Think for a moment," says Eeshlith. "With this news spreading around, the fortress is probably restless. There are too many eyes that could spot us leaving. If we tried to escape now, we'd be recaptured or killed before we could sneak out of the building."

"What do you propose?" asks Darderos.

"This will take careful planning and timing," says Eeshlith. "We must remain here for a few more weeks and plan this out. We can't just flee. We have to know where we are going."

"Shukrat is a generous soul," says Shudgluv. "He might be willing to grant us sanctuary."

"I'll be heading straight to Castle Demonicus," says Darderos. "The king must get my report before it is too late."

"That settles the destinations," says Eeshlith. "But for the rest, we must be patient."

CHAPTER 21

Several weeks pass, and the eve of the Grand Tourney arrives. Pelagius and the others rest in the common area of their opulent prison-guest quarters. They sit at the table conversing and playing a game of cards. Aldtaw emerges from his bedchamber. Having aged several more years, he stoops over and walks with a cane. Much of his hair has turned gray, especially around his muzzle, and a long white tuft of beard-like hair extends down from his chin. Despite his tired and haggard appearance, he hobbles over to join the others.

The door unlocks and Mughan enters. He grins warmly as he sees his charges. "Good evening, my fine prisoners."

"It's not often that we see you at this time," says Pelagius. "What brings you here, Mughan?"

"It is the eve of the Grand Tourney," says Mughan, "A grand feast is being held for all guests, dignitaries, and competitors, and King Demonicus has invited you to join the festivities. You will be carefully watched, of course, but you are welcome to come."

Pelagius grins as he rises to his feet. Kevnan, Alithyra, and Ralkgek follow suit.

"Thank you, Mughan," says Pelagius. "We would be honored."

Aldtaw takes a seat and rubs his snout, his head sagging toward his chest. "I think I shall remain here. I must rest."

Mughan frowns and gives the aging canin a look of pity. "As you wish. Since you are not a prisoner, the door will remain unlocked for you if you should feel up to joining later. The rest of you, come with me."

Mughan leads them out of the guest quarters and to the great hall. The room has been lavishly decorated, and several tables have been set out, all laden with food. The chamber is full of people of all species milling about, conversing with one another and dining on the scrumptious delicacies. Pelagius and the others weave through the crowd, heading for the nearest empty table.

"Pelagius, aren't you a sight for sore eyes," says a familiar voice as he reaches the table.

Pelagius turns and instantly recognizes the elderly centaur walking in his direction.

"Celemrod!" exclaims Pelagius. "It is great to see you."

"Same to you, my friend," says Celemrod. "You must tell me of your journey. Where are Bojan and Adotiln?"

Pelagius shakes his head and lowers his eyes to the floor. "Sadly, Bojan and Adotiln are no longer with us."

"I'm sorry to hear that," says Celemrod. "What happened and why are the guards staying so close to you?"

Pelagius relates his tale, starting with his departure from Austracene. Celemrod listens intently, as do several other guests surrounding them. A look of shock crosses the old centaur's face as he learns of Pelagius's current situation.

"Quite a spot you're in," says Celemrod. "Good luck to you, Pelagius."

"Thank you, Celemrod," says Pelagius. "I'll certainly need it."

As Celemrod takes his leave, a young man, possibly in his early thirties, wearing fine, blue silk clothing, approaches Pelagius. Accepting a goblet of wine from a passing servant, he smiles as he approaches the table. "Pelagius, right?"

"Yes," says Pelagius.

"I apologize, but I couldn't help but overhear your story," says the stranger. "Quite a fascinating tale. I'm sorry for the bind it put you in. Have you met any of the competition?"

"Not yet," says Pelagius. "Are you competing?"

The stranger smiles. "I am. While I do not wish to condemn a man such as yourself to whatever fate your trial has in store for you, I hope you understand that I can't just let you win if we face each other."

"I understand," says Pelagius. "It is a competition, after all. I would not wish for anybody to throw a fight just for my sake."

"Very honorable," says the stranger.

"May I ask your name?" asks Pelagius.

"Forgive me, sir," says the stranger. "Where are my manners? Sir Jabbleth at your service."

Pelagius and his companions take a step back in shock at the man's name.

"Sir Jabbleth?" asks Kevnan. "You are the current Black Knight?"

"I see my reputation precedes me," says Jabbleth.

"It does," says Pelagius. "Legendary as your deeds are, they are also horrific and vile. Why so polite when you know we are on opposing sides of the conflict?"

Jabbleth chuckles. "I am a knight, sir. Rudeness is not a part of my character. We may be enemies ideologically speaking, but we share no personal enmity. I have nothing but respect for you, Pelagius."

"Forgive me," says Pelagius. "I am more accustomed to enemies who are not so civil."

"I think you'll find that not all of us whom you consider evil are rude or, to put it bluntly, psychotic," says Jabbleth. "Alas, I must be off. There are others to meet and mingle with. Good luck, Pelagius. Perhaps we will meet on the field."

Jabbleth extends his hand. After a second of hesitation, Pelagius accepts, and the two men engage in a firm handshake.

"If we do, I look forward to the challenge," says Pelagius.

"As do I, my friend," says Jabbleth. "Farewell for now."

Sir Jabbleth slips off into the crowd. Pelagius and the others spread out around the room to mingle. As he scans the crowd, Pelagius spots an older orc wearing purple priest's robes streaked with gold. The orc is speaking with a wizened elf and a regal-looking, middle-aged neanderthal. As Pelagius moves in to get a closer look, a man roughly his own age, wearing a suit of armor, deliberately blocks his path.

"Please don't disturb Archpriest Bothurg," says the man. "He is engaged in an important conversation."

"So, he is the Archpriest," says Pelagius. "I thought that might be him, but I wasn't sure."

"It is," says the man. "He is taking some much-needed leisure time to attend the Grand Tourney."

"You are his bodyguard, correct?" asks Pelagius.

The man chuckles. "In a manner of speaking. As the Grand Inquisitor of the Order of the Divine Hand, that is but one of my duties."

Pelagius's eyes grow wide as he realizes who he is speaking to. "Grand Inquisitor Rynmor! Forgive me, sir. I didn't recognize you."

"No worries, my friend," says Rynmor. "We've never met before, so there is no reason that you would recognize me. You are Pelagius, a Crusader of Ender, are you not?"

"I am, sir," says Pelagius. "Although I chose to be an independent crusader rather than join the Order of the Divine Hand."

"In a way it is a shame," says Rynmor. "From what I have heard of your accomplishments, had you decided to remain with the Order you would have been promoted to Knight Crusader within a year and Chevalier within ten. It is possible that you may have even become the Lord Chevalier of Ender's Waskan branch of temples by now. I realize, though, that working for the Order is not for everyone. You wanderers are an essential part of Sarcasca's society."

"Just Lord Chevalier?" asks Pelagius jokingly. "You don't think that I would have made Knight Templar or even Inquisitor by now?"

Rynmor shares a laugh with him.

"Knight Templar is possible, but unlikely," says Rynmor. "Inquisitor is very unlikely, since there is only one per kingdom, and no positions have opened up in your lifetime."

"I see," says Pelagius. "Who is the Archpriest conversing with, if I may ask?"

"The elf is King Sylwyn of Eosurwood," says Rynmor. "His eldest son Prince Matheral is competing as well. The other is King Bloodsworth VII of Battallia."

"It must be very important then," says Pelagius. "I shall be going. Best of luck to you, Grand Inquisitor."

"Thank you," says Rynmor. "To you as well."

Pelagius slips away and rejoins his companions. As the night goes on, he speaks with more competitors and dignitaries. His companions also mingle with many important people. Kevnan converses with a well-known dwarven Waskanian hero named Baron Skadgral, who represents the kingdom of Waskan in the tournament. Alithyra spends much of the night interacting with a nervous-looking young human warrior and a gruff-looking, battle-hardened satyr. At one point, Pelagius spots Koskru in the crowd, but is too far away to approach him for conversation.

Ralkgek has less luck with the mingling. Unable to see, he gets jostled about in the crowd. As Ralkgek tries to stumble away from some of the guests, he bumps into a young, finely dressed elf, who wheels around and shoves him away.

"Watch where you are going, daemon," says the young elf. "You should learn to respect your superiors."

"Forgive me, sir," says Ralkgek. "I am recently blind and could not see you. I meant no disrespect."

"If you cannot see, you should not join such a party," says the young elf. "You inferior species are such bothersome beasts. Why did they let you in?"

Ralkgek balls up his fists and sharply inhales. He slowly exhales before addressing the elf again. "Insults are unnecessary. Who do you think you are that you can be so blatantly rude?"

"How dare you?" says the young elf. "I am Prince Matheral, heir to the throne of Eosurwood. You have no right to speak to me in such a manner. In fact, you have no right to speak to me or any of your elven superiors at all."

"My elven superiors?" asks Ralkgek.

"I will not lower myself to explaining the intricacies of elven superiority to an inferior such as yourself," says Matheral.

Before Ralkgek can respond, King Sylwyn comes over. He steps between Ralkgek and Matheral, crosses his arms, and glares disapprovingly at his son. "Matheral! Mind your tongue!"

"I said nothing wrong, Father," says Matheral. "I was simply stating the truth."

Sylwyn scrunches his face and exhales slowly. "Your truth is not what I taught you. Apologize to this man."

Matheral scoffs. "I will not apologize. Not to one such as this thing that is so far beneath me."

Sylwyn slaps Matheral hard across the face. "I can still withdraw your name from the tournament. Learn your manners, Matheral, or our kingdom will forfeit this year."

Matheral sneers and turns to Ralkgek. "I apologize for my words and behavior."

The young prince turns and stomps away, disappearing into another room. King Sylwyn turns to Ralkgek. "I sincerely apologize for my son. He is young and misguided. I am trying to break him of this superiority phase."

Ralkgek bows. "Think nothing of it, Your Majesty."

King Sylwyn embraces Ralkgek and exchanges a firm handshake. He goes to the other room, presumably to set Matheral straight. The festivities continue with no more incidents. Finally, close to midnight, the feast comes to an end. The guests exit the main hall, heading to their quarters or the nearest inn. Mughan escorts Pelagius and the others back to their chambers, locking them in for the rest of the night.

Chapter 22

Grimadert stands by a small table upon which rests a piece of leg-shaped iron, mostly hollow in the center. Using a hammer and chisel, he slowly chips away pieces of the interior. Grabbing a large pair of tongs, he then places the leg in a nearby fire until it is red hot. He removes it and pounds on it with a hammer, smoothing out the interior and bending it into an improved shape. When Grimadert is satisfied, he dips it into a pool of water, rapidly cooling it down and setting off a torrent of steam. He removes it from the water and looks it over. Grinning, he uses his chisel to split it open down the middle and walks over to Iriemorel.

"Let's give this one a try," says Grimadert. "Fitting attempt number fifty-three. All previous attempts have been either far too big or too small to be of any use."

Grimadert lifts one of Iriemorel's legs and places the object under it. He lowers the leg, easily sliding it into the opening. He places the other half over the leg, fitting perfectly. Grimadert burst into maniacal laughter. "Finally! A perfect fit! Now that we have the sizing correct, we can start on the suit in earnest."

Iriemorel looks at him, unnerved by the laughter. "Suit? I thought that it was just going to be leg coverings."

Grimadert grins and pats him on the head. "Unfortunately, no. The leg pieces are useless if they're not attached to something other than your body. We're going to have to create an entire golem suit for you. Not to worry: we may be able to make the helmet and upper body removable, but the lower portion will have to be grafted to your flesh."

"So, I am to be fully encased in iron?" asks Iriemorel.

"Afraid so, my friend," says Grimadert, grinning madly. "You will be the Iron Dwarf. Has a nice ring to it, don't you think?"

Iriemorel stares up at the ceiling. "I'm not sure I like this idea, but if it's the only thing that will allow me to walk again, then so be it."

"On the plus side, if you have any enemies amongst the fae, you will be physically invulnerable against them," says Grimadert. "Rogi, Giro! Let's get started, boys."

Grimadert returns to the forge, followed by his assistants. Using the successful fitting as a guide, they create a mold for the pieces that they must now fabricate. They work late into the night and well into the early morning.

As dawn breaks outside, they finally finish the golem body that they intend to use in their procedure. Having completed the first part of his project, Grimadert breaks into his mad laugh, but a large yawn interrupts his glee.

"Flaming zombie minotaur!" says Grimadert. "We were at it all night. Well done, boys. Get some rest. We'll need to replenish our strength before we continue."

Rogi and Giro slip out the door, headed for their chambers. Grimadert climbs onto one of his equipment tables and curls up amongst the tools. He falls asleep quite quickly, despite his choice of a bed looking agonizingly uncomfortable.

CHAPTER 23

Shudgluv returns to the dungeon, having gone up to the main fortress to scout the area. He walks up to the cells as Eeshlith and Darderos rise to greet him.

"What did you learn?" asks Eeshlith.

"Tonight seems to be the best opportunity," says Shudgluv. "The soul hunters will be out on a mission. Alasdar is allowing many of the mortal guards to attend the opening ceremony of the Grand Tourney. They'll be gone for a few days, so the only ones on guard will be Charndergh, Yilrig, Glakchog, and any umbra warriors that are not otherwise occupied."

"Sounds like they'll be working with a skeleton crew on guard," says Darderos.

"Thankfully not literally," says Shudgluv.

They share a chuckle at this remark.

"Unfortunately, it's still not a small number," says Eeshlith. "There will still be thousands of umbra warriors spread out throughout the fortress."

"How will we escape then?" asks Darderos. "It sounds like the gate will be thoroughly covered."

Shudgluv and Eeshlith think for a moment.

"I have an idea," says Eeshlith. "I heard that Pelagius and his friends got into Devil's Den via a secret entrance in the dungeon. We may be able to get out through there."

"I once heard Thakszut and Nyogsutt talking about it," says Shudgluv. "It's very risky. We'll have to use impeccable timing, because it leads through Manthysbia's lair."

A look of horror crosses Eeshlith's face.

"Who is Manthysbia? asks Darderos.

"An old and powerful dragon who formed a loose alliance with Babu a long time ago," says Eeshlith. "Nobody is really sure which was here first: Manthysbia and his lair or Devil's Den. Either way, nobody messes with him."

Darderos gulps. "So, our options are to try to sneak past the guards at the gate or go through a dragon's lair?"

"I'm afraid so," says Eeshlith.

"Personally, I'd rather deal with Manthysbia than face Alasdar's wrath if we get caught," says Shudgluv. "At least with the dragon, our deaths will be swift."

"If we wait until he leaves to hunt, we should be able to slip through unnoticed," says Eeshlith. "None of the guards ever patrol the wall by his lair out of fear of being eaten. Even the umbra warriors avoid that area."

"We're all in agreement then?" asks Shudgluv.

Eeshlith and Darderos nod.

"Very well," says Shudgluv. "Tonight, we brave the dragon's lair."

Chapter 24

Mughan escorts Pelagius and the others out of the castle and leads them to a massive stadium. It was obviously recently built to accommodate the tournament. From the exterior, it appears to be a massive but simple wooden structure. He leads them to a huge set of double doors on one side of the arena, where the other contestants filter in.

"This is where I must leave you," says Mughan. "Join the other competitors inside and wait for the doors to open. I shall escort Aldtaw and Ralkgek to the stands."

The competing and noncompeting heroes exchange a few farewells and good lucks, then Mughan leads them away. Pelagius, Alithyra, and Kevnan follow the other combatants into a large but still cramped waiting area inside the arena. Pelagius hears the cheers of the crowd on the opposing side of a set of massive doors. A pair of horns blow, and the doors open, allowing the contestants to enter the arena.

The interior is far more elaborate than the exterior. Makeshift barricades divide a massive field in the center into several different sections, presumably for different types of games. In one section, a deep pit has been dug and a slender board laid across it. Another section has several enormous logs, and another has several large targets set to varying ranges. Roughly half the field is one large section, most likely for jousting and other contests involving horses. A network of barriers surrounds the field, behind which stands a massive crowd stretching back for several yards.

Behind the standing crowd are several levels of stands and seats, followed by a large balcony section extending around the entire structure. Above even these, a series of private boxes line the walls, permitting the nobility to remain separate from the crowd and yet allow their presence to be known. One of these boxes holds Ralkgek and Aldtaw, along with Shukrat and several guards. A few others are empty, with a rope across their entrances indicating they are reserved for someone who has not yet arrived.

At the very top and center of the stadium stands a large private platform which seats King Demonicus and the dignitaries representing the governments of the other kingdoms. This section has been heavily reinforced; the representative of Bratenro is a giant who sits at the very back of the box. King Demonicus is front and center, flanked on his sides by King Sylwyn and Archpriest Bothrug. The other dignitaries sit farther down either side, with a goblin dressed in robes similar to the Archpriest's, presumably the Grand Priest of Barbicon, at the opposite far end. King Bloodsworth sits on the other side. Necrotia's representative wears sorcerer's robes and is clearly undead, most likely a lich.

King Demonicus rises to address the crowd. "Ladies and gentlemen!" His voice booms across the stadium thanks to the excellent acoustics. "Welcome to the Grand Tourney!"

The crowd below erupts into a cacophony of cheers.

"Over the next few days, our chosen contestants will compete for your entertainment and their personal glory!" says Demonicus. "Bragging rights and the great prize of a legendary magical weapon await the one who is named champion. There are many entries this year. We started out with over two hundred hopefuls. Thanks to last week's preliminary rounds, we have that number down to sixty-four. However, there can only be thirty-two in the finals, so let's get the games started."

The crowd cheers again.

"Today, we will hold several contests," says Demonicus. "Horseback ring catching, archery, javelin tossing both on foot and horseback, and feats of strength are but a few of the possibilities. The contestants will be divided into eight groups of eight so that several games will occur at the same time. At the end of the games, the worst performers of each group will be eliminated, and the remaining hopefuls will move on to the next game. Once we have only sixteen eliminations to go, the jousting contest begins. The jousting will continue until we are down to thirty-two finalists, or the sun goes down, in which case the games will resume in the morning. Let the games begin!"

The crowd bursts into cheers and raucous applause as the contestants emerge onto the field. Mughan and several other guards enter the arena and divide the combatants into different groups. Pelagius breathes a sigh of relief when he learns that he will not be in the same group as Sir Jabbleth, Prince Matheral, or any of the giant-size participants. One member of his division does give him pause: a young human male. He does not seem to be an imposing figure. He is average height for a human with a stocky and slightly pudgy build. This bushy-bearded individual doesn't even have the look of a warrior, but his brow-furled expression and piercing eyes hint at a barely-contained rage hidden under his apparently calm facade.

The guards lead Pelagius's group to the largest section of the field, which has a wooden barrier running down the middle. Five suspended boards containing rings of varying sizes and heights are interspersed across the field. There are eight horses and several lances close by. The horse master steps forward as the group approaches.

"Here are the rules of the game," says the horse master. "You will each be provided with a horse and a lance. One at a time, you will ride down the field as fast as the horse can go. Using the lance, you are to catch as many rings as possible from their posts before you reach the end of the field. You will then turn around and repeat the run. You will be judged based on the precision of the catches and how many rings you acquire. Any questions?"

Nobody speaks.

"Good," says the horse master. "Let's begin."

The horse master first selects Kevnan, who mounts the largest horse and takes a lance from the weapons master. At the horse master's signal, he charges down the field, almost in a blur as the horse gallops at top speed. He easily catches the first ring and fourth rings, but misses the second, third, and fifth. On his return trip, moving just as quickly, he manages to snag all five rings for a total of seven.

"Very good," says the horse master. "A little sloppy at first, but not bad. Men, reset the track."

Several underlings quickly return the rings to their perches. The young man with rage-filled eyes is next up. He misses the first two rings, but easily collects the last three. Like Kevnan, he snatches up all five on the way back, bringing in a total of eight.

"A bit of a rough start," says the horse master. "But excellent overall."

Trial by Tournament: Champion of Valor

After another reset, the other members of Pelagius's group go. Most of them do fairly well, although none collect any more rings than Kevnan. Pelagius goes second to last. Steadying his lance and focusing deeply, he charges down the field. He collects all five of the first set of rings with ease. Turning around, he urges his horse on and manages to snag all five of the others on the way back.

"Perfect ten," says the horse master, impressed. "Most excellent."

The last member of Pelagius's division mounts the horse. He charges down the field, snagging the first ring, but missing all the others. Clearly flustered, he tries to turn the horse without slowing down and is flung from the saddle. He gets back on and charges down the field, but his frustration gets the better of him and he swings the lance around wildly, missing every ring on the way back. He drops the lance to the ground and slides off the horse, dejected.

The horse master places his hand on the contestant's shoulder. "I'm sorry, sir, but clearly you are eliminated. Better luck next time. You are welcome to join the spectators for the rest of the tournament."

The young man slinks off into the crowd. As they wait to move on to the next game, Pelagius watches the other groups finishing up. Sir Jabbleth and Prince Matheral are quite clearly dominating their respective divisions, and Alithyra easily scores highest at the archery contest, but with most of the others it's quite a bit closer.

As the round draws to a close, King Demonicus addresses the masses. "Exciting stuff, is it not, people?"

The crowd applauds in agreement.

"Now that the first round is over, the contestants shall take a small break while we clear the field," says Demonicus. "But don't wander off. The next round begins very soon."

Chapter 25

The contestants return to the field ten minutes later. The guards lead Pelagius's group to the far side of the field, where an archery range has been set up. Seven sets of three targets at three different ranges line the field. The bowman steps up to greet the group.

"As you can see, we will be having an archery contest," says the bowman. "All of you will fire at once. You will first be using the closest target. Each contestant will fire five arrows at that target. You will be judged based on your overall skill with the bow as well as how close you get to the center with how many arrows. After that, you will move on to the middle target, again with five arrows, and then to the farthest one. The criteria will be the same for both. Whoever has the worst score at the end shall be eliminated. Is that understood?"

"Yes, sir," say the contestants.

"Good," says the bowman. "Pick a target set and step up to the line."

The competitors spread out and step up to the line on the ground as the bowman hands out bows and places quivers of fifteen arrows beside them. The bowman gives them the signal to begin, and they let the arrows fly. The closest target is the easiest, and all seven competitors do very well. After expending the five arrows, several underlings move the first targets off the field. Once they are clear, the arrows fly once more.

Most do an average job, but the angry young man does exceptionally well. Pelagius does quite poorly, missing one shot completely and landing the rest on the outer edges. As he looks around at the other targets, he notices that one of the others also did just as badly. The squires remove middle targets, and the final round begins.

Pelagius pulls back on the bowstring, arrow notched, the fletching tickles his cheek. It is an older recurve bow, and the draw is heavy enough that he feels the strain in his shoulders. He takes a breath and tries not to think of how long it has been since he last let an arrow fly.

His stance steady, he releases the last of his arrows, and watches in despair as it pierces the target at the very edge.

Not enough. Is this what will trip him up and condemn him? The grim realization of his failure threatens to rise and overwhelm him, but he swallows it down. He sees the bowman approach their group.

The bowman points at Pelagius and the other struggling competitor. "You two. You are tied for last. We can't have a double elimination, so we are going into sudden death. We will use the farthest targets. One arrow each. Whoever lands their shot closest to the center wins. The other is eliminated."

Pelagius and his new rival are each handed one arrow, and they return to the line. The bowman gives the signal. The other contestant looses his arrow immediately, striking the outermost ring. Pelagius observes him, taking his time to focus. He slowly pulls back the drawstring and aims, taking deep breaths as he concentrates. After almost a minute, he releases his arrow. It soars through the air and hits the target just a few inches below his opponent's. All around, the crowd erupts into a raucous frenzy of cheers and applause.

The bowman steps forward grinning. "Congratulations, Pelagius. You are still in the game. Just barely." He turns to the other contestant. "Good effort, but he just barely beat you out. Better luck next time."

The dejected contestant disappears into the crowd. As the other groups complete their rounds, King Demonicus once again addresses the crowd.

"Congratulations to those who remain," says King Demonicus. "We must take a recess to clean the field and set it up for the jousting competition. This will also allow the competitors to don their jousting armor. For everyone else, some entertainment has been arranged outside the arena. The horns will sound when the field is ready."

The crowd filters out of the arena. Mughan approaches with several other guards to help escort the competitors to the feast if they wish.

"Close one, Pelagius." Mughan sneers. "For a moment, I thought I would be escorting you and your friends back to the dungeon." He glances back at Pelagius to check if the little dig has landed.

Pelagius resists the urge to roll his eyes. He steps to Mughan and looks up, right into Mughan's eyes. "As did I. Sorry to disappoint you." A smirk sneaks out and the corner of his lips curl at the absurdity of his lucky reprieve.

Mughan glares at Pelagius. He chuckles and pats him on the back hard enough to knock the wind out of him. "On the contrary. I'm quite pleased that you weren't eliminated. I want to see you in action."

Chapter 26

Rogi and Giro return to the laboratory to find Grimadert already working at hollowing out the golem body. The mad gnome looks over at them.

"What kept you?" asks Grimadert. "I've been at this for hours. Get over here and help me with this."

The twins join their mentor and resume work on their project. Hollowing out the pieces goes significantly faster with the three working together. After several hours, and multiple heatings, poundings, and coolings, they finally have the golem suit ready for the next step.

Grimadert approaches Iriemorel. "This next step is a multiple day process. Grafting this to your flesh and using the golem animation ritual is not a quick procedure. It must be done with the utmost care and precision, or the consequences of failure will be disastrous. Are you certain that you wish to continue?"

Iriemorel ponders the situation and emits a heavy sigh. "I am. Please begin the procedure. Let's just get it over with."

Grimadert emits a deranged giggle. "Excellent. Then let's get started."

Grimadert picks up a large knife and begins cutting an incision around the uppermost part of Iriemorel's thigh.

"What are you doing?" asks Iriemorel.

"Relax," says Grimadert. "This is necessary for the procedure. Besides, you won't feel a thing."

Grimadert starts by slicing into the flesh of Iriemorel's leg and runs the incision all the way down the leg, finishing at the end of the center toe. A mad grin plastered across his face, he starts to cut away the skin in long strips until Iriemorel's entire leg, foot included, is completely skinless. He covers the knee with the golem knee joint before he encases Iriemorel's foot with a boot-shaped piece. He covers the lower and upper leg in their respective components and magically superheats the entire leg covering. It sizzles, and the stench of burned flesh fills the air as he uses the heat to weld the seams shut and fuses the metal to Iriemorel.

He then repeats the entire process on his other leg. Rogi and Giro select more pieces to hand to Grimadert, but he holds up his hand and they stop.

"No," says Grimadert. "That's it for today. We must let these first parts settle."

Iriemorel sighs in relief.

"Tomorrow we'll start on the hips and waist," says Grimadert. "Don't worry though. I'll be sure to make a few pieces removable so as not to interfere with certain bodily functions. We wouldn't want you to make a mess in your suit."

"What do we do with the skin?" asks Rogi.

Grimadert thinks for a moment. "Heat up some oil and fry it. I'm sure we can find somebody who likes dwarf rinds." Grimadert laughs madly and disappears down a hallway, presumably to either rest or work on other projects.

CHAPTER 27

As the horns sound to signal that the jousting contest will soon begin, Pelagius and the other contestants gather by the door to await their entry. The armor they wear appears to be full plate, but it is bulkier and twice as heavy as the version worn for combat. Most of their suits are essentially the same with a few exceptions. Some of the contestants are of a species requiring special design changes to fit into the armor. Looking over the competition, Pelagius wonders how any of the larger contestants will even be able to participate. Sir Jabbleth has clearly brought his own armor, since his is completely black.

As the doors open to allow the competitors onto the field, King Demonicus stands and addresses the gathering crowd. "Welcome back, ladies and gentlemen! We shall soon begin today's final competition, the jousting contest. Hopefully, we can complete this round today so that we can move on to the main event tomorrow." Demonicus gestures toward the combatants. "Let's hear it for your brave entertainers."

The crowd erupts into a loud cheer.

"Before we begin, I must go over the rules," says Demonicus. "To start with, anybody intentionally striking their opponent's horse will be disqualified. Second, all lance strikes must be aimed for the shield or the torso. No head strikes will be allowed. Third, everyone must complete their own run themselves. No substitutions, with a few exceptions."

Demonicus gestures to the cyclops, a rhinoran, and a giant. "Because they are too large to ride a horse, and in the interest of fairness to the others, the giant-size competitors have been allowed to choose a champion to represent them in the joust, but only in the joust. As for the games themselves, we all know how jousting works. For this tournament, each match will be a best of five points. A competitor gains a point for shattering their lance on their opponent's shield or body. If both lance's break, that run is a draw. However, knocking your opponent off their horse is worth three points and therefore an instant victory. If you are injured or simply do not wish to continue, a yield or forfeit will be accepted. Is everyone ready?"

The audience once again erupts into thunderous applause.

Demonicus smiles and raises his hands into the air. "Very well. Let the games begin!"

Several guards and squires assist the competitors in mounting their horses, divide them into two groups, and lead them to opposite ends of the field. The contestants draw lots to determine the order of their jousts, with Pelagius drawing the one to go last. The first from his group is a dwarf who, judging from the scars, is clearly either a veteran soldier or a seasoned adventurer.

Grasping his lance tightly to his body, the old dwarf lines up and prepares himself. Looking down the field, Pelagius sees that the dwarf's opponent is Sir Jabbleth. King Demonicus gives the signal and the two contestants' horses bolt down the field as fast as possible. The jousters lower their lances as they close in on one another. Jabbleth deflects the dwarf's lance with his shield before landing a solid blow to the center of the dwarf's body, shattering his own lance and sending the dwarf tumbling from his horse to the ground. The crowd bursts into wild cheers as Jabbleth slows his horse to a stop.

"Ladies and gentlemen, your first winner," says Demonicus. "Sir Jabbleth!"

The infamous Black Knight slides off his horse and walks to his fallen opponent. To everyone's surprise, he helps the defeated dwarf to his feet before embracing him and exchanging a hearty handshake. The dwarf slinks off the field, and Jabbleth exits the arena, having decisively qualified for the finals. Beside Pelagius, Prince Matheral sneers.

"Foolish stubby dwarf," says Matheral. "That's what you get for challenging your betters."

"Is there anybody you don't hate?" asks another elf in the group.

"Elves, of course," says Matheral. "We are longer lived, smarter, more graceful, and much better looking than any of the other mortal species. We are superior, and should be ruling these inferiors and undesirables. I hope that I get to face this Sir Jabbleth in the tournament. I'll show this so-called Black Knight who the true legend is."

The elf laughs. "You versus the Black Knight? I'd pay to see that."

"With any luck, you'll get to see it for free," says Matheral. "I suspect it will be a very one-sided contest in my favor. Now, if you'll excuse me, my loyal subject, I believe it is my turn."

The elf bends down in an over exaggerated bow. "Oh, please, show us how it is done, Your Majesty."

Matheral glares at him and coaxes his horse up to the starting line. Glancing down the field, his opponent appears to be a busurin, judging by the built-in lump on the back of the armor.

"One of the deformed ones?" says Matheral. "They insult me with such a pitiful opponent."

At King Demonicus' signal, they charge down the field, lowering their lances as they draw near. Matheral loses his grip at the last moment and nearly drops the lance but manages to hold onto it. This causes him to miss his target entirely, and his opponent's lance shatters against his shield.

As Matheral slows his horse to a stop at the other end of the field, the horse master approaches. He adjusts the prince's grip. "Try grasping it like this."

Matheral slaps his hand away. "I know how to joust, peasant. I just thought I'd allow that pitiful soul a brief moment of hope before I crush his dreams."

The horse master crosses his arms. "From my view, it looked like you lost your grip."

"You are incorrect," says Matheral. "One so superior as myself could never make such a basic mistake."

The horse master chuckles. "Just try not to give him too many 'sporting chances' before you decide to get serious."

Matheral starts to retort but sees the signal to start before he can say anything. Distracted, he charges down the field. He and his opponent come to blows, both shattering their lances on one another. Reaching his end of the field, he slows his horse to a stop as a squire hands him a new lance.

"So, where's your superior jousting skills, your highness?" asks the elf, mockingly.

"Do not mock me, peasant," says Matheral. "I was giving him a sporting chance. You are about to see what I can really do."

The two combatants charge each other once more. At the last second, Matheral leans back, ducking under his opponent's lance and shattering his own against the busurin's shield. The horse master hands him another one.

"It's a tie at the moment," says the horse master.

"Of course it is," says Matheral. "I didn't want to bore the crowd with another decisive victory immediately after Jabbleth's. Unlike our so-called Black Knight, I seek to entertain the people."

"Whatever you say, Your Highness," says the horse master.

At the king's signal, the two combatants charge once more. This time, both riders remain solidly in position as they begin their final approach. They clash, shattering their lances against one another's bodies and both topple off their horses. Matheral manages to grab onto his saddle at the last moment, hanging from the side of his horse as he reaches the end. The busurin is not so lucky and tumbles to the ground. As the crowd cheers, Matheral releases his grip and drops to the dirt. He looks back at his opponent and sneers before leaving the field.

The next several bouts are nowhere near as suspenseful, with two contests going to point based decisions. The angry young man has a victory just as decisive as Jabbleth's on the first run. Grand Inquisitor Rynmor and Koskru also win their bouts quite easily. Kevnan, clearly not used to wearing such heavy armor, has more difficulty, but manages to pull off a win.

Alithrya's new friends, the nervous young man and the battle-hardened satyr, are both victorious as well, with the satyr scoring a decisive victory and the young man knocking his opponent off his horse in the third run. Despite needing to manually adjust her prosthetic, Alithyra wins her joust with ease, knocking her opponent off his horse on the second try. The competition continues late into the afternoon and the sun is beginning to set as the second to last bout comes to an end. As Pelagius rides up to the line, King Demonicus addresses the crowd.

"What an exciting afternoon!" says Demonicus. "I know that it is beginning to get late, but don't go anywhere yet. We only have one more bout to go, and I believe it should be over before dark. The final joust begins now."

Trial by Tournament: Champion of Valor

Pelagius looks down the field at his opponent, who appears to be a medium-sized canin, although he cannot determine what breed. Demonicus gives the signal and both contestants charge down the field as fast as their horses will go. As they approach one another, they lower their lances for the opportune strike. They land solid blows on each other, shattering their lances and nearly knocking each other off their horses, but both remain in the saddle. Replacing their lances, they barrel down the field again.

Pelagius deflects the blow with his shield and lands a solid strike on his opponent's torso, causing his lance to practically explode. Reaching the opposite end and receiving a new lance, he charges back down the line. His aim is off, and he misses his opponent, who shatters his lance against Pelagius's chest. Once more, they speed toward one another, lances poised to strike the final blow. Neither one bothering to block, they each land a solid strike simultaneously, their lances shattering on impact. The crowd bursts into frenzied cheers as the two competitors look to King Demonicus about what happens next.

"Ladies and gentlemen, we have a draw!" exclaims Demonicus. "However, we must have a clear victory, so we are going into sudden death. Figuratively speaking, of course. In sudden death, simply shattering your lances will not be enough. Whoever can knock his opponent from the horse first wins."

The two opponents charge down the field, lances once again poised to strike the victorious blow. Pelagius fails to react with his shield in time and his opponent's lance goes straight for his chest. However, at the last second, he repositions himself so that the lance glances off his armor. He leans forward, driving his own lance into the other rider's chest. The lance explodes with a force strong enough to knock the rider clear out of the saddle, hitting the ground with a thud. The spectators burst into a raucous, thunderous applause.

"We have our winner!" exclaims Demonicus. "Congratulations to all who have qualified. That is all for tonight, but the tournament will continue tomorrow. Everyone, spectators and competitors both, are welcome to join us in the grand hall for a magnificent feast. For those who wish to return home, have a good night."

Demonicus departs with the other dignitaries following suit. As the crowd filters out of the arena, Pelagius slides down from his horse and follows the remaining contestants back into the arena's combatant waiting area, where the servants and squires assist in changing out of his bulky armor. Mughan meets Pelagius at the doors and escorts him back to the castle.

Chapter 28

Mughan leads Pelagius and the others into the great hall, which was set up for the feast hours ago and is already packed with guests. Looking around, Mughan spots another guard waving him over. Following him, Pelagius can't help but flash a wide smile when he sees his companions sitting at one of the long tables, along with several other spectators and contestants including Alithyra's new friends. Even Aldtaw is in attendance tonight, but Shukrat is absent. Aldtaw notices him approaching first and greets him with a firm handshake. The others quickly follow suit.

"Congratulations," says Aldtaw. "We were rooting for you the entire time."

"Thank you, my friend," says Pelagius.

"You gave us quite a scare in the archery contest," says Alithyra. "We all thought for certain that you had lost."

"As did I," says Pelagius. "I was quite relieved when I had not let you down."

"They were more concerned for you than themselves," says the nervous young man. "Doubtless that their sentences would be far more lenient than yours."

"I appreciate that," says Pelagius. "You did very well yourself."

"Thank you, sir," says the nervous young man. "Delradi of the village of Wolfsbane."

Pelagius shakes his hand.

The battle-hardened satyr looks over at him. "Hasn't the village of Wolfsbane been abandoned for ten years?"

Delradi fidgets nervously. "It has. I meant that I was born in Wolfsbane."

Sir Jabbleth, who had been conversing close by, approaches the table and places his hand on the satyr's shoulder. "Come now, Hexeron. No need to interrogate the young lad. We all have our stories, and many of us are from small settlements that no longer exist."

"While I don't recall inviting you to our conversation, you have a point," says Hexeron.

"A mercenary's manners to the end," says Jabbleth. "Still more polite than Prince Matheral, though. If you'll excuse me."

Sir Jabbleth disappears into the crowd and Pelagius turns to Hexeron.

"Mercenary?" asks Pelagius.

"Ah yes, forgive me. Hexeron, founder and leader of the Wargoats mercenary band."

"I've heard of them," says Ralkgek. "They have an honorable reputation, only taking jobs from those who are completely honest about what they want done."

Hexeron nods and goes back to his drink.

"So, where's Shukrat?" asks Pelagius. "I know I saw him in the crowd earlier."

"He returned to Ethor," says Alithyra. "He said that he had some important business to take care of but would return for the games tomorrow."

"It's a good thing he is a master of transport magic," says Kevnan. "Especially considering that Ethor is a few days away on foot."

"Who do you think you'll be competing against tomorrow?" asks Ralkgek.

"I honestly don't know," says Pelagius. "King Demonicus hasn't yet announced how the next round will be structured."

"I hope I get Prince Matheral," says Hexeron. "I'd like to knock his superior butt down a few pegs."

As they continue conversing, King Demonicus appears at his seat and addresses the crowd. "Good evening, ladies and gentlemen. Today was a very exciting day. Tomorrow will be even more exhilarating, for the tournament begins in earnest. I know many of you have questions as to how the lineup will be determined, but that is for tomorrow. For tonight, eat, drink, and have a great time."

The evening continues with food and drinks continually served. At one point in the evening, Celemrod joins the heroes at their table, congratulating Pelagius and the others on qualifying for the main tournament. After several hours, the festivities come to an end. Many drunk guests simply sleep where they fall, while others leave, preferring a bed. As Celemrod bids them goodnight, Mughan and several guards approach Pelagius's group and escort them back to their quarters.

Chapter 29

As night falls, Shudgluv takes a quick walk around Devil's Den, surveying the opposition they may face if their escape attempt fails. Satisfied that Charndergh is absent and most of the umbra warriors are elsewhere in the fortress, Shudgluv walks away to return to the dungeon. As he walks away, Yilrig spots him and approaches.

"What are you doing away from your post?" asks Yilrig in multiple echoey, simultaneous voices.

Shudgluv slightly jumps and stops. He takes a moment to compose himself and faces Yilrig. "I needed some fresh air. It's not like the prisoners are going anywhere."

"We do not want to hear your excuses," says Yilrig. "Return to your duties or we will be forced to report you to Alasdar."

"Yes, sir. Right away."

"You are dismissed. Don't let us catch you away from your post again."

Yilrig rejoins the guards on the wall and Shudgluv returns to the dungeon. Bolting the door behind him, he unlocks Eeshlith and Darderos's cells.

"No problems?" asks Eeshlith.

"A brief encounter with Yilrig, but he suspects nothing. At least, I don't think he does. It's impossible to read an umbra warlord since they never take off their helmets. Regardless, we should go now while we have a chance."

"Quietly," says Darderos. "We don't want to attract attention."

The three escapees proceed to the farthest end of the dungeon, which has gone unused for decades at least. Locating the broken cell that Alithyra entered through, they find a secret door in the back wall.

TRIAL BY TOURNAMENT: CHAMPION OF VALOR

"How did Babu not know this was here?" asks Shudgluv.

"From what I've gathered, he's not the original owner of Devil's Den," says Eeshlith. "The fortress is old and much of the dungeon hasn't been used in centuries."

Opening it with extreme caution, they discover a tunnel leading down. Closing the door behind them, they follow the tunnel until it ends at another door. Shudgluv cautiously cracks the door open and peeks through. On the other side, he sees Manthysbia snoozing on a pile of gold, his tail right next to the door. Shudgluv immediately freezes and observes the massive dragon.

Shudgluv gulps. "He's right on the other side." Shudgluv speaks in a whisper with a shakiness in his voice. "We'll have to wait until he leaves."

"How long will that be?" whispers Darderos.

"It could be minutes or hours," whispers Eeshlith. "We just need to be patient."

Shudgluv keeps his eye to the door as he continues to observe the dragon. After a few hours, Manthysbia finally stirs, yawning and stretching as he rises. He glances at the door and moves his head for a closer look. Shudgluv freezes in terror as the dragon eyes their only means of escape.

Manthysbia pushes the door closed with his massive paw. "Stupid secret door." Manthysbia's booming voice reverberates around his chamber. "I need to have Alasdar fix it. It keeps opening on its own."

As he hears Manthysbia's steps moving away, Shudgluv cracks the door open again and watches the dragon disappear out his exit tunnel. After a few moments, Manthysbia takes to the sky outside the cave. Shudgluv motions to the others and opens the door. "Whatever you do, do not take anything. Manthysbia will notice that something is missing and will conduct a violent search of the countryside."

The three escapees quickly move through the dragon's lair, leaving through the cave and setting foot outside. They quietly creep toward the swamp, not wanting to catch the attention of any guards farther down the wall. Manthysbia returns just as they slip into the trees. The dragon sniffs the ground and surveys the area. He looks directly at their hiding spot and watches it for several minutes. He gives a wicked grin and slips back into his cave as multiple, red-eyed ravens gather. The three escapees breathe a sigh of relief.

"What now?" asks Eeshlith.

"I must return to the castle as quickly as possible," says Darderos. "The king will need to hear my report immediately."

"We'll head for Ethor as per our plan," says Shudgluv. "With any luck, we should get there in a few days."

"I thought that Ethor was only a day's journey," says Darderos.

"Normally it is," says Eeshlith. "But we will be moving through the thickest part of the swamp for a while, which will delay us. And we will be moving slowly and quietly, so as not alert any of Alasdar's spies that he may or may not have posted."

"I see," says Darderos. "Good luck."

"You as well," says Shudgluv. "Farewell, my friend."

Darderos turns and bolts through the trees as fast as he can run. Eeshlith and Shudgluv silently head the other way, failing to notice the appearance of General Charndergh on the wall above Manthysbia's cave.

Chapter 30

Charndergh shoves open the doors to Alasdar's throne room and enters with urgency. He quickly bows as he reaches the center of the room. "Forgive the abrupt entry, My Lord. The king's messenger has escaped, along with Shudgluv and Eeshlith."

Alasdar leans forward, intrigued by the news. "So Shudgluv finally grew a spine. I've been waiting for him to turn on us for some time. How did they get out?"

"Through Manthysbia's lair while he was out," says Charndergh. "It would seem that the rumors of a secret entrance there are true."

"It takes brave or foolhardy individuals to try to use that," says Alasdar. "No matter."

"What shall I do, My Lord?" asks Charndergh. "Shall I send some men to intercept them?"

Alasdar grins. "No. Everything is going according to plan. Let them think that they have gotten away. The messenger's escape was always part of the plan."

"What of Shudgluv and Eeshlith?" asks Charndergh.

"Give them a slight head start," says Alasdar. "When Hazgor and Garu return, have them take Glakchog and a few umbra warriors to pursue them. There is only one place in the area that they could go."

"What about the Green-Eyed Man?" asks Charndergh.

"He shall remain here," says Alasdar. "Now that things have been set in motion, I want at least one soul hunter at the fortress at all times. At least until the army marches to the castle."

"Very well, sir," says Charndergh. "Are we to recapture Shudgluv and Eeshlith?"

"Only if they come quietly," says Alasdar. "If they resist, then Hazgor and Garu are free to do as they wish. We may as well subjugate Ethor while we're at it."

"What of Shukrat?" asks Chandergh.

"He is too loyal to the king," says Alasdar. "As an example to the rest of the town, execute him."

Chapter 31

The next day, the remaining combatants return to the arena waiting area to change into their armor. This time it is not the bulky jousting armor. Instead, most competitors wear chainmail or half plate. Sir Jabbleth wears a suit of black full plate with a pair of large, curved spikes extending from the shoulders, sharp points covering the sleeves and knuckles of the gauntlets and a helmet designed to look like a morag's head.

Pelagius approaches him. "I thought that magic weapons and armor were banned from the tournament. Why are you wearing your Nightshade Armor?"

"I'm not," says Jabbleth. "This is a mundane replica of the Nightshade Armor. Even in a tournament, people expect the legendary Black Knight to bear a certain appearance."

"Fair enough," says Pelagius. "Good luck, Sir Knight."

"Thank you, Pelagius," says Jabbleth. "Good luck to you as well."

They exchange a firm and hearty handshake before Pelagius returns to the other side of the room. After a few minutes, the doors open, admitting the contestants onto the field and the loud cheers of the spectators. As he scans the audience, Pelagius notices that some of the eliminated contestants now occupy a few of the previously empty private boxes.

King Demonicus rises, scares off a few red-eyed ravens, and once again addresses the crowd. "Good morning, ladies and gentlemen. Today we begin the tournament in earnest. This time, every round of the finals will be one-on-one personal combat. The exact type of contest will be determined by one of the combatants chosen randomly at the start. Killing one's opponent is forbidden, and will result in the killer's immediate removal from the competition. First, we must determine who fights whom and in what order. In the middle of the field, we have a jar full of numbers and a chart. Each contestant will draw from the pot and place their name in the spot they have drawn. Gentlemen, you may proceed."

The contestants line up and proceed to draw numbers to determine the order of their battles. Sir Jabbleth manages to draw spot number one, placing him in the first match and Prince Matheral ends up with spot number three. Pelagius reaches in and grabs a piece of folded parchment. He opens it and reveals number thirty-one, placing him in the last match of the round.

"Why do I always go last?" asks Pelagius.

Once the drawing of numbers is complete, the guards take the order chart up to the king's box. King Demonicus examines the chart thoroughly and turns back to the crowd.

"Ladies and gentlemen, we are in for a treat," says Demonicus. "The first match will be the Black Knight, Sir Jabbleth, versus Grand Inquisitor Jarlak, representative of Barbiconia and head of the Divine Hand of Barbicon."

Archpriest Bothrug rises from his seat. "The Divine Hand of Barbicon? Barbicon copied the Order of the Divine Hand and named it after himself? His blasphemy knows no bounds."

The goblin in priestly robes stands and steps up to the Archpriest. "Mind your tongue. The Divine Hand of Barbicon is the true Divine Hand. The God-King has declared this himself."

Demonicus forces himself between them. "Gentlemen, please. This is not the place for a holy war. Try to tolerate one another's presence for a few more days." The two dignitaries return to their seats and Demonicus turns his attention back to the crowd. "Forgive the interruption, good people. In the interest of neutrality, Sir Jabbleth shall choose the game for his match."

"I choose quarterstaffs over the pit," says Jabbleth.

"Very well," says Demonicus. "The rules of this game are simple. The two combatants will be using quarterstaffs and must balance on a beam over a twenty-foot-deep pit. Whoever can knock their opponent into the pit wins. Take your places when ready, gentlemen."

Sir Jabbleth grabs a quarterstaff, a long wooden pole about six feet in length, and steps up to the pit. Grand Inquisitor Jarlak, a goblin in heavy armor, steps up to the balance beam on the opposite side. The weapon master signals them to start, and they cautiously step onto the beam, which is only about two feet wide. They carefully walk toward each other, mindful of their footing. When they meet in the middle, they swing their staffs at each other, connecting with a loud crack. They exchange several blows, with Jabbleth pushing Jarlak back a few feet. The goblin nimbly maintains his balance and pushes back against Jabbleth, who nearly loses his balance, but manages to regain his footing. They clash again. As Jarlak pushes against Jabbleth's staff, Jabbleth suddenly pulls his staff away, throwing the goblin off balance. Jarlak stumbles and nearly falls into the pit. In one quick movement, Jabbleth sweeps his staff under Jarlak's feet. The goblin falls back first onto the beam and bounces off. Jarlak manages to grab onto the beam at the last second and tries to pull himself back up. Jabbleth actually grabs his hand and helps him regain his stance on the beam. Realizing that Jarlak has dropped his quarterstaff, Jabbleth tosses his weapon aside.

"There's no sport in using a weapon against an unarmed opponent," says Jabbleth.

"Hardly an even match, but the thought is appreciated," says Jarlak.

The goblin attacks Jabbleth's shins, although the strikes are not particularly effective due to his armor. Jabbleth kicks Jarlak in the chest and the goblin slips off the beam, plummeting into the pit below. The crowd erupts into a frenzy of cheers and applause. As Jabbleth makes his way across the beam, the squires lower a ladder into the pit, allowing the unlucky goblin to climb out. The two combatants exchange a firm handshake before leaving the field.

"Ladies and gentlemen, your winner is Sir Jabbleth," says Demonicus. "What a great match, and what sportsmanship shown by the Black Knight. The first match is over, but don't go anywhere. The second match begins very soon."

CHAPTER 32

After giving the squires a few minutes to retrieve the quarterstaffs from the bottom of the pit and straighten up the field, King Demonicus and the other dignitaries check the board to determine the next match. Following a brief consultation, Demonicus addresses the crowd.

"Ladies and gentlemen," says Demonicus. "Our next bout shall be Prince Matheral versus Grundoc. Competitors, please enter the field."

Grundoc, a fairly large orc, comes out first to a chorus of cheers. Prince Matheral follows suit and is immediately greeted with a cacophony of jeers and boos. Understanding their ire, King Sylwyn cracks a sympathetic grin, but Matheral sneers indignantly.

"How dare you boo me?" says Matheral. "I am the Prince of Eosurwood! By rights, I should be ruling over all of you peasants!"

As the crowd settles down, Demonicus consults with the other dignitaries.

"As unanimously agreed upon by myself and all the other dignitaries, Grundoc shall choose the game for this match," says Demonicus.

"Unanimous, wow," says Pelagius. "I would never have expected Archpriest Bothrug and Grand Priest Ekdrig to agree with one another."

"Nor would I have ever expected King Bloodsworth to agree with King Demonicus on anything," says Hexeron. "Matheral must have gotten under everyone's skin."

Matheral looks up at the dignitaries with a shocked expression. "Even my father agreed with this? No matter. I can handle whatever game this animal decides upon."

"Grundoc, how would you like to proceed?" asks Demonicus.

"I choose hand-to-hand combat," says Grundoc.

"Typical barbaric orc," says Matheral.

"Very well," says Demonicus. "Take a moment to prepare and then let the games begin."

The two combatants square up in the center of the arena, staring each other down as they prepare themselves for the fight.

"To think I have to lower myself to fight an orc," says Matheral. "As a superior elf, I should win this by default."

"I hope you're prepared to eat your words, Prince," says Grundoc.

"You may as well yield now, orc," says Matheral. "I am better than you in every way."

"Let's see if you can back up your claims," says Grundoc impatiently.

"I shouldn't need to back up anything," says Matheral. "Elves are the superior lifeforms. That does not need to be proven."

"Shut up and fight," says Grundoc.

Grundoc lunges forward and throws the first punch, which Matheral blocks with ease. Matheral retaliates, punching Grundoc in the stomach, but Grundoc does not react at all, prompting a nervous grin from the smug prince. Grundoc slugs him across the face, sending Matheral sprawling to the ground. The orc stands over him as he rises to his feet.

"You're so busy boasting about your own superiority that you forgot one thing," says Grundoc. "Orcs are stronger than elves. You can't match me in terms of physical power."

Matheral grins arrogantly. "That first strike was just a test. I was holding back. I don't need to be stronger than you to outmatch you."

Grundoc takes another swing at Matheral, who quickly ducks under his fist. Matheral punches Grundoc in the side to little effect. Grundoc backhands Matheral across the face, sending him to the ground. Grundoc looms over Matheral, staring down at the prince. "Who is the superior one now?"

Matheral spits. "I am, of course. I already know how to win this."

Grundoc lifts his leg and stomps down toward Matheral's chest. Matheral rolls out of the way and hops up. Before the orc can do anything else, the prince kicks him in the crotch as hard as he can. Grundoc's eyes go wide as a wheeze of pain escapes his mouth. He grabs the afflicted area and drops to his knees as the crowd erupts into a frenzy of boos.

"That was dirty," says Grundoc squeakily. "Poor sportsmanship."

"It wasn't outlawed in the rules presented," says Matheral. "You should have worn plated pants."

Before Grundoc can recover, Matheral rapidly slugs him across the face several times. He punches Grundoc right in the nose and uppercuts him under the jaw. Despite the barrage, Grundoc does not fall. He attempts to stand, but Matheral hits him with another low blow. Grundoc doubles over in pain. Matheral steps around him and jogs ten feet back. He turns and runs at Grundoc at full speed. He leaps into the air and grabs Grundoc by the back of his head. Using his momentum, Matheral drives Grundoc face first into the ground. When the orc does not stir, one of the squires runs out to check on him.

"He is unconscious!" shouts the squire in the direction of King Demonicus.

"Then Prince Matheral is the winner," says Demonicus, clearly disgusted by the manner in which the prince was victorious.

The crowd bursts into another round of jeers and boos as Prince Matheral celebrates his victory. As Grundoc regains consciousness, the squires help him to his feet.

Matheral approaches Grundoc, flashes an arrogant smile, and pokes him in the chest. "I told you we were superior. This victory proves that."

Grundoc glares angrily at Matheral and turns away. "The only thing this proves is that you are a dirty fighter and a coward." He exits the field as the crowd cheers him.

Matheral smugly struts out of the arena, encountering Sir Jabbleth at the doors.

"You have no honor," says Jabbleth, disgusted.

"Honor has no place in combat," says Matheral. "It is a weakness to be exploited."

As Matheral disappears into the inside of the arena, the dignitaries convene with one another.

"I apologize for my son's unscrupulous tactics," says Sylwyn. "His lack of honor shames me to no end. If you wish to disqualify him and reverse the decision, I have no objections."

"Technically, we never said that low blows were illegal," says Bloodsworth. "It is, however, generally assumed that nobody would stoop so low as to use such a disgraceful tactic. I say we let him keep this victory and outlaw low blows from here on out."

"What say the rest of you?" asks Demonicus.

The discussion continues for several minutes. Once they have reached a conclusion, Demonicus addresses the crowd. "After much debate, we have come to a decision. On a vote of seven to five, Prince Matheral's victory stands." The crowd bursts into a frenzy of jeers and boos as Matheral reappears in the doorway and grins.

Demonicus raises his hands in a gesture to the crowd to quiet down. Once the audience calms, Demonicus continues. "However, it has been unanimously agreed upon that from here on out, low blows are illegal in the tournament and any more use of them will result in immediate disqualification. This rule shall be extended to all future Grand Tourneys as well. As further penalty for his actions, Prince Matheral will not be allowed to choose the game for any of his further rounds and, although he will be allowed to continue in this tournament, shall from here on out be banned from competing in the Grand Tourney for life. As compensation for the controversial and unfairly dishonorable nature of his departure, Grundoc will automatically be qualified for the final thirty-two of the next Grand Tourney."

The spectators cheer wildly as the grin fades from Matheral's face. He slinks back into the competitors' waiting area to sulk.

"Since we do not wish the next bout to be marred by this distasteful turn of events," says Demonicus, "we will be taking a ten minute break."

Chapter 33

Iriemorel lies on his operating table, his arms still strapped down and his entire lower body now covered with the prosthetic golem suit. Rogi, Giro, and Grimadert stand around him, adjusting the most recently installed pieces. As they finish up these tweaks, Grimadert leaves the table.

"Finish up for me, boys," says Grimadert. "Then we're done with him for today. I have something else I need to work on."

Grimadert leaves the laboratory and walks down the nearest hallway. He enters the preservation room and approaches a table upon which lie the dismembered pieces of several halflings. On another table nearby is what remains of Adotiln, her most intact parts crudely sewn back together. Her head, minus the lower jaw, has been reattached to her neck, and placed back on the shoulders. The arms and legs have also been reassembled and set approximately where they would normally go if the rest of the body was there. Both hands are nearby, although one is missing the last two fingers, and the other is only half of a hand. Lying where the chest would be is a heart-shaped glowing object constructed of metal and glass. Inside, a strange liquid flows through the structure and around the soul gem. Grimadert examines the recently acquired halfling parts and jots something on a piece of parchment.

"The remains of the one known as Adotiln have been pieced back together as sufficiently as possible," says Grimadert. "However, many parts were missing or too badly damaged to be of further use. A few halfling funerals were recent enough to send Rogi and Giro to their graves after the mourners had departed, but while many of them are usable, not all of them are fresh enough. Fortunately, a few halfling drifters recently wandered by, so we acquired their services as well. Hopefully nobody notices that they are missing."

Grimadert looks through the various parts covering the table. After a while, he picks up the head of a young female and examines it in great detail. He grabs a surgical knife and carefully removes the lower jaw. Grimadert takes it to the table containing Adotiln and places it into the proper spot, making small adjustment cuts to ensure a perfect fit. Once he is satisfied, he slowly sews it in place. He retrieves two fingers and attaches them to the mostly intact hand, which he sews onto the wrist of the proper arm. Looking over the half hand, he tosses it to the side and simply retrieves a whole one from the pile and attaches it to the other arm. Grimadert glances over his work and looks back at the pile.

"Now comes the hardest part," says Grimadert. "Determining the best pieces for the torso and the best organs to use. Nobody has ever created a biogolem without a full or partial mindwipe before. I relish the challenge to create life from death with full memories."

Grimadert flashes a deranged smile and carefully sorts through the many pieces of halfling bodies, in search of the perfect fit.

Chapter 34

As the intermission comes to an end, the dignitaries once again consult the board. Demonicus grins and turns to the crowd. "Ladies and gentlemen, our next match is about to begin. It shall be Ubzon versus Balric."

A cyclops walks out onto the field, followed by the angry young man, whose opponent dwarfs him by roughly ten feet in height.

Demonicus looks at the angry young man. "Balric, you shall be the one to choose the game for this match. Additionally, due to the size and strength difference between you and your opponent, you may choose to combine this match with the next one for a four-person battle to even the odds a bit."

Balric glances up with his eyes, not bothering to raise his head. "No. I choose to take on the cyclops one-on-one."

"Very bold," says Demonicus. "Name your choice of battle."

"Club duel," says Balric. "Victory upon surrender or knock out."

"The decision has been made," says Demonicus. "Squires, bring out the weapons."

The squires pull out a cart of several clubs, including a single club large enough for a cyclops to use. Balric picks out one covered in spikes that is large enough for him to need two hands to wield. As the squires clear the field, Demonicus gives the signal to begin. Balric charges Ubzon, smashing his foot on the first strike. Ubzon cries out in pain and brings his club down upon Balric, who quickly sidesteps it. He swings sideways at the young warrior, who moves to block it. The force of the impact knocks him partway across the field as a result. Balric rises to his feet and glares angrily at the cyclops, breathing heavily through his clenched teeth. He rushes forward and brings his club down on Ubzon's foot. The cyclops grunts and kicks him away before bringing his own club down in an underhand arc. He lands a solid blow on Balric and sends him flying across the field.

Balric rises to his feet and emits a primal scream that shakes the entire arena to the core, silencing the crowd. His rage boiling over, Balric charges at the cyclops, deflecting a club strike on the way. He rapidly strikes Ubzon across the shin multiple times, completely ignoring the cyclops' own attacks. Ubzon brings his club down directly on top of Balric, driving him into the ground. Somehow, the enraged warrior springs to his feet, ignoring what should have been a devastating blow.

Balric leaps up and smashes his club into Ubzon's leg. The blow connects with a sickening crunch and Ubzon cries out in pain as he drops to one knee. Balric jumps up onto the cyclops' thigh, now parallel to the ground, and bashes his club across Ubzon's face. The stunned cyclops topples to the ground and Balric is upon him in an instant, repeatedly pummeling his face. Ubzon blocks a blow with his hand and tosses the raging warrior aside. Flipping onto his stomach, Ubzon starts to stand, but Balric leaps onto the back of his leg and resumes bashing in his knee. Swatting him off, Ubzon crawls away, his injured leg clearly in no condition to allow him to stand. Balric charges back around and slams his club into Ubzon's cheek, sending the cyclops sprawling onto his back. Balric starts bashing in his other leg before running back around and smashing his club into the side of Ubzon's head.

"Stop!" cries Ubzon. "I yield! I yield!"

Balric smacks him in the head one more time before regaining a semblance of control. The crowd sits in stunned silence at the overwhelming victory of this angry warrior. King Demonicus breaks the silence.

"Ladies and gentlemen, the winner is Balric," says Demonicus, clearly as stunned as everyone else.

Balric reverts to his previously calm demeanor, but despite the outpouring, his eyes show that his rage has not truly subsided and remains barely contained. Balric drops his club and returns to the waiting area. The other contestants quickly clear a path as he enters. Balric pauses as he passes Matheral and turns to glare at him, daring the outspoken prince to say something. Matheral gulps and steps out of Balric's reach, wisely choosing to keep his mouth shut. The angry young man resumes his trip to the back.

Once Balric is off the field, the squires come out with a priest in tow, who proceeds to heal Ubzon's injuries. The crowd cheers Ubzon for his valiant attempt as he dejectedly slinks off the field.

"Well, I think we can all agree that went unexpectedly," says Demonicus. "Our next bout is Slythskin versus Kevnan."

Kevnan arrives on the field, followed by a cecropsan. Demonicus thinks for a moment. "Kevnan, you shall choose the game."

"I choose quarterstaffs over the pit," says Kevnan. "First to fall in loses."

"Very well," says Demonicus. "It shall be done."

The two opponents obtain their weapons from the squires and, upon Demonicus' signal, make their way onto the balance beam. Kevnan nearly trips on his own foot and stumbles for a few steps. He swings his arms wildly, takes a step back, and regains his balance. Slythskin, on the other hand, has no problems whatsoever; his lower half is the body of a snake. The two exchange a few blows with their staves, neither one gaining any particular advantage. As they lock weapons and push against each other, Kevnan headbutts Slythskin right in the face. Stunned, the cecropsan nearly topples into the pit, but manages to wrap his tail around the beam as he falls. Using his own momentum, Slythskin swings around the beam by his tail and gets back on it.

"You'll have to do better than that," says Slythskin.

Kevnan lunges forward and strikes at Slythskin. The cecropsan easily parries the attack and retaliates. He blocks the blow and pushes Slythskin's quarterstaff away. Kevnan attempts a leg sweep but connects with the base of Slythskin's tail with no effect. Slythskin jabs his staff forward, striking Kevnan in the gut, causing him to groan in pain and double over. As Kevnan recovers, Slythskin wraps the end of his tail around his ankle and pulls his leg out from under him. Kevnan drops with his legs on either side of the beam and cries out in agony as he lands. Slythskin remains in place, grinning, until a squire steps forward.

"Stop! A rules check is in order." The squire turns to the dignitaries' box. "Your Majesty, does that constitute an illegal attack?"

Demonicus consults with the other dignitaries. "No. I believe his intention was for Kevnan to fall into the pit. Such an accident could easily occur on the beam in any circumstances. Therefore, that was not an intentional move. The match continues."

As Demonicus speaks, Kevnan carefully rises to his feet and takes a moment to regain his balance. Slythskin strikes first and Kevnan narrowly blocks the attack. He takes a step back, ducks under another swing from Slythskin, and lunges forward. He jabs at him and connects just under the chin. Slythskin falls from the beam but manages to wrap his tail around it. He attempts to swing around in the same manner as before, but Kevnan lands a solid blow on his back as he tries to right himself. Slythskin swings back below the beam and comes to a stop upside down. As Slythskin pulls himself back up, Kevnan stomps on his tail. Slythskin loses his grip and plummets into the pit.

The crowd cheers as Demonicus declares Kevnan the winner.

Chapter 35

Kevnan and Slythskin exit the arena, and King Demonicus addresses the crowd. "Next we have Stalgorax versus Gnarzak, the representative of the Necrotian Empire."

A gaki enters the area, munching on a large chunk of meat. A minotaur quickly follows. The two turn to face Demonicus as the gaki swallows the rest of his snack whole.

"In the interest of fairness, Stalgorax shall choose the stipulation for the round," says Demonicus.

The gaki looks at the minotaur and turns back to the king. "I choose hand-to-hand combat, Your Majesty."

"Very well," says Demonicus. "You may begin when ready."

Stalgorax and Gnarzak turn to face one another and slowly walk in a circle. Arms raised and fists clenched, they glare at each other, each daring the other to make the first move. After a few minutes, the crowd grows restless and boos the two combatants. Stalgorax lunges forward, throwing the first punch. Moving his arm into position, Gnarzak blocks the blow. Pushing his opponent back, Gnarzak punches Stalgorax in the stomach, causing the gaki to double over.

Taking advantage of the situation, Gnarzak raises his leg and pushes forward in a large step. His hoof connects with the side of Stalgorax's head. The gaki spins and tumbles to the ground. He shakes his head a few times as he rises. Unable to regain his focus, he stumbles. Gnarzak lowers his head and charges, driving his horns into Stalgorax's belly and sending him crashing to the ground several feet away. When Stalgorax feebly attempts to stand, Gnarzak rushes forward and slams his hoof into the side of the gaki's head. Stalgorax's eyes roll back, and he crumples to the dirt, unconscious. A squire rushes over to check on him and confirms that Stalgorax is out.

Demonicus rises from his seat. "Ladies and gentlemen, the winner is Gnazak."

The crowd cheers as Gnarzak exits the field and a priest rushes out to heal Stalgorax. After a minute, the gaki's eyes open and he leaves the arena.

"Next up, we have Ashisat, representing the kingdom of Ranwald, against the dragon slayer Koskru," says Demonicus.

Koskru emerges onto the field, followed by a human in armor constructed of multiple thick pieces of leather stitched together with heavy straps. Demonicus addresses them. "Koskru, you shall select the match type."

Koskru grins. "I choose a wrestling match. Victory upon pin or incapacitation."

"Very well," says Demonicus. "Let the match begin."

Koskru and Ashisat turn to each other and lock arms, each combatant grabbing onto the other's shoulders. They struggle for several minutes, attempting to push and pull the other one to the ground. Koskru pushes forward, forcing Hashisasto to walk backward. As they continue moving around the arena, they come dangerously close to the pit. Koskru pushes downward, sending Ashisat sinking onto one knee at the edge of the hole.

Glancing back, Ashisat grins and looks Koskru in the eyes. When Koskru renews his attempts to force Ashisat to the ground, Ashisat pulls on Koskru's shoulders. Koskru loses his balance and stumbles forward. Using this momentum against him, Ashisat rolls to the side and yanks on his arms. He releases his grip and Koskru tumbles into the pit.

Demonicus rises to his feet. "We have our winner!"

The squires lower a ladder into the pit. When Koskru reaches the top, Ashisat assists him in climbing out. The two shake hands and exit the arena. Demonicus turns his attention to the crowd. "Our next match features the Wargoat himself, Hexeron, against Diablos's own Raimdon."

Hexeron enters the arena, followed by a blue-skinned daemon sporting a pair of curved horns.

"In this situation, I believe that it is only fair to allow Hexeron to choose the stipulation," says Demonicus.

"I choose a simple duel with any weapon we can get our hands on," says Hexeron. "Victory upon yield or incapacitation."

"Very well," says Demonicus. "The squires shall distribute the weaponry. Choose your starting weapons, gentlemen."

The squires pull a cart of weapons out onto the field. Raimdon approaches and pulls out a longsword and a shield. Hexeron rummages through the cart for a few minutes until he decides to match his opponent. The two combatants take their positions in the center of the arena while the squires spread the remaining weapons across the grounds.

When they complete their task and make their exit, Demoncius gives the signal to begin. Hexeron and Raimdon circle one another, sizing each other up as they formulate their strategies. They charge, their swords clashing with a metallic clang. They strike again with the same result.

The two men continue to exchange blows, blocking with their shields and parrying strikes. Hexeron increases the intensity of his swing and knocks Raimdon's blade to the side, nearly causing Raimdon to lose his grip. Hexeron brings the blade around in an overhead arc. Raimdon raises his shield and Hexeron's sword strikes it hard enough that a metallic crack rings through the arena. Both men take a step back and look over their respective items. Unable to determine which one was damaged, they continue their battle. Raimdon swings his sword around and Hexeron moves his weapon to parry. Hexeron's blade shatters on impact. Dropping the broken weapon, Hexeron positions his shield in front of him, blocking multiple blows from Raimdon's strikes. He slowly backs away, searching for a new weapon. The first item he finds is a large axe. Blocking another blow, Hexeron glances at the weapon.

Grasping his shield with both hands, Hexeron lunges forward, surprising his opponent. Raimdon blocks the charge with his own shield, but the blow forces him several feet back. Hexeron rapidly backs up to the axe and retrieves it. He rushes forward, swinging the weapon at Raimdon, who regains his footing and raises his shield to block the blow. The axe strikes the same spot as the sword earlier and embeds itself in the shield. Unable to dislodge the axe, Hexeron abandons it and rushes off to obtain another new weapon. Raimdon attempts to remove the axe from his shield but is also unsuccessful and drops the damaged item to the ground. He pursues Hexeron to continue the fight. As Raimdon approaches, Hexeron glances down at a long wooden handle connected to a chain, at the end of which is a spiked ball. *A flail. That should do.*

Hexeron picks up the weapon and raises his shield in time to block a blow from Raimdon's sword. He swings the flail at Raimdon, who desperately jumps back to avoid it. Ducking under another swing, Raimdon rushes forward to get inside the flail's striking range. He grabs Hexeron's shield and rips it from his grasp.

Before Raimdon can reposition the shield to use it himself, the head of the flail strikes it with a clang, knocking the shield from his hands. He swings his blade at Hexeron, who uses the wooden handle to parry. Hexeron brings the flail back around, and Raimdon positions his sword to block. The chain wraps around the blade, entangling the two weapons. The two combatants tug at their weapons, trying to pull them apart. Raimdon grasps the hilt with both hands and yanks as hard as he can, wrenching the flail from Hexeron's hand and flinging it to the side. Raimdon steps forward and kicks Hexeron in the chest, sending him crashing to the ground. Raimdon plants his foot on Hexeron's torso and holds the tip of his sword to his opponent's throat.

"Well played," says Hexeron. "I yield."

The crowd cheers as Raimdon helps Hexeron to his feet. While the two exit the field, King Demonicus addresses the crowd. "What an amazing match! Next up, we have Grand Inquisitor Rynmor, the representative of Rodaria, against Halfhill's Waltgaud."

Demonicus turns to the others and consults with them. "It has been agreed upon that Grand Inquisitor Rynmor shall choose the game."

"Your Majesty, I choose quarterstaffs on the balance beam," says Rynmor.

Demonicus nods. "Very well. Take your positions."

Rynmor and Waltgaud go to opposite ends of the pit. They each grab a quarterstaff and position themselves on the beam. Demonicus raises his hand. "Begin!"

Rynmor jabs at Waltgaud, who quickly ducks under the strike. Waltgaud spins in a circle, swinging his staff at Rynmor's legs. The blow connects, sweeping Rynmor off his feet. The Grand Inquisitor plummets into the pit. A stunned silence fills the arena until Demonicus rises to his feet. "A short and sweet match. Waltgaud wins!"

While the squires lower a ladder into the pit, Waltgaud slowly makes his way to the exit, pausing to strike a victory pose several times. Rynmor climbs out of the pit, glances up at the dignitaries' box, and lowers his head shamefully. He quickly exits the arena.

Observing Rynmor's departure, Archpriest Bothrug rises. "Pardon me, gentlemen. I must be off. Rynmor seems deflated by his loss. If he is too humiliated to stay for the rest of the tournament, then I will have to depart as well."

"Best of luck to you, Archpriest," says Demonicus.

Bothrug disappears through the curtain at the back of the box, and Demonicus turns his attention to the crowd. "Ladies and gentlemen, you are in for a real treat with this next bout. Our combatants are Count Vuzenkhord, Lord Champion Gladiator of Battallia, versus Baron Skadgral of Waskan."

The crowd bursts into frenzied cheers as a neanderthal and a dwarf enter the arena. Reaching the center, the neanderthal raises his hands, prompting the audience to cheer again. He grabs the dwarf by the wrist and raises his arm, eliciting the same reaction.

Waiting for the raucous to quiet, Demonicus consults with the other dignitaries. Once the audience has calmed, King Sylwyn addresses the crowd. "As a neutral party, I give the choice of game to Baron Skadgral." He motions to the dwarf. "What say you, baron?"

"A sword duel, Your Majesty," says Skadgral.

"Very well," says Sylwyn. "Demonicus, if you please."

Sylwyn returns to his seat. While the squires hand the combatants their weapons, Demonicus addresses them. "Begin now."

The two contestants stare each other down, circling as they prepare for combat. Vuzenkhord twirls his sword in his hand three times, stops, points the blade in Skadgral's direction, and raises it in the air. The crowd cheers wildly while Skadgral's brow furrows.

"What are you doing?" asks Skadgral.

"Playing to the crowd," says Vuzenkhord. "There is a certain amount of showmanship expected of such an event."

Skadgral groans. "Next time you do that, I'll just strike. You're stupid to leave yourself open like that."

"That would be a breach of decorum," says Vuzenkhord. "I will be prepared for it, though. Shall we begin?"

The two combatants approach each other, and their blades collide. They clash again and separate. Vuzenkhord twirls his blade and parries a blow. He pushes Skadgral back and raises his sword in the air, posing for the crowd. Skadgral charges and swings his sword in a horizontal arc. Vuzenkhord immediately repositions his blade mid-pose and parries the strike. He sidesteps the still-moving dwarf. Grabbing Skadgral's arm, Vuzenkhord pulls him in a circle and sweeps the dwarf's legs with his foot. Skadgral drops his sword and crashes to the ground. Instead of going for the win, Vuzenkhord retrieves Skadgral's weapon and raises both swords in the air. Skadgral rises to his feet and Vuzenkhord hands him his blade.

Skadgral raises an eyebrow. "Why? You had the fight won."

"The last match was far too short," says Vuzenkhord. "These people seek to be entertained. Therefore, we must continue."

"Don't expect the same courtesy from me," says Skadgral.

"Of course not," says Vuzenkhord.

The two men clash again, pushing against each other's swords. Vuzenkhord pulls away, catching Skadgral off guard. The dwarf loses his balance and stumbles while Vuzenkhord strikes him in the back with the flat of his blade.

Skadgral turns to face his opponent, clenching his fist as his face turns red. "Stop playing around!"

"I'm playing to the crowd, baron," says Vuzenkhord. "I mean no disrespect."

"You're not taking this seriously, count," says Skadgral.

"On the contrary," says Vuzenkhord. "I fight gladiatorial battles for a living. What I'm doing is part of the job."

"This is not one of your battles for show," says Skadgral.

Vuzenkhord glares at the dwarf. "For show? You think my gladiator fights are fake simply because I seek to entertain?"

"Prove me wrong, Vuzenkhord. Get serious and fight."

"Are you certain you want that?"

"Yes."

"Very well. You asked for this."

Vuzenkhord's expression morphs into a look of stoic focus. The two men charge, and their swords collide. Before they separate, Vuzenkhord grabs Skadgral's wrist and twists his arm around. Skadgral drops his weapon as Vuzenkhord rapidly spins behind him, still grasping his arm. Before Skadgral can react, Vuzenkhord has the edge of his blade against the dwarf's throat. Vuzenkhord brings his head to Skadgral's ear. "You wanted serious, so you got it. If we were fighting back home, I would have already slit your throat."

Skadgral gulps. "Point taken. I yield."

A nearby squire rushes to the combatants and confirms Skadgral's surrender. As Vuzenkhord releases his defeated opponent, the squire turns to the dignitaries' box. "Baron Skadgral has conceded the match! Vuzenkhord wins!"

The crowd bursts into wild applause as the two combatants exit the field. Demonicus rises to address the crowd. "Next, we have the young Delradi versus the representative of Bratenro, Drosk."

Delradi nervously enters the arena, followed by a large ogre. Drosk looks over his opponent and grins. Demonicus gestures to Delradi. "In the interest of fairness, Delradi shall choose the game."

Delradi thinks for a moment. "I choose a duel over the pit with each combatant using the weapon of their choice."

Demonicus glances at the other dignitaries. "An excellent choice. Contestants, choose your weapon and take your positions."

Delradi and Drosk walk to opposite ends of the pit. Drosk chooses a large club while Delradi picks a a swordstaff, a quarterstaff with a two-foot sword blade on the end, then wraps a meteor hammer around his waist.

When Demonicus gives the signal to begin, they make their way onto the beam. Drosk struggles to balance himself but gets his footing after a few seconds. When Drosk approaches, Delradi jabs at him with the swordstaff, forcing him to back away. Delradi attempts to sweep Drosk's legs, but the ogre steps back to avoid the trip attempt.

As Delradi continues to maintain a distance, Drosk grows frustrated. He aggressively pushes forward. When Delradi lunges at him, Drosk allows the blade to strike him in the chest and grabs the shaft. He brings his club down on the pole, snapping it in two, and tosses the bladed end into the pit. Delradi drops the broken weapon and quickly retrieves the meteor hammer. He twirls it around his head, slowly letting more rope out as it spins. This tactic forces Drosk to duck and back away. Delradi tosses the hammer end at his opponent, striking Drosk in the chest. The impact knocks Drosk off balance and he nearly falls off the beam. Retrieving the dangerous piece, Delradi continues spinning the weapon. He brings it around in a circle toward Drosk's legs, entangling him. Drosk desperately tries to keep his balance, but Delradi yanks on the rope and pulls Drosk's feet out from under him. Drosk crashes onto the beam and drops into the pit.

"Our next match should be an exciting one," says Demonicus. "We have Barglok versus the representative of Drago, Sir Galzra of the Dragon Protectors."

Two figures emerge onto the field. One is a busurin, with the typical bald head, uneven facial features, and hunchback associated with the species. The other individual appears humanoid, but his skin is scaly with a gray tint, and his golden eyes possess a reptilian quality. The busurin looks over his opponent. "Of course, Drago's representative would be a dracian."

"Is that a problem, Barglok?" asks Galzra.

"Not at all," says Barglok. "It's just what I would have expected from that kingdom."

"Enough," says Demonicus. "Barglok, you have been selected to choose the game."

Barglok thinks for a moment. "I choose a fist fight, Your Majesty."

"I see," says Demonicus. "Very well. Remove the upper portions of your armor and begin."

With assistance from the squires, Galzra and Barglok remove their gauntlets, breastplates, and arm coverings. Once their helpers have cleared the field, both men raise their arms and ball their fists. They circle one another, waiting for the other to strike first. After several minutes, Barglok lunges forward and Galzra easily blocks his punch. Galzra retaliates and the busurin blocks in turn.

They continue this process for nearly ten minutes. The crowd grows restless and boos both combatants. Barglok grits his teeth and lunges more aggressively. Instead of blocking, Galzra sidesteps his attack, sending Barglok off balance. Galzra grabs Barglok's arm and punches him across the face five times. Galzra releases his grip and Barglok crumples to the ground. When he doesn't move, a squire runs onto the field to check on him.

"He's unconscious!" says the squire.

"Then this fight is over," says Demonicus. "Galzra wins!"

The crowd boos as Galzra exits the field. Barglok regains consciousness and leaves as well, with the same reaction.

"Ladies and gentlemen, I apologize for such a slow, uneventful fight," says Demonicus. "Next up, we have Alithyra versus Jarkam of Industria."

A small, bearded creature, too short to be a dwarf, enters the arena. Alithyra quickly follows.

"I have consulted with my fellow dignitaries," says Demonicus. "Jarkam shall choose the game."

Jarkam grins. "I choose a club duel, Your Majesty."

"Interesting choice," says Demonicus. "Very well. Choose your weapons."

The squires wheel out a cart filled with clubs. Alithyra chooses a club that only requires one hand to wield. Jarkam picks one that is larger than his own body.

Demonicus shakes his head. "This will be quick if he can't even lift his own weapon. Let the match begin!"

Jarkam drags his oversized weapon toward Alithyra, who stands there with an amused grin. "You can barely lift that. How are you going to beat me?"

"You'll see," says Jarkam.

Alithyra rushes to Jarkam and swings her club at him. Jarkam lifts his club with all his might and blocks the blow. He spins as quickly as he can, swinging his weapon in a circle. It connects with Alithyra's club and knocks it from her hand. The club lands ten feet away.

Jarkam stands in place and grins. "Go on." Jarkam stifles a laugh. "Go get it."

Alithyra eyes him suspiciously. "You have the advantage. Why let me retrieve it?"

"I have my reasons."

While Alithyra jogs over to retrieve her weapon, Jarkam pulls a stone out of his pocket and strikes the slender end of his club. He lifts it and mounts it on his shoulder, pointing it at his opponent. When Alithyra turns to return to the battle, the end of Jarkam's club explodes. Alithyra's breastplate sparks as a round piece of metal connects and bounces off, leaving a large dent.

Alithyra steps back in shock and glances down at her armor. "What was that?"

The crowd falls silent and Demonicus stands. "Stop the match!"

Confused, uneasy mutterings echo through the arena, and several of the other contestants filter out to see what is happening.

Demonicus glares at the gnome. "Jarkam, what was that? Explain yourself!"

Jarkam grins. "Just a little experiment that I snuck in with the clubs. Aside from being unable to penetrate her armor, it worked quite well."

Demonicus turns to a gnome seated a few feet away. "Can you explain this, Togpym?"

Togpym nods. "It would appear that he has concealed a culverin inside the club. I was unaware that he had done this." Togpym glares at Jarkam. "You disappoint me, Jarkam. You're making our kingdom look bad."

The grin fades from Jarkam's face. "High Guildmaster Togpym, surely you understand the need for these field tests."

"Not in a setting such as this," says Togpym. "Excuse us while we decide what to do."

The dignitaries leave their seats and consult with one another. After a few minutes, they return to their chairs.

Demonicus addresses the combatants. "It has been unanimously decided that Jarkam is disqualified. Alithyra advances to the next round."

Jarkam's smile fades. "There wasn't an official rule against it. Oh well. At least it worked." He slumps his shoulders and leaves the field. Alithyra returns to the waiting area.

"For our next match, we have Tanazhan against Hulkonis," says Demonicus.

The crowd cheers as two large figures emerge onto the field. One is a troll, who, despite his height nearing nine feet, is dwarfed by his opponent; a massive rhinoran nearly twice his size. When they reach the center of the arena, Demonicus observes them silently for a moment. He turns to the troll. "Hulkonis, you shall choose the game. Considering the size difference, you may, if you wish, combine your match with the next one."

Hulkonis shakes his head. "Hulkonis enjoy the challenge. Hulkonis choose wrestling."

"How shall victory be determined?" asks Demonicus.

"Give up or knock out," says Hulkonis.

"Very well," says Demonicus. "You may begin."

Hulkonis charges at Tanazhan and crashes into him. The rhinoran does not budge as Hulkonis grabs his sides and pushes with all his might.

Tanazhan glances at the crowd and looks down at his opponent. "You've bitten off more than you can chew. You might as well quit now. You can't move me."

Hulkonis glances up, flashing an expression of confusion. "Hulkonis not bite yet."

Tanazhan groans and shoves Hulkonis away. The troll flies back several feet and lands on his back. Hulkonis jumps up and rushes Tanazhan, who raises his leg and lunges forward. Hulkonis runs directly into Tanazhan's foot and slams to the ground. He rises to his feet, shaking his head. He locks into another grapple with Tanazhan, who simply lifts him in the air and smashes him into the dirt. Tanazhan stomps on Hulkonis's torso and presses down. Hulkonis cries out in pain and struggles under his opponent's weight, desperately trying to wiggle free.

"I've got you pinned," says Tanazhan. "Just give up."

"Hulkonis never give up."

Tanazhan sighs. He lifts his foot and stomps on Hulkonis's head. Looking down at his opponent, he sees Hulkonis shake his head and stand.

"I should end this before he can initiate a troll emergency regenerate," says Tanazhan.

A look of confusion crosses Hulkonis's face. "Huh?" His expression changes to one of realization. "Right. Hulkonis is troll. Hulkonis can heal self in bad situation."

Hulkonis closes his eyes and begins to inhale deeply, but Tanazhan grabs him by the neck. Tanazhan lifts Hulkonis in the air and throws him halfway across the field. Hulkonis crashes to the ground just feet from the pit.

When Hulkonis stands, Tanazhan charges in his direction. The rhinoran's aim is off and he rushes right past the troll, skidding to a stop just short of the pit. Hulkonis charges at Tanazhan again, but the rhinoran once again catches him by the throat. Tanazhan lifts Hulkonis into the air, turns, and drops him into the pit. Hulkonis lands headfirst, falling unconscious immediately.

"The winner is Tanazhan!" says Demonicus. "Get a priest down there to heal Hulkonis. In the meantime, we'll take a short recess."

The dignitaries leave their box, only to return five minutes later.

"For our next match, we have the demon slayer, Viscount Kingston versus Gremlack," says Demonicus.

Pelagius watches as an orc in regal golden armor and a silver-skinned daemon emerge onto the field. Delradi appears next to him. "Demon slayer? Why is a demon hunter here?"

Pelagius shrugs. "I couldn't tell you. Certainly, his motives are a mystery to me."

"Do you know him?"

"Not personally, but I have heard of him. He's a Crusader of Karaugh, or he was, at least. Most of Karaugh's crusaders follow his justice aspect, but Kingston is more inclined to vengeance. Rumor has it that he has killed innocent demonkin on more than one occasion and was stripped of his title by the Order of the Divine Hand as punishment."

"I guess that hasn't stopped him."

When Kingston and Gremlack reach the center of the field, Demonicus rises to greet the crowd. "Nobody is more surprised than I to see you here, Viscount Kingston."

The orc smirks. "My reputation precedes me. Rest assured, Your Majesty, I will do no demon slaying in your kingdom as long as the tournament goes on."

"Be advised, Kingston, that any unprovoked attack on me people will be considered murder," says Demonicus. "If you slay anyone without just cause, you will not leave this kingdom alive."

"Strong words, Demonicus," says Bloodsworth. "I'm impressed."

"You would do the same in your kingdom, Bloodsworth."

"Oh, we would do much worse. His death would not be quick or merciful in Battallia."

"Back to the matter at hand," says Demonicus. "The majority has decided that Kingston shall choose the terms of the game."

Kingston looks at his opponents and sneers. "I choose a fight to the death."

Demonicus stands and glares at Kingston. "No! This is strictly a non-lethal tournament. Choose something else."

"Very well," says Kingston. "I choose a pit fight. First to climb out of the pit wins."

Demonicus turns to the other dignitaries to discuss the matter. After a few minutes, he returns his attention to Kingston. "Very well. Ladders shall be placed around the pit. In order for the spectators to witness the fight, five sorcerers shall surround the pit and magically transmit the images to the crowd. Choose your weapons and descend."

The squires approach with a cart of weaponry. Kingston chooses a longsword and shield while Gremlack chooses to wield a pair of axes. While they climb down a pair of ladders, five sorcerers take their positions around the pit and begin chanting and waving their arms. When the two combatants reach the bottom, a cloud forms over the hole and the image of the contestants appears.

Demonicus raises his hand. "Begin the match!"

Kingston and Gremlack circle the pit, glaring at one another. Kingston strikes first, charging his opponent. He swings his sword in a downward arc, but Gremlack blocks his blow. Pushing the blade aside, Gremlack then strikes at Kingston with his second axe, but his blade bounces off Kingston's shield.

The two continue to trade blows, blocking and parrying each other, for several minutes. Kington raises his shield and lunges at Gremlack. The daemon raises his axes to block, but the blow knocks him to the ground. Kingston is upon him quickly, holding his sword to Gremlack's throat.

"Do you yield?" asks Kingston.

"That was not a condition of victory," says Gremlack. "By your own choice, one of us must escape the pit to win."

"Right," says Kingston. "That slipped my mind." Kingston smacks Gremlack across the face with the flat of his blade. "Stay there. I shall take my leave."

Kingston turns to leave. When Gremlack rolls over to stand, Kingston rushes back and kicks him in the head. Gremlack collapses into the dirt, and Kingston approaches one of the ladders. He attempts to climb but finds that the shield is in his way.

Dropping the shield, Kingston sheaths his sword and begins his ascent. When Kingston is only ten feet up, Gremlack rises, shaking his head, and bolts to the ladder. Gremlack chops the ladder on both sides, and it collapses, sending Kingston plummeting to the ground. Gremlack then tucks his axes into his belt and climbs up another ladder. Before he can get very far, Kingston grabs him and yanks him off. Gremlack lands on his feet and draws his axes just in time to parry a blow from Kingston's sword.

"You will not defeat me, demon scum," says Kingston. "I have slain demons far more powerful than you."

The crowd boos and Gremlack sneers. "Any true demons? From what I've heard, you've only killed a few demonkin and innocent demonfolk."

"True demons don't dare challenge me and no being of demonic descent is innocent."

"Arrogant fool."

The two resume trading blows, parrying and blocking one another's strikes. Gremlack lands a blow on Kingston's arm, but his armor prevents any damage. Kingston grabs the axe that struck him and pulls it from Gremlack's hand. Tossing it aside, he parries another attack, and punches Gremlack in the face with his free hand. Stunned, Gremlack stumbles, leaving an opening for Kingston.

Kingston slashes Gremlack across the face and Gremlack falls to the ground, clutching the wound. Kingston sheaths his sword and climbs the nearest ladder. When Kingston is halfway up, Gremlack jumps to his feet, chops the ladder out from under Kingston, and climbs the next nearest one. Kingston hits the floor with a thud. He stands with difficulty and pursues Gremlack up the same ladder.

When Gremlack is nearly at the top, Kingston draws his sword and chops at the ladder above himself. Just before Gremlack reaches the top, the ladder collapses under him and he plummets back into the pit. With Gremlack falling straight toward him, Kingston leaps to another nearby ladder and continues climbing. Gremlack lies at the bottom of the pit in a heap, stirring just as Kingston reaches the top and climbs out. The crowd bursts into frenzied boos as Kingston raises his arms in celebration.

Demonicus scowls as he stares at the victor. "Ladies and gentlemen, the winner is Kingston."

"Why so disgusted, Your Majesty?" asks Kingston. "I gave everyone a good show."

"Do you really think that none of us heard your remarks down there?" asks Demonicus. "Not only that, we all saw how you conducted yourself. You have not ingratiated yourself to me or the people, viscount."

"I stand by my words," says Kingston.

Kingston exits the field. After a few minutes, Gremlack emerges from the pit and a priest comes to heal his injuries.

Once the squires clear the field, Demonicus rises to address the crowd. "Two matches remain for this round. Our penultimate bout features Darfindrin against Gribthak."

An elf and a dwarf emerge into the arena to a loud cheer from the audience. When the cacophony dies down, Demonicus points to the dwarf. "Gribthak shall choose the game."

Gribthak looks at Darfindrin and grins. "Your Majesty, I choose a weapon-of-choice duel. Victory by first blood."

"Very well," says Demonicus. "Squires, bring out the weapons cart and help them remove the armor from their upper bodies."

The squires wheel the cart onto the field and proceed to remove the contestant's armor. Once complete, Gribthak and Darfindrin approach the cache. Darfindrin chooses a pair of small axes. He walks away to take up his position on the field. When Darfindrin turns back to his opponent, he sees Gribthak pull a scythe from the cart. Gribthak grins while the squires remove the cart from the arena and Demonicus gives the signal to begin.

Gribthak charges Darfindrin and swings the scythe at him. Darfindrin barely parries the blow and nearly loses one of his axes. Gribthak attacks again and Darfindrin desperately leaps back to avoid the blade. Darfindrin steps forward to attack, but once again dodges the sweeping scythe.

Gribthak smirks. "How do you expect to win? You can't get near me without being struck by my blade. You may as well surrender, Darfindrin."

"I'll figure something out. The scythe is not unbeatable."

Darfindrin continues blocking and dodging blows from the scythe, stepping back each time. Gribthak raises the scythe above his head and

TRIAL BY TOURNAMENT: CHAMPION OF VALOR

brings it down in an overhead arc. Darfindrin leaps back to avoid it and rushes to the side. While Gribthak pulls his blade from the ground, Darfindrin throws one of his axes at the dwarf. Gribthak spins around to avoid the axe, swinging wildly. Darfindrin ducks under the blade and rushes forward until he is right next to Gribthak. Before the dwarf can back away, Darfindrin buries his remaining axe in Gribthak's shoulder. Gribthak screams in pain and drops the scythe.

"Darfindrin wins!" shouts Demonicus. "A priest will be along shortly to heal Gribthak's wound." As the squires clear the field, Demonicus rises and addresses the crowd. "It has certainly been an exciting day, ladies and gentlemen. The day shall soon draw to a close, but we have one more match before night sets in. Our final bout for the day will be Pelagius versus Taratagi."

The crowd bursts in thunderous applause as Pelagius takes to the field. He turns to see his opponent; a tengu with gray tips on his black feathers and a purple scar running the length of his red beak, following suit. Taratagi walks to the center of the field, eyes down, not once acknowledging the crowd.

Demonicus consults with the dignitaries before turning his attention back to the field. "Taratagi, you shall be the one to choose the game."

Taratagi looks up at the king. "Swords, Your Majesty. Victory by first blood."

A hushed murmur breaks across the crowd.

"Two first blood matches in a row?" asks King Sylwyn.

Bloodsworth smiles. "There's no rule against that. In fact, the bloodier, the better. It's the next best thing to a death match."

"Taratagi, why do you want a first blood bout so soon after another one?" asks Demonicus.

Taratagi scans the crowd and shudders. "I just want to get this over with quickly."

Demonicus shrugs. "Very well. The squires will remove the chest pieces of your armor. The first to leave an obvious bleeding slash across the torso or one of the arms wins. No strikes at the neck or head will be tolerated."

The squires take to the field and assist the combatants in removing their breastplates and chain shirts. They offer the combatants several choices of weapons. Pelagius chooses a longsword and a shield while Taratagi picks a pair of shortswords. The two square up, waiting for the signal to start.

As soon as Demonicus starts the match, Taratagi lunges at Pelagius, who blocks the blow with his shield. Pelagius retaliates, striking at Taratagi with all his might, but the attempt is easily parried. The two trade blows back and forth, neither one able to penetrate the other's defenses. Taratagi goes for a rapid stab, but Pelagius raises his shield. At the last second, Taratagi releases his grip on his second sword and uses his momentum to grab the edge of the shield, yanking it away from the surprised crusader.

Taking advantage of the shock, Taratagi slashes at Pelagius's chest, but Pelagius leaps back in time, the blade barely missing his flesh. They trade blows back and forth for several strikes, seemingly evenly matched. Pelagius notes that, although he is not using it, Taratagi has not dropped the shield. They lock blades and glare at each other.

"Well played on the shield grab," says Pelagius. "Certainly an unorthodox tactic."

"You'll find my fighting style quite unpredictable," says Taratagi. "Whereas I can read you like a book. I know your every move before you make it."

"Is that a fact?" asks Pelagius, skeptical. "I'll show you how unpredictable I can be, then."

Pelagius backs out of the blade lock, causing Taratagi to lose his footing and stumble. He regains his balance just as Pelagius strikes, blocking another blow. They lock blades once again and this time Taratagi rapidly withdraws. Expecting this, Pelagius pretends to stumble, and Taratagi swings the shield at his face as hard as he can. Pelagius ducks under the attack, and Taratagi throws himself off balance with his own momentum.

Before he can recover, Pelagius swings his sword in an upward arc, catching the tengu in the side of the stomach. He slices a deep cut diagonally across his torso and the crowd cheers wildly as the blood starts to flow.

"Ladies and gentlemen, the winner is Pelagius!" says Demonicus. "Congratulations to all who have advanced to the next round. Once again, everyone is invited to a grand feast in the great hall. Tomorrow, the games continue."

The squires return to the field to retrieve the weapons, bringing a priest along with them. Once the priest heals Taratagi's wound, he and Pelagius exchange a firm handshake. After changing from his armor into ordinary clothing, Pelagius meets with Mughan, who escorts him back to the castle.

Chapter 36

Mughan enters the great hall and leads Pelagius to the table, where his companions have already taken seats. Each congratulates him excitedly on his victory.

"Thank you, my friends." Pelagius turns to Kevnan and Alithyra. "Congratulations to you two as well. Excellent victories today by all of us."

The captain turns to leave as the servant approaches and hands him something. Mughan looks it over, thanks the servant, and turns back to the group. "Congratulations on your victory, Pelagius."

Mughan departs. As Pelagius takes a seat, Delradi and Hexeron join him and the others at the table. Looking around the area, Pelagius sees Koskru conversing with Celemrod as well as several other contestants mingling with the guests. Grand Inquisitor Rynmor is not present, most likely not wanting to face the public after his humiliating loss. When he turns back to his friends, Shukrat appears at the table.

"Well done, Pelagius," says Shukrat. "A hard fought victory if I ever saw one."

"Thank you," says Pelagius.

Shukrat turns to Alithrya. "Now that we have the opportunity, we can work on your arm more after the feast. Back in your quarters, I can go through the ritual that will allow you to magically link with your prosthetic and control it as though it were the real arm."

"Thank you, Shukrat," says Alithyra. "I'm getting used to doing things with one hand, but it will be nice to have two again."

As they converse, Celemrod makes his way over to the table. "Great fight today, Pelagius. Keep up the good work."

"Thank you," says Pelagius. "I'll do my best. There is some stiff competition, though."

"I just hope you don't have to face Balric," says Kevnan. "The anger he fights with is terrifying."

Pelagius nods. "As soon as I saw him, I knew there was something off about him. His rage bubbles just under the surface, ready to explode at the slightest provocation. Aren't you fighting him tomorrow, Kevnan?"

Kevnan gulps and fidgets nervously. "I'm afraid so. I don't know if I can defeat him, but I will do my best."

Pelagius places his hand on Kevnan's shoulder. "I'm sure you will. Nobody is unbeatable. I'm sure you'll find a way."

Jabbleth works his way through the crowd, politely taking a tray full of goblets from a servant. He reaches Pelagius's group and hands one to everyone in the vicinity. Jabbleth lifts his in the air. "Well fought victories, everyone! A toast to those of us advancing to the next round!"

Pelagius and the others raise their glasses. Vuzenkhord steps next to Jabbleth and follows suit. "To victory and glory! To the Grand Tourney!"

The combatants emit an exuberant cheer and down the wine in their goblets. Pelagius and his friends sit at a nearby table to enjoy a meal.

The feast continues into the late hours of the night with guests and contestants occasionally leaving. As the festivities draw to a close, Mughan escorts Pelagius and the others back to their quarters. Pelagius, Kevnan, Ralkgek, and Aldtaw retire for the night, but Alithyra decides to remain in the common area with Shukrat and the dwarven smith who created the arm. As Mughan locks the door to the main chamber, the dwarf unwraps a parcel that he brought with him. Inside is a harness similar to the one Alithyra already uses to attach her prosthetic arm, but the part that covers the shoulder has a clamp-like device connected to a single strap with a lever crank in the center. He removes the prosthetic and original harness before replacing it with the new one and fastening the arm.

"This harness will keep the arm more securely attached to your body, but is easier to get in and out of," says the dwarf. "When you crank the lever, the clamps will tighten around the shoulder joint. Once they have reached a tightness that is secure and comfortable, push the lever down and lock it in place. When you need to remove the arm, say for sleeping, simply unlock the lever and allow the clamps to loosen."

He and Alithyra go through the process of securing her prosthetic. While they do this, Shukrat sets up a ritual in the center of the room. He completes his preparations as they finish the basics of the new harness and calls them over.

"The ritual I am about to cast will infuse your prosthetic arm with magic," says Shukrat. "Allowing you to control it as though it were truly attached to you whenever you are wearing it. It will not be in effect whenever you take it off, but it will reactivate when you put it back on."

Alithyra sits in the center of Shukrat's prepared circle, which he touches and begins to chant. He continues his incantation for several minutes and the circle glows. As the glow increases in intensity, the prosthetic arm and harness shine as well. Pulsating light encases Alithyra's entire body. After several more minutes, the glow fades away.

"Now concentrate," says Shukrat. "Try to move the arm."

Alithyra inhales deeply as she focuses her attention. Her metal arm moves, bending the elbow upward and the fingers curl into a fist. She continues moving the arm, hand, and fingers for several seconds. She stands and walks to the table and tries pulling out a seat. She grasps the seat so hard that the wood cracks, and she accidentally flings it across the room when she pulls it back.

"It's going to take some practice," says Shukrat. "But you should get used to it in a few days. Additionally, since it is infused rather than imbued, the magic is temporary. It will still last longer than if it was enchanted. It should last at least ten years, rather than only working once, but it will need to be recharged eventually."

"Thank you, gentlemen," says Alithyra, smiling. "This means a lot to me."

"Due to its composition, it is extremely durable," says the dwarf. "Even more so now that it is magically enhanced. However, it is not indestructible. Tomorrow, I will teach you how to do maintenance, but for now, I must return home and get some rest."

"I must be going as well," says Shukrat. "Good night, my friends."

Shukrat opens a portal and steps through, with the dwarf following quickly. As the portal closes, the heroes go off to their bed chambers for a good night's sleep.

Chapter 37

Matheral storms into his quarters with his father close behind. Clearly agitated by the day's events, he paces back and forth across the room. He slams his fist on a table, knocking over a pair of empty goblets and shaking a nearby pitcher. "How dare they ban me from future tournaments? They have no right."

Sylwyn closes the door. "They do have that right. They are the rulers of their respective kingdoms and representatives of the ones that were unable to come."

"No matter. Once I am king, I can lift the ban myself."

Sylwyn sets the goblets back up, picks up the pitcher, and pours some wine. "Actually, you can't. The ruling was made by the combined kings of all the kingdoms. Only a unanimous agreement of all can reverse it."

Matheral pouts. "How could they do this?"

Sylwyn picks up a goblet and takes a sip. "You brought it upon yourself, Matheral. Using such unsportsmanlike tactics to win is heavily looked down upon."

Matheral crosses his arms. "They just fear my superiority. Those tactics were perfectly legitimate until I used them."

"While they were not technically against the rules, not using them was an unspoken gentleman's agreement. You violated that trust with such dishonorable actions."

Matheral grabs the remaining cup. "A gentleman's agreement applies only to two gentlemen. My opponent was no gentleman. He was an orc. Nothing but an inferior savage."

"Everyone who competes is subject to a gentleman's agreement."

Matheral sneers and takes a swig of wine. "The vote was seven to five. At least I know you stood up for me."

Sylwyn shakes his head. "Actually, I voted to disqualify you and reverse the decision. Your actions on the field were shameful. I was also the one who suggested banning you from future tournaments and giving Grundoc a chance in the next one as compensation for his unfair loss."

Matheral spits out his wine and looks over at his father, an expression of shock and betrayal on his face. "You? It was your idea? Why would you do this to me?"

Sylwyn offers Matheral a rag. "Your scandalous actions brought great embarrassment upon our house and kingdom. I almost forfeit in shame, but the other dignitaries talked me out of it."

Matheral wipes the wine from his chin. "It doesn't really matter. Once I defeat Sir Jabbleth and go on to win the tournament, I will show them how little their opinions matter. We are superior, Father. We should be able to overrule any of the others at our whim. When I am king, I will show them just how wrong they are to do this to me."

Sylwyn glares at his son. "It would be humiliating for you to win this tournament as a representative of our kingdom. I don't know where you got this elven supremacy mindset, but I will break you of it even if I have to beat it out of you. You will learn humility, young prince, and losing this tournament is a good way to start that lesson."

Matheral sets his wine down. "Humility is for the weak. This 'all species are equal' mindset of yours is baffling to me. It will be the first thing stricken from the kingdom once I am king."

Sylwyn turns his back on Matheral. "I wouldn't count on being king anytime soon. You are not my only heir. You may be the eldest, but you have shown me that you are the least fit to rule. You are a disgrace to Eosurwood, Matheral, and I am seriously rethinking your place as my successor."

Stunned by this statement, Matheral gives him a look of utter betrayal. He slaps the goblet off the table, enters his bedchamber, and slams the door.

Chapter 38

Grimadert, Rogi, and Giro finish hollowing out the torso of the golem suit when a crank turns and pulls back a log attached to the wall of the laboratory. Once the crank stops, the log releases and slams into a large gong. Grimadert places his tools on the table and starts heading to the main entryway.

"Keep working on that, boys," says Grimadert. "I've got to get the door."

Iriemorel turns to watch him leave and notices something large lurking in the shadows. Grimadert walks down the hallway and pulls a lever, opening the main door. Outside is a creature dressed in a hooded robe, obscuring its identity.

"Can I help you?" asks Grimadert.

"Those crates that were delivered to you a while back, do you remember them?" asks the stranger.

"Yes," says Grimadert.

"My master sent me to inquire as to the status of the order for the parts within them," says the stranger.

Grimadert grins. "They are coming along. I've been working on multiple projects at once, so they are not yet complete. I should have them finished within a couple of weeks."

"My master wants them in one week."

Grimadert unfurls a scroll and shakes his head. "I was not informed that this was a rush job. The work is far too delicate to be successful in one week. I can have them ready in two weeks."

The stranger crosses his arms. "He will be most disappointed with your lack of progress, but two weeks will be sufficient. Not a day longer."

Grimadert rolls up his scroll. "The halfling should be ready in a few days. She's almost fully reassembled, so I could have her delivered separately."

The stranger shakes his head. "The halfling pieces were spare parts. She was not part of that order."

"I see. Since the pieces came with the others, I naturally assumed that they were with them."

"The confusion is understandable, but no more delays. Two weeks and not a second longer."

"They will be on his doorstep the moment I have them completed. Grimadert never fails." Grimadert smiles, beaming with pride.

"I seem to recall that you have a dungeon filled with failed experiments."

Grimadert's grin fades and he thinks for a moment. "I stand corrected. Grimadert almost never fails. Now, if you don't mind, the longer we stand here chatting, the less time I have to fill your master's order."

The stranger bows and takes his leave, with Grimadert closing the door behind him. The mad gnome returns to the laboratory, arriving just as Rogi and Giro complete their task.

"Excellent," says Grimadert. "Now we can finish with the torso."

Grimadert grabs a large knife and approaches Iriemorel. "I'm afraid that we'll have to use the same procedure that we used with your legs. Given that your upper body still works, this is going to hurt. A lot."

With Rogi holding up the dwarf's beard, Grimadert cuts a large slice across Iriemorel's chest, causing him to shriek in pain. He cuts several slices down Iriemorel's chest to the bottom of the stomach before slicing off the flesh in long strips, then does the same to his sides. Iriemorel's screams echo throughout the castle.

"I need to get his back," says Grimadert. "Undo his restraints and hold him up."

Rogi and Giro remove the straps from Iriemorel's wrists and help him to sit up. They grasp his arms as he flails attempting to get away. As the twins hold him steady, Grimadert slices the skin from his back, despite the protests and screams of the dwarf. When he has finished this task, he directs one of the twins to retrieve the back piece of the torso. Rogi readjusts his stance to grasp both arms while Giro fetches the piece.

He places the backplate on the table and the twins lower Iriemorel into it, replacing the restraints on his arms. They retrieve the chest and stomach pieces and place them in the proper spots, holding up his beard so it doesn't get caught inside the chest piece.

Grimadert mutters a brief chant and superheats the torso to the point that it is glowing white hot. Iriemorel shrieks in absolute agony as the metal seers his flesh and the pieces magically weld together, connecting with the lower body now as well. As the heat fades, Iriemorel sobs on the table.

"You mad, sadistic little rockhopper!" cries Iriemorel.

"I told you it would be painful," says Grimadert. "I take no pleasure in your pain. We only have the arms and gauntlets left now, but he will need a few days to recover. Boys, see to it that he is well taken care of. I've got other things to attend to."

Grimadert leaves the laboratory and heads down the hallway. He opens a door and disappears into a completely different area of the castle.

Chapter 39

The next morning, Pelagius and the other remaining contestants gather in the arena's waiting area and don their armor. The cheers of the crowd penetrate the doors as the contestants wait to emerge onto the field. The doors open, and the combatants enter the arena.

King Demonicus rises to address the excited crowd. "Good morning, ladies and gentlemen. Welcome to the second round of the Grand Tourney finals. Today is certain to be an exciting day, and we have several excellent bouts lined up. I know many of you have been looking forward to our first match, so let's get started. Our first fight shall be Sir Jabbleth versus Prince Matheral."

Sir Jabbleth walks out onto the field to a chorus of cheers. Matheral follows and is immediately greeted by a cacophony of jeers and boos.

Matheral crosses his arms and pouts. "These fools should be cheering me. I am their superior."

Jabbleth smirks. "You should try ingratiating yourself to them. It's much easier to be applauded when they actually like you."

"I don't need advice from you, knight. You are nothing but a servant. I should be fighting your lord, not you."

"My lord is not here. He wishes to remain anonymous. I was given leave to compete."

"Your lord must be humiliated to have such a pathetic worm as you as his servant."

Jabbleth shakes his head and shrugs off the comment, waiting for the next part of the proceedings.

Demonicus rises. "Since Prince Matheral is not allowed to choose the type of game, the task falls to Sir Jabbleth. What say you, Sir Knight?"

Jabbleth looks at Matheral and grins. "A sword duel, Your Majesty. Victory upon surrender or incapacitation."

Matheral gives him a surprised look. "A sword duel? Do you really think you can best me in combat?"

Jabbleth's grin grows wider. "We're going to find out."

Demonicus gestures to the crowd. "You heard him, ladies and gentlemen." He turns his attention to the squires standing along the arena wall. "Squires, bring out the weapons and let the match begin."

The squires wheel out an assortment of different types of swords. Both combatants pick the longsword and shield combination. Matheral struggles with the weight of the longsword for a moment before establishing his grip.

Jabbleth chuckles. "You're not going for something lighter?"

Matheral turns up his nose and flashes an arrogant grin. "I know this is your preferred style. I'm going to prove my superiority to you by defeating you with your own specialty."

"Keep telling yourself that, your highness."

King Demonicus gives the signal to begin and the two combatants circle the field, sizing each other up. Matheral is the first to strike, charging forward and swinging his sword at the Black Knight, who easily blocks the blow with his shield. Matheral attacks again, but Jabbleth parries the strike. The two exchange blows for several minutes, with Jabbleth remaining on the defensive.

Matheral points his blade in Jabbleth's direction. "See? You can't even get in an attack. I am clearly the better fighter."

Jabbleth rolls his eyes. "I haven't tried to attack. I'm getting my measure of you and your style is sloppy."

Rage fills Matheral's eyes. "How dare you!"

Matheral strikes once more and Jabbleth parries again. Matheral's next swing is so wide that he leaves himself open, and Jabbleth smashes him in the face with his shield, sending him stumbling back a few feet.

Matheral drops his sword and grabs his face. "Dirty move! I call dirty move!"

Demonicus gives Matheral a thumbs down gesture. "Actually, that is quite clean. Using your shield as a weapon is a legitimate strategy and is highly encouraged among sword and shield style warriors. Stop whining and show us what you've got, prince."

Matheral retrieves his weapon, glares angrily at Jabbleth, and charges him. He brings his sword down in an overhead arc and is once again blocked by the shield. He backs away and advances again, making several wild swings that are easily blocked and parried. Matheral lunges forward for a stab, but Jabbleth ducks under the strike. Catching Matheral in the chest with his shield, Jabbleth uses Matheral's momentum against him and flips him over himself through the air. Landing on his back and losing his helmet, the prince quickly jumps to his feet. He charges again, swinging wildly at the Black Knight, who effortlessly blocks every blow.

"Getting frustrated, are we?" asks Jabbleth.

"Silence!" shouts Matheral. "You have no right to speak to me in such a manner!"

Matheral raises his sword too high, leaving himself open and once again gets his face smashed by Jabbleth's shield. He stumbles back a few feet and flings his shield at Jabbleth, who deflects it easily. Standing there glaring at his opponent, Matheral tosses his sword aside.

Jabbleth raises an eyebrow. "Surrendering?"

"Never," says Matheral. "But I know that you would never attack an unarmed opponent with a weapon. You're far too honorable for that."

Jabbleth drops his shield and tosses his sword aside. He removes his helmet to give Matheral a better chance. "You are correct. Shall we continue?"

Matheral charges Jabbleth and tries to slug him in the face. Jabbleth easily blocks the attack and punches him across the jaw. Stunned, Matheral is unable to defend himself from several more punches, bloodying his face. Jabbleth then kicks him in the chest, sending him toppling to the ground. "Do you yield?"

Matheral sits up and spits at Jabbleth's feet. "I will never yield to the likes of you."

Matheral struggles to his feet and attacks Jabbleth again. This time, he manages to land a blow on Jabbleth's face. However, the punch is weak, and Jabbleth simply gives him a pitying look, completely unfazed by the attempt. He punches Matheral in the stomach, causing him to double over before uppercutting him and sending him sprawling to the ground. As Matheral rises to his feet, he sneakily picks up a nearby sword and swings it around at his opponent. Jabbleth uses his armored arm to block the attack and grabs Matheral by the wrist.

"That was cowardly." Jabbleth punches the elf in the face a few more times before releasing his grip. Retrieving his own sword, Jabbleth slowly walks toward his opponent. Matheral strikes to slash at him, but Jabbleth quickly parries and deflects the blow, throwing the young elf off balance. Taking advantage of the opening, Jabbleth brings his sword around in an upward diagonal arc and slashes Matheral across the face. Matheral crumbles to the ground and Jabbleth is on top of him almost immediately. He plants his boot in the center of Matheral's chest and pins him to the ground as he holds the tip of his sword against Matheral's throat.

"You are beaten," says Jabbleth. "Yield."

Matheral sneers and spits in Jabbleth's face. "Never!"

Jabbleth sighs and removes the sword from Matheral's throat. Dropping the sword, he punches him in the face as hard as he can, driving Matheral's head into the ground and knocking him unconscious. The crowd erupts into the biggest frenzy of cheers that the tournament has ever seen.

"Ladies and gentlemen, the winner is Sir Jabbleth!" says Demonicus.

The squires enter the field with a priest in tow, who heals Matheral, while the squires collect the weapons with Jabbleth's assistance.

Matheral stands and turns to a squire. "What happened, servant? Why is everyone acting like the fight is over?"

"It is over, Your Highness. You were knocked unconscious."

Rage crosses Matheral's face. "What are you saying, peasant?"

"Incapacitating one's opponent was a victory condition. You lost, sire."

Matheral grabs the squire by the collar. "No! I did not lose!" He shoves the squire away and turns to the dignitaries' box. "As an elf, I am superior to this lowly human! There is no possible way that I could lose!"

"Let it go, your highness. The match is over. There is no shame in defeat." Jabbleth turns and starts to leave the field.

Matheral gestures toward Jabbleth. "He cheated! That's the only possible way he could have won!"

A hush falls across the crowd as Jabbleth, just about to enter the doorway, comes to a stop. Jabbleth glances back at Matheral with a menacing glare. "Would you care to repeat that, your highness?"

Matheral points accusingly at Jabbleth. "I don't know how, but you cheated!"

Jabbleth furrows his brow and crosses his arms. "Are you questioning my integrity? Do you really want to call my honor into question? Choose your next words carefully, Prince."

"In a fair fight, I would have won! You could never beat me in a real battle! You only won because you cheated! No human could ever best their elven superiors! This match has been tainted by fraudulent tactics and the decision must be reversed! I demand satisfaction!"

Jabbleth turns and quickly strides up to Matheral, stopping inches from the elf's face. "Are you challenging me to a duel?"

Matheral takes a step back. "You are a weak, pathetic, worm of a human! I could easily defeat you anytime and anywhere!"

Jabbleth removes one of his gauntlets and slaps Matheral across the face with it. He grabs the young prince by the throat and lifts him into the air, slamming him into a nearby wall. Jabbleth tightens his grasp as he glares at the young prince. "If you wish to challenge me to a duel, I will gladly accept. Anytime and anywhere. If you like, we can do it right here after we've changed into our proper combat attire. Keep in mind, Matheral, that in a real fight, I would be wearing my Nightshade Armor, and I would not be holding back for the entertainment of the crowd. Do you truly wish to challenge me to a fight to the death?"

A look of terror crosses Matheral's face.

"Answer me, Matheral. Are you challenging me?"

Matheral lowers his gaze to the ground, avoiding Jabbleth's harsh eyes. "No." Matheral speaks with a noticeable tremor in his voice.

Jabbleth pulls Matheral away from the wall and shoves him back against it. "Well, you should have considered that before you opened your mouth. You have called my honor and integrity into question. Therefore, I am challenging you to a duel. Do you accept?"

Still avoiding Jabbleth's glare, Matheral shakes his head to the extent possible with Jabbleth's hand wrapped around his throat. "That won't be necessary."

"So, you are declining my challenge?"

"I decline your challenge. I have no interest in battling you to the death."

The crowd emits a series of jeers and boos. Jabbleth releases his grip, dropping Matheral to the ground. "Gutless, dishonorable coward." Jabbelth squats down to Matheral's level, grabs him by the face, and pulls him forward. "Don't ever besmirch my character again, young prince. Next time, I will not be so kind as to let you back out of your own challenge. Try it again, and I will kill you on the spot." Jabbleth shoves Matheral's face into the dirt and stands. He exits the field and disappears into the arena interior. The other contestants give him a wide berth as he comes through.

Matheral stands and looks up at the dignitaries' box. King Sylwyn rises to his feet and glares down at his son. "Matheral, your outburst is humiliating. Your inability to gracefully accept defeat is a disgrace to Eosurwood and all elvenkind. As much as I would like to remain for the rest of the tournament, your attitude and behavior is too shameful for us to stay and represent our kingdom. We will be returning to Eosurwood immediately so that I may properly put you in your place." Sylwyn turns to the other dignitaries. "Pardon me, gentlemen. I must be going."

King Sylwyn disappears from the dignitaries' box and Matheral quietly slinks into the arena interior.

Chapter 40

As the squires finish clearing the field, King Demonicus rises to address the crowd. "Wasn't that an exciting match, ladies and gentlemen?"

The crowd applauds in agreement.

"And I think we can all agree that it ended exactly how everybody wanted it to," says Demonicus. "Time to move on, though. Are you ready for the next bout?"

The crowd cheers in excitement.

"Very well." Demonicus checks the board. "Our next match will be Balric versus Kevnan."

The crowd cheers as the two combatants enter the field. Balric comes out first, oblivious to the crowd's adulation. Kevnan follows nervously, clearly not wanting to trigger Balric's rage. Demonicus consults with the other dignitaries before turning his attention back to the contestants. "After some discussion, we have decided that Kevnan will choose the game."

Kevnan looks over at Balric. "I'd like to make this as quick as possible. Sword duel. Victory upon first blood."

Demonicus nods. "Very well. Like yesterday, a simple scratch will not be enough. The first to leave an obvious cut on the limbs or torso wins."

The squires bring the swords back onto the field as the two combatants remove their breastplates. Kevnan picks a shortsword and a shield, while Balric grabs a greatsword. The squires leave the field and Demonicus gives the signal to start the match.

Balric strikes first, bringing his sword down upon Kevnan, who blocks the blow with his shield. Kevnan retaliates with a slash of his own, which Balric easily parries despite the size of his sword. They continue to trade strikes back and forth, neither opponent gaining a clear advantage. Balric's growing frustration is evident by the angry grunts and teeth-clenched breathing.

Kevnan sees an opening and moves in to take advantage. He slips inside of Balric's reach and goes for a stab. Balric's sword hilt deflects the strike, and he barely nicks the warrior's arm, not enough for a victory. Kevnan kicks Balric in the chest to try to get some distance between them. Balric unleashes a fury-filled primal scream as his rage boils over, causing an expression of pure terror to form on Kevnan's face.

Kevnan gulps and steps back. *Flaming zombie minotaur! This is going to be bad!*

Balric rushes forward, striking at Kevnan with all his might. Kevnan blocks the blow with his shield, but Balric makes several more rapid strikes, keeping him on the defensive. An opening seems to appear and Kevnan goes in for the attack. Balric brings his sword around and slams it into Kevnan's blade, shattering it completely.

"Not good," says Kevnan, horrified.

Balric continues striking at Kevnan's shield. The outmatched elf cowers behind it until the enraged warrior grabs it and rips it from his hand. Before Kevnan can react, Balric swings his sword in a horizontal arc, cutting deeply into his chest. Kevnan drops to the ground as the sword finishes its slash. Balric brings his sword around, positioning it for another strike. The squires rush the field and grab Balric's arms to prevent the attack. It takes seven people to hold him in place until his rage subsides.

"Ladies and gentlemen, the winner is Balric," says Demonicus.

The crowd, terrified by Balric's anger, is silent for a moment before issuing a weak cheer. Balric drops his sword and exits the field as a priest comes out to heal Kevnan.

Once healed, Kevnan leaves the arena. Pelagius meets him at the doors.

"Good effort. You almost won at one point."

Kevnan shudders. "His fury is like nothing I've ever seen. I knew going in that I likely didn't stand a chance."

Pelagius gives Kevnan a light pat on the back. "Well, you made it to the second round. That is bragging rights in and of itself."

Kevnan smiles. "It certainly is."

Demonicus consults the board and turns to the crowd. "Our next match is Gnarzak versus Ashisat!"

Ashisat enters the field, followed by his much larger opponent. Demonicus turns to the other dignitaries for a moment. Once the hushed discussion is complete, Demonicus returns his attention to the combatants. "It has been decided that Ashisat shall choose the game."

"I choose a katana duel, Your Majesty," says Ashisat. "Victory upon incapacitation or yield."

"So be it," says Demonicus. "Gentlemen, choose your weapons."

The squires bring out a pair of katanas. Ashisat chooses one and unsheathes it to inspect the blade. Satisfied, he sheathes the sword and fastens it to his belt.

Gnarzak grasps his katana. His hand covers the entire hilt, the blade looking comically small in his grip. "Do you have any of these in a larger size? This thing is more like a dagger for me."

A squire nods. "We may. I'll check with the weapons master." The squires rush off the field and out of sight. Ten minutes later, they emerge carrying a katana the size of a greatsword. "It took some time to find. It was buried in the back of the armory. Clearly it hasn't seen much use."

Gnarzak trades his normal size katana for the giant one. He draws the sword, which squeaks shrilly on the way out. The blade has three rust spots along its length. Ashisat frowns at the sight. "That's no way to treat such a blade. What a shame."

Gnarzak shrugs. "It'll have to do." He spits on the blade, wipes the saliva across it, and sheathes the sword. "I'm ready if you are, Ashisat."

Demonicus gives the signal to begin. Ashisat positions one leg in front of himself, steps back with the other foot, and slightly bends his knees. He places one hand on the hilt and the other on the sheath. Gnarzak observes him and copies the stance. The two contestants circle on another, staring at the other. Ashisat charges and Gnarzak follows suit. They draw their swords just before they reach each other and their blades clash. They withdraw and strike again, parrying each other's blows.

Gnarzak pushes downward on his sword, forcing Ashisat down to one knee. Ashisat pulls the sheath from his belt and swings it around, striking Gnarzak in the ribs. Caught off guard by this maneuver, Gnarzak bellows in pain and steps back, releasing Ashisat from the blade lock. Ashisat retreats across the field. Gnarzak grunts angrily and runs after him. In one swift motion, Ashisat turns and rushes Gnarzak. He swings his sword just as he reaches Gnarzak, who desperately attempts to position his blade to parry. Gnarzak's reflexes are too slow and Ashisat's sword slashes him across the thigh. Ashisat skids to a stop and Gnarzak tumbles to the ground. The angry minotaur stands immediately and inspects the wound.

"There's nothing to worry about," says Ashisat. "It's just a shallow cut, nothing life-threatening. The battle would be over right now if I had chosen first blood as the victory condition, though."

Gnarzak scoffs. "You'll have to cut deeper if you want to incapacitate me, Ashisat. I won't hold back, and neither should you."

"A full-strength strike with this sword will remove a limb. I do not wish to kill you."

"A dismembered limb can be magically reattached as long as it is mostly intact. Unless you decapitate me or slice me in half, you won't kill me."

"Both are possible. I certainly won't aim for the head."

"You can't win against me if you're not willing to hurt me. Seems like victory is already mine."

"If that's how you want it, Gnarzak. Shall we continue?"

Gnarzak nods and charges at Ashisat. When Gnarzak draws near, Ashisat sidesteps the attack, and the minotaur goes right past him. Ashisat casually swings his sword at his passing opponent, leaving a gash on his side. Gnarzak snorts angrily and turns to face his opponent, parrying another strike. He grasps his sword in both hands and raises it above his head. Ashisat takes advantage of the opening and slashes Gnarzak across the stomach.

Ignoring the pain, the minotaur brings his katana down in an overhead arc. Ashisat jumps back to avoid the blow and the blade crashes into the ground. He runs up the sword using it as a ramp and cuts into Gnarzak's shoulder, jumping to the side before the minotaur raises the weapon again. Ashisat falls back to the far side of the arena, expecting Gnarzak to follow. When his opponent remains in place, he waits. After a minute, Garzak bellows and charges at Ashisat. He swings his sword around, but

Ashisat ducks under the strike and lunges forward. Ashisat's blade cuts deeply into Gnarzak's leg, slicing it off in one blow. He screams in agony and falls to the ground.

Demonicus instantly rises to his feet. "That counts as an incapacitation! Ashisat wins!"

A priest and a squire rush out onto the field. The squire picks up the severed leg and holds it to the stump while the priest prays. After a few seconds, the priest glows blue and transfers the energy to Gnarzak. As the glow fades, Gnarzak's wounds heal and the leg reattaches.

"Ladies and gentlemen, next up is Raimdon versus Waltgaud!" says Demonicus.

The two combatants emerge and enter the center of the arena. After a minute of discussion from the dignitaries, the lich rises. "As a neutral party, I declare that Raimdon shall choose the stipulations."

Raimdon looks at his diminutive opponent. *There's no way I can beat him in a contest of speed, dexterity, or athleticism. Perhaps a test of strength.*

"Your Majesty, I have a request," says Raimdon. "Rather than direct combat, I would like two stone targets set up. Whoever smashes their target first wins. The largest mauls available are necessary to achieve this task."

The lich turns to Demonicus. "A test of strength hardly seems fair, but that is not my concern."

Demonicus nods and looks at the halfling sitting a few seats away. "What say you, Marquis Faromar?"

Faromar grins. "I say allow it. We halflings are clever. There are more ways to win a test of strength than sheer, brute force."

Demonicus nods. "As you wish, then." Demonicus turns to the lich. "Make the announcement, Maldorus."

Maldorus returns his attention to the arena. "The request is approved. The bout will begin as soon as the preparations are complete."

After twenty minutes, the squires drag two life-sized, dwarf-shaped statues into the middle of the field. They leave the arena and return with a cart containing two massive mauls. Raimdon lifts his with some difficulty. The squires hand the other to Waltgaud, who immediately drops to the ground when the full weight hits his arms.

Waltgaud stands and looks over the weapon. "How is this fair?" I can't even lift this."

Raimdon shrugs. "That's your problem. I just considered my options and determined the best way to win. If you had been selected, you would have played to your strengths, too."

Demonicus gives the signal to start the match. Raimdon strikes his statue multiple times in quick succession. Waltgaud struggles and strains to even lift his maul. He drags it as close to his target as possible and swings it across the ground, striking the base. It takes all his might to reposition the giant hammer to strike another blow.

An hour passes and Raimdon's statue barely cracks. The crowd grows restless, and a smattering of boos fills the air. Raimdon looks around before his next strike. *Perhaps I should have chosen something a little less robust.*

Glancing around, Waltgaud breathes heavily as sweat pours down his face. *Perhaps another tactic is in order.*

Waltgaud grasps the maul in the middle of the handle and, with every ounce of strength he can muster, lifts it over his head. He turns and brings it down on Raimdon's foot. The head impacts with a loud crunch.

Raimdon screams in pain, grabs his foot, and hops to the side. "That was a cheap shot! He should be disqualified for that."

"Technically, you never stated in your rules that we couldn't attack each other," says Waltgaud. "Can't smash a statue if you're incapacitated."

Demonicus gives a thumbs up. "I'm going to allow this."

Raimdon limps back into position. "Fine. Play it like that if you want. Either way, I'm going to finish this match in four strikes."

Waltgaud laughs. "I would love to see that. You've barely cracked the head."

"Then stand by and watch if you like."

"Very well. Proceed."

Raimdon stands in front of his statue and lifts the maul. "One." He strikes the statue with all his might and knocks off a tiny chunk.

Waltgaud chuckles. "If that's all you can manage, it's going to take more than four."

"Two." Raimdon pulls his maul back and swings again with the same result. "Three." He strikes once more, smashing in the nose.

Waltgaud bursts into hysterical laughter. "There's no way you're going to win with one more hit."

Raimdon positions his maul off to the side of his head. "Four!" He turns toward Waltgaud and swings the weapon in an underhanded arc. The giant hammerhead impacts the halfling's ribs with a loud crunch and sends Waltgaud flying through the air. Waltgaud slams into the ground and lies motionless for a few seconds. He curls into a fetal position and wheezes as he tries to catch his breath.

A squire emerges onto the field and rushes over to check on him. "Are you all right, sir? Do you think you can continue?"

Waltgaud gasps as he tries to form words. "I yield."

The squire turns to the dignitaries' box. "Waltgaud is unable to continue. Raimdon wins."

The audience emits a smattering of applause. A priest runs into the arena and heals the contestants' injuries. Waltgaud approaches Raimdon with a scowl on his face. He glares at his opponent, but his expression quickly changes to a wide grin. "Well played, Raimdon. Good luck in the next round."

The two combatants exit the arena. As they step through the doors, Demonicus checks the board and turns his attention back to the crowd. "Next up, we have the Lord Champion Gladiator of Battallia, Count Vuzenkhord against Delradi."

Vuzenkhord and Delradi emerge. Vuzenkhord walks to Delradi and extends his hand. Delradi hesitates, eying the outstretched palm nervously, before accepting the offer. Vuzenkhord clasps their hands firmly and the two exchange a hearty handshake. The crowd cheers in approval.

"What sportsmanship!" says Demonicus. "In the interest of fairness, Delradi shall decide what stipulations shall be in play."

Delradi looks over his opponent, deep in thought as he fidgets nervously. "Your Majesty, I have an idea. A duel with dual shortswords. Victory upon incapacitation or surrender."

Vuzenkhord roughly pats Delradi on the back, causing him to yelp in surprise and stumble forward. Vuzenkhord smiles. "Sorry, lad. Excellent choice, my friend."

"Very well," says Demonicus. "A dual-wielding duel it is then."

Two squires emerge onto the field, each carrying two shortswords. They hand the weapons to the combatants and quickly scurry away.

Demonicus gives the signal to begin and Delradi immediately enters a defensive stance with both swords crossed in front of him. Vuzenkhord twirls both weapons simultaneously and raises them into the air. The crowd shouts its adulation and Vuzenkhord turns to the next section. He repeats the process until he has turned in a full circle and once again faces Delradi.

Delradi blinks in confusion. "What was that?"

Vuzenkhord twirls his swords, tosses them in the air and catches them, much to the delight of the audience. "Showmanship. This battle is for entertainment. We should do our best to get the crowd excited."

"Well, I'm not really a showman. It looks fun, though. Do you mind?"

Vuzenkhord grins. "By all means, do try."

Delradi turns to face part of the crowd and raises his sword in the air. The audience does not react. Delradi turns to another section and tries again to the same response. He dejectedly lowers his sword and looks at his opponent.

Vuzenkhord grins. "It takes some practice. We could continue, but we should probably start the match. Would you like to make the first strike, or shall I?"

Delradi's breathing slows and his eyes narrow. He takes a deep breath and lunges at Vuzenkhord with a single swift strike. Vuzenkhord brings up a single sword in a flourishing wide arc, easily parrying the blow. Delradi jabs his other hand forward attempting to stab his opponent, but Vuzenkhord quickly blocks the attempt with his other blade and pushes the weapon aside.

Delradi takes a step back and attacks again, swinging both swords in a horizontal arc. Vuzenkhord calmly leans back slightly, and the tips of the blades narrowly miss his nose. He steps forward, slashing at Delradi's shoulder. Delradi is unable to react in time due to his wide stance and the blade connects with his flesh, slicing a deep gash in his shoulder. Vuzenkhord twirls around and swings both of his weapons at Delradi, who quickly raises his blades to parry. The weapons lock against one another and the two combatants push against each other. Vuzenkhord's experience and large muscles allow him to rapidly overpower Delradi, forcing him down to one knee.

"I've got you practically pinned, Delradi. Do you yield?"

Delradi closes his eyes. "No." He takes a deep breath and his muscles bulge, seemingly increasing in size. He opens his eyes and, with a single mighty shove, pushes Vuzenkhord back. The gladiator stumbles several feet away.

Delradi sighs with relief, and his muscles return to normal size. Delradi closes his eyes and takes a few deep breaths, whispering to himself. "I am in control. The beast has no power over me." Delradi opens his eyes as Vuzenkhord approaches.

"I've never seen anything like that before," says Vuzenkhord. "How did you do that?"

"That is a secret," says Delradi. "One that causes me a great deal of shame and anguish."

Vuzenkhord narrows his eyes in contemplation and cocks his head. "Intriguing. I won't pry, but you have me quite curious. Shall we continue?"

The two contestants charge each other and their blades clash. Delradi alternates his strikes, swinging both blades individually. Vuzenkhord parries every attack with ease. Delradi swings one blade in a horizontal arc, and Vuzenkhord moves to block the blow. At the last second, Delradi pulls the blade back and strikes with the other one, catching Vuzenkhord off guard and slicing his arm.

Vuzenkhord glances at the wound and smiles. "Not bad. Nothing worth surrendering over, but landing a blow on me is impressive for a non-gladiator."

Delradi lunges forward with both swords. Vuzenkhord blocks both blows and pushes outward, causing Delradi to lose his grip. Vuzenkhord slashes at Delradi in a diagonal arc. He catches Delradi just above the jawline and cuts a deep gash up his cheek and across the bridge of his nose. Dropping his swords, Delradi cries out in pain, spins, clutches the wound, and falls to the ground. Delradi tries to crawl away as Vuzenkhord stands over him.

"Do you yield?" asks Vuzenkhord.

Delradi pulls his blood-soaked hand away from his face and looks at it. His eyes narrow, his face scrunches, and his lips curl into a snarl. As his muscles bulge, his eyes flash an animalistic yellow and growls. The wounds on his face and shoulder slowly start to close. His eyes quickly return to normal and grow wide, his muscles revert to their regular size, and the healing stops. "No!"

Vuzenkhord stares blankly at Delradi and blinks. "What's going on? You don't surrender, then?"

Delradi remains on the ground, rapidly whispering to himself. "I am in control. The beast has no power over me. It will not take over. I must remain in control." Delradi takes several deep breaths and stands. He turns to face Vuzenkhord, who looks over him with a puzzled glare.

"What was that?" asks Vuzenkhord. "I heard you mumbling about remaining in control. What are you trying to control?"

Delradi lowers his eyes. "My secret. I hope to never reveal it here."

"You're very mysterious," says Vuzenkhord. "Your wounds seem smaller than I thought they would be."

Turning his gaze back to Vuzenkhord, Delradi gulps nervously and shrugs. "I guess they weren't as bad as you meant them to be."

Vuzenkhord's eyes narrow in suspicion as he continues to stare at his opponent. "Perhaps. Either that or whatever you're hiding is responsible." Vuzenkhord offers one of his swords to Delradi. "Shall we continue?"

Delradi eyes the weapon nervously and reaches out to grasp the hilt. When Vuzenkhord does not strike, Delradi tightens his grasp and accepts the blade. "Thank you."

"There's no sport in attacking you unarmed."

Delradi strikes at Vuzenkhord, who flashily parries the strike. Before Delradi can withdraw, Vuzenkhord pushes down on the blades with all his might, forcing Delradi down onto both knees. Unable to extricate himself, Delradi closes his eyes, takes a deep breath, and whispers those familiar words.

He opens his eyes, his muscles bulge, and he forces Vuzenkhord's sword up. As Delradi rises to his feet, Vuzenkhord withdraws his weapon and slashes Delradi across the same shoulder. Delradi cries out in pain, but the wound quickly begins closing up. His eyes flash yellow and he snarls at Vuzenkhord.

A look of panic appears on Delradi's face, and his eyes return to normal. Delradi rapidly chants his mantra repeatedly until the healing stops and his body returns to its usual state.

"Why would you stop the healing?" asks Vuzenkhord. "It would seem you have a gift."

"It's more like a curse." Delradi drops his weapon and summons a squire. "I yield."

"Are you certain, sir?" asks the squire.

"Yes. I dare not continue."

The squire turns to the dignitaries' box. "Delradi concedes the battle. Count Vuzenkhord wins."

The crowd cheers quietly, not certain of how to react.

"That was anticlimactic," says Demonicus. "Very well. Count Vuzenkhord is the winner."

As two priests emerge to heal the combatants, Vuzenkhord approaches Delradi. "Why did you stop? This fight could have continued."

Delradi shakes his head. "My secret was dangerously close to revealing itself. If I continued, there would have been great peril for everyone in attendance."

Vuzenkhord nods. "I see. You've revealed more than you meant with that statement."

"Don't tell anyone."

"As long as you remain in control, your secret is safe with me."

Pelagius stands by the door as Delradi and Vuzenkhord exit the field. As Delradi passes by, Pelagius stops him. "What happened? You didn't appear to be badly injured. You could have easily continued."

Delradi glances at Pelagius and turns his eyes to the ground. Outside, King Demonicus' voice pierces the air. "Next, we have Sir Galzra of Drago versus Alithyra."

Alithyra and Galzra immediately head toward the field, stepping around Pelagius and Delradi. The remaining competitors approach the entryway to watch the match.

Alithyra emerges onto the field to a chorus of cheers. Sir Galzra follows suit to a similar reaction. Demonicus grins and glances at the other dignitaries. "The crowd seems to like both combatants. It will be interesting to see what they come up with."

After speaking with the other rulers for a moment, Demonicus returns his attention to the field. "Alithyra, you shall choose the stipulations."

Alithyra thinks for a moment. "Your Majesty, I choose a bow duel. First to three successful hits wins."

"As long as none of the arrows score a lethal hit, that should be fine," says Demonicus. "Squires, retrieve two bows and two quivers of arrows."

A pair of squires leaves the arena, returning minutes later with the proper equipment. Alithyra and Galzra meet in the center of the field and the squires hand them their weaponry. The two combatants turn their backs to each other and knock an arrow.

Demonicus raises his hand. "Walk twenty paces and begin." He lowers his hand.

Alithyra and Galzra slowly start their walk. After twenty steps, they turn to face one another. Galzra and Alithyra loose their arrows simultaneously. Alithyra's arrow strikes Galzra in the shoulder while Galzra's bounces off her prosthetic. Both combatants glance at the dignitaries' box in confusion.

"Does that count?" asks Galzra. "Do we both get a point?"

Demonicus consults with the other dignitaries.

"It has been decided that hitting the prosthetic does count as a hit," says Demonicus. "Since it is attached to her body, it counts as a limb. Therefore, one point each."

"Fair enough," says Alithyra.

"Another ten paces," says Demonicus.

Alithyra and Galzra turn and walk farther down the field. Upon reaching the proper step count, they wheel around to face each other. Galzra nocks an arrow and looses it at his opponent. Alithyra quickly reaches up with her prosthetic arm and catches the arrow. She nocks Galzra's arrow along with one of her own and looses both. The arrows soar through the air and strike Galza in the arm and thigh.

"Two strikes in one," says Demonicus. "Alithyra wins! A priest will be out shortly to heal Galzra's wounds."

Chapter 41

Pelagius leads Delradi to the center of the chamber to avoid the traffic by the door.

"So, what happened?" asks Pelagius.

"I'd rather not talk about it," says Delradi. "I made a decision. That's it."

"I see," says Pelagius. "Are you certain there's nothing you wish to discuss?"

The competitors standing in the doorway emit a loud cheer. A squire approaches and taps Pelagius on the shoulder. "Pardon me, sir, but Delradi has been eliminated from the competition. He must either leave for home or join the other former competitors in their box to watch the tournament. He is no longer allowed back here."

"My apologies," says Delradi. "I'll be on my way."

The squires help Delradi out of his armor. Delradi gets dressed and turns to leave. As he approaches the door, Balric comes through carrying a large turkey leg. The two warriors collide, and Balric nearly drops his snack. Balric seethes and glares angrily at Delradi, who shrinks back.

"Excuse me, sir," says Delradi. "I'm on my way out."

Balric reaches out and grabs Delradi by the shirt, drawing him in. His rage-filled eyes pierce the young warrior's soul. "Stay out of my way or I will crush your skull against the ground."

Delradi gulps. "I don't think you want to do that. It would end badly."

Balric snorts. "For you."

Pelagius walks up to them. "Take it easy, Balric. It was an accident. There's no need for you to lose your temper."

Balric glares at Pelagius. "Stay out of it, old man. This is between me and him. Interfere at your own peril. Angering me further would not end well for you."

While Pelagius continues to try to calm Balric down, Sir Jabbleth approaches. "It would not end well for you either, friend. Remember the rules of the tournament. Any fighting outside of a sanctioned bout will get you disqualified. I would hate to miss out on a challenging match because you can't control yourself."

Balric grunts angrily and releases his grasp on Delradi, dropping him to the ground. "Fine. I'll save it for the battlefield … if I can."

Balric stomps away, to sit alone in a corner on the far side of the room. Pelagius and Jabbleth help Delradi to his feet.

"Are you all right?" asks Pelagius.

"I'm fine," says Delradi. "Thank you both for the assistance. I should go to the eliminated competitors' box now."

Delradi leaves through the outside door. The remaining competitors watching the fight groan as Demonicus' voice pierces the air. "Alithyra wins!"

Jabbleth frowns and turns to Pelagius. "We missed the whole fight."

Pelagius nods. "That one was short."

Pelagius returns to the doorway as the two fighters return to the preparation area. Demonicus scans the crowd before addressing them once more. "For our next match we have Viscount Kingston against Tanazhan!"

The crowd roars with applause as the massive rhinoran emerges onto the field. The cheers quickly morph into jeers and boos when Kingston appears.

Kingston sneers as he looks around. "Ungrateful rabble. I will be the one who frees you from demonic rule."

"What was that?" asks a nearby guard. "Did you just threaten the life of our king?"

"No, sir," says Kingston. "I wouldn't think of it."

Kingston quickly jogs to the center of the field, joining his immense opponent. Demonicus' eyes narrow as he observes the size difference. "In the interest of fairness, Kingston shall name the stipulations." The crowd boos, but the king ignores them. "Viscount Kingston, if you like, you may combine your match with the next one to make up for the difference in size."

Kingston scoffs. "I've fought morags one-on-one. I can handle this brute."

"Very well," says Demonicus. "Name the game."

"I'll take a longsword," says Kingston. "He can have a club. Victory upon incapacitation."

"So be it," says Demonicus.

The squires wheel out two carts. Swords fill one and the other holds a single massive club. Kingston takes his time looking at several blades until he finds one he likes. Demonicus addresses the fighters. "Let the match begin!"

Tanazhan turns toward Kingston and charges. Kingston jumps to the side, barely avoiding a trampling. Tanazhan skids to a halt and brings his club around. He connects with Kingston and sends him flying across the field. Kingston lands with a thud and stands quickly. He charges his opponent, dodging another blow from the club. Kingston swings his sword at Tanazhan's leg and connects with a solid hit, but his blade bounces harmlessly off his thick skin.

Kingston glances at his sword and looks up nervously at his opponent. Tanazhan jabs at him with his club, striking him in the chest and knocking him to the ground. The rhinoran raises his foot and brings it down upon Kingston, stomping him across the chest and stomach with a sickening crack. Kingston screams in pain and spits up a large gush of blood. Tanazhan withdraws his foot, and the demon hunter rolls onto his side, clutching his gut and coughing up more blood.

A squire runs onto the field and kneels next to him. "Sir, do you need me to stop the fight?"

Kingston gags and sputters as he tries to catch his breath. The squire stands and faces the dignitaries' box. "I believe that Kingston is unable to…"

Before the squire can finish, Kingston grabs him by the arm and pulls him to the ground. "Don't. I'm not done yet." Using his sword for support, Kingston slowly fights back to his feet.

The squire turns back to the king. "Kingston claims that he can continue. I have my doubts."

Demonicus shrugs. "If he thinks he can keep going, that's his prerogative."

Kingston limps toward Tanazhan and swings his sword at his leg. The strike connects with the same result. Tanazhan looks down at Kingston and frowns. He lightly swats Kingston with his club and the orc crashes to the ground. Kingston fights to regain his footing.

Tanazhan shakes his head. "Stay down, Kingston. You're far too injured to win this."

Kingston winces in pain. "I've won fights in worse condition. I will keep going as long as I can stand."

Kingston chops at Tanazhan's leg with his sword. After several strikes, a small cut appears. Tanazhan shakes his head and lunges forward, kicking Kingston to the ground. He stomps again, his foot landing solidly across Kingston's legs. Upon impact, Tanazhan presses down with all his might and two loud cracks echo through the arena.

Kingston screams in agony. "My legs! I can't move my legs!"

The squire returns and quickly assesses the situation. "Kingston is most definitely unable to continue. Tanazhan wins!"

The crowd remains silent for a moment before bursting into applause.

"A decisive victory if there ever was one," says Demonicus. "Get the priests out there quickly. Kingston needs healing immediately."

A priest runs onto the field, kneels next to the screaming Kingston, and heals his wounds. Upon completion, the priest leaves and Kingston rises to his feet. He looks up at the dignitaries' box. "Tanazhan should be disqualified for that! He nearly killed me by stomping on my gut!"

"If that stomp was meant to be fatal, it would have been," says Tanazhan.

Demonicus shakes his head and gives Kingston a thumbs down. "There was no intent to kill, and you survived. The decision stands."

"Demon scum!" shouts Kingston.

"Be careful what you say, Kingston," says Demonicus. "Keep that train of thought going if you want to be seen in the same light as Prince Matheral."

"I am not like that spoiled prince," says Kingston.

Demonicus glares at Kingston. "Then show some dignity and accept defeat."

Kingston looks around and lowers his head. "Fine. I accept the outcome. I will take my leave now."

Kingston exits the arena through the crowd, mounts a horse, and disappears into the horizon.

Chapter 42

"Another great day of exciting bouts draws to a close," says Demonicus. "However, we have one more match before the day is through. Our final contest of the day is Pelagius versus Darfindrin."

The crowd lets out a raucous cheer as Pelagius enters the field. His opponent joins him almost immediately.

Demonicus consults the other dignitaries and turns his attention back to the fighters. "Darfindrin, you shall choose the game."

Darfindrin looks over at Pelagius, deep in thought as he considers his options. "So, how is your balance, old man?"

Pelagius grins knowing full well what the elf has in mind. "Well, I'm not as spry as I used to be, but I'd say it's fair."

"Your Majesty, I choose the balance pit with quarterstaffs," says Darfindrin. "Sorry, Pelagius, but I've always been taught to take advantage of an opponent's weaknesses."

Pelagius suppresses a smirk. "No apologies necessary. I'm sure I'll manage."

Pelagius and Darfindrin each retrieve a quarterstaff and take their places at opposite ends of the beam. Upon Demonicus' signal, they carefully step onto the beam and head toward one another. As soon as they meet, Darfindrin goes for a leg sweep, but Pelagius blocks it effortlessly. Darfindrin attacks again, still going for the legs, only for Pelagius to deflect it. Pelagius jabs his staff at Darfindrin's face, catching him off guard and nearly sending him into the pit. The elf manages to regain his footing and remains on the beam.

"Well played, Pelagius," says Darfindrin.

The two trade blows back and forth, forcing each other back on the beam several times. Darfindrin keeps trying to go for the legs, but

Pelagius has grown wise to this tactic and effortlessly blocks each attempt. Darfindrin swings his staff upward and connects with the center of Pelagius's staff, snapping it in two. Pelagius readjusts his grip on both halves and continues the match.

"Your balance is better than anticipated," says Darfindrin. "I thought you would have fallen off the beam by now for sure."

"Did you really think that I would give you accurate information on my strengths and weaknesses?" asks Pelagius. "You underestimated my abilities, Darfindrin."

They trade a few more blows before Darfindrin once again goes for Pelagius's legs. Pelagius easily parries the strike with one half of his broken weapon and swings the other half in an upward arc. He lands a blow right under Darfindrin's chin, sending him stumbling backward. As Darfindrin tries to regain his footing, Pelagius smashes him across the face and sends him plummeting into the pit. The crowd goes completely wild, bursting into applause.

Demonicus rises to his feet. "Ladies and gentlemen, the winner is Pelagius! Congratulations to those who remain. The festivities continue tonight in the great hall." Demonicus turns to a nearby servant. "Please inform Captain Mughan that with this victory, Kevnan has been cleared of all charges."

Chapter 43

Pelagius joins his companions at a table in the great hall along with several other guests, including Hexeron, Delradi, and Koskru. They converse about the matches of the day, congratulating Pelagius and a few other contestants on their victories.

"So Kevnan, what do you plan to do now that you are no longer a prisoner and you're out of the tournament?" asks Hexeron.

"I would like to seek someone to train me in the art of using a katana," says Kevnan. "I have learned the basics, but recently lost a fight to an expert. I would like to challenge him to a rematch after I learn more."

"You should ask Ashisat, the representative of Ranwald," says Koskru. "He's a raimasu, and they specialize in that weapon."

"Would he be willing to?" asks Kevnan. "He won his match today, so he's still in the tournament."

"It's worth a try," says Pelagius.

"I suppose it is," says Kevnan. "I think I saw him on the other side of the room. I'll go mingle my way in that direction."

Kevnan rises and leaves the table, but he doesn't go very far. Instead, he stops and engages in conversation with a few nearby guests. After several minutes, he moves on to another group a bit farther away, repeating this process throughout the night. He reaches Ashisat later in the evening, shortly before the festivities come to an end. The Ranwaldan contestant notices him approaching.

"How can I help you, my friend?" asks Ashisat.

"Congratulations on making it this far in the tournament," says Kevnan. "Your matches have been very impressive."

"Thank you," says Ashisat. "It is an honor to know that I have kept the people entertained."

Kevnan engages Ashisat in conversation for the rest of the evening. As the festivities draw to a close and those guests who haven't passed out leave, Ashisat moves to excuse himself. "If you'll excuse me, my friend, I must be going. I need to be well rested for my match tomorrow."

"Before you go, I have one question," says Kevnan. "I've always wanted to learn how to use a katana. I know the basics, but I need someone to teach me more advanced techniques. Would you be willing to instruct me in the art?"

Ashisat smiles. "Of course, my friend. We can start as soon as the tournament is over, or once I am eliminated. Whichever comes first."

"Thank you, Ashisat," says Kevnan.

"Think nothing of it," says Ashisat. "It brings me great honor to pass along my knowledge to another. Until tomorrow."

Ashisat leaves the great hall and Kevnan returns to the others, who are meeting with Mughan to return to their quarters for the night.

Chapter 44

Grimadert returns to the preservation room, followed by Rogi. Instead of going back to working on Adotlin, whose stitched-up corpse lies nearly complete on its slab, Grimadert goes through a door on the other side of the room. He holds it open long enough for Rogi to grab Thakszut and follow him through, shutting it as soon as the busurin is in the chamber. In this room, which is still part of the preservation area, is a live fiendling chained to the wall. The unfortunate little demonfolk struggles futilely to break free.

"Let me go," says the fiendling. "You said you needed my assistance. Why do you hold me prisoner?"

Grimadert grins madly. "I do need your assistance. You see, I need to restore this fiendling to health, but due to a severe injury, his body is useless. I need a new body for his brain to inhabit, and your sacrifice will allow a greater being to live on."

The fiendling's eyes grow wide in horror as he doubles his efforts to get loose. Grimadert attempts to get close to start his experiment, but the fiendling's flailing makes the task impossible.

"Rogi, sedate him, if you please," says Grimadert.

Rogi walks to the struggling fiendling and grabs him by the chest, immobilizing him against the wall. He punches the poor demonfolk in the face, causing his head to bounce off the stone and knocking him unconscious.

"Excellent," says Grimadert. "Now we just need to immobilize him so he can't struggle when he regains consciousness."

Rogi grabs more chains and shackles from a nearby storage container and proceeds to fasten the fiendling to the wall more securely. When he finishes, there isn't room for the unconscious demonfolk to shift even slightly whenever he wakes. Grimadert sets up a system of thin metal tubes connected to a pump operated by a collection of gears. One of the tubes ends over a large tub and the other has a needle in it. Poking various spots on the fiendling's body, he grins when he finds what he is looking for and inserts the needle into that spot. Grimadert pulls a switch, and the gears and cogs turn, causing the pump to move up and down with a suctioning sound.

Within minutes, blood drips out the tube's end, into the tub. After a few minutes, the fiendling regains consciousness. Unable to move, he shifts his eyes in the direction of the sound and the sight horrifies him.

"What are you doing?" asks the fiendling.

"Draining your blood," says Grimadert. "If I were to simply transplant his brain into your body, it may reject the foreign blood. Or it may not. This is an experimental procedure, and it may work either way or it may not work at all. But if it were to reject your blood, the brain would die. This way, I can keep the brain from destroying itself before the experiment is complete."

"You're mad!" says the fiendling.

Grimadert cackles madly. "Perhaps so, but I'm also a genius, and both traits are highly beneficial when combined for the sake of science."

As time passes, the fiendling watches helplessly as his blood drains from his body, filling the nearby tub. After an hour of the slow procedure, he grows woozy, and his visible skin becomes pale. As time passes, he grows weaker and weaker until he loses the fight to remain conscious.

After another hour, he stops breathing as the last of his blood drains from his body. Rogi unshackles his lifeless body as Grimadert stops the machine and removes the needle from the fiendling's corpse. They place him on a nearby table.

"Do we transfer the blood from Thakszut now, Master?" asks Rogi.

"Not yet. We need to replace the heart first." Grimadert picks up a large knife and carefully cuts open the fiendling's chest. He removes the heart, handing it to Rogi for disposal. He casts a spell on Thakszut before opening his chest and removing his still beating heart. He places it where the original heart was, connects it to the surrounding valves, and sews the chest back up.

"The stasis spell should keep him alive while we finish transferring his blood and brain to his new body." Grimadert opens the fiendling's skull and removes the brain, tying off the blood vessels as well. "Now we transfer Thakszut's blood. We could transfer the brain first, but it will be less messy this way."

They reinsert the needle into the fiendling's body before attaching a needle to the other end and placing it in Thakszut. Grimadert reactivates the machine, and they wait a few hours while the blood transfers. After the machine has done its job, they deactivate it and remove the needles from both bodies.

Grimadert opens Thakzut's skull and carefully removes his brain, transplanting it into the other fiendling's now empty skull. One at a time, he carefully unties the blood vessels and attaches them to the proper locations, before setting the top of the cranium back and sealing the bone before sewing the head up.

"Shall I take him to the main laboratory, Master?" asks Rogi.

"No," says Grimadert. "We need to let everything settle for a few days before we commence with the next step. Even in stasis, his heart may stop completely if we move him too early. In the meantime, we have other experiments to see to."

Rogi and Grimadert leave the room, shutting the door behind them and disappearing into a dark room at the end of the hall.

CHAPTER 45

As he waits by the doors, Pelagius hears the excitement of the crowd as they cheer and applaud, despite none of the competitors having entered the arena.

After a few minutes, the doors open, admitting them onto the field as the crowd roars with approval. As Pelagius looks up at the dignitaries' box, he sees King Sylwyn, Archpriest Bothrug, Grand Priest Ekdrig, and High Guildmaster Togpym have departed, but the rest remain, even if their champion no longer competes.

A grinning King Demonicus rises to give his opening address. "Good morning, ladies and gentlemen. Welcome to the Grand Tourney Quarter Finals! It has been an amazing past few days, and the excitement shall continue. Our first match is sure to be especially interesting. We have the legendary and vile Black Knight, Sir Jabbleth, versus the raging beast, Balric! Who shall prevail in this clash of the titans?"

"If I were a betting man, I'd put my money on Sir Jabbleth," says King Bloodsworth. "He's far more disciplined and composed."

Maldorus nods. "Perhaps, but Balric seems unstoppable once his rage breaks. He took hits that would have put the other competitors out of the competition and still won."

"Would you care to place a wager then, Archduke Maldorus?" asks Bloodsworth. "It would make it even more interesting."

Malorus grins, his dried skin and exposed muscles creaking. "Why not? I'll put twenty gold pieces on Balric."

"I'll match that," says Bloodsworth. "Anybody else care to place a bet?"

The other dignitaries decline the offer. Demonicus shrugs and turns his attention back to the field as the contestants emerge. "Sir Jabbleth,

TRIAL BY TOURNAMENT: CHAMPION OF VALOR

you shall be the one to choose the game for this match. How would you like to proceed?"

Jabbleth removes his helmet. "I'd like it to be somewhat even. I choose hand-to-hand combat."

A shocked muttering washes over the crowd. Archduke Maldorus' desiccated face creaks as he grins. "I think I'll up the ante, Bloodsworth. I'm increasing my bet to one hundred gold pieces."

"I'll match your new bet," says Bloodsworth.

"Very well, then," says Demonicus. "Let the first bout of the quarter finals begin."

Demonicus gives the signal to start and the two competitors square up, each daring the other to make the first move. After several seconds, Balric charges in and throws the first punch, which Jabbleth easily blocks. The Black Knight gives him a stiff palm thrust to the chest, pushing him back a few feet.

Balric rushes back in and attempts to slug Jabbleth a second time, but the Black Knight blocks and deflects his attack in the same manner. Balric emits a seething, teeth-clenched breath and charges back in. Jabbleth sidesteps him, and grabbing his arm, tosses Balric aside, using his momentum against him. Balric grunts furiously, rising to his feet and glaring at his opponent. He aggressively stomps toward Jabbleth and stares down the Black Knight without making another move.

Balric throws a wild punch, which Jabbleth easily ducks. His frustration building, he throws several rapid punches at Jabbleth, who easily blocks each one. Balric's rage boils over and he emits his signature scream of fury. He pounds on Jabbleth as hard as he can, but the Black Knight remains on the defensive and blocks every blow.

Seeing an opening, Jabbleth lunges and lands two hard punches across Balric's face. The angry young warrior is unfazed and continues his assault, landing a blow across Jabbleth's jaw and sending him sprawling to the ground. Balric is upon him in an instant and Jabbleth raises his arms to protect his head from the furious assault.

As Balric pulls back for another punch, Jabbleth takes advantage of the brief pause and flings him off. Rising to his feet, Jabbleth notices Balric charging at full speed. He ducks under a wild punch and slams himself into Balric's torso, lifting him up and slamming him into the ground. Jabbleth slugs his enraged opponent across the face several times, but Balric shrugs off the assault and pushes him away. Balric throws another punch, which Jabbleth dodges.

Before Balric can make another move, Jabbleth grabs onto his arm and twists it behind Balric's back. Using his free hand, Jabbleth locks in the other arm and slams the young warrior into the ground, holding him in place.

"You're tough, I'll give you that," says Jabbleth. "But rage can only be sustained for so long. Sooner or later, you'll burn out."

After a brief struggle, Balric manages to get one arm free and tosses Jabbleth over his shoulder, slamming him into the ground. Jabbleth quickly rolls out of the way of a stomp and rises to his feet. As Balric continues his assault, Jabbleth keeps his defenses up. They continue trading blows for a few minutes as Jabbleth tries to wear down his opponent, but Balric shows no signs of coming out of his rage.

Jabbleth weaves to the side, avoiding another punch as he considers the situation. *He's keeping this up far longer than should be possible. Perhaps there is something fueling his anger. He may burn out eventually, but I don't know if I can outlast his fury. I need a new strategy.*

Jabbleth deflects another blow and sends Balric sprawling several feet across the field. The angry young warrior hops up and charges, throwing a punch as he draws near. Jabbleth ducks under the strike and flips Balric over himself, slamming him into the ground.

Before Balric can stand, Jabbleth grabs one his arms from behind and twists it around. He pulls it behind Balric's back and repeatedly pulls and slams his elbow down onto it until a sickening snap echoes through the arena. Balric emits a pained shout of fury and uses his body to throw Jabbleth off. When he rises to his feet, one arm hangs limply by his side. His eyes bloodshot from his out-of-control rage, Balric blindly charges Jabbleth, who ducks his punch and slams into his legs.

As Balric crashes to the ground, Jabbleth grabs one of his ankles and rapidly drops to the ground, wrapping his legs around Balric's knee. He uses his entire body to wrench the leg back and forth while Balric thrashes trying to dislodge him. Jabbleth twists Balric's ankle completely around and rapidly jerks his knee to the side with several sickening snaps. Despite his injuries, Balric pulls his leg free and struggles to his feet, but Jabbleth kicks him in his good knee, sending him crashing to the ground.

Trial by Tournament: Champion of Valor

Jabbleth is upon Balric in a flash, holding his good arm behind his back before twisting it beyond its normal range of motion. Balric flops on the ground like a fish, screaming in anger as he continues to try to assault Jabbleth. The Black Knight sighs, plants his knee on Balric's spine, and wraps his arms around the young warrior's throat. Balric continues to thrash for several minutes, but finally comes down from his rage. Jabbleth releases his grip as Balric returns to his calmer state.

"Do you yield?" asks Jabbleth.

Balric rocks back and forth until he manages to flip over onto his back. He glares at Jabbleth. "I never yield."

Jabbleth plants his foot on Balric's chest and bends down. "I'm not going to give you the opportunity to build your fury back up. I'm sorry."

Jabbleth punches Balric in the face hard enough to instantly knock him unconscious. A shocked silence falls across the crowd for several seconds. They burst into a cacophony of applause as a priest emerges to heal Balric's injuries. The squires remain cautiously behind until they are certain that they are safe from Balric's fury. Archduke Maldorus begrudgingly makes a quick count of his coins and hands a bag to King Bloodsworth.

"Ladies and gentlemen, the winner is Sir Jabbleth!" says Demonicus.

As the priest completes his task, Balric regains consciousness. He grabs the priest by the throat and tosses him several feet away. He rises to his feet and looks around. Without a word, Balric disappears into the interior of the arena, with the remaining competitors keeping a safe distance. He retrieves a large axe from the weapons master and departs.

While the squires clean up the field, Ashisat turns to Raimdon and smiles. "We're up next, my friend. Are you ready?"

"Of course," says Raimdon. "No hard feelings when I win?"

Ashisat laughs. "No hard feelings regardless of who wins."

Raimdon and Ashisat stand by the doorway, awaiting their cue to enter the arena. King Demonicus rises to address the crowd. "Ladies and gentlemen, our next match is Ashisat of Ranwald versus Raimdon of Diablos!"

The two combatants enter the field to thunderous applause. Demonicus consults the other dignitaries and returns his attention to the contestants when the noise dies down. "In the interest of fairness, Ashisat will decide the stipulations."

"I choose a tether duel, Your Majesty," says Ashisat.

Demonicus glances at the other dignitaries and gives a quizzical look. The dignitaries all shrug, including King Bloodsworth.

Demonicus smirks. "Really, Bloodsworth? There's a form of combat you are not familiar with? You? The Warlord King?"

Bloodsworth shoots Demonicus a humorless glare. "Don't antagonize me, Demonicus. While I am familiar with many styles of battlefield and gladiatorial combat, this is a new one to me."

Demonicus turns his attention back to Ashisat. "Explain, please."

Ashisat bows. "Of course, Your Majesty. We shall be tied together with a rope, leather strap, or chain, depending on what the squires can find. Twelve feet total in length, although once both of us are tied it will likely be closer to nine or ten feet. Tethered as such, we will duel with shortswords. Victory upon incapacitation or yield. Cutting the bonds indicates a surrender."

"Very well," says Demonicus. "Squires, find the appropriate bonds."

Several squires leave the arena. After a few minutes, they return with a leather strap of appropriate length. Two squires wrap the ends of the strap around the waist of each competitor and tie them off, ensuring the knot is tight and the strap is snug. Another squire carries a pair of shortswords onto the field, handing one to each contestant. When they are certain that the strap is securely fastened, the squires leave the field and Demonicus gives the signal to start. The two men put as much distance between each other as possible, grasp the strap, and engage in a tug-of-war. Both combatants pull on the strap as hard as they can, each unable to overpower the other. Ashisat releases his grip and charges Raimdon, who loses his balance and stumbles back at the sudden slack.

Raimdon regains his composure just in time to parry a strike from Ashisat's sword. They trade blows, dodging and parrying each other's attacks for several minutes. Ashisat grabs a section of the strap with his free hand and whips it into Raimdon's face. Stunned, Raimdon stumbles as Ashisat uses the strap to entangle Raimdon's legs and trips him up. Raimdon crashes to the ground and hops to his feet, quickly disentangling himself.

"What was that?" asks Raimdon.

"The strap is part of the fight," says Ashisat. "It too can be used as a weapon."

"Good to know," says Raimdon.

Raimdon yanks on the strap, pulling his opponent off his feet. Ashisat hops up, blocks an attack from Raimdon's blade, and counterattacks, striking the hilt of the daemon's sword and knocking it from his hands. Ashisat holds the tip of his sword to Raimdon's throat. "Do you yield?"

Raimdon grins. "Not yet."

Raimdon swings the strap into Ashisat's face and retreats as far as he can. Ashisat grasps the strap and pulls, but Raimdon plants his feet and does the same. Ashisat grins and charges. As Ashisat draws nearer, Raimdon gathers more of the strap into his hands. Ashisat begins the final approach of his charge, sword at the ready to strike. Raimdon drops some of the slack and pulls, entangling Ashisat's legs and tripping him.

Ashisat stumbles and tries to regain his balance as he blunders past Raimdon. Raimdon grabs Ashisat by the shoulder and kicks him in the back of the knee, sending Hashsiato down on one knee. Raimdon takes up some of the strap's slack, wraps it around Ashisat's neck, pulls it tight, and holds it in place. Ashisat gasps for air and swings his sword wildly in a vain attempt to escape. Unable to strike Raimdon or break free, Ashisat' vision grows fuzzy and his foot slips, nearly sending him crashing to the ground. Raimdon holds tight, not allowing Ashisat to break free.

"My turn to ask," says Raimdon. "Do you yield?"

Unable to respond, Ashisat continues trying desperately to break free. He gags as his vision fades in and out. Growing weaker and on the verge of losing consciousness, Ashisat grabs a loose piece of the strap and forms a loop in his hand. He slides the blade of his sword into the loop and cuts the strap. Raimdon releases his grasp and Ashisat crashes to the ground, gasping and coughing.

"Ladies and gentlemen, Raimdon wins!" says Demonicus.

A pair of priests emerge onto the field, but Raimdon is uninjured and Ashisat waves them off as he stands. Ashisat extends his hand to Raimdon, and the two combatants exchange a hearty handshake.

"Well played, my friend," says Ashisat. "Good luck to you in the next round."

"Thank you, sir," says Raimdon.

Ashisat and Raimdon exit the field and enter the competitors' staging area. Pelagius and Sir Jabbleth greet them.

"Good show, my friends," says Jabbleth. "Quite an innovative match."

"Thank you," says Ashisat. "It's a fairly common form of duel in Ranwald. Thought I'd give it a try."

"Too bad it backfired," says Jabbleth.

"You win some, you lose some," says Ashisat. "I should head to the eliminated competitors' box. Good luck to the rest of you."

Ashisat leaves the area. Pelagius's attention diverts to the arena doorway as Demonicus' voice pierces the air.

"That was an exciting bout," says Demoncius. "Our next match is Count Vuzenkhord of Battallia against Alithyra."

Count Vuzenkhord enters the arena, slowly walking to the center as he stops several times and raises his arms to excite the crowd. Alithyra passes by Vuzenkhord as he turns to each section to incite a cheer.

"I'm not an impatient person, but we don't have all day," says Alithyra.

"There's no need to rush, my friend," says Vuzenkhord. "Always best to play to the crowd."

"I see no strategic value to playing to the crowd, but it seems like fun," says Alithyra.

"For someone in my profession, support from the audience is everything. I've seen gladiators rise and fall based on changing reactions from the stands."

The crowd falls silent when Demonicus rises to address the competitors. "It has been unanimously agreed upon that Count Vuzenkhord shall decide the stipulations of the game."

Vuzenkhord thinks for a moment, glances at his opponent, and grins. "Your Majesty, I have an usual request."

"Name it," says Demonicus.

"This will require the assistance of mages," says Vuzenkhord. "I request a series of stone pillars twenty feet high placed throughout the arena. We will race across the pillars from one end to the other, pausing to duel with weapons placed on certain ones at random intervals. Victory is determined in two ways. The first is by reaching the final pillar first. The second is causing your opponent to fall from the pillars three times.

Whichever is achieved first will decide the victor."

"Does missing a jump count as a fall?" asks Alithyra.

"Of course, but only if you hit the ground. If you manage to catch the pillar before then and climb back up, no points are awarded."

"That sounds intriguing," says Demonicus. "You are quite creative, count."

Bloodsworth chuckles. "You should see what he comes up with at the Grand Coliseum when death matches are allowed."

"Very well then," says Demonicus. "Clear the field while the sorcerers make preparations."

Alithyra and Vuzenkhord return to the entry gate. After several minutes, ten sorcerers emerge onto the field. Positioning themselves around the arena, they chant in unison. The sorcerers simultaneously place their hands on the ground and the field glows. The ground rumbles as multiple mounds of stone and dirt clump together throughout the entire area.

The mounds form into cylindrical pillars and rise twenty feet into the air, expanding in diameter as more debris attaches to the sides. When the ritual finishes, the glow fades and the pillars cover the field, the distances between each one ranging from five feet to eight feet. The squires wheel a cart of weapons onto the field. With help from the sorcerers, they place the weapons randomly on top of the pillars. Upon completion, everyone involved departs, and Demonicus addresses the combatants. "Approach the pillar closest to you."

Alithyra and Vuzenkhord emerge and walk up to different pillars.

Demonicus raises his hand in the air. "Upon my signal, begin your ascent." He rapidly drops his arm down. "Go!"

The two combatants begin climbing. Alithyra has difficulty getting a grip, but Vuzenkhord draws a pair of daggers and repeatedly drives them into the sides of the pillar, using them as climbing tools. Seeing this, Alithyra grabs a nearby piece of the leather strap left from the previous match. She wraps it around the pillar and uses it to ease her ascent. Vuzenkhord reaches the top first and waits for Alithyra, who arrives shortly after.

"You had a head start," says Alithyra. "Why allow me to catch up?"

"Where's the sport in an early lead?" asks Vuzenkhord. "That wouldn't be very exciting for the audience."

"It would have been when I caught up," says Alithyra.

The two combatants leap to the next closest pillars, easily landing. Finding no weapons, they continue to the next one. Due to differing distances, Vuzenkhord nearly doesn't make it, but manages to grab onto the side and pulls himself up. Alithyra finds a spear on her platform and jabs at Vuzenkhord as he clambers up. Reaching the top, Vuzenkhord picks up a pair of small hatchets and uses it to deflect the blows.

Realizing that her jabs are ineffective, Alithyra decides to move on to the next pillar. She backs up to the edge of his pillar and rushes forward. She drives the end of the spear into the ground and uses it as a pole vault for an extra push. Vuzenkhord leaps to the next pillar, tossing a hatchet at Alithyra as she lands. The handle strikes Alithyra in the face as her feet touch the pillar, knocking her off balance. Driving the spear into the dirt, Alithyra prevents herself from falling, but the spear snaps when Vuzenkhord throws his remaining hatchet at it. Unable to regain her balance, the sudden loss of the spear under her weight causes Alithyra to teeter over the edge and plummet to the ground.

"One point to Count Vuzenkhord," says Demonicus.

Vuzenkhord stands in place, playing to the crowd as Alithyra climbs back up. Both combatants leap to the next pillar. Alithyra lands easily, but Vuzenkhord's destination was farther than he anticipated, and he falls to the earth below.

Demonicus addresses the crowd. "One point to Alithyra."

Alithyra leaps to the next pillar as Vuzenkhord returns to the top. Finding a net at the top, he grabs it and continues on his way. Alithyra lands on another pillar and nearly loses her balance, allowing Vuzenkhord to catch up. Ignoring the sword at her feet, Alithyra leaps to the next pillar. Vuzenkhord tosses his net at Alithyra, catching her in midair and stopping her progress. Entangled, Alithyra falls to the ground.

Vuzenkhord leaps to the next platform while Alithyra disentangles herself from the net and climbs back up. Grabbing the sword, Alithyra leaps to the next pillar and quickly jumps across to Vuzenkhord's side. Caught by surprise, Vuzenkhord barely grabs the nearby mace and parries Alithyra's attack.

Striking with the blade, Alithyra waits for Vuzenkhord to block the blow before she balls up her metal fist and lunges forward. Impacting

Vuzenkhord's chest, Alithyra punches Vuzenkhord off the edge. Vuzenkhord hits the ground with a thud and jumps to his feet, climbing back up as quickly as possible. Alithyra jumps to the next pillar just before Vuzenkhord reaches the top. The count quickly follows.

"Well played, my friend," says Vuzenkhord.

Alithyra jumps to the next pillar with Vuzenkhord close behind. Still wielding their previous weapons, the two combatants engage in a brief duel before continuing. With the final pillar in sight, Alithyra makes one final leap. Vuzenkhord flings his mace and strikes Alithyra in the side mid-jump. The force of the blow stuns Alithyra and changes her trajectory. She slams face first into the side of the pillar and plummets to the ground. The crowd erupts into thunderous applause.

"Final point!" shouts Demonicus. "Vuzenkhord wins!"

Vuzenkhord descends his pillar to the ground and helps Alithyra to her feet. "Close contest. If I had missed, you would have won."

Alithyra smiles. "Lucky shot."

Alithyra leaves the field. Vuzenkhord slowly walks to the back, pausing every few feet to raise up his arms and play to the crowd. After five minutes, he disappears through the doorway.

"Ladies and gentlemen, wasn't that exciting?" says Demonicus. "We will take a break for a few minutes while the sorcerers return the field to its normal state. Then, we can start the final match of the day."

Chapter 46

King Demonicus rises to address the crowd, silencing the restless mutterings. "Our final match of the day is Pelagius versus Tanazhan."

Pelagius arrives on the field, his smile fading when he sees his opponent. Although he had watched his previous matches, Pelagius just now realizes who he will be facing. Demonicus surveys the scene, realizing that he overlooked the mismatching of sizes in this bout.

"Pelagius, in the interest of fairness, you shall choose the game," says Demonicus. "You may, if you wish, also choose two of the other remaining competitors to join and make it a four way double elimination match."

Pelagius is silent for several moments, clearly in deep thought as to his options. "I think I'll stay with one-on-one, Your Majesty, and for this bout, I have an unusual request."

Demonicus shifts in his seat and leans forward. "Name it."

"I'd like to have this match in the style of a bullfight," says Pelagius. "Tanazhan will be unarmed, and I will be armed with a sword and a cape. Victory upon yield or incapacitation."

Demonicus turns to the other dignitaries and discusses the request. When they have concluded their dialogue, he turns back to the competitors.

"What do you think of this stipulation, Tanazhan?" asks Demonicus.

Tanazhan grins. "I like it."

"Very well," says Demonicus. "This match shall be in the style of a bullfight. Take your places on the field."

Tanazhan goes to the far end of the stadium, and the squires bring Pelagius a selection of swords. Being most familiar with it, Pelagius chooses the longsword. It takes the squires a few minutes to locate a red cape, but once they find one, they bring it out immediately.

After draping it over Pelagius's shoulders, the squires leave the field. Once they are clear, Demonicus gives the signal to begin. Pelagius waves the cape in a dramatic flourish, grabbing Tanazhan's attention. The rhinoran squints to get a better look, fighting his naturally poor vision to target his opponent. After pinpointing Pelagius's location the best he can, he charges down the field. Unprepared for this surprising swift movement, Pelagius is nearly trampled, but manages to just barely jump aside. Pelagius swings his sword as Tanazhan passes by, connecting with his leg.

Unfortunately, the rhinoran's tough hide easily deflects the blow. Tanazhan smashes through a barrier, causing the members of the standing crowd to scatter. He turns and tries to reestablish visual contact with his opponent. Staying out of his line of sight for a moment, Pelagius moves farther down the field before waving his cape to catch the rhinoran's attention. Having spotted his target, Tanazhan charges again, barely missing Pelagius as he jumps to the side. The standing crowd scatters as he plows through the barricade. Unable to stop due to his momentum, Tanazhan slams into the lower stands, scattering several members of the audience and collapsing the remaining section.

"Sorry," says Tanazhan. "I went a bit too fast."

As the rhinoran turns, Pelagius again relocates. Tanazhan spots him as he waves his cape and goes barreling across the field. Pelagius easily leaps out of the way, and Tanazhan runs right past him. Having failed to notice the surrounding area due to his lousy sight, Tanazhan steps onto the balance beam, which snaps and sends him tumbling headfirst into the pit.

Although the hole is only two feet higher than him, Tanazhan's horn imbeds in the soil at the bottom, causing him to struggle to free himself. Tanazhan is unable to reposition himself to escape the pit as one of the squires counts to ten. The crowd falls into stunned silence before erupting into wild applause.

"Ladies and gentlemen, the winner is Pelagius!" Demonicus glances around the arena, a look of concern on his face as he beholds the damaged stands. "Priests will be along shortly to heal those who were injured during the match."

Several priests follow the squires out onto the field and head for the stands. As the priests heal the injured spectators, a pair of giants grab

Tanazhan by the feet and pull him out of the pit. Clearly embarrassed, he leaves the stadium and disappears into the horizon.

"It has certainly been an exciting few days," says Demonicus. "Tomorrow, we will have the semi-finals, followed by the finals later in the evening. Be sure to come back. You don't want to miss the exciting conclusion to this Grand Tourney. As before, everyone is welcome to join us in the great hall for more festivities. Be cautious on your journey home tonight. A storm is coming from the east."

Demonicus turns to one of his servants. "Have Captain Mughan inform Pelagius that Alithyra and all his companions who fell during his attack on Devil's Den shall receive full pardons for their roles."

The servant bows and disappears from the platform as Pelagius leaves the field.

Chapter 47

A desperate pounding on the front door wakes Shukrat from a deep sleep. He groggily lights a lantern and moves through the house to answer. "Now who could that be at this hour?"

The elderly goblin opens the door to find Shudgluv, who seems to have aged a few years, and Eeshlith standing outside. Shukrat's sleepy eyes spring wide open and he enters a defensive stance, electricity crackling in his hands. "What do you want? Did your master send you?"

Eeshlith raises her hands to show that she is not armed. "No. We have defected from Alasdar's service and fled Devil's Den. We need your help."

"Your service to the Green-Eyed Man is well known," says Shukrat. "How do I know that this is not a trick?"

Shudgluv ducks and peers through the doorway. "We have valuable information regarding Alasdar's plans. Please, just hear us out."

Shukrat thinks for a moment, and then relaxes his stance and dismisses his spell. "Please, come in. It seems that you two have a chance at personal redemption."

The two former henchmen enter the house, and Shukrat directs them to a parlor. As they sit in the comfortable chairs, Shukrat disappears from the room. He returns with tea, which is gladly accepted by the two refugees.

"Now tell me everything you know," says Shukrat.

Shudgluv and Eeshlith relay their story, starting from the attack on Inolutet. A look of horror crosses Shukrat's face as they describe Alasdar's recent activities and overarching goal.

"This is serious," says Shukrat. "What he's doing is treason of the worst kind. We must inform the king immediately."

Shudgluv and Eeshlith gather around Shukrat. Their forms blur as they begin to teleport to the castle, but they flicker and remain in place, failing to vanish. A look of concern crosses Shukrat's face and he makes the motions to open a portal, but nothing happens.

"That's bad," says Shukrat. "Alasdar must have a spy in Ethor."

"How would that affect your powers?" asks Shudgluv.

"The spy must be a sorcerer," says Shukrat. "I'm guessing that when they saw you arrive, they placed an anti-transport bubble around the town. People can teleport in, but we can't transport out. We'll have to leave the town's borders before I can use my transport powers."

The door to the hallway flies open, and a halfling dressed in sorcerer's robes steps through. He points at Shukrat. "You're not going anywhere. Bound to earth, you travel no more. In one spot you shall stay until the hour of twenty-four."

As the halfling finishes his chant, a beam of purple energy shoots from his finger and strikes Shukrat in the chest. The elderly goblin flies across the room as the energy engulfs his body. Thinking quickly, Eeshlith grabs a large knife and flings it at the attacker. She catches the halfling off guard and the blade strikes him in the chest, embedding itself deeply. The attacker stumbles backward and slumps against the wall.

Glancing down at the knife in his chest, he starts laughing. "It doesn't matter. I have completed my task."

The halfling laughs again before emitting a final choking breath. Shudgluv and Eeshlith rush to Shukrat, who rises to his feet as they arrive.

"I'm all right," says Shukrat.

"What did he do?" asks Eeshlith.

Shukrat focuses for a moment. "I've been cursed. Even if we get beyond the dimensional barrier, I cannot use transport magic for twenty-four hours. I do not know what would happen if I tried, but I do not wish to find out."

Shudgluv moves toward the door. "Then we should leave immediately. We have to get to the castle."

Shukrat shakes his head. "Castle Demonicus is a few days' ride away. We may as well wait here until the curse runs its course. In the meantime, we should…"

A large bell rings outside, interrupting Shukrat.

"It's just as I thought," says Shukrat. "Ethor is about to come under attack. Grab some weapons from Ralkgek's chest and help me rally the guards and militia."

As Eeshlith and Shudgluv go to another room to arm themselves, Shukrat rushes out the door.

Chapter 48

Dark clouds roll ominously into town as Shudgluv and Eeshlith join Shukrat outside. Shudgluv wields a maul and a longsword. Eeshlith has several weapons. One is a handheld repeating crossbow, which can fire up to ten bolts within a few seconds due to attaching a cartridge containing multiple bolts to the firing mechanism. She also carries an unusual item that at first appears to be a shortsword but has a morningstar's spiked ball at the end of the hilt. Two bandoliers cross her chest, one full of knives and the other containing more bolt cartridges. A strange coil of thin metal wraps around her waist like a belt; a hilt-like handle protruding from one side.

Shukrat directs several individuals in their placement of the defenses. Some of the guards, militia, and other townsfolk place pikes in the ground, while others set up walls of sandbags or building makeshift wooden walls, platforms, and other such defenses. Shudgluv and Eeshilth approach him.

"How many are we dealing with?" asks Eeshlith.

"We're outnumbered for certain," says Shukrat. "Between the guards, militia, and able-bodied townsfolk, we've got around one hundred defenders, plus us three. From what we can see, there are at least one hundred and ten umbra warriors on the march being led by a busurin."

Eeshlith and Shudgluv shoot each other a concerned glance.

"So Glakchog is leading the assault himself," says Shudgluv. "Why am I not surprised?"

"Are there any soul hunters?" asks Eeshlith.

"None that we have spotted," says Shukrat.

"Strange," says Shudgluv. "One hundred and ten against one hundred and three is not a particularly large numbers advantage. Alasdar must have something else up his sleeve."

"Everybody get in position!" shouts one of the guards. "They're beginning their advance."

Several defenders grab a bow and a quiver of arrows. They then climb up onto the platforms and makeshift walls. Others grab the embedded pikes and steady themselves. Eeshlith, Shudgluv, and Shukrat join the archers and look across the field. Glakchog stands on a rock elevated above the umbra warriors pouring out of the swamp and lining up. As the last warrior takes his place in line, rain falls from the sky and a blast of thunder breaks the silence.

As the drizzle increases to a downpour, Glakchog glares at the defensive line. "Fools. Their pitiful defense will not hold against the perfect soldier. Men, it would seem that we must teach these townsfolk a lesson." Drawing his hookswords, Glakchog points in the direction of Ethor. "Charge!"

The umbra warriors charge across the field, weapons drawn and ready to cut down their opponents. As they draw near, the archers unleash a barrage of arrows, killing about a quarter of the charging forces. As they loose another round, Shukrat flings a fireball amidst a large group of them.

The ensuing arrow storm and explosion wipe out half of the remaining warriors. The ones who were quick enough to avoid the barrage rush forward and impale themselves on the pikes. Just as always, the bodies vanish into a blue mist. Glakchog observes the battle from his position as the defenders cut down the last of his force.

"This seems too easy," says Shudgluv. "What is he planning?"

Glakchog looks into the swamp and emits a loud whistle. A blast of thunder cuts through the air, and a flash of lightning reveals movement beyond the trees. Within seconds, even more umbra warriors emerge from the swamp, flooding the field.

"Another wave," says Shukrat. "Maybe his plan is to overwhelm us with rounds."

As the defenders cut down more and more umbra warriors, a loud bellowing catches their attention. From a different grove of trees, Hazgor emerges and charges across the opening. He is upon the defenders in an instant as arrows bounce off his hide.

He tramples several pikemen and smashes through the main barricade, sending Shukrat and several others flying. The elderly goblin slams into a wall and hits the ground with a thud. Hazgor's momentum carries him partway into town as he smashes through several houses.

With the defenders distracted by the charging rhinoran, the umbra warriors close the gap and pour into town. Shudgluv joins the defenders in combating the ever-increasing wave. Eeshlith glances across the field and notices Garu joining Glakchog. Both advance on the town at a slow walk. Eeshlith leaps into the fray, taking down several warriors with her bizarre double headed weapon.

As the fight continues, Shukrat rises and flings spells at individual warriors so as to not catch any of the defenders in a large blast. A flash of lightning reveals a shadow looming over him, and he barely leaps out of the way as Hazgor brings down a massive club. Shukrat sends a blast of electricity at Hazgor, but the rhinoran is barely affected.

"Normally, that works against rhinorans," says Shukrat nervously.

Hazgor flashes a malevolent smile. "Part of my special abilities from my soul hunter pact was gaining a heavy resistance to magical attacks. You can't hurt me, Shukrat." Hazgor brings his club around in an underhanded arc. He lands a direct hit on Shukrat in the side and sends him flying halfway across town.

As the defenders overwhelm the umbra warriors, whose numbers have ceased increasing, Glakchog and Garu arrive. Garu swings his massive horsebreaker sword, cutting through several townsfolk and umbra warriors in one swing. One defender, who had disappeared when Hazgor barreled through, comes charging in on a horse. As he draws near, he readies his weapon to strike at Garu. The soul hunter swings his enormous blade in an upward arc. He connects with the underside of the horse's chest, cutting clean through and slicing the rider in half in one strike.

Taking advantage of Garu's very intimidating moment, Glakchog rushes forward to engage the shaken defenders. As he mows through the defenses, Glakchog advances intently toward Shudgluv. Hazgor charges through the line, forcing Glakchog to dive aside and causing attackers and defenders to scatter.

He turns and charges through again and the troll leaps onto the side of a half-destroyed house to avoid him. The startled troll climbs up onto the roof to regroup, and Glakchog immediately follows him. Eeshlith moves to help Shudgluv, but Garu blocks her path. Shudgluv and Glakchog stare each other down.

"I should have known it would come to this," says Shudgluv. "The tension between us has been building for years."

"Yes," says Glakchog. "It would seem that we were destined to fight one another. Prepare yourself, Shudgluv."

Glakchog lunges forward, swinging both swords over his head. Shudgluv easily blocks the attack and pushes him back before retaliating. Glakchog parries the blow and uses one of his swords to hook the end of Shudgluv's maul, yanking it out of his hands with ease. He turns the sword so that the hook is facing backward and slashes Shudgluv's arm with the long side of the blade.

Blocking his other swing, Shudgluv pushes him away and stabs at him, attempting to use his greater reach to his advantage. Out of immediate range, Glakchog interlocks the hooks of his swords and swings them in Shudgluv's direction. Shudgluv blocks a few blows, but others connect, cutting deeply into his flesh. One slashes the troll's hand, causing him to drop the sword. Glakchog continues swinging his connected blades, slicing Shudgluv's arms, legs, and chest to ribbons. He grabs the hilt and separates the swords before continuing his assault.

Turning his hands so the hilt faces his opponent, he uses the small protruding blades at the end to viciously stab Shudgluv before he continues slashing at him. He pauses briefly, and the severely injured troll drops to his knees. Glakchog turns his swords so that the hooks are facing his opponent and brings them down on opposing sides of his head. He pulls back, driving the hooks deep into Shudgluv's shoulders and causing the troll to cry out in pain. Glakchog yanks the swords out, leaving deep, ragged gashes in the troll's shoulders. Shudgluv slumps forward slightly, breathing heavily as his injuries appear to overcome him.

Glakchog scowls as he looks over Shudgluv. "I was hoping for more of a challenge. I'm disappointed that it was so easy to kill you."

Glakchog raises his weapons, prepared to strike the fatal blow.

Chapter 49

As the rooftop battle goes on, Eeshlith desperately tries to avoid Garu's massive blade. She jumps back every time he takes a swing, and is unable to close the gap between strikes. As she leaps back once more, she finds herself surrounded by ten umbra warriors.

Making a quick survey of her situation, she grabs the handle of her new metal belt and pulls on it, unwrapping herself and revealing the entire thing to be roughly eight feet in length. Eeshlith swings it around and over her head in a whiplike motion. This unusual weapon is made of metal but is so thin that it moves with a whip's flexibility. Its sharp edges catch Garu across the face, leaving a deep laceration and causing him to back up. Eeshlith lashes out with the whip-sword, striking down every umbra warrior around her before advancing on Garu.

Unable to defend himself due to the size of his sword, the bizarre weapon slices the daemon soul hunter to pieces. Bringing it back around, the thin blade cuts deeply into Garu's throat, causing him to collapse.

"That should put him out of the fight for a while," says Eeshlith. "If he weren't immortal, it would be for good."

She moves into the main fray, striking down several umbra warriors as they overwhelm the dwindling defenders. Hazgor comes barreling toward her, scattering everyone in his way. She lashes at him, but his thick hide harmlessly deflects the blade. He is upon her in an instant, knocking her down and stamping down hard with one foot. She screams in pain as he pins her to the ground; several row her ribs crack under the rhino-ran's weight.

"Garu, we should probably start harvesting these souls," says Hazgor. "Now that Eeshlith is incapacitated, she shouldn't be a problem."

Garu rises to his feet, his injuries completely healed. His immortality has revived him after a fatal blow. "Very well. Take hers as well ... while she is still alive."

The two soul hunters summon their urns and remove the lids. Several blue beams shoot out of each urn and connect with the bodies of the fallen defenders, ripping out their souls and drawing them in. Still under Hazgor's foot, Eeshlith desperately tugs at a few weapons. She retrieves the hand crossbow and fires several bolts at Hazgor and Garu. A single bolt strikes each of the soul hunters' urns, shattering them in an explosion of blue energy and releasing all the souls within.

"No!" cry the soul hunters.

Stunned, Hazgor steps back, releasing Eeshlith from his grasp. Rolling away, she retrieves Garu's horsebreaker sword and holds her position. Hazgor charges at her, his already poor eyesight now red with fury. At the last moment, Eeshlith thrusts the massive sword forward, striking Hazgor in the chest. Hazgor's momentum carries him forward and he impales himself on the enormous blade.

As he is almost upon her, Eeshlith releases the hilt and drops down, allowing him to pass harmlessly over her. Hazgor stumbles to a stop and drops to his knees. Looking down at the blade in his body, he chuckles weakly before toppling over. His body hits the ground with a thud, and he emits a final wheezing breath.

Chapter 50

An explosion distracts Glakchog, halting his fatal strike. Glancing in the direction the sounds came from, he sees the aftermath of the destruction of Garu and Hazgor's urns. He watches in amazement as Eeshlith strikes down the massive rhinoran.

"Impressive," says Glakchog, turning back to Shudgluv. "But it won't save you. Garu is still in the fight and there are still several umbra warriors for her to deal with."

Despite his injuries, Shudgluv starts laughing.

"What's so funny?" asks Glakchog.

"I'm a troll, remember?" says Shudgluv. "And as a troll, I have one special ability that you seem to have forgotten about."

Shudgluv closes his eyes and concentrates for a moment. He takes a deep breath and every wound on his body instantly heals. Grabbing his sword, he rises to his feet and glares at Glakchog, who takes a step back in alarm.

"Emergency regeneration," says Glakchog, nervously. "I admit that it slipped my mind that you could do that. You can only do it one more time, though. Either I'll kill you before you have the chance to use it, or I'll kill you after you've run out of them. Either way, I win."

Shudgluv angrily lunges forward, attempting to run Glakchog through. The cunning busurin easily sidesteps the attempt and brings the back end of one sword up, slashing Shudgluv across the throat, barely missing his jugular vein. He brings the hooked end of his other sword around, driving it deep into Shudgluv's belly. He pulls back on the sword, leaving a deep jagged gash across the troll's stomach. Pushing away, Shudgluv scrambles to the other side of the roof and initiates another emergency regenerate, closing the wounds. However, this time he is visibly drained and looks quite exhausted.

"You may as well surrender, Shudgluv," says Glakchog. "We both know that you can't heal yourself a third time, and you are clearly too fatigued to continue."

"I will never surrender to you," says Shudgluv.

Taking a moment to catch his breath, Shudgluv tries desperately to gather the energy to continue. However, Glakchog advances immediately, determined to put an end to his former friend. As the busurin brings his swords around for another attack, Shudgluv gets his second wind and deflects the blow. With a surprising ferocity, he advances on Glakchog, striking several times in quick succession and driving the shocked busurin back.

As the intensity of Shudgluv's attacks increases, Glakchog goes on the defensive, forced back by the strength of the blows. Shudgluv swings his sword in an underhand arc. Glakchog manages to deflect the strike, but the force of the blow sends him tumbling backward, landing on his back at the edge of the roof.

Shudgluv is upon him in an instant and brings his sword down. Crossing his blades, Glakchog parries the blow, and the two opponents lock swords. Shudgluv pushes down with all his might, and it takes every ounce of Glakchog's strength to prevent him from forcing the blades onto his body. Glakchog places one foot against Shudgluv's chest and rapidly withdraws his swords from the blade lock.

Unprepared for this move, Shudgluv loses his balance and Glakchog manages to roll aside to dodge his blade. He catches Shudgluv's ankles with the hooks of his swords and pulls his feet out from under him. Shudgluv topples off the roof and plummets to the ground. He lands on his back; one of the house's broken support beams impales him through the chest.

Chapter 51

Glancing up at the roof after defeating Hazgor, Eeshlith grins as she watches Shudgluv regenerate and catch Glakchog by surprise. Confident that her friend has that fight handled, she retrieves her whip-sword and rejoins the fray, striking down umbra warriors in droves. A shocked Garu can only stand there, aghast as to what has just occurred.

As Eeshlith cuts down the warriors' numbers to the point that the remaining defenders can easily handle them, she glances up at the roof just in time to see Shudgluv topple off. She watches in horror as a broken support beam runs him through.

"No!" shouts Eeshlith.

She rushes to Shudgluv's position and finds that he is still alive, despite the obviously fatal wound. Glakchog hops down from the roof, grinning smugly. Eeshlith glares angrily as he looms over them.

"I told you it would end this way, Shudgluv," says Glakchog. "You could never win against the perfect soldier."

Eeshlith looks him right in the eyes. "You are hardly perfect at anything, and you are definitely not the perfect soldier. You never were and you never will be."

A flash of lightning illuminates the sky as the two former friends stare each other down.

"You'll regret those insults," says Glakchog. "I shall prove you wrong."

Glakchog advances toward Eeshlith, swinging his swords in an overhead arc. Eeshlith leaps back, avoiding them, and backflips several feet away. As Glakchog moves to close in the gap, she flings several knives in his direction. He deflects most of them, but one reaches its target, embedding itself in his shoulder. He interlocks the sword's hooks and swings them around, trying to take advantage of the better reach. Eeshlith backpedals away, staying out of range. Reloading her repeating crossbow, she rapidly fires ten bolts at Glakchog. Once again, he spins the swords around and deflects the bolts.

As the fight continues, Garu comes out of his stupor and looks around. "Glakchog, we should retreat. We're almost out of umbra warriors, and the defenders will soon be coming for us."

"Call in the third wave, you fool," says Glakchog.

Garu retrieves a horn from his belt and turns to face the swamp. He blows the horn, emitting a low bass blast. The trees sway as another two hundred umbra warriors emerge and march across the field. The defenders brace for another assault.

Eeshlith flings more knives at Glakchog, who deflects them with ease. She retrieves her whip-sword and lashes in his direction. Glakchog moves his swords to parry the strike, but Eeshlith moves its trajectory at the last second. The thin blade loops over the two hookswords and slashes him across the face. Eeshlith strikes again, wrapping the blade around Glakchog's weapons.

Unfamiliar with this bizarre sword, Glakchog fails to react in time to deflect it and the whip-sword cuts deeply into his arm, causing him to drop his swords. Eeshlith slashes at him several more times, leaving deep gashes all over his body. She swings the whip-sword in a horizontal arc, slashing Glakchog across the throat. Grabbing at the wound, Glakchog hastily retreats. He stumbles several feet before collapsing just on the edge of town. He drags himself away as he desperately tries to keep himself from bleeding out.

Glakchog manages to drag himself over a nearby small hill and around a tree. Propping himself up against the trunk, he desperately tries to stop the bleeding, however, his strength is fading rapidly. As he attempts to pinch the wound closed, Brelgvu drops out of the tree and approaches.

"Brelgvu, help me," begs Glakchog. "It wasn't supposed to end this way."

"I can't help you as you are," says Brelgvu. "I'm afraid that this is your fate."

Glakchog's shoulders slump and tears form in his eyes. "Then, I'm not the perfect soldier."

Brelgvu gives Glakchog a mischievous look and places his hand on the busurin's chest, causing a red glow to engulf his body. The bleeding stops, but the wound does not close.

"What did you do?" asks Glakchog. "What's happening?"

"No, you are not the perfect soldier," says Brelgvu. "Not yet. It is something that could not be achieved in this life."

"What do you mean?" asks Glakchog, fearfully.

Brelgvu drags Glakchog away from the tree and, using his claws, draws a circle around him.

"What are you doing?" asks Glakchog.

"With my help, you will finally become the perfect soldier," says Brelgvu. "Time to go home, my friend. Malferno awaits."

Glakchog's eyes grow wide with horror as Brelgvu's hands glow fiery red. As Brelgvu touches the circle, a wreath of fire surrounds Glakchog and the mud beneath him becomes a dark void. Brelgvu hops onto Glakchog's chest, and they slowly sink into the darkness.

"No, please," begs Glakchog. "Not this! This isn't what I wanted!"

"You wanted to become the perfect soldier," says Brelgvu. "The deal you made to achieve that goal cannot be completed without this final step."

"I'd rather die than be dragged to Malferno," says Glakchog. "Please, call off the deal and let me pass on. At least that way, I pass on to Amyrus. Even being sentenced to the Byzonis Abyss would be better than Malferno."

Brelgvu laughs. "Don't be so dramatic. The deal stands. Your death is necessary for the transition to occur, but I need to start the process immediately. Once we arrive in Malferno, I will allow you to die."

"No!" begs Glakchog. "Please don't do this to me!"

Glakchog shrieks in horror as he disappears into the abyss.

Chapter 52

Garu grins malevolently as the third wave of warriors descends upon Ethor. As Glakchog crawls away, Eeshlith joins the remaining defenders in preparation for the final assault.

"I don't like these odds," says one of the defenders. "This could be it."

"If we're going to fall, then let it be valiantly defending your homes," says Eeshlith.

As the umbra warriors pour into town, Eeshlith and the defenders charge forward. They each strike down several warriors, with Eeshlith taking down five at a time. However, the sheer numbers overwhelm them, and they are quickly surrounded.

Watching from where he fell, Shudgluv's expression goes from a look of pained-approaching-death to one of determination. Using his remaining strength, he pulls himself off the broken beam and stumbles toward the battle. Ready to collapse at any moment, Shudgluv closes his eyes to concentrate and takes a deep breath. He initiates a third emergency regenerate, and the hole in his torso closes. With a look of pure focus, he tears through the ranks of the umbra warriors, shrugging off hits that should easily take him down. Their morale restored by this miraculous resurgence, the defenders redouble their efforts. The pushback continues as the defenders overtake the umbra warriors. Eeshlith leads the charge, cutting down as many as five attackers at a time.

Shudgluv continues his unstoppable rampage, completely ignoring any and all attacks while destroying more umbra warriors than any of the others combined. As the warriors' numbers whittle down, the grin on Garu's face fades into a look of deep concern.

Retrieving his horsebreaker from Hazgor's corpse, he retreats, into the swamp. Seeing this, the normally unflappable umbra warriors fall back. A massive explosion incinerates most of the remaining attackers, and Eeshlith smiles as Shukrat steps around a corner. Finally, the last attacker falls and the townsfolk pour out of their homes, cheering for the defenders. Eeshlith rushes to Shukrat and gives him a celebratory hug. She turns to Shudgluv.

"I thought I'd lost you for certain," says Eeshlith. "I thought that trolls couldn't regenerate a third time."

"We can't." The determined expression on Shudgluv's face fades, and his skin turns ashy gray. His knees buckle and he collapses into the mud. The cheering comes to an abrupt stop, and a horrified Eeshlith runs to her friend. Dropping down, she cradles his head in her arms.

"What's happening?" Eeshlith's voice quivers.

"I'm afraid it's over for me," says Shudgluv weakly. "I used my remaining life force to force a third emergency regenerate."

"So, a third regenerate kills the troll who uses it?" asks Eeshlith.

"Normally, a third regeneration is outright impossible," says Shudgluv, growing weaker. "Only through sheer force of will and by expending one's remaining life can we achieve it."

"If you knew it was going to kill you, why did you do it?" asks Eeshlith, her voice breaking as she fights back tears.

"I was dying anyway," says Shudgluv. "At least this way, my death had meaning."

Tears stream down Eeshlith's face. "You could have survived. You could have been healed."

"No, a priest would not have gotten to me in time," says Shudgluv. "By using what life I had left, I was able to help save the day."

"Yes, you did," says Eeshlith, crying.

Shudgluv smiles. "Perhaps redemption is possible after all."

Shudgluv goes limp as he emits a final exhale, and the light fades from his eyes.

Eeshlith hugs his head to her chest. "Don't leave me like this. You're all I've got left. Please come back, my friend."

With no response from the fallen troll, Eeshlith hugs him even tighter, bawling uncontrollably. Shukrat comes to her and places a comforting hand on her shoulder as the townsfolk gather around.

Chapter 53

An hour later, the townsfolk finish moving the wounded into the makeshift hospital in the guest quarters of Shukrat's house. Shukrat is busy grinding various herbs into a paste as Eeshlith assists the several of the townsfolk in bandaging the injuries of the defenders.

The locals who aren't helping with medical needs bring in the bodies of the fallen. They place them on empty beds and cover each with a sheet. Due to his size, it takes four of the townspeople to carry Shudgluv's body. The bed shudders under his weight as they place him upon it. Eeshlith shoots a concerned look in their direction.

"Sorry," says Shukrat. "None of these beds were built with trolls in mind. I rarely get guests larger than humans."

The townsfolk cover Shudgluv with a sheet, only to discover that they need a second sheet to completely cover him. Eeshlith assists them in their task, sitting next to the bed when they have finished. Shukrat applies an herbal salve to one of the defender's wounds and goes to her.

"I'm sorry, Eeshlith," says Shukrat. "He meant a lot to you, didn't he?"

Eeshlith tearfully nods. "He was my best friend. Actually, he was like a brother to me. These past sixty years have changed the others too much. My friendship with Glakchog ended years ago due to his insistence on following all military protocol to the absolute letter, and casting us aside as pawns. My attempts to bring out the Green-Eyed Man's humanity have failed, so that friendship is over. I doubt that Aldtaw will ever forgive me for allowing the Green-Eyed Man to imprison him for sixty years, and don't even get me started on Alasdar. Only Shudgluv stayed true to who he was before all of this happened."

"I promise you that his sacrifice will not be in vain," says Shukrat. "I will do everything I can to ensure that his final moments were meaningful."

"Thank you, Shukrat," says Eeshlith. "But first we need to heal the wounded and warn the king."

Shukrat sighs. "Unfortunately, most of the town priests either fell during the battle or were not here at the time. Until the curse wears off, we'll have to make do with mundane medicine. Once I can use my transport powers again, I'll fetch a priest from the nearest town. Then you and I can head to Castle Demonicus to inform the king of these recent events."

"When will that be?" asks Eeshlith.

"Either during or after the Grand Tourney finale," says Shukrat. "Depending on how long the final match goes. I should get back to work. More herbs are needed for the wounded."

Shukrat returns to his table full of medicinal herbs. Eeshlith remains by Shudgluv to mourn for a few more minutes before she goes to help the townsfolk treat the wounded.

Chapter 54

Garu steps through a portal and stumbles into the main courtyard of Devil's Den, startling a few of the guards. He rushes down the hall toward the throne room. Throwing open the doors, he barges in, clearly interrupting a meeting between Alasdar and the Green-Eyed Man.

"This had better be important, Garu," says Alasdar. "We were in the middle of a mission report."

Garu bows and takes a moment to catch his breath. "My Lord, I bring ill news. Our mission to Ethor has failed."

A look of rage crosses Alasdar's face as he rises to his feet, causing the Green-Eyed Man to nervously back away.

"What?" inquires Alasdar. "What happened? Give me the full report."

Garu proceeds to inform him of events of the battle, leaving out the situation between Glakchog and Brelgvu since he did not witness it. Alasdar listens intently as he finishes.

"It wasn't a total failure," says Alasdar. "Having forced a third regeneration, Shudgluv is certainly dead, and you killed a large number of the townsfolk."

"Thank you, my Lord," says Garu, relieved.

"Do not mistake my interpretation for forgiveness," says Alasdar. "Overall, it was still a failure. Shukrat likely still lives, and you did not capture Eeshlith. Plus, Hazgor is dead, Glakchog is missing, and you lost over four hundred umbra warriors."

Garu lowers his eyes and shuffles his feet. "I am sorry. They were better prepared than we expected."

"No excuses," says Alasdar.

Alasdar motions to the Green-Eyed Man, who obtains a horrified look of realization. The Green-Eyed Man leaves the throne room, shutting the doors behind him.

Alasdar approaches Garu. "You said that your urn was destroyed, am I right?"

"Yes, Master," says Garu. "I fled because I needed to survive in order to give you the report."

"Pity," says Alasdar. "You are no longer a soul hunter, and I have no use for a coward. Your services are no longer required, Garu."

Fear crosses Garu's face and he flees to the doors. However, he finds that the Green-Eyed Man has barred them from the other side. Pressing his back to the doors, he watches as Alasdar approaches. The soulborn's flesh squirms and roils as he slowly walks toward his terrified minion.

"I can still be of use, My Lord," says Garu.

"How so?" asks Alasdar.

"I am still a seasoned warrior," says Garu. "Killing me would be a waste of resources, especially since Glakchog is no longer around to lead the army."

Alasdar's skin bulges and slightly cracks. "Convince me, Garu. Why should I give you another chance?"

Garu closes his eyes and inhales. He opens them again and looks directly at Alasdar. "I have never failed Master Babu, and I will not fail you again. You need experienced troops like me to coordinate the army. The Green-Eyed Man will need my assistance."

Alasdar pauses as his flesh returns to normal and ponders his failed minion's words. "Very well. I will give you one more chance." Alasdar turns to the door. "You can come back in now."

The door opens and the Green-Eyed Man sheepishly enters. His eyes widen in surprise when he sees that Garu is still alive. "You spared him?"

"He convinced me he can still be useful."

The Green-Eyed Man nods nervously. "I see. What do you wish of me, My Lord?"

"Gather the conscripts from the surrounding settlements," says Alasdar. "The army begins its march tonight. Since Glakchog is most likely dead, you and Garu shall be leading the charge."

"There are no conscripts, sire," says the Green-Eyed Man. "None of the hamlets and villages we visited showed any compliance."

Alasdar clenches his fist and seethes, breathing deeply and exhaling. "No matter. We still have six thousand umbra warriors. We only lost a small percentage. Conscripts would have been insignificant anyway. Now carry out my orders."

"I will not fail you," says the Green-Eyed Man.

"I know you won't," says Alasdar. "And just to be certain, I shall be joining you."

"I do not believe that will be necessary, sir," says the Green-Eyed Man, nervously.

"My presence is simply insurance," says Alasdar, "I will not be involved in the battle, just an observer ... as long as everything goes smoothly. Now, let us be off. Inform General Charndergh that he is in charge while I am away."

"It shall be done, My Lord," says the Green-Eyed Man.

"One other thing," says Alasdar. "I have one more stop in mind before we go to the castle."

Chapter 55

The crowd erupts into frenzied cheers as the final four competitors emerge onto the field. As the ruckus dies down, King Demonicus once again addresses the audience.

"Ladies and gentlemen, welcome to the Grand Tourney semi-finals," says Demonicus. "Today is the last day of the tournament. We will be holding the finals later this evening, after the two semi-final bouts. As a reminder, the winner of the tournament shall receive the Knight's Honor, a legendary magical sword that has been wielded by the greatest military leaders in history. Our first match today is Sir Jabbleth versus Diablos' representative, Raimdon. In the interest of fairness, one of the other dignitaries will choose the competitor who will pick the type of match."

Demonicus turns to the remaining dignitaries, and they enter into a lengthy discussion. After a few minutes, King Bloodsworth rises and steps forward. "To show that we are not completely hostile to our Diablosian neighbors, at least until we can declare war, Raimdon shall pick the type of match. What say you, Raimdon?"

Raimdon looks over his opponent, fully aware of the challenge in front of him. He remains silent for a few minutes, deep in thought as he considers his options. "I choose a sword battle on horseback. Victory by yield or incapacitation."

Bloodsworth grins and takes a seat, gesturing to Demonicus to take over. King Demonicus stands and addresses the crowd.

"So be it," says Demonicus. "We will take a few minutes while the squires ready the horses and assist the competitors in mounting them. The combatants must only strike at each other. Attacking the horses will result in immediate disqualification for the offender."

TRIAL BY TOURNAMENT: CHAMPION OF VALOR

The crowd cheers as Raimdon and Jabbleth leave to prepare for their match. As Demonicus takes his seat, Bloodsworth turns to him and grins.

"With any luck, our representatives will face each other in the finals," says Bloodsworth. "You remember our deal, right?"

Demonicus nods. "How could I forget? If our kingdoms' champions face each other in the finals of a Grand Tourney, the future of the kingdoms' relationship hangs in the balance."

"Yes," says Bloodsworth. "If my champion wins, then we finally get to declare war on Diablos and avenge the slight from long ago."

"A slight that neither kingdom remembers," says Demonicus. "And if my champion wins, Battallia lifts its embargo, yields all rights to declare war on Diablos unless we violate the agreement, and enters into negotiations so that diplomatic relations can resume."

"How humiliating that would be," says Bloodsworth. "Diplomacy is for the weak. The strong settle their conflicts with war."

"Then why have you not simply invaded?" asks Demonicus.

"We're not stupid," says Bloodsworth. "Since the insult has been long forgotten, our allies have declared that they will not support us in a war against Diablos unless we can prove that there is a real reason to do so. We know that if we were to invade without our allies' support that we would get crushed by the overwhelming numbers of Diablos and its allies. We are strong and our army is large, but I know that even we cannot stand up to the might of multiple kingdoms simultaneously."

"Quite the predicament," says Demonicus.

Bloodsworth begins to respond, but a loud cheer from the crowd interrupts him. The two kings return their attention to the field to see Jabbleth and Raimdon emerge on horseback. Jabbleth circles the arena, sword in the air, several times as he riles up the audience.

Raimdon, realizing that he can't compete with Jabbleth's showmanship and charisma, simply directs his horse to one end of the field and waits for the match to start. After a minute of playing to the crowd, Jabbleth takes his position at the opposite end of the arena. The crowd grows silent and waits with anticipation for the coming clash. As the tension rises to a boiling point, Demonicius gives the signal to begin.

The two combatants urge on their horses and charge down the field as rapidly as the animals can go. They are upon one another in an instant, their swords bouncing off each other with a loud clang as they ride by. They turn their horses and begin their duel, striking and parrying as they circle around. When neither combatant can penetrate the other's defenses, they withdraw and ride to the ends of the field. They charge once again, swords clashing with a loud bang as they meet. The force of the blow briefly throws Raimdon off balance, and he nearly drops his sword. He regains his stability just as Jabbleth turns his horse in his direction, barely blocking a strike from the Black Knight's blade.

"You fight well on a horse," says Jabbleth. "You have cavalry training, I take it?"

"Captain of the Tenth Cavalry," says Raimdon, proudly. "I am quite experienced with combat on horseback."

"As am I, Captain," says Jabbleth. "You do not have as large of an advantage as you believe."

"I'm not taking this bout lightly, Sir Knight," says Raimdon. "I'm well aware of your skills."

The two clash once more, striking at each other with their swords and parrying each strike. After a few moments, they withdraw to opposite ends of the field and charge. Again, they clash at top speed, their blades slamming into each other with loud clangs. The unusual angle of Jabbleth's strike causes Raimdon to briefly lose his grip.

Before he can regain control of his sword, Jabbleth's blade scrapes him across the armored chest. Already off balance, the force of the blow knocks him from his horse and sends him tumbling to the ground. Without a rider, Raimdon's horse flees the field, returning to the stable hand inside the arena.

Rising to his feet, Raimdon raises his sword to parry a strike by Jabbleth, barely deflecting the blow in time. The two exchange blows for a few moments, striking and parrying one another. Despite Jabbleth's height advantage upon his horse, Raimdon manages to hold his own. Jabbleth withdraws to the end of the field and charges. Raimdon parries the incoming strike, the force of the blow knocking him to the ground.

Jabbleth slides off his horse, which returns to its handler, and stands over his opponent. Raimdon grabs his sword, but Jabbleth is on him before he can rise to his feet. As he parries another strike, Raimdon notices that there is a large crack in his blade. Distracted, he fails to notice

Jabbleth's sword sweeping in. The force of the collision knocks Raimdon's blade from his hand. Jabbleth then points his sword at Raimdon's throat and holds it in place.

Raimdon exhales and turns his eyes down. "I yield."

The crowd bursts into a cacophony of applause as King Demonicus rises to announce the results. "The winner of this bout is Sir Jabbleth. Congratulations on advancing to the finals." Demonicus turns to King Bloodsworth. "It's always disappointing to see your own champion eliminated, but I guess this means that our representatives won't be fighting for the fates of our kingdoms after all."

Bloodsworth nods disappointedly. "It's a shame, really. I was actually looking forward to the match. No matter which champion emerged victorious, it would have been an amazing bout."

Jabbleth helps Raimdon to his feet as the squires arrive to clear the field. After discerning that he has no injuries, they wave the incoming priest away. The two combatants exit the arena.

Chapter 56

As King Demonicus waits for the wild cheers of the crowd to die down, Pelagius emerges onto the field. He is quickly followed by his opponent, Count Vuzenkhord. Once the raucous settles, Demonicus addresses the crowd.

"Ladies and gentlemen, the last match of the semi-finals is upon us," says Demonicus. "This bout features Pelagius of Waskan versus Count Vuzenkhord, Lord Champion Gladiator of Battallia."

The crowd bursts into another frenzy of cheers.

"In the interest of fairness to our Battallian neighbors, I will be letting one of the other dignitaries choose which fighter will pick the game," says Demonicus.

Demonicus turns to the remaining dignitaries and begins a quiet discussion. After a few minutes, Archduke Maldorus rises and addresses the crowd.

"As a completely neutral party in this matter, I will determine who shall pick the game," says Maldorus. "Count Vuzenkhord, you shall have the honor of choosing what type of match this shall be."

Vuzenkhord thinks for a moment, then grins and turns to Pelagius. "I think we should do something special. We should try to outdo that last match in every way. What say you?"

"I agree," says Pelagius. "It would be foolish to follow up such a spectacular bout with something ordinary."

Vuzenkhord nods and turns back to the dignitaries. "My Lord, I have something quite extraordinary in mind. We shall hold a chariot battle race. Six laps around the arena, followed by a joust and duel in the chariots, with the absolute victor determined by best of three. Victory in the race is determined by who finishes first or by who is still in their chariot if the other's is put out of commission. Victory in the joust shall be determined by who breaks the most lances, or knocking the opponent from the chariot. Victory in the duel, if necessary, shall be by yield or incapacitation."

"Very well," says Maldorus. "Demonicus, the floor is yours."

Maldorus takes his seat and Demonicus steps back to the forefront as Pelagius and Vuzenkhord leave to prepare.

"This should be quite exciting," says Demonicus. "The chariots shall be pulled by two horses, each with teams of three. Both Pelagius and Vuzenkhord will be allowed to choose two companions to assist them. These companions will serve as driver, shield bearer, or weapons master, with Pelagius and Vuzenkhord taking the position that the others do not. Of course, Pelagius and Vuzenkhord can switch between positions during the race, but must be the main combatants during the joust and duel portions."

Demonicus pauses and takes a breath. "During the joust and duel, the other two shall serve only as driver and shield bearer and must leave the field if their contestant is knocked from the chariot. Attacking the horses will result in immediate disqualification, but targeting the chariots is fine. Combat may take place during the race as well. Victory can also be achieved if one of the contestants is incapacitated during the race."

As Demonicus' speech draws to a close, Pelagius and Vuzenkhord enter the contestants' waiting area inside the arena. Vuzenkhord disappears down a hallway as Mughan approaches Pelagius.

"Your bout is certain to be quite the spectacle," says Mughan.

"Indeed," says Pelagius. "A three part match is definitely not what I was expecting."

"Count Vuzenkhord is a professional gladiator," says Mughan. "He's a natural showman and wants to give the crowd something to remember. He's also incredibly skilled at both chariot racing and combat, so you're in for a challenge."

"Well, I guess I'll just have to beat him at his own game," says Pelagius.

"Good luck," says Mughan. "Do you know who you want to join you in the chariot?"

"If possible, I'd like my partners to be Alithyra and Kevnan," says Pelagius, "I'm sure they'd jump at the chance to help me."

"Very well," says Mughan. "I'll retrieve them and help them get ready."

Mughan leaves the area. Pelagius goes over to the squires to get their assistance in donning the proper armor for the event.

Chapter 57

Mughan enters the doorway leading to the spectators' area. Bypassing the entryway to the bleachers, he ascends a long winding stairway. He walks down a hallway, peeking through doors as he goes, searching for Alithyra and Kevnan's box. After disturbing a few nobles, he locates the correct box. The guards salute as he enters. This private box also holds several eliminated competitors, and he finds Pelagius's friends sitting with Koskru, Hexeron, and a clearly extra-agitated Delradi, who glances up at the sky on several occasions.

"Would you stop looking at the sky?" asks Hexeron. "Nothing is going to drop onto us out of nowhere."

"I'm not concerned about something falling from the sky," says Delradi. "It's … something else."

Mughan halts his approach, intrigued by the conversation.

"What exactly are you so concerned about?" asks Hexeron.

"Don't worry," says Delradi, nervously. "It's nothing."

"Clearly it's not nothing," says Hexeron. "Something has you on edge even more so than usual. If you know something important, you need to share that information."

"It's not important," says Delradi. "At least it shouldn't affect anyone here."

"What does that mean?" asks Hexeron. "You're clearly hiding something. What are you so concerned about?"

"There's a bad moon tonight," says Delradi.

"A bad moon?" asks Hexeron. "What are you talking about?"

"Just a personal superstition," says Delradi unconvincingly. "Nothing more."

Hexeron emits an exasperated sigh. "Fine. Be that way."

As the conversation draws to a close, Mughan approaches the group.

Alithyra spots Mughan and stands. "Can we help you, captain?"

"Yes," says Mughan. "You and Kevnan need to come with me. Pelagius has selected you as his chariot team."

Alithyra grins and rises to her feet. Kevnan, clearly not paying attention, notices her standing up.

"Where are you going?" asks Kevnan.

"Didn't you hear Mughan?" asks Alithyra.

"I was a bit preoccupied," says Kevnan. "Shukrat hasn't shown up today, and I'm a little concerned as to why."

"Now that I think about it, he's right," says Aldtaw. "He said he was going to be here."

"Hopefully something just came up," says Ralkgek.

Alithyra glances around worriedly. "I hope he's all right too, but you and I have something else of more immediate concern. Pelagius wants us to be on his team for this match."

A wide smile crosses Kevnan's face as he stands. "Well then, who am I to say no?"

"Excellent," says Mughan. "Follow me."

Mughan turns to leave with Kevnan and Alithyra following behind. He leads them out of the spectator's quarters and into the interior of the arena. They approach the squires just as they finish helping Pelagius suit up. He wears light gladiator style armor with a leather chest piece, leather arm and shin guards, a light plate pauldron on one shoulder, and a helmet that covers his face.

The squires turn to assist the elf and canin, dressing them in similar gear. They then lead the three heroes over to the horse master, who hitches two horses to their chariot containing a small round shield, a large iron tipped spear, and a shortsword.

The chariot itself is fairly basic, painted red and consisting of two wheels supporting a semi-oval shaped floor with a waist-high guard wall covering the front and sides. The entire thing is just barely large enough to fit three people, and probably better suited to hold two. The horse master proceeds to go over the basics of controlling and driving the conveyance.

After a few minutes, he directs them to the competitors' entrance, where they join Count Vuzenkhord and his team, who wear similar armor to theirs. Although its basic design is the same, Vuzenkhord's chariot is more ornate; it's a golden color with accents of red and purple. Vuzenkhord controls the reins, while his two assistants wield the weapons and shield. Seeing this, Pelagius takes the reins, directing Kevnan to the shield and Alithyra to the weapons.

"Nice ride," says Kevnan.

"Thank you," says Vuzenkhord. "I took the liberty of bringing my personal war chariot along in case the opportunity arose to use it."

"You came prepared," says Pelagius.

"Being prepared is critical in my line of work," says Vuzenkhord.

The doors open, and the contestants ride onto the field to the wild cheers of the crowd.

Chapter 58

The two teams drive up to a newly drawn line on one side of the arena, slowing to a stop as they approach. As the applause dies down, King Demonicus addresses the crowd once more. "Ladies and gentlemen, I apologize for the wait. Now that our combatants have been prepared, the final match of the semi-finals can begin."

King Demonicus gives the signal to start, and the drivers urge the horses, which take off like a shot.

Vuzenkhord takes an early lead, flying around the arena as fast as his horses can go. Pelagius trails behind, urging his horses to go faster. Vuzenkhord completes the first lap unopposed and continues around the track as Pelagius tries desperately to catch up. As Vuzenkhord makes his turn for the second half of the second lap, Pelagius finally closes in on him. The horses are neck and neck as they complete the second lap and begin the third.

Pelagius briefly pulls ahead, but Vuzenkhord matches him before the end of the third lap. His weapons master thrusts a spear in their direction, which Kevnan barely blocks with the shield. Alithyra retaliates with her own spear, which is also parried. The attempts to jab each other with the spears continue as they round the corner to finish the third lap.

Vuzenkhord's weapons master readjusts his grip on the spear and looks down it as though aiming it before hurling it straight at Pelagius. As it draws near, Kevnan leaps in front of it, blocking the blow with his shield. As Vuzenkhord's weapons master draws his sword, Vuzenkhord directs the horses to put some distance between the two chariots.

"I think it's time for our secret weapon," says Vuzenkhord.

The count pulls a lever next to the reins and three spiked metal balls attached to chains pop out from the center of the wheels on either side

Trial by Tournament: Champion of Valor

of his chariot. He directs the horses back toward Pelagius's chariot and the spinning flails begin inching their way toward the chariot's wheels. As they draw near, Kevnan desperately thrusts his shield downward to block their advance.

The balls connect with the shield, emitting a piercing metallic screech and sending sparks flying with each strike. With Kevnan in a vulnerable position, the weapons master takes a swing with his sword, but Alithyra parries the blow with her spear. Kevnan continues blocking the advance of the spinning flails, but the force of the blows nearly causes him to lose his grip on the shield.

"I can't keep this up much longer," says Kevnan. "If I lose this shield, our chariot is finished."

Pelagius directs the horses to try to pull away from Vuzenkhord's chariot, but the count follows suit. Thinking quickly, Alithyra flings her spear in Vuzenkhord's direction. As the shield bearer blocks the attack, Alithyra draws her sword and leaps out of Pelagius's chariot, landing on the edge of Vuzenkhord's. Caught off guard, the weapons master barely parries a strike from her blade. The two exchange blows for several seconds until the shield bearer recovers from the shock. He lunges forward with the shield, striking at Alithyra's legs. Alithyra jumps over the attack, withdrawing her sword from a blade lock and knocking the weapons master off balance. Regaining her footing, she rapidly reaches out and grabs the edge of the shield with her prosthetic arm. Alithyra yanks the shield away, sending the shield bearer tumbling out of the chariot. The weapons master reengages, attempting to strike her with his sword, but she easily parries.

Vuzenkhord casts a worried glance behind him at the unexpected close quarters battle. "Hurry up and get rid of her."

Alithyra and the weapons master exchange a few more blows before locking blades once again. They continue pushing against each other as the chariots cross the line to enter the final lap of the race, still neck and neck. As they fly around the track and enter the final push, Alithyra leans back, once again disrupting the weapons master's balance, and kicks him in the chest. He slams into Vuzenkhord, driving him forward into the lever and withdrawing the flails.

Stunned, the count loses his grip on the reins and the horses slow their pace. As the weapons master and Vuzenkhord desperately try to untangle themselves from one another, Alithrya hops back to her team's chariot. Pelagius pulls ahead, and Vuzenkhord's horses slow to a near stop. As the count regains control of the reins and urges his horses back into action, Pelagius crosses the finish line.

Chapter 59

Pelagius slows his chariot to a stop, and the crowd erupts into a wild cacophony of cheering. Even the dignitaries, including King Bloodsworth, stand and applaud. As the applause continues, Count Vuzenkhord rides up and, stopping his chariot, joins in the revelry with a big smile on his face. He grabs Pelagius by the wrist and raises his hand into the air, causing the cheers to grow even louder.

"Well done," says Vuzenkhord. "That was a very unorthodox tactic. I can honestly say that I wasn't expecting that."

Pelagius laughs. "Neither was I. She surprised me just as much as you."

"I see." Vuzenkhord turns to Alithrya. "You are a natural, my dear. If you should ever wish to compete at the Grand Coliseum in Battallia, look me up. You would become an instant favorite among the people."

"Thank you, sir," says Alithyra. "Bloodsports are not my cup of tea, so please forgive me if I decline."

"I understand," says Vuzenkhord. "It's certainly not for everyone."

As the raucous finally dies down, King Demonicus addresses the public. "What an exciting race! Pelagius wins round one. Next up is the chariot joust. Contestants, please take your positions."

Pelagius and Vuzenkhord drive their chariots to opposite ends of the arena, with Vuzenkhord picking up his shield bearer on the way. Having reached their starting positions, they switch places with one of their assistants. Vuzenkhord trades tasks with his weapons master and Pelagius switches with Alithyra. Both shield bearers plant their shields firmly in front of the combatants' torsos as the squires bring over three lances to each contestant, handing them one immediately.

Once the preparations are complete, the squires leave the field, and King Demonicus gives the signal to begin. The drivers urge the horses forward, and they fly down the field at full speed. As they approach one another, Pelagius and Vuzenkhord position their lances, aiming for the shields. They clash as they drive past one another, the lances of both opponents shattering as they collide with the shields.

Reaching the ends of the field, they turn and reposition themselves for another run, retrieving a new lance. They charge back down the field, intently focusing on the task at hand. They clash in the middle, but Vuzenkhord's aim is slightly off, and his lance deflects off the shield while Pelagius's shatters on impact. Coming around, they repeat the run once more, but this time Vuzenkhord's lance breaks and Pelagius's remains intact.

"The joust is all tied up, ladies and gentlemen," says Demonicus. "This next run shall determine the victor of the round and possibly the match."

Pelagius and Vuzenkhord start their final run, driving toward one another at full speed. As they approach, both perfectly position their lances for an optimal strike. Pelagius's chariot hits an unexpected bump, causing Pelagius to briefly lose his grip and throw off his aim. He misses his mark completely, and Vuzenkhord's lance strikes the center of his shield, shattering spectacularly on impact. The crowd bursts into cheers as they bring their rides to a stop.

"Ladies and gentlemen, round two goes to Count Vuzenkhord," says Demonicus. "This final round shall determine the winner of the match: who shall advance to face Sir Jabbleth for the championship."

Retrieving their swords and spears, the two teams line up like they did for the start of the race. As soon as King Demonicus signals them to start, both chariots charge forward. As they circle the track, Pelagius and Vuzenkhord trade blows with their swords, parrying one another frequently. Occasionally, the shield bearers step in to block a blow. As they continue around the arena, Vuzenkhord motions to his driver, who pulls the lever to bring out the spinning flails. Seeing this, Alithyra directs the horses away from the other chariot while Kevnan once again places the shield in their path. Sparks fly off the shield each time the spiked balls make contact.

"Do something," says Kevnan. "We're not going to last much longer if this keeps up."

"I can't leap over this time," says Alithyra. "It's up to Pelagius."

Pelagius thinks for a moment as he parries a few sword strikes. Retrieving the spear, he steps out of range of Vuzenkhord's swing. Pelagius positions the spear, concentrating as he looks down the shaft, and jabs it in Vuzenkhord's direction. The count's shield bearer moves to protect his leader from the attack, but Pelagius is not aiming at Vuzenkhord. Pelagius thrusts the spear into the path of the spinning flails and the chain wraps around the shaft, entangling the two weapons.

Pelagius retrieves the spear, grasps it on either side of the chain, and pulls with all his might, ripping it from the center of the wheel. He disentangles the flail, holds it at the base of the chain, and twirls it around. He lobs it at the damaged wheel, striking it exactly where the flail was once attached. The spikes of one ball lodge in the wood and the chain tangles in the spoke. The remaining flail heads spin with the wheel, striking it with each rotation until the wood shatters. The damaged wheel collapses, sending the chariot off balance and careening out of control. It topples over as they round a corner, sending Vuzenkhord and his men tumbling to the ground.

As Pelagius comes back around, Vuzenkhord rises to his feet. He retrieves a net and a trident as his men exit the field. While his opponent's chariot bears down on him, Vuzenkhord flings his trident at Kevnan, causing him to bring up his shield to deflect it. With Kevnan distracted, Vuzenkhord throws his net at Pelagius, entangling him, and pulls him from the chariot. Seeing this, Alithyra directs the horses off the field.

Pelagius struggles to disentangle himself while Vuzenkhord retrieves his trident and approaches his downed opponent. He drives the trident downward toward Pelagius, who rolls out of the way. As the prongs embed in the ground, Pelagius frees one foot from the net and sweeps Vuzenkhord's legs out from under him, sending him crashing to the ground. As the count rises to his feet, Pelagius finally untangles himself and throws off the net.

Pelagius rushes to the side to grab a spear and turns to face Vuzenkhord, who once again flings the net at him. This time, Pelagius manages to sidestep it and deflects a jab from the trident with his spear. He jabs back in retaliation, but his strike is also blocked. Keeping their distance, they trade blows back and forth until Vuzenkhord catches Pelagius's spear between two prongs of his trident. Using the extra grip as leverage, he wrenches the spear from Pelagius's hands and flings it to the side.

Vuzenkhord lunges at his unarmed opponent, who sidesteps the attack, grabbing the trident. Using Vuzenkhord's momentum against him, Pelagius sweeps his legs out from under him, causing the count to lose his grip on the weapon and tumble to the ground.

As Vuzenkhord stands and turns around, Pelagius flings the net at him, entangling Vuzenkhord in his own weapon. As Vuzenkhord struggles to break free, Pelagius kicks him in the chest and uses the trident to sweep him off his feet once again. He hits the ground with a thud, and Pelagius is upon him instantly, pressing the trident up against Vuzenkhord's throat.

Vuzenkhord takes a moment to survey the situation, grins, and raises up his hands. "Well done. I yield."

The crowd bursts into a frenzy of cheers and applause. As Pelagius helps Vuzenkhord disentangle himself from the net, King Demonicus addresses the audience.

"Ladies and gentlemen, the winner is Pelagius," says Demonicus. "Congratulations are in order for our two finalists. We will be adjourning for now, so that our combatants may get some rest, but we will be reconvening for the final bout later this evening. Be sure to come back for the exciting conclusion to this year's Grand Tourney."

Demonicus turns to one of his servants. "Please inform Captain Mughan that Ralkgek is now cleared of all charges."

The servant bows and leaves the dignitaries' box as Demonicus turns his attention back to the field. As Pelagius turns to leave the arena, Vuzenkhord grabs him by the shoulder and stops him.

"Wait," says Vuzenkhord. "Don't leave just yet."

Vuzenkhord turns to face part of the audience, bringing Pelagius with him. As the crowd begins to filter out, Vuzenkhord grabs Pelagius by the wrist and raises his hand into the air. Seeing this, the crowd stops in its tracks and bursts into another round of wild applause. The two men turn to another section and Vuzenkhord raises Pelagius's hand again, earning the same reaction. They repeat this with every section of the arena, getting louder and louder cheers each time. As the applause finally dies down, the two combatants exchange a hearty handshake before departing from the arena.

Chapter 60

Mughan leads Pelagius back to his quarters within the castle. Entering the parlor, he finds the others already there along with Koskru, Hexeron, and Celemrod. He does, however, notice the absence of Shukrat, Ralkgek, Delradi, and Aldtaw. As Pelagius enters the room, the others immediately come forward to greet him.

"Well done, Pelagius," says Celemrod. "That was a most outstanding match."

"Indeed, it was," says Hexeron. "It takes a lot of skill to best a professional gladiator at his own game."

"Thank you," says Pelagius. "It was quite exhilarating. I'm just glad that I was able to get the charges for everyone dismissed."

Alithyra approaches smiling. "Only one more bout and you'll be exonerated as well."

"Hopefully," says Pelagius. "All I have to do is defeat the Black Knight in combat. Easy, right?"

Everyone chuckles.

"Where is everyone else?" asks Pelagius.

"Aldtaw is taking a nap and Ralkgek went into his chamber," says Kevnan.

Pelagius looks around. "I know I saw Delradi in the stands with you. What happened to him?"

"He went home," says Hexeron. "He said he couldn't stay for the finals. Something about a bad moon tonight. He said he would come back in the morning for the festivities."

"How strange," says Pelagius. "And Shukrat? I haven't seen him all day."

"Neither have we," says Alithyra, clearly concerned. "He never showed up this morning."

"Really?" says Pelagius, worriedly. "I hope he's all right."

As they continue to converse, Ralkgek emerges from his room carrying a large satchel. Using a walking stick, he heads for the door and places his bag next to it.

"Where are you going?" asks Pelagius.

Ralkgek turns in the direction of Pelagius's voice. "Nowhere just yet. I'm just preparing for a journey. Since I am no longer in legal jeopardy, I shall be taking my leave once the tournament is over. Thank you for everything you've done for me, Pelagius."

"You're going to leave?" asks Alithyra. "Why? What is your destination?"

"I won't be staying in Diablos," says Ralkgek. "Even though I was cleared, being accused of treason will give me a stigma that will cause those who are aware of the events to shun me. I must seek out someone elsewhere, who can teach me how to hone my remaining senses to make up for the loss of my sight."

"You can do that on your own," says Hexeron. "Where are you really going?"

Ralkgek sighs in annoyance. "Fine. If you must know, then I'll tell you. That was part of the truth, but there is more. I have heard rumors of the legendary sword Blindstrike surfacing somewhere in the Necrotian Empire. I'm going to try to find it. With its powers, my lack of sight will no longer be a problem."

"You don't need a legendary artifact to make up for losing your sight," says Pelagius. "There's no guarantee that it's even in Necrotia."

"Thank you for your sentiment, but I've made up my mind on this," says Ralkgek. "It's a chance that I can't pass up. I have to try."

"If you must, then so be it," says Pelagius. "When will you depart?"

Ralkgek thinks for a moment. "I'm not certain yet. I may leave after the final match, or I might attend tomorrow's feast."

Pelagius nods. "I wish you luck, my friend."

Pelagius extends his hand and grabs Ralkgek's. The two exchange a firm handshake.

Chapter 61

Iriemorel lies on Grimadert's operation table, still strapped down and now completely encased in his golem suit. The helmet covers his entire head, leaving eye holes and an opening around his chin so that his beard is not stuck inside. The sun shines directly into his face as the table is currently sitting on the fortress' roof.

Grimadert stands next to the table, looking up at the sky with a scowl. "There's never a lightning storm when you need one."

Iriemorel glances at him nervously. Grimadert pulls a lever next to the table and a loud cranking sound starts as the floor lowers, revealing itself to be a platform. They descend back into the main laboratory and the ceiling swings shut above them. Rogi and Giro approach as the platform settles back into the floor.

"What now?" asks Giro.

"We switch to Plan B," says Grimadert. "We'll have to create the lightning we need ourselves."

"Why do we need lightning?" asks Iriemorel.

"It's an essential part of creating a golem," says Grimadert. "When the electricity mixes with the magically and alchemically enhanced inscriptions within the golem, the resulting reaction creates an enchantment that brings the golem to life. We must use this same technique to animate your suit. Boys, you know what to do."

Rogi and Giro move to opposite ends of the laboratory and simultaneously pull on a pair of levers. Turning gears crank and grind and pull open a pair of panels on the walls. As the devices continue turning, a set of enormous strange-looking metal spiraled prongs emerge from the holes and move across the room.

They stop a few feet from one another and lower until they are about a foot above Iriemorel's head, which they flank. When they pull another switch, a section of each wall slides open and a pair of strange machines with hand cranks emerge into the room. On the back center wall, another device emerges and connects with the other machines and objects. This thing is oval and made of metal, with thick wire-like tubes and prongs poking in all directions. The middle of the oval slides open, revealing a seat and a pair of metal handles on each side. Rogi and Giro take their positions next to the cranks as Grimadert places himself in the seat and grabs the handles.

"At my signal, begin turning the cranks," says Grimadert. "Be sure to start at the exact same time or it will throw off the entire procedure."

Grimadert closes his eyes and concentrates. After a few minutes, he chants in a language unknown to Iriemorel. As his chant continues, electric sparks arc out of his body, zapping the prongs around him. These bursts become more powerful as the chanting goes on until he is practically glowing white with electric power. Drawing energy from the gnome's magic storm, the machine groans and jolts.

As electricity begins arcing between the various prongs, Rogi and Giro turn the cranks. Managing to start simultaneously, they start off slow, but gradually increase their pace. Electricity arcs between the prongs above Iriemorel as the dwarf watches nervously. Grimadert emits a massive surge, and the prongs launch their power at Iriemorel.

The blast engulfs the dwarf, who screams in agony as the electricity flows through his body. As the charge dies down, the prongs send out another jolt, renewing the flow of power. The few external runes on Irimorel's suit glow, and the light from the ones inside the metal body shines through the iron.

As another bolt shoots out of the prongs, Grimadert issues a veritable lightning storm, pouring power into the machine. The flow of power from the prongs stops coming in bursts and becomes a constant stream of electricity. Iriemorel's screams echo through the hallways as the power flows through his entire body, further merging him with the suit. The inscriptions glow so brightly that the dwarf cannot be seen through the light, which fades after about a minute. As the glow dies down, Grimadert stops chanting and the lightning storm slowly comes to a stop. Rogi and Giro continue turning their cranks until the prongs no longer emit any electric blasts. His hair sticking out in all directions and his body smoking, Grimadert steps down from his seat and pulls another lever. The entire contraption splits and returns to its spots within the walls.

Grimadert walks toward Iriemorel but collapses after only one step. Rogi and Giro rush to their master's side and help him up. Grimadert glances at them and smiles reassuringly. "I'm fine, boys. I just channeled a little too much magical power to create that storm. Let's check on our work."

As Grimadert and his twin assistants approach, Iriemorel lies completely still on the table. Grimadert pokes him and receives no response. "What a pity. There was no guarantee that he would survive, but I would have liked to succeed. Well, best take him to the preservation room until we can figure out what to do with the body."

Rogi and Giro reach out to undo the restraints on Iriemorel, but his eyes fly open. The dwarf jolts and inhales sharply. An elated Grimadert laughs madly. "It worked! It's alive!"

The twins give Grimadert a confused glance.

"What?" says Grimadert. "I've always wanted to say that. Let him off the table, boys."

Rogi and Giro remove Iriemorel's restraints. The dwarf looks over at Grimadert.

"Try to stand up," says Grimadert. "Let's see how well you can do."

Iriemorel moves his arms to test their mobility and is shocked to discover that the iron encasing his body is almost as flexible as his own skin. As he stirs, he successfully bends his knees and flexes his feet.

"Amazing," says Iriemorel. "It actually worked."

Iriemorel sits up, removes the helmet, and swings his legs over the edge of the table. Sliding off, he finds that he can actually stand, even if he is a bit wobbly. He takes a few steps forward and stumbles. Rogi and Giro catch him before he can hit the ground and help steady him.

"Easy now," says Grimadert. "It will take some time to get used to this. You're going to have to learn how to walk again. We've prepared a room for you where you can stay while you regain your strength. The boys will help retrain you whenever they are not assisting me. For now, get some rest."

"Thank you, Grimadert," says Iriemorel. "I just hope it was worth the pain."

Rogi and Giro help Iriemorel as he leaves the laboratory, heading to his quarters. As Grimadert looks back at the table, a deranged grin spreads across his face.

Chapter 62

Eeshlith drops the last shovel full of dirt onto the freshly covered grave. Glancing around the newly expanded cemetery, she sees several funerals in progress as the survivors mourn the fallen. Turning back to the grave she had been attending, Eeshlith approaches the newly placed stone. Retrieving a nearby hammer and chisel, she carves an epitaph.

Upon completion, she steps back and looks over the writing, which reads "Here lies Shudgluv. A hero to the end and proof that redemption is possible. May his conflicted soul finally find peace."

Eeshlith wipes tears from her eyes. "I can't believe you're gone. Even knowing that I would have outlived you and the others by centuries if we had all aged naturally, it still feels like I lost you too soon."

As she speaks, Shukrat and some of the villagers approach to pay their respects.

"Even though I'll miss you, I want you to know that I'm proud of you," says Eeshlith. "Thanks to your heroic sacrifice, we were able to defeat Garu and Glakchog's forces. It was also thanks to your courage that we finally defected from Devil's Den. You have found your redemption, my friend. It is time for me to attempt to earn mine. Goodbye, Shudgluv."

Eeshlith leaves Shudgluv's grave and goes to assist the villagers in burying the last of the fallen heroes. Once this task is done, she returns to Shukrat's home and changes the bandages of some of the wounded. Shukrat joins her shortly and applies a newly mixed salve to their injuries. Eeshlith appears to be deep in thought as she goes about her task.

"We should consider evacuating the town," says Eeshlith. "Alasdar will not react well to the loss and will most likely send General Charndergh or the Green-Eyed Man with a much larger force."

Shukrat gives her a concerned glance. "You may be right. I'll speak with the village leaders and see what can be done. Some of these people are too injured to move, though, so it may not be feasible until we can get a priest to heal them."

Shukrat leaves the building to go speak with the villagers. He returns a few minutes later as Eeshlith is completing the task of changing bandages.

"The elders are reluctant to leave," says Shukrat. "They say that there is no proof that a retaliatory strike will be sent and that the injured should not be moved."

"Fools," says Eeshlith. "Alasdar is far more vengeful than Babu. He will send the Green-Eyed Man to exact revenge."

"Why are you still calling him the Green-Eyed Man?" asks Shukrat. "Since you know his real name, shouldn't you be using it to refer to him now that you are free of his influence?"

"Unfortunately, I can't remember his name," says Eeshlith. "It's strange, but about a day after we fled, my memories of life before joining Babu grew fuzzy. I can remember basic details, but the Green-Eyed Man's name and most of my memories involving him before he became a soul hunter have faded."

Shukrat frowns as a look of concern crosses his face. "It must be a contingency spell. One of the Green-Eyed Man's greatest weapons is the mystery that surrounds him. He must have wanted to ensure that his mysterious nature would remain intact if you and the others defected. To do that, when he magically prevented you from aging, he must have cast a mindwiping spell set to trigger if you ever left his service. The rapid aging of Aldtaw, and to a lesser extent, Shudgluv, might be one as well."

"That does make sense," says Eeshlith. "Poor Aldtaw must think he's going senile. Can you break those spells?"

Shukrat shakes his head. "Without knowing the nature of the magic involved, there's nothing I can do."

"His urn must be the key," says Eeshlith. "He used it to stop the aging process on us, so it has to be the source of the other spells too."

"Then you know what you must do," says Shukrat. "It will not be easy, though. He's likely going to be extra cautious after you were able to destroy the urns of Garu and Hazgor."

"Then I'll have to play it safe and wait until the right moment," says Eeshlith.

Chapter 63

As dusk sets in, Mughan escorts Pelagius back to the arena. The path is well-lit with torches, and the glow of several fires emanate from within and atop the coliseum. As Pelagius glances into the darkening sky, he notices that not only is the moon full tonight, but a sliver of red has begun creeping across its surface.

"Another eclipse," says Pelagius.

"Pardon?" inquires Mughan.

"This is the second lunar eclipse this year," says Pelagius. "There was a red moon the night I entered Devil's Den as well."

Mughan glances up at the sky. "How odd. Red moons normally occur once a year at most."

As they arrive at the combatants' entrance, Pelagius takes a quick look around.

"Well, good luck, Pelagius," says Mughan.

"Thank you, Mughan," says Pelagius. "I'll need it."

"You most certainly will," says Mughan.

Mughan departs, heading for the main entrance so that he may stand guard during the finals. As Pelagius turns to go inside, he glances up and notices that the moon is now half covered in red.

After properly donning their armor, Pelagius and Jabbleth emerge onto the field to a wild cacophony of cheering. A crimson glow bathes the field as they come to a stop, and the moon is almost completely red.

King Demonicus rises to address the crowd. "Good evening, ladies and gentlemen! Welcome to the final bout of the Grand Tourney. As you all know, the final match shall be the much-anticipated Sir Jabbleth versus Pelagius!"

The crowd erupts into thunderous applause.

"The rules and match type of this fight shall be simple, since I doubt that we can top the last two in terms of wild stipulations," says Demonicus. "This shall be a simple duel with the weapons of their choice. Victory shall be achieved by yield or incapacitation via either or the inability to stand before the count of ten."

"Or death!" shouts King Bloodsworth.

"No!" interjects Demonicus. "This is not a fight to death. No killing will be allowed. If one combatant intentionally slays his opponent, he shall be disqualified, and the one slain shall be awarded the championship posthumously."

"It's not a proper conclusion without a death match," grumbles Bloodsworth.

"Save it for when you host the Tourney," says Maldorus.

"Gentlemen, choose your weapons," says Demonicus.

Pelagius and Jabbleth approach the weapons cart as the squires roll it onto the field. Both men choose a longsword and a round shield. As the squires exit, the two combatants square off in the center of the arena, waiting for the signal to start.

"It seems we have two contestants with similar fighting styles," says Demonicus. "Let the match begin!"

Pelagius and Jabbleth charge one another, closing the gap between them rapidly. As their swords clash for the first time, the eclipse completely overshadows the moon, making it entirely red. The glow of the eclipse bathes the arena as their blades lock. The two combatants stare each other down, daring one another to make the next move. They withdraw simultaneously and clash, striking at one another repeatedly.

"You fight well, Pelagius," says Jabbleth. "The stories of your skill are quite accurate."

"The tales describing you do not disappoint either, Sir Knight," says Pelagius.

"How I wish I could have faced you in your prime," says Jabbleth. "That would have been quite the show."

"It certainly would," says Pelagius. "But I believe my experience will triumph over your youth."

The two opponents lock blades once again. Jabbleth suddenly withdraws his sword and takes a step back. Unprepared, Pelagius stumbles forward, throwing his arms outward to catch his balance. With his opponent temporarily defenseless, Jabbleth strikes. He smashes Pelagius in the face with his shield, stunning him long enough to completely lower his guard.

Jabbleth brings his shield around in an underhand swing, striking the underside of Pelagius's chin with the top edge, knocking off his helmet and sending him tumbling to the ground. Pelagius lies motionless for a few moments as he tries to regain his senses; one the squires begins counting to ten. His vision blurred and head spinning, Pelagius flips himself over onto his belly and tries to push himself up, but collapses. As the squire's count reaches seven, Pelagius fights his way back to his feet. Pelagius looks over at Jabbleth and enters a defensive stance.

Jabbleth smiles. "I'm glad you managed to get back up. It would have been disappointing for our match to be that short."

"It was close, but I'm tougher than that," says Pelagius.

Jabbleth points his sword toward the crowd and raises his shield, palm up, in Pelagius's direction, inciting wild cheers from the audience.

Jabbleth smiles. "Those in attendance appreciate your grit, too. Shall we continue?"

Pelagius nods and lunges forward, prompting Jabbleth to block the blow with his shield. Their blades collide with a clang, and the two men step back and forth as they fight across the field. Their swords clash and Jabbleth continues pushing his blade, forcing himself and Pelagius to spin their weapons in a circle and separate. Pelagius pushes forward, striking Jabbleth's sword and shield with all his might, forcing the Black Knight back until he is near the edge of the pit.

Jabbleth glances back nervously, distracting him long enough for Pelagius to land a solid blow across his breastplate. Knocked off balance, Jabbleth swings his arms wildly to prevent himself from falling into the pit, but tumbles backward. Jabbleth leaps to the side as he falls and manages to catch hold of the balance beam. Sword and shield still in hand, he pulls himself up. He looks at Pelagius, smiles, and slams his sword into his own shield three times.

"Impressive strategy, Pelagius," says Jabbleth. "You almost had me there."

"I thought it was worth a try," says Pelagius.

"Come on out, then," says Jabbleth. "Let's keep going."

Pelagius steps out onto the beam and inches toward Jabbleth. The Black Knight strikes first, swinging his sword in an overhead arc. Pelagius blocks the blow with his shield and attempts to stab Jabbleth, who uses his own shield to great effect. The swords collide and separate multiple times as the two men move across the beam.

Upon reaching the center, they deflect one another's blows, and their swords bounce off the beam, splintering it with each hit. After a few minutes, a loud crack distracts the combatants from one another. They glance down as the wood slightly buckles. While they look at each other nervously, the beam snaps and both men plummet into the pit. They rise and brush themselves off.

"What now?" asks Pelagius.

Jabbleth shrugs. "That's up to the king, I suppose."

Pelagius and Jabbleth look up and listen for Demonicus' voice.

"Ladies and gentlemen," says Demonicus. "Both combatants have fallen into the pit. Normally, I would consider this a draw. However, since this is the final round, there must be a decisive winner. Squires, lower several ladders into the pit as per a previous match. Pelagius and Jabbleth may continue their bout in the pit, but the victor must be decided on the open field. The fight continues!"

The squires place multiple ladders around the pit. Several sorcerers surround it and cast the view spell, allowing the crowd to witness what goes on below. Pelagius and Jabbleth turn their attention back to each other.

"So, I guess we fight our way up," says Pelagius.

"It would seem so," says Jabbleth. "Let's make it exciting but try not to run out of ladders."

Pelagius nods. Jabbleth charges and the two combatants cross blades again. They step around each other in a circle, blocking and parrying blows. Their swords collide with a clang, and Pelagius pushes his weapon against Jabbleth's. The Black Knight rapidly withdraws and sidesteps, causing Pelagius to stumble and fall to the ground.

Jabbleth rushes to the nearest ladder and begins his ascent. Pelagius rises to his feet and goes up the ladder directly next to Jabbleth's. When Pelagius catches up, his opponent drops his shield and quickly switches his sword to his off hand. He strikes at Pelagius, who leans back and narrowly avoids the blade. Releasing his shield to keep a better grip on the ladder, Pelagius retaliates with his own attack, which Jabbleth blocks.

They slowly climb up their ladders, trading blows along the way. Pelagius swings his weapon too hard and loses his grip on the ladder. His foot slips off the rung, and he plummets back to the mud of the pit floor. Pelagius stands and pulls Jabbleth's ladder backward, causing the Black Knight to fall. Pelagius sheathes his sword and makes his way up the next ladder. Both men reach the top around the same time. Jabbleth motions to a nearby squire, who brings new shields to both combatants.

"Tipping the ladder wasn't necessary," says Jabbleth. "Reaching the top first wasn't a victory condition."

"I got caught up in the moment," says Pelagius.

Jabbleth shrugs. "Happens to everyone, I suppose. Shall we continue?"

Pelagius and Jabbleth walk away from the pit to the center of the field before resuming their bout. Their blades clash once again, metallic clangs ringing through the arena. Pelagius's breathing grows heavier with each attack and his strikes slow.

Stepping back to take a breather, Pelagius trips on his own discarded helmet. He stumbles backward and barely regains his balance in time to prevent himself from falling. Glancing down at the helmet, Pelagius grins. He thrusts his sword inside the hole, lifts the helmet, and flings it at Jabbleth. The Black Knight brings his shield around and bashes the helmet in midair, deflecting it back in Pelagius's direction. It smashes Pelagius in the face, stunning him enough to drop his sword and sends him crashing to the ground. Jabbleth is upon him in an instant, pressing the tip of his sword to Pelagius's throat.

"Do you yield?" asks Jabbleth.

Pelagius shakes his head. "You know I can't. There is too much at stake for me to surrender."

Jabbleth frowns. "Then, I will do what I must to finish the fight."

He backs away and offers a hand to Pelagius, who hesitantly accepts. Jabbleth helps him to his feet and allows Pelagius to retrieve his weapon. He strikes as hard as he can, knocking Pelagius's sword to the side. He smacks Pelagius across the side of the head with the flat of his blade and smashes him in the face with his shield. Pelagius hits the ground with a thud and lies motionless for a few seconds, prompting the nearest squire to start counting. Pelagius stirs as the squire reaches five and flips over onto his stomach.

He pushes up as the squire reaches seven, but his foot slips, sending him back to the dirt. Pelagius shakes his head and pushes up again, but the squire reaches ten before Pelagius can even get on his knees. A stunned silence falls over the crowd before they burst into thunderous applause. Pelagius's head finally clears as King Demonicus stands.

"Ladies and gentlemen," says Demonicus, somewhat solemnly. "The winner of the Grand Tourney is Sir Jabbleth!"

Pelagius freezes and his eyes grow wide as the king's words echo through his mind. His mouth falls open as he stares at the ground in disbelief. The crowd cheers as Kevnan and the others sit in stunned silence. Jabbleth helps Pelagius to his feet and the two share a hearty handshake.

"Congratulations," says Pelagius. "A well fought victory."

"Thank you, sir," says Jabbleth. "I truly apologize for whatever fate I have condemned you to."

A pair of priests emerge onto the field and heal any injuries the two combatants sustained. When they are finished with their task, Demonicus waves them away and turns to Mughan.

"Captain Mughan, please escort Pelagius to the grand hall," says Demonicus. "We will conclude his trial after the victory ceremony."

Mughan approaches Pelagius and shackles his hands before leading him off the field. Entering the competitors' staging area, Mughan pauses.

"Why are we stopping?" asks Pelagius.

"He told me privately that if this scenario were to arise, you would be allowed to watch the victory ceremony if you desired," says Mughan.

"Very well," says Pelagius. "I shall observe."

Standing in the doorway, Pelagius watches Sir Jabbleth walk to the center of the field. After a few minutes, several squires with long horns line up by a doorway on the opposite end of the arena. They simultaneously raise their instruments and blow several musical notes. The door opens and King Demonicus emerges onto the field, followed by a few of the other dignitaries and several bodyguards. A squire follows behind pushing a cart covered with a tarp. Demonicus approaches Sir Jabbleth, who kneels into a bow.

"Congratulations on your victory, Sir Knight," says Demonicus.

"Thank you, Your Majesty," says Jabbleth. "It was an honor to entertain you and your people."

Demonicus turns to the squire and motions for him to approach. The squire wheels the cart closer and removes the covering, revealing a plain-looking shortsword. Demonicus picks up the sword and a bright light covers the weapon. When the light clears, the sword has transformed into a red-bladed greatsword.

Demonicus turns the sword on its side, resting the blade on his free hand, and extends it toward Jabbleth. "Sir Jabbleth, for winning the tournament, I present to you the legendary sword, the Knight's Honor. It shall take on the appearance and properties of any weapon you need or desire at the time."

Jabbleth reaches to accept the weapon, but Demonicus does not hand it to him. Instead, the king raises the sword to his own face. "Knight's Honor, I relinquish ownership of you. You now belong to Sir Jabbleth, the legendary Black Knight. Serve him well."

Demonicus gently lays the sword into Jabbleth's hands, and the weapon glows once more. When the light clears, Knight's Honor takes on the appearance of an ornate black longsword. Its hilt is inset with several red, blue, and green gems.

Jabbleth smiles. "Thank you, Your Majesty. I shall treasure this legendary weapon as long as I live."

Demonicus motions for Jabbleth to stand. "Rise, Sir Knight." Jabbleth rises to his feet and sheaths his new sword. Demonicus turns in a sweeping motion, gesturing toward the palace. "Celebrate your victory and enjoy the feast. I will join the festivities as soon as I take care of some business."

Mughan glances at Pelagius. "That's our cue. We must go now and complete your trial."

Chapter 64

Eeshlith assists Shukrat in tending to the wounded when the town bell rings. Shukrat rushes outside to investigate, bathed in crimson as the moon turns red. Retrieving her whipsword and Glakchog's hookswords, Eeshlith soon follows.

"What's happening?" asks Shukrat, approaching the captain of the guard.

"There are several umbra warriors on the outskirts of the swamp," says the captain. "It looks like another attack."

"Gather anybody remaining who has the strength to fight," says Shukrat.

As the defenders gather and reinforce the barricades, more and more umbra warriors come into view. The Green-Eyed Man appears and surveys the horizon as Garu emerges behind him.

"That's not good," says Eeshlith.

"I told the elders that we should evacuate," says Shukrat. "Why does nobody listen to me?"

Hundreds of umbra warriors pour out of the swamp and run in different directions. However, none of them head toward the town.

"What are they doing?" asks the captain.

As the umbra warriors continue to spread out, Shukrat comes to a horrific realization. "They're encircling the town. The Green-Eyed Man intends to attack from all sides."

The captain turns to some of the others. "Go tell the other defenders to spread out across town. We must protect every entry point."

Several defenders scamper off as more and more umbra warriors encircle the town.

"We must evacuate before it is too late," says Shukrat. "Even once my curse is lifted, I cannot transport the entire town."

One of the defenders returns. "Sir, the town is completely surrounded."

"It would appear that it is already too late," says the captain. "We must hold them off for as long as we can. Once your curse lifts, you and Eeshlith teleport to the castle and warn the king."

The defenders emit audible gasps as Alasdar makes his presence known; he stands behind the Green-Eyed Man.

"Flaming zombie minotaur!" exclaims the captain. "That's very bad."

Eeshlith absentmindedly taps the hilt of her whipsword. "How long before you can teleport again?"

"A few minutes," says Shukrat. "Let's hope we can hold out that long."

"Head to the center of town," says the captain. "That should buy you a little time."

The Green-Eyed Man summons his urn and points his sword toward the town. "Charge!"

As the eclipse covers half the moon, the umbra warriors immediately rush toward the town. As they close in, the defenders begin volleying arrows. They down a few at a time, but there are too few of them to do any real damage to the attackers' numbers. The army crashes into the barricades, forcing the defenders to hold them in place. Shukrat flings fireballs, obliterating groups of ten at a time, and Alithyra decapitates a few with her whipsword. However, the sheer numbers overwhelm the defenders and the barricades collapse.

The captain rushes into the fray. "Center of town! Now!"

As the umbra warriors pour into town, Shukrat and Eeshlith slowly back away toward the town square, fighting off umbra warriors as they go. The Green-Eyed Man and Alasdar walk across the field.

"We need to go now," says Shukrat.

The two turn and run to the town square, putting as much distance between themselves and the invaders as possible. As they come to a stop, Shukrat begins to concentrate.

"I should be able to get us out of here in another minute," says Shukrat.

"We may not have that long," says Eeshlith.

As Shukrat desperately tries to activate his powers, Eeshlith strikes down any umbra warriors that reach the square. After a while, the remaining defenders, including the captain, surround the area, desperately fighting off the invaders as the Green-Eyed Man comes into view.

"A valiant attempt," says the Green-Eyed Man. "I must admit that I'm impressed by your efforts, feeble though they are."

As the Green-Eyed Man approaches, Shukrat continues to try and fail to cast a transport spell. The captain of the guard rushes the Green-Eyed Man, locking swords with him.

"You're very brave," says the Green-Eyed Man. "Commendable."

For a few seconds, the captain holds his own against the soul hunter, but the Green-Eyed Man slashes him across the chest and kicks him to the ground. He steps over the captain. "If you'll excuse me."

As the Green-Eyed Man closes in on his targets, the captain forces himself to his feet and rushes him. Hearing him coming, the Green-Eyed Man sighs and turns to face him, running him through with his sword. A shimmering portal opens in the middle of the square, and Eeshlith and Shukrat dive through just as the umbra warriors reach them. The portal closes before anybody else can enter.

Chapter 65

Kragus and Tohirata, with shovels in hand, stroll down a massive roadway just south of a large swamp.

"Are you sure it's around here?" asks Kragus.

"Lord Scirrhus' spies were quite specific," says Tohirata. "It should be close."

As the moon turns red, they stop at a grave by the side of the road.

"Here it is," says Tohirata. "Are you sure you're ready for this?"

"I'm not sure that I'm strong enough to raise him the way I wish to," says Kragus. "But at the very least, we can exhume his corpse and preserve it to prevent further decay."

"Are you certain that he won't have completely rotted away by now?" asks Tohirata. "It has been a few months since his death."

"No, but I'm confident that there will still be some flesh," says Kragus. "Burials are rarely permanent among followers of Ender. Instead, they are temporary placeholders until the body can be retrieved for a proper cremation. As such, part of a burial ritual involves magically preserving the corpse. It will not be fully preserved though; just enough to slow down the process of decomposition."

The two begin digging, slowly piling dirt beside the grave as the eclipse continues. After several minutes, they locate what they came to find.

Kragus sets his shovel aside and hops into the grave. "Here he is. Help me get him out."

Tohirata reaches down as Kragus lifts out a shroud-wrapped form, a large lump extending from the area of the face. The moon turns completely red as they place the body on the ground. Kragus places his hand on the motionless form and concentrates.

"The decay is extensive, but not too far advanced," says Kragus. "As long as we can prevent him from rotting further, I should be able to raise him as planned."

"Step back for a moment," says Tohirata.

Kragus backs away as Tohirata mutters something under his breath. He extends his hand and a white mist sprays from his fingers. It envelops the corpse, freezing it solid.

"Now use your stasis spell," says Tohirata.

"Stasis and freezing seems unnecessary," says Kragus. "But we can't be too careful."

Kragus whispers under his breath and touches the corpse, which briefly glows a sickly purple.

"We should return to your master's fortress," says Kragus. "That way we can properly store him until I have the strength to pull this off."

Tohirata opens a portal as Kragus hoists his prize over his shoulder. The two then step through.

Chapter 66

Pelagius stands before the throne in a situation that is now all too familiar to him. As the crowd stops filing in, Barbox and Demonicus enter, with Demonicus sitting in the throne.

Barbox steps forward. "Presenting His Royal Highness, King Demonicus IX."

Demonicus motions for everyone to take a seat.

"We all know why we are here," says Barbox. "Pelagius has been accused of the assassination of Marquis Babu. Tonight, we conclude this trial. Your Majesty, what is the verdict?"

"Pelagius's co-conspirators have all been found not guilty and are free to go," says Demonicus. "However, Pelagius, you were not victorious in the Grand Tourney. Therefore, I have no choice but to find you guilty of all charges."

The crowd bursts into a small frenzy of whispers.

"I'm afraid that I cannot show leniency in this regard," says Demonicus. "Pelagius, for your crimes against the Diablosian Crown, I hereby sentence you …"

"Your Majesty, I bear grave news!" The doors to the grand hall fly open with a loud crash and Darderos bursts into the room.

Demonicus jumps to his feet, his eyes wide with surprise. "Darderos, where have you been?" He returns to his seat. "I'm relieved to see you alive, but I am about to sentence the prisoner. Can the news wait?"

"I'm afraid it cannot, Your Highness," says Darderos.

"Very well," says Demonicus. "Speak."

Darderos relays his story, giving all the information he was told and including his treatment afterward.

"Disturbing," says Demonicus. "How large of a force does he have?"

"Approximately five thousand umbra warriors," says Darderos. "Possibly more."

"How long until he attacks?" asks Demonicus.

"I do not know, sire," says Darderos.

"In that case, we must put the matter of this trial to rest immediately and then deal with Alasdar," says Demonicus. "Pelagius, as I was saying, I sentence you …"

A portal opens in the center of the room, interrupting Demonicus once again. Eeshlith and Shukrat tumble out and crash to the floor.

"Shukrat?" says Demonicus. "What is the meaning of this rushed entry?"

Shukrat rises to his feet. "Your Highness, Ethor has fallen. Alasdar's forces are on the move. They will be here within a few days."

A series of shocked whispers pass through the crowd.

"Then Pelagius's sentencing will have to wait," says Demonicus. "We must gather our forces for a counterattack."

King Bloodsworth grins smugly. "Need I remind you that any mobilization of the Diablosian army will be considered an act of war? If your forces gather, we will have no choice but to consider it a threat and declare war."

"Surely we must defend ourselves," says Demonicus.

"You are free to defend yourselves, of course," says Bloodsworth. "But an official gathering of your military will still be considered an act of war by my government. Proceed as you please."

"This changes everything," says Demonicus, frustrated. "A moment while I figure this out."

Demonicus consults with Barbox for a few moments.

"Since we cannot mobilize the military, we must take an unorthodox approach," says Demonicus. "Pelagius, I sentence you to defend the castle. You will be in charge of the defense force. Whether you live or die, your sentence will have been carried out. What say you?"

"It is my fault that you are in this situation," says Pelagius. "It is a fair ruling."

Demonicus turns to Bloodsworth. "The entire defense force will be composed of a third party. Is that satisfactory or will that somehow still be seen as aggression."

"It is not an army loyal to you," says Bloodsworth. "It is acceptable."

"This trial has ended," says Demonicus. "Captain Mughan, please escort Pelagius to his quarters. He has much to think about and little time to do it."

Chapter 67

The next morning, Pelagius sits in the common room. He is contemplating his next move as Alithyra and Kevnan enter.

"We will help," says Kevnan.

"You two have done enough," says Pelagius. "This is my burden."

"We said we were with you to the end," says Alithyra. "The death of Babu was only the beginning of the quest. We're not finished."

Pelagius grins. "I appreciate that. I need an army. Hopefully we can recruit a few of the others."

Eeshlith enters the room. "I would like to help."

"Are you the only one who defected?" asks Pelagius.

Eeshlith fights back tears. "No. Shudgluv defected with me and gave his life to save Ethor during the first assault. I wish to honor his memory, and I believe that Shukrat will be willing to help as well."

"Very well," says Pelagius. "I will accept your offer. Who else can we recruit?"

"We won't recruit anybody by sitting here," says Kevnan. "We need to head to the Grand Hall."

"You're right," says Pelagius. "Let's go."

They leave their area and head to the great hall.

CHAPTER 68

Grimadert stands in his lab as Rogi and Giro carry in Adotiln and Thakszut. The two assistants place the bodies on tables side by side and strap them down. They pull a pair of levers, activating the same machine that he used to animate Iriemorel's armor and take their places by a pair of cranks.

"Now to see if I can do what the priests cannot," says Grimadert. "Boys, begin turning."

Grimadert begins his chant and summons a magical electric storm twice as powerful as the previous one. As the machine shakes, nearly tearing itself apart from the power channeling in, Rogi and Giro turn their cranks.

Electricity dances between the prongs, striking the two motionless forms in quick bursts. Grimadert unleashes all the built-up power into the prongs simultaneously and the bodies are hit with a constant stream of electric blasts, spasming violently as the power surges through them.

After several minutes, Grimadert pulls the lever to deactivate the machine, which folds back into the walls and collapses. Rogi and Giro squat over his motionless form. After a minute, Grimadert stirs and sits up. "Remind me not to do that again, boys. I might disintegrate myself if I push my boundaries any further. Let's check on our experiments."

The three look over at Adotiln and Thakszut. Rogi and Giro undo the straps securing them to the tables. For a few moments, the forms lie motionless. Adotiln suddenly takes a deep gasping breath and sits up, shrieking in agony.

After a few seconds she stops and takes in her surroundings. "Where am I? How am I alive?"

Adotiln looks at her chest and finds no visible wound. Looking over the rest of her body, she clearly sees the scars and stitch marks keeping her together. "What is this? What have I become? Who did this to me?"

Grimadert stands, wincing in pain, and approaches her. "Take it easy, my dear. You were badly injured. I saved your life."

Adotiln glares at the wizened gnome. "You did this? You're the one who pulled me out of the Underworld?"

"I am," says Grimadert, proudly.

"I'm supposed to be dead," says Adotiln. "Undeath is unnatural. What you have done is a crime against nature. Rasthor will not be pleased when he learns that a soul was stolen from the Underworld."

"My dear, you are not undead, and Rasthor will not know of this unless it is brought to his attention; you never crossed his threshold," says Grimadert. "I put you back together and revived you with a combination of magic and science."

Adotiln stares at him. She lowers her eyes and looks over her body. "So, I'm a construct now?"

Grimadert nods, then thinks for a moment and shakes his head. "Yes and no. In a way you could be considered a biogolem, but your memories are fully intact, so you are still you and not a slave. It may be more accurate to call you a fleshforged."

Adotiln bursts into tears. "Then I'm an abomination. I may not even be allowed to be a priestess anymore."

"Yes, the rules of life and death are quite fuzzy in this situation," says Grimadert.

As they converse, Thakszut stirs. He emits a pained shriek as his hair turns white and he increases in size, knocking over Adotiln's table. Thakszut rapidly sits up and takes in his surroundings as Grimadert calmly explains the situation.

"This is unexpected," says Grimadert. "It appears that something in the procedure has permanently activated your Demonic Potential."

As Adotiln rises to her feet, Iriemorel comes loudly clomping into the room and sees Thakszut. "It worked. Excellent." He turns his head and comes to a stop as he sees her. "Adotiln?"

She lowers her head in shame. "Yes."

Iriemorel glares angrily at Grimadert. "You were specifically told to let her rest in peace. You stole her head and revived her anyway?"

Grimadert smiles, beaming with pride. "I did. It was a challenge I couldn't resist."

"You lying psychopath!" shouts Iriemorel. "Happy as I am to see her alive, I should tear you apart for this!"

Iriemorel charges at Grimadert, but something rushes out of the shadows and slams into the enraged dwarf, pinning him to the ground with a massive foot. This creature is humanoid in shape but is ten feet tall and hairless, with dark gray skin and solid white eyes.

Grimadert walks to Iriemorel and bends down. "Iriemorel, meet Molgbrim. He's my bodyguard."

"A skemguri," says Iriemorel. "Excellent choice for a bodyguard. I yield."

As Molgbrim releases Iriemorel, Adotiln backs away fearfully.

"I see you still have your sense of self preservation," says Grimadert.

"You seem to think that I am suicidal," says Adotiln. "I may disagree with what you have done to me, but I do not wish to die. That being said, I am disgusted by what I have become and would have preferred to remain dead unless resurrected by the Archpriest."

"Well, you'll just have to come to terms with your new life then," says Grimadert, grinning. "Or find another opportunity to sacrifice yourself."

Grimadert turns and begins to leave, followed by Rogi and Giro.

"Molgbrim, keep an eye on them," says Grimadert. "Adotiln and Thakszut need a few days to gather their strength. Now, if you'll excuse me, I have a delivery to make."

Chapter 69

Pelagius is in the grand hall, conversing with Hexeron, as many others go about their business.

"How many of your troops can get here before Alasdar's army arrives?" asks Pelagius.

"I have about fifteen hundred camped within a day's ride," says Hexeron. "If I send word now, they should get here in time. With any luck, they'll send word to another camp as well."

"Unfortunately, I can't pay you," says Pelagius. "But I will do my best to make sure you are compensated."

"This one is on the house, Pelagius," says Hexeron. "This is a matter of justice."

As they converse, a confused Delradi approaches. "Where's the feast? I thought there was to be a grand festival after the tournament."

Pelagius explains the situation.

"I see," says Delradi. "Well, I'm in if you'll have me."

"I can use all the help I can get," says Pelagius.

Kevnan and Alithyra come through the crowd and join them.

"Well, Koskru, Celemrod, and Ashisat are in," says Kevnan. "Unfortunately, King Bloodsworth and Count Vuzenkhord have already left."

"No surprise there," says Pelagius. "Considering the animosity between the two kingdoms, I doubt that Bloodsworth would be willing to assist anyway."

"Sir Jabbleth has already departed as well," says Alithyra. "He apparently has pressing business elsewhere."

"That's a shame," says Pelagius. "Having him as an ally in this endeavor would have been a significant advantage. What of the others?"

"Adltaw claims that he can still fight," says Kevnan. "If we can keep him in the rear, that would be best."

"We need more sorcerers," says Pelagius. "There are surprisingly few magic users in the city at this time."

"Shukrat is searching for more," says Alithrya. "He and Ralkgek have an idea for a magical trap if things go wrong. Eeshlith is recruiting as many of the locals and remaining tournament contestants as possible."

"Very well," says Pelagius. "Continue scouting out potential recruits. We have only a few days until the attack begins and we must be fully prepared."

CHAPTER 70

Adotiln sits in an empty chamber with her legs crossed. Her eyes closed and she is deep in thought. The space around her shifts as the stone walls vanish, replaced by an empty, white void. A chill wind blows and snow flurries around her as a mountain materializes in front of her. Adotiln opens her eyes and rises to her feet as she ascends the seemingly treacherous slope.

After what seems like hours, she reaches the peak, upon which sits a massive stone monastery. She approaches the door and knocks three times. The door opens on its own accord, and she steps inside.

Upon crossing the threshold, an older man of incredible height greets Adotiln. His hair and beard are turning gray, and he wears brown robes.

"Welcome back to Osica Monastery, my child. How may I be of service to my loyal follower?" The man looks her over and a stunned expression crosses his face. "Adotiln? You're supposed to be dead. You should be awaiting your eternal rest pending Rasthor's judgment."

Adotiln bows. "My Lord Ender, God of Valor. I have been returned from the dead by unusual means, and I seek your council."

"Speak, child," says Ender, puzzled.

Adotiln explains the situation that led to her death and the circumstances of her return from the grave. Ender looks disturbed as he absorbs the information.

"As I believe that I have become an abomination, I do not know if you would consider me worthy of being your follower, let alone willing to grant me any powers," says Adotiln. "I need to know if I can still serve you."

"This is unprecedented," says Ender. "I must speak to some of the other gods. Wait here while I seek counsel."

Ender walks out the monastery door and vanishes. Moments later, he reappears. "The gods are gathering to form a council to discuss this matter. You must end your current prayer."

"Why?" asks Adotiln. "Can't you transport my consciousness to Castle Ordatras with you?"

"Yes," says Ender. "However, it will take time for the gods to gather. You must fetch Thakszut, since he is in a similar situation, and rejoin me at Castle Ordatras in a few hours. Farewell for now."

Ender disappears and the surroundings fade out until Adotiln stands in a white void. She kneels and closes her eyes, finding herself back in her chamber in Grimadert's fortress upon opening them.

Chapter 71

Kragus enters Scirrhus' chamber and approaches the throne. The sickly carcinomancer leans forward as he approaches and motions for Tohirata to intercept him.

"What do you want, Kragus?" asks Scirrhus. "It is not yet time to begin the next phase of my plan."

"I wish to perform a ritual on the corpse we exhumed," says Kragus, "I believe I am strong enough to pull off what I have in mind."

"If you are mistaken, you could destroy yourself," says Scirrhus. "Are you certain you wish to proceed?"

"I am," says Kragus.

"Very well," says Scirrhus. "Tohirata, fetch the subject."

"Yes, Master." Tohirata exits through a nearby door, returning several minutes later carrying something wrapped in a brown cloth. He places it on the ground and removes the cloth, revealing Bojan's frozen corpse.

Scirrhus snaps his fingers and Bojan instantly thaws. The body is severely decayed. Most of the feathers are missing and bone shows in several places.

Kragus kneels to examine the corpse. "Excellent. He is in just the right state for what I have in mind. Scirrhus, I have need of an assistant, preferably someone you consider expendable."

Scirrhus motions to a nearby guard, who approaches Kragus.

"How can I be of service?" asks the guard nervously.

Kragus extends his bony hand. "I require your sword."

The guard hesitantly draws his sword and hands it to Kragus, who inspects the blade thoroughly. "Excellent weapon. I think I shall be keeping this. I need a new one anyway."

"But I need that to do my duty," says the guard.

"Your current duty does not require it," says Kragus.

"What do you wish of me?" asks the guard.

"Just hold still. This won't take long." Kragus slashes the guard across the throat. Bleeding out rapidly, the guard collapses.

"Why did you do that?" asks Tohirata.

"Watch and learn." Kragus dips his hand in the rapidly forming pool of blood and draws a circle around Bojan's corpse. He draws lines from the outside into the center, moving the body when necessary, before using more of the blood to inscribe indecipherable symbols on the corpse's chest, arms, legs, and head.

Scirrhus leans forward, his expressionless face never changing. "A blood magic ritual. I am intrigued."

Kragus approaches Bojan's body and kneels. He places his hand on the corpse's chest and quietly chants. After a few moments, a purple glow surrounds him before expanding into the body and outward in the circle. The blood vanishes as the magic consumes it, and Bojan's dead eyes open.

Soon, the glow fades, except for the eyes, and Bojan slowly sits up. He plants his feet on the ground and pushes up, bending his back unnaturally before he straightens, stands, and turns to a very drained-looking Kragus.

"I am ready to serve, Master," Bojan says with a dry rasping voice.

"Excellent," says Kragus.

"What is my first task?" asks Bojan.

"For now, nothing," says Kragus. "You are powerful, but only freshly arisen. You must gather your strength."

"As you wish, master." Bojan walks to a nearby bench and sits, the purple glow fading from his eyes as he enters a state of deathly hibernation.

Kragus struggles to his feet and sits close by.

"I see that the ritual has weakened you," says Scirrhus.

"Severely," says Kragus. "Without the use of blood magic, that ritual likely would have destroyed me. I must now, once again, regain my strength."

"Was it worth the effort to raise an intelligent zombie?" asks Tohirata.

"That is no zombie," says Kragus. "Bojan is now a mort. He is incredibly powerful, but completely under my control."

"I've never seen morts created with a blood magic ritual," says Scirrhus.

"I needed that ritual to enhance him," says Kragus. "I have given him a special ability. Aside from me, no being, living or undead, can kill him."

Chapter 72

A pale elf opens a massive door and enters a large chamber. This room is circular, and its exact size seems immeasurable. The walls extend so high that darkness conceals the ceiling. Several pillars, apparently made of bone, extend upward out of sight. A line of semi-transparent beings of all species extends from the door to the end of the room.

At the end of this line, an imposing figure nearly thirty feet in height sits on a throne made of bones. This man is pale and emaciated. He wears a black, hooded cloak, and a large scythe leans against the wall close by. The elf approaches him.

"What is it?" asks the figure. "I'm busy judging souls."

"Pardon the intrusion, great Rasthor," says the elf. "One of the recent arrivals wishes to speak with you."

"Can it wait?" asks Rasthor. "I have thousands of interviews and judgments to make today."

"He says it's urgent, sir," says the pale elf.

"Fine," says Rasthor. "Send him in."

The elf leaves. A few minutes later, a semi-ghostly, semi-solid form of Bojan comes through. Bypassing the line of clearly confused and agitated spirits, he approaches Rasthor's throne.

"What is it, Bojan?" says Rasthor.

"Oh Mighty God of Death, please hear me out," says Ghost Bojan. "My former body has been desecrated and corrupted. I fear the worst should it be allowed to exist."

"How do you know of this corruption?" asks Rasthor.

"I may have been using the crystals in the Golden Palace to scry and caught a glimpse of my grave being plundered," says Bojan, sheepishly.

"This breach of the rules shall be forgiven for now," says Rasthor.

"However, what your body does now should be none of your concern. You are dead and you have come here. You should be enjoying your eternal rest."

"I fear that as a mort, my body could cause widespread destruction and death," says Ghost Bojan. "I must be allowed to return to the world of the living and help dispose of its threat."

"Absolutely not!" shouts Rasthor. "There are too many wandering spirits as it is. I will not allow another that has already come here to leave."

"This is of the utmost importance," says Ghost Bojan. "I beg you to let me do this. I swear upon my own soul that I will do anything you ask of me in return."

Before Rasthor can answer, the pale elf returns.

"Pardon the interruption, My Lord," says the pale elf. "You are needed at Castle Ordatras for an important meeting."

Rasthor rises from his throne. "It seems that we must continue this discussion later. I shall consider your request, but I make no promises."

"Thank you, My Lord," says Ghost Bojan.

Rasthor turns to the pale elf. "Escort Bojan back. Fetch one of my reapers to judge souls in my stead. I shall be off."

Rasthor vanishes as the pale elf leads Ghost Bojan back through the door.

Chapter 73

Back in the form of a small red monkey, Thakszut enters Adotiln's chamber and finds her sitting in the middle of the floor.

"You called for me?" asks Thakszut.

"I see you managed to change back to normal," says Adotiln.

"For now," says Thakszut. "It took a lot of effort and concentration to do it, and it is taking everything I have to keep my powers under control. Did you need me for something?"

Adotiln explains her conversation with Ender.

"Are the gods going to help us?" asks Thakszut.

"I don't think so," says Adotiln. "Not in the way you're thinking, anyway. I just know that Ender said they will want to speak with us."

"How do I join you?" asks Thakszut.

"Sit by me, close your eyes, and concentrate," says Adotiln. "I'll take care of the rest."

Thakszut sits next to Adotiln in a cross-legged position, closes his eyes, and instantly transforms into a giant, white monkey with streaks of black and gray. Adotiln takes his hand and sits in the same position. The terrain shifts around them until they appear to be sitting in a meadow. Adotiln opens her eyes and stands.

"You can open your eyes now," says Adotiln. "We're here."

Thakszut's eyes open and he finds that they are in front of a massive castle, one far larger than any that exists in the Material Realm.

Looking at himself, he discovers that he is in his normal form. "How am I like this? Without concentrating on keeping my powers low, I should be in my larger form."

"Your astral form always looks like the true you," says Adotiln. "We should go now. They'll be expecting us."

As they move forward, the drawbridge comes down. A humanoid figure emitting a slight glow meets them.

"Welcome to Castle Ordatras, home of the gods," says the servant. "The meeting is already in progress. Come with me."

They follow the servant across the bridge and inside. They continue down massive stone corridors until they reach a gigantic wooden door. Indecipherable muffled voices can emanate from the other side. The servant stops and turns to them.

"You will find the gods through here," says the servant. "They are expecting you, but many of them are unhappy with the situation. Good luck."

The servant opens the door, and the two heroes enter a massive chamber resembling a great hall. In the center is a large table high enough to seat giants. Around the table are twenty-one individuals of immense proportions. Most are humanoid in shape, but not all appear human. Ender and Rasthor are at one end of the table, flanking a regal dwarf-like deity. Close by the dwarf is another god who greatly resembles Ender but looks far older.

In an alcove behind them is a twenty-second individual in the form of a dragon far larger than any dragon has ever seen. Adotiln kneels respectfully. Thakszut stares in awe before the halfling pulls him down to the floor. The gods stop talking and look in their direction.

"And here they are," says Ender. "What should we do about this situation?"

"They cheated death and disrupted the balance of the universe," says a human-looking deity. "To restore the balance, they must be destroyed."

"Easy, Hoven," says the dwarf-like deity. "We have not yet come to a decision."

"I rarely take sides in order to maintain balance, Zargan," says Hoven. "That is how grave I feel the situation is."

"They did not intentionally cheat death," says Ender. "This state of life was forced upon them."

"Then we should destroy the one who created them," says Hoven. "This so-called scientist is a threat to universal balance."

"He will meet his fate in due time," says Rasthor. "He is not our current concern."

Zargan turns to the elderly-looking god. "Andrinor, what is your take on this? Should they be destroyed to restore universal balance or allowed to live and continue to serve?"

"Technically, Thakszut never truly died," says Andrinor.

Rasthor produces a scroll and looks over it. "He is correct. His heart stopped, but not long enough to be completely dead."

"Then we must destroy Adotiln," says Hoven. "I will do it if I must, and then I will accomplish a good act to restore balance."

"Kill me if you must," says Adotiln. "By all rights, I should be dead and standing before Rasthor for judgment."

"True," says Ender. "However, it is not your fault that you were restored to a mockery of life."

The gods continue to argue for at least an hour. Each deity has something to say, except for the massive dragon, who does not appear to care. After a while, Zargan has clearly had enough. Zargan stands and slams his hands on the table. "This bickering is getting us nowhere. We need a solution." Zargan turns to the dragon. "Bralagon, you have yet to say anything. What is your opinion?"

"I do not care what the rest of you do in this matter," says Bralagon. "I'm only here on ceremony. I have more important matters to attend to."

"I believe I have an idea, sire," says Andrinor.

Andrinor whispers something in Zargan's ear. Zargan nods and motions for Ender and Rasthor to join the secret conversation. After several minutes, they seem to reach an agreement.

"We have come to a compromise," says Zargan. "Adotiln, step forward."

Adotiln rises and approaches the gods.

"We have determined that you will be allowed to live and will continue to serve Ender as a priestess," says Zargan. "However, you will also be serving Rasthor."

"How will that work?" asks Adotiln. "Only the Archpriest can get power from more than one god."

"Your service to me will not be as a priestess," says Rasthor. "Instead, for the remainder of your life, you will serve me as a living reaper. I will assign one of my reapers to you. They will give you missions, and you are to hunt down wayward souls and destroy those who have cheated death. Once you die, your reaper supervisor will personally escort your soul to me, and your service will have been fulfilled."

"As you wish, My Lord," says Adotiln. "When do I begin?"

"That is yet to be determined," says Rasthor. "For now, rest and regain your strength."

"What about me?" asks Thakszut.

"You may assist her if you wish," says Rasthor. "However, you have no debt to balance and are free to do as you like."

"This meeting has been concluded," says Zargan. "Everyone, return to your godly duties. Adotiln and Thakszut, you may go."

"Thank you, My Lord," says Adotiln. "Thakszut, follow my lead."

Adotiln sits on the floor and closes her eyes, joining hands with Thakszut when he sits next to her. When they awaken, they are back in Adotiln's chamber.

Chapter 74

A few days later, Pelagius and Hexeron stand atop the barbican above the main gate, looking at the horizon. Eeshlith positions herself on one of the towers flanking the gate while several of the others walk the battlements. Several steaming cauldrons sit on the floor behind Hexeron with a few mercenaries close to each one.

"I'm surprised they're not here yet," says Hexeron.

"They should be here soon," says Pelagius.

"Do you think we stand a chance?" asks Hexeron.

"It's a slim chance, honestly," says Eeshlith.

Several hours of tense silence pass. As the sun sets, Delradi calls out. "I think I see them. They're emerging from the marsh on the left."

Pelagius rushes along the battlement to check the situation. Sure enough, a relatively small group of umbra warriors march out of the swamp west of the castle. The umbra warriors stream out of the swamp, stretching from the left of the castle all the way around to the front.

"They're flanking us," says Pelagius. "They've got us covered on two fronts."

As the umbra warriors continue to swarm out of the marsh, nine catapults and a trebuchet come wheeling through the trees, followed by twelve siege towers. The army comes to a halt as the Green-Eyed Man and Garu emerge from the tree line and begin coordinating the troops. After an hour, the army's forces loop around to the right side of the castle, flanking the heroes on three sides and spreading the siege towers evenly among the ranks. They wheel the trebuchet around to face the front gate, along with three of the catapults. Three catapults remain on the west side, while the invaders take the last three to the east.

"This setup is taking a while," says Delradi. "Shouldn't we try to destroy their siege engines before they attack?"

"They're staying out of range of even the sorcerers," says Hexeron. "Attacking now would expose us."

"He's right," says Pelagius. "We're outnumbered and on the defensive. This battle must begin on the Green-Eyed Man's terms."

"They will most likely wait until morning," says Hexeron. "It will be night soon, and even umbra warriors have no tactical advantage in a full-scale battle after dark."

"I agree," says Pelagius. "We must remain vigilant throughout the night, but they most likely won't make a move until sunrise."

Chapter 75

As the sun rises, a loud horn blast echoes from outside the walls. Pelagius and Hexeron peer over and see the umbra warrior line begin to advance. Several individuals push and pull the siege towers behind them.

"It is beginning," says Pelagius. "Give the signal."

Hexeron grabs a nearby torch and lights the contents of a steaming cauldron, which bursts into a large fire visible along the entire castle wall.

"Everyone to your positions!" shouts Hexeron.

As the defenders take up arms, the attackers continue to advance. Peering out over the horizon, Pelagius notices that large boulders are being loaded into the catapults and trebuchet. Archers and sorcerers line the walls of the battlements, with Eeshlith directing their movements.

"Hold your fire," says Eeshlith. "We must wait until they are closer."

As the line continues to advance, the siege engines unleash their loads. A few boulders slam harmlessly into the lower section of the outer wall.

As the warriors operating the siege engines reload and recalibrate, the line continues to advance. As they close in, Pelagius puts a hand in the air. After nearly a full minute, he extends his hand forward.

"Fire!" shouts Eeshlith. "Archers, take down the infantry! Sorcerers, concentrate on the siege towers!"

The archers simultaneously release a volley of arrows, nearly blacking out the sky. A few dozen umbra warriors fall as the arrows descend. Several explosions rock the siege towers as the sorcerers fling fireballs and various other magical attacks, but none topple. The archers unleash more volleys of arrows as the umbra warrior army continues to advance. The siege towers continue their approach despite a few catching on fire. Even killing the umbra warriors pulling and pushing them along does little to slow their progress and those felled are quickly replaced.

"Those towers are tough," says Delradi. "They may have been enhanced with some magic resistance."

"Possible, but not likely," says Hexeron. "They may just be very well constructed."

The siege engines unleash another volley of boulders.

"Incoming!" shouts Pelagius.

Several boulders slam into the side of the castle wall, shaking the ground beneath the defenders' feet. One lands directly on a battlement, smashing the walkway and crushing several archers and mages.

"We need to take out those siege engines," says Pelagius. "They're going to bring the whole wall down if they are allowed to continue."

"They're out of range of the sorcerers," says Hexeron.

"There are ballistae on the towers at the east and west corners," says Pelagius. "Get those loaded and start firing back!"

Hexeron passes along the command and several defenders rush to each ballista, which looks like a giant crossbow, and begin the arduous task of loading in their massive bolts. As the line continues to advance, one of the siege towers pulls ahead of the others and rapidly approaches the wall.

"We can't allow that to get close," says Hexeron. "Who knows how many soldiers each one holds."

"Sorcerers, concentrate all attacks on that tower!" commands Pelagius.

All the sorcerers in the immediate area, numbering roughly twenty, fling magic attacks at the offending siege tower. Finally, they all launch fireballs at the base and destroy the foundation; the siege tower collapses in a flaming heap.

"That's one down," says Pelagius. "Hopefully we can do that with the rest."

The siege engines unleash another volley of boulders. Most of the stones smash into the walls, but one boulder obliterates one of the towers flanking the barbican. Eeshlith barely leaps to safety. Another stone smashes through the top of a wall and plows through a battlement, crushing and scattering several soldiers. The boulder bumps into Delradi and sends him plummeting into the courtyard. As the siege engineers reload the catapults, some of the umbra warriors tinker with the trebuchet.

"We can't take much more of those boulders," says Pelagius.

"The archers and sorcerers are eliminating as many of the enemy troops as they can," says Eeshlith. "Their numbers are just too many."

Chapter 76

Alithyra watches as the army marches forward with the rising sun. Ashisat stands nearby, longbow in hand, waiting to give the archers the command to loose their arrows. After several minutes, the umbra warriors charge, and the siege towers move toward the wall. Before any enemy troops come into range, the catapults unleash their loads. Two boulders crash into the base of the wall. The defenders on the battlement scatter and duck as one flies right over, barely missing the battlement and slamming into the courtyard.

"Everyone back in position!" shouts Alithyra. "We need to be ready soon."

Celemrod walks down the line, helping troops to their feet and handing them dropped weapons. "Get ahold of yourselves. Get back on the wall."

As the defenders reposition themselves, the line of umbra warriors moves ever closer. Ashisat glances at the archers and sorcerers and holds up one hand. "Steady now. Just a little closer."

When the wave advances further, Alithyra readies her own bow and turns to Ashisat. "Now."

Ashisat rapidly drops his hand and raises his bow. "Fire!"

The archers loose a volley of arrows, felling several umbra warriors, and the sorcerers unleash a wide variety of magical attacks. The catapults fling another round of boulders, which slam into the wall, shaking the battlements enough for a few troops to temporarily lose their balance. As the archers continue launching arrows, Alithyra notices the siege towers are drawing uncomfortably close. Looking around, she sees some defenders from the front wall running toward the ballista on the corner tower. She looks to the other side of the wall and sees that there is a ballista mounted there as well.

Alithyra turns to Celemrod and Koskru. "Take some troops and load that ballista. We need to get it working so we can take out the siege engines. Koskru, take command of the forces on the battlement."

Celemrod takes a few defenders, rushes down the wall to the ballista, and starts loading it. Alithyra turns her attention to the battlefield and notices one siege tower drawing closer more rapidly than the other three. "Ashisat, have the sorcerers concentrate on that tower!"

Ashisat nods. "All magic users, focus your attention on that siege tower!"

The sorcerers look over at the approaching tower and release a maelstrom of magical energies. Between all the lightning bolts, fireballs, and other forms of magical energies, the tower explodes and collapses, sending dozens of umbra warriors crashing to the ground. The catapults unleash another barrage of boulders, damaging the wall and nearly destroying a section of the battlement.

With the ballista loaded, Celemrod turns it toward the nearest siege tower and fires. The massive bolt slams into the side of the tower and knocks it over, sending it crashing to the ground.

Celemrod grins. "Reload!"

A large wave of umbra warriors reaches the base of the wall and attempts to scale it. With few handholds, most are unsuccessful, and the attackers that do manage to climb are quickly felled by the defenders. The umbra warriors operating the catapults wheel them closer to get a better shot. Two sorcerers fling a fireball at the closest catapult and the siege engine explodes, showering the area with burning debris. The boulder it was about to launch slams into the bottom of a siege tower, destroying its base. The tower collapses, crushing a nearby catapult.

Alithyra grins at the sight. "Well done. That was a lucky hit."

Several umbra warriors stop charging and rummage through the wreckage of the siege towers. They pull a pair of intact ladders from the least damaged tower and rush toward the wall. Setting up the ladders, they quickly scale the wall, and several defenders meet them at the top. Swords clash as both sides strike and parry one another. Koskru swings his large blade, decapitating multiple umbra warriors in one swing. Alithyra kicks one umbra warrior in the face as he appears at the top of the ladder, and the warrior flies off the wall and plummets to the ground.

Five umbra warriors reach the top and surround Ashisat. Dropping his bow, Ashisat rapidly draws his katana and spins, slicing through all five opponents in a single strike. One of the sorcerers turns his attention to the ladders and hits them with a fireball, igniting the climbing equipment and incinerating several attackers.

Taking advantage of the distraction caused by the troops ascending the ladders, the final siege tower draws nearer to the wall. When it is nearly close enough to deploy, Celemrod unleashes a bolt from his ballista into the center of the tower. Although it does not topple, it is briefly knocked off balance, forcing the warriors pushing it to stop. The sorcerers blast the base of the tower with multiple fireballs, igniting the tower until it collapses on itself. The umbra warriors survey the scene and change course, heading around to the front of the fortress.

"Where are they going?" asks Ashisat.

"With the towers out of the way, they can't effectively climb up," says Alithyra. "Take out as many warriors as you can, but concentrate on destroying those catapults. They're the main threat right now."

Alithyra joins the archers in loosing another volley of arrows, felling a few dozen invaders. Ashisat and Koskru lead the melee fighters on the defense, cutting down any umbra warriors reaching the top and knocking over the ladders. The catapults fling another series of boulders. Two slam into the base of the wall, but the third boulder skims the top of the battlement, killing several defenders and barely missing Ashisat. Celemrod lines up his ballista and looses a bolt, destroying one of the catapults.

As Celemrod reloads, the umbra warriors operating the two remaining siege engines load more rocks into their catapults. One fires immediately, damaging the base of the wall. The siege engineers of the second catapult reposition it to face the ballista tower. Celemrod and the enemy catapult unleash their loads simultaneously. The ballista bolt slams into the base of the catapult, snapping the ropes and destroying the crank.

Celemrod approaches the ammunition pile to grab another bolt and sees the boulder flying toward him. "It looks like this is where I fall. I have no regrets." Celemrod closes his eyes in preparation for his demise. The boulder sails over his head and smashes the ballista.

Celemrod opens his eyes and looks around. He glances down at himself and sets his hands on several points of his body. "Perhaps not. The battle continues." Seeing that the impact destroyed the ballista, he runs down the battlement to rejoin the rest of the battle.

Alithyra approaches Celemrod. "Are you all right?"

"I'm fine. Unfortunately, the ballista has been destroyed."

Alithyra nods. "Hopefully the sorcerers can take care of that last catapult." She turns to Koskru. "Have the sorcerers concentrate on that last siege engine."

"Very well. I will relay the order." Koskru walks up the mage line. "All sorcerers, focus your attacks on that catapult!"

The sorcerers turn their attention to the catapult as it unleashes another boulder, which crashes into the wall with a loud crack. The mages point at the siege engine and then position their hands so that everyone's pointer fingers are touching. They chant in a language the rest of the defenders don't understand, and a bright glow forms around their fingers. The sorcerers step back, allowing space between their fingers, and the glow forms into a ball.

The energy increases in size as they continue chanting. When the energy ball is the size of a human head, the chant stops, and the mages release it in the direction of the siege engine. It collides with the catapult and explodes, incinerating the entire device and disintegrating any umbra warriors within ten feet. The remaining invaders pause and survey the scene. They abandon their attack on the west flank and run north toward the main gate.

"Excellent," says Alithyra. "Send a message to Pelagius and Hexeron that the west flank is clear. Ask if they need any reinforcements."

Chapter 77

Kevnan observes the wall of umbra warriors march toward his position. He firmly grasps the hilt of his sword and nervously adjusts its position on his belt. He turns to Raimdon, who stands nearby. "Any thoughts on what we should do first?"

Raimdon glances at him. "You're in charge of this flank, not me. You should make a decision."

"I'm an adventuring minstrel and storyteller, not a military commander," says Kevnan. "Why aren't you in command?"

"Because of King Bloodsworth's decree," says Raimdon. "If I were to take charge here, any Battallian spies could interpret that as the Diablosian military leading the defense, which Battallia would purposefully interpret as an act of war. As a simple volunteer recruited by Pelagius, I can assist in the defenses without provocation."

"Incoming!" shouts a nearby archer.

Kevnan and Raimdon duck behind the wall as a boulder sails over their heads. They glance over the battlement as the siege towers move forward and three more stones slam into the wall.

"Better figure something out quick," says Raimdon.

Kevnan looks around and notices Eeshlith on the corner loading a ballista. Turning his attention to the other side of his battlement, he sees an unmanned giant crossbow on a tower at the farthest end of the wall. "Send someone to operate that ballista. We can use that against the siege engines."

"You'll have to give the order," says Raimdon. "If I even relay a command, Battallia could use it against us."

Kevnan sighs. "Very well." He looks around and sees Sir Galzra directing the mages. "Sir Galzra, take some troops and get that ballista operational."

"I'm on it," says Galzra.

Sir Galzra motions to several others, runs the length of the wall, and loads the ballista. Several others follow, but a boulder crashes into a section of the battlement and plows through, killing several troops and leaving a large gap in the floor.

Kevnan turns the archers and mages. "Archers, fire at will. Sorcerers, target the nearest siege engine."

The archers loose a volley of arrows, felling a dozen umbra warriors. The mages fling a variety of spells at a nearby siege tower, damaging it, but not enough to halt its approach. A siege tower wheels closer to the southmost end of the wall. Galzra turns his ballista toward it and fires. The massive bolt slams into the tower, knocking it off balance and briefly stopping its advance. The umbra warriors pushing the siege tower manage to rebalance it and resume their approach. One umbra warrior motions to a nearby catapult, pointing at the ballista tower. The warriors operating that catapult reposition it and carefully adjust its aim.

Galzra turns to his helpers. "Reload. We need to take those things out." With help from the others, Galzra hoists up another ballista bolt and they race to lock it in place as the siege tower draws ever nearer. When the tower is almost next to the wall, Galzra turns the ballista in its direction and fires. The bolt slams into the tower at nearly point-blank range and the force of the impact causes the tower to topple over and slam into the ground.

Galzra sighs with relief. "Well done, everyone. That was too close."

The catapults unleash their boulders, two of which crash into the center of the wall. One boulder lands directly on top of the battlement, obliterating several archers and most of the mages attacking a siege tower. The final stone hurls toward the ballista tower. Galzra's eyes grow wide as he sees it approach.

"Run!" shouts Galzra.

A few of the troops manage to leap to the main battlement before impact. Before Galzra and two others can get to safety, the stone slams directly into the tower, smashing through the wall and going straight through. The impact destroys the ballista and collapses the top section of the tower, sending Galzra plummeting through the crumbling floor. The remains of the tower crumble and collapse under the weight of the boulder. Kevnan and Raimdon take in the sight in horror.

"That's bad," says Raimdon. "The loss of Galzra and his ballista crew, along with most of our mages, leaves us nearly defenseless against the siege engines."

A nearby mercenary approaches Kevnan. "Sir, the north flank is sending some mages over."

Kevnan nods. "Thank you. That will be somewhat helpful. Have them and the remaining other mages take out as many towers as they can. Instruct the surviving archers to target the umbra warriors pushing the towers."

The mercenary nods and rushes down the line. The archers peek over the battlement and take aim at the bases of the siege towers. They loose their arrows, felling most of the umbra warriors steering the large structures, bringing the towers to a halt. The surviving mages regroup with the new arrivals and target the most damaged tower with a multitude of different spells, destroying it. Any umbra warriors close to the siege towers break off from the advancing line and restart the towers' approach, but most are quickly picked off by the archers.

Kevnan grins as he observes the attempt to halt the towers. "Good. This appears to be working fairly well. With the towers stalled, we may not have to deal with any warriors making it up here."

"What about the catapults?" asks Raimdon.

Kevnan's smile fades as the catapults unleash another volley of boulders. The stones all slam into the wall in the same vicinity, causing the battlement to jolt and shake. The umbra warriors quickly reload and fire off another round, severely damaging the structure.

"We can't take much more of that," says Raimdon.

"Sorcerers, target the catapults!" shouts Kevnan.

Three of the catapults fling another volley of stones. Raimdon's eyes grow wide as they close in. "It may be too late."

Three of the stones slam into the wall, causing a massive crack to form between the already damaged sections. The fourth catapult unleashes its load. The massive boulder crashes into the center of the damaged wall and plows straight through, collapsing the battlement and leaving an enormous hole in the defenses. Kevnan and Raimdon leap to an undamaged section of the walkway just before the floor beneath them collapses. They turn to survey the damage.

"Sound the retreat," says Kevnan. "We must fall back."

Chapter 78

A large explosion rocks the battlefield as two more siege towers explode and collapse. Another volley of arrows slays a dozen more umbra warriors, but the line continues to advance. More boulders smash into the walls, dealing additional damage to the beleaguered structure. The defenders arming the ballistae fire off a pair of bolts, destroying two of the catapults.

"How is the west flank faring?" asks Hexeron.

"About the same as us," says Eeshlith. "All the siege towers on their side have been destroyed, but those catapults are still an issue."

"What of the east flank?" asks Hexeron.

"Their wall is taking a massive beating," says Eeshlith. "The siege towers are getting too close for comfort over there."

"Send some of our sorcerers to reinforce them," says Pelagius. "We can spare a few."

Hexeron relays the command and several mages rush to the east flank. As the hours drag on, the umbra warrior army continues to close in, and the siege engines do more and more damage to the walls. The ballistae continue loosing bolts, destroying a few catapults and damaging several siege towers until they topple over. A messenger approaches Hexeron and hands him a note.

"The west flank is clear," says Hexeron. "They want to know if we need their assistance."

"Good," says Pelagius. "Tell Alithyra to bring half of her remaining forces over here. The rest should stay there in case some of the army decides to try the west flank again."

As Pelagius turns his attention back to the battlefield, a single siege tower wheels right up to the wall.

"How did this one get through?" asks Pelagius.

"The sorcerers must have been concentrating on the others," says Hexeron.

"Everyone, to me!" commands Pelagius.

A large metal structure on the front of the siege tower folds down and forms a bridge onto the battlement as dozens of umbra warriors swarm out. A huge melee breaks out as the defenders rush to repel these invaders. As more enemies pour out of the siege tower, Eeshlith leaps into the nearest ballista and turns it to face the threat. Defenders and invaders fall in droves as she lines up her shot.

She unleashes the ballista bolt, which collides with the side of the enemy tower and sends it toppling to the ground, cutting off the remaining ground forces. Eeshlith then joins the fray with her whip-sword, cutting down umbra warriors in droves. As the defenders repel the invaders, the remaining siege engines unleash another volley of boulders, scattering the defenders as the stones slam into the side. Then, the trebuchet, which had apparently been undergoing repairs of some kind, unleashes a massive boulder.

"Everybody, brace for impact!" shouts Pelagius.

The stone slams into the outer gate, obliterating the gatehouse and nearly collapsing the barbican as it plows through and comes to a stop in the courtyard. Another crash from the east flank draws Hexeron's attention.

"The walls have been breached!" shouts Hexeron.

"Everyone fall back to the inner wall!" commands Pelagius. "Now, before we are overrun!"

Receiving the order, the remaining defenders climb down into the courtyard and make a mad dash to the inner gate as umbra warriors swarm through the openings. As Pelagius reaches the ground, he finds Delradi groggily rising out of a haystack.

"How are you alive?" asks Pelagius. "That fall should have killed you."

"I don't know," says Delradi unconvincingly. "Just lucky, I guess."

"It doesn't matter," says Pelagius. "Fall back."

Pelagius and Delradi join the other defenders in their retreat, rushing through the gate as quickly as possible. As the Green-Eyed Man and Garu arrive at the smashed outer wall, the inner gate slams shut.

"What do we do now?" asks Alithyra. "We are at a severe disadvantage now."

"Find Shukrat and Ralkgek," says Pelagius. "Tell them to gather the remaining sorcerers and prepare themselves."

Chapter 79

The Green-Eyed Man surveys the scene from the hole in the main gate. Noticing that the sun is beginning to set, he motions to the umbra warriors in the courtyard to fall back.

"What are you doing?" asks Alasdar, hiding in the shadows. "Victory is nearly ours."

"The sun is setting," says the Green-Eyed Man. "The defenders have held up inside the inner walls and, as such, have a tactical advantage over the courtyard when the sun goes down."

"So, you will resume the attack at dawn?" asks Alasdar.

"Of course," says the Green-Eyed Man. "In the meantime, the umbra warriors can salvage the remains of the siege towers and the destroyed catapults. We should be able to construct something from any usable parts."

The Green-Eyed Man summons his urn and opens the lid. Hundreds of blue beams erupt from within and draw in the souls of the fallen defenders.

"How many of the souls from the fallen umbra warriors can you recapture?" asks Alasdar.

"Maybe a quarter of them," says the Green-Eyed Man. "The earliest casualties will have already gone beyond my reach and moved to the afterlife."

"Get as many as you can," says Alasdar. "We will need to create more soldiers once this is over."

After stealing the souls of the dead defenders, the Green-Eyed Man concentrates for a moment until his urn glows. Several hundred more blue beams shoot out and wave around the courtyard and battlefield, pulling in any wayward souls they can find. Once the task is complete, the Green-Eyed Man closes the lid and dismisses his urn.

"Perhaps we could demoralize them more," says Alasdar.

"How so?" asks the Green-Eyed Man.

"Continue the assault with the remaining siege engines and destroy more of the outer wall," says Alasdar. "That should give them a sleepless night and allow for easier entry for your forces in the morning."

"Excellent idea," says the Green-Eyed Man. "We are laying siege, after all."

"Well, I shall be off then," says Alasdar.

"Where are you going?" asks the Green-Eyed Man.

"I'm returning to Devil's Den," says Alasdar. "You seem to have this battle well in hand. If something should go wrong, send Garu back with a message."

"Why me?" asks Garu.

"Because you're the one most likely to run away if the battle goes wrong anyway," says Alasdar. "Giving you that task will at least put your cowardice to use if the situation arises."

Alasdar opens a portal and steps through as the Green-Eyed Man returns to base camp to plan out his next move.

Chapter 80

As the sun rises, the defenders gather on the battlements and towers of the inner wall to survey the battlefield. More boulders lay strewn around the outside of the castle with several new holes in the front section of the wall. A few towers have collapsed, and the original two breaches have grown.

"This is a problem," says Kevnan with a yawn. "They can nearly stroll right into the courtyard."

"That's likely their goal," says Pelagius.

As the defenders take up their positions, a horn blast washes over the battlefield and the enemy forces advance. While the trebuchet remains in position, some of the catapults wheel closer to the castle.

"Archers, ready your bows!" orders Pelagius. "Sorcerers, stand by!"

As the horde closes in, the catapults unleash their loads and boulders sail into the courtyard and slam into the inner wall. As the front of the line comes within range, the archers unleash a volley of arrows, downing a few dozen umbra warriors. Enemy soldiers trickle into the outer courtyard. The archers eliminate many umbra warriors, but more pour in as the catapults continue launching boulders into the inner wall. As the day wears on, these assaults continue until the siege engines suddenly stop.

"Why did they stop firing?" asks Kevnan.

Several more umbra warriors slip through the gaps carrying ladders. Those that make it past the archers line their ladders against the inner wall. The umbra warriors scurry up the ladders as the defenders rush to repel them.

Although the defenders knock down a few ladders, they are set back up almost immediately, and several soldiers make it to the top of the battlements. The defenders immediately engage in combat, swords and other weapons bouncing off each other and shields as troops on both sides fall.

With the defenders distracted by the invaders, another group of umbra warriors enters the courtyard carrying a large log attached to a pair of chains and suspended from two mounted beams. They approach the gate and begin slamming the log against it.

"Someone, take out that battering ram!" orders Pelagius.

Freeing themselves from the melee, Eeshlith and Alithyra leap onto the towers flanking the gate and loose arrows at the ram operators. The defenders slay several warriors, but they are quickly replaced as more umbra warriors flood into the courtyard. As the gate splinters, the flood of incoming umbra warriors ceases and the Green-Eyed Man and Garu appear at the main gate. Repelling an attacker, Pelagius quickly surveys the scene.

"Get rid of those ladders!" shouts Pelagius. "Sorcerers, burn them down!"

A pair of sorcerers appear on the towers next to Eeshlith and Alithyra and unleash several fireballs, destroying the ladders and setting the battering ram ablaze. When the defenders repel the last of the invaders on the wall, Pelagius looks out over the battlefield. A sea of umbra warriors inhabits the courtyard, jostling against each other as they try to advance further. A few of them even attempt to scale the wall.

"It looks like the entire army is inside the courtyard," says Kevnan.

"They are," says Pelagius. "Everyone fall back to the keep!"

The defenders abandon their positions as they flee into the interior of the castle. Pelagius enters last, ensuring that everyone has made it inside. As the doors close, Pelagius turns to Shukrat.

"Shukrat, now," says Pelagius.

Chapter 81

As the defenders fall back, the umbra warriors attempt to scale the wall, and some bash at the damaged gate.

The Green-Eyed Man grins wickedly as he observes the chaos. "They have abandoned their attempts to defend the castle. The cowards are likely in the keep awaiting a pathetic last stand."

"It seems too easy," says Garu. "They fled before we could even break through."

"They knew their defeat was inevitable," says the Green-Eyed Man. "It was easy because we overwhelmed them with numbers."

The Green-Eyed Man steps forward, summons his urn, and begins to collect the souls of the fallen defenders, as well as recapturing any fallen umbra warriors he can. The umbra warriors continue bashing the gate, doing little damage, but slowly extending the cracks. A few of those attempting to scale the wall even manage to climb to the top. As the blue tendrils continue extending from the urn, Shukrat, Ralkgek, and several sorcerers teleport onto the tops of the towers surrounding the inner and outer courtyards and chant in a strange language. The Green-Eyed Man is too focused on his task to notice, but Garu realizes that something is not right.

"What are they doing?" asks Garu.

The Green-Eyed Man closes his urn and looks around as the sorcerers continue their ritual. As he observes, the mages simultaneously draw daggers and deeply slice their palms, allowing a stream of blood to fall to the ground.

"A blood magic ritual?" asks Garu.

The Green-Eyed Man nods. "I don't recognize it, but whatever they are planning, we need to put a stop to it." He launches a fireball at the nearest sorcerer, and it explodes on impact. "That's one down."

As the smoke clears, the sorcerer is still in position, a small bubble of light flickering around him.

"A shield spell," says the Green-Eyed Man. "They were prepared for magical attacks."

"Those shields can only take so many hits," says Garu. "Maybe you could bring it down with a few more."

"Not fast enough to stop all of them. This calls for a different approach." The Green-Eyed Man turns his gaze to the umbra warriors still attacking the inner gate. "Forget the gate! Get to the top of the wall and eliminate those sorcerers!"

The umbra warriors on the wall rush toward the nearest sorcerer, while the ones on the ground scatter to the walls, desperately trying to scale them in any way they can. As the umbra warriors attempt to slay their chosen sorcerer, the ground in the courtyards and the battlements atop the walls glow a faint red. Garu and the Green-Eyed Man eye the floor nervously as the glow increases in intensity.

A look of horror crosses the Green-Eyed Man's face, and he flees toward the gate. "Everybody, fall back!"

Garu quickly retreats, passing the Green-Eyed Man and rushing out of the fortress. The umbra warriors pause briefly and abandon their attack as they scramble toward the main gate. The normally unflappable minions seem to be in a near panic as they stumble over one another in their attempt to escape. As the red glow reaches its full intensity, it flashes and pulses until the sorcerers vanish. The Green-Eyed Man leaps through the main gate as a massive blast of magical energy explodes, engulfing both courtyards and the walls in its maelstrom.

Chapter 82

As the smoke clears, Garu and the Green-Eyed Man peek through the gateway. Although the structures are still standing, not one umbra warrior remains. The Green-Eyed Man panics as he rushes into the middle of the outer courtyard and desperately tries to recapture the fallen umbra warriors.

"We should retreat," says Garu, remaining outside the wall. "They wiped out our entire army."

"That was a suicide attack," says the Green-Eyed Man. "They decided to take us down with them."

"Then why isn't your urn collecting more souls?" asks Garu.

Pelagius appears on the battlement. "Because we were protected from that blast."

Garu shrinks back as the defenders reappear atop the battlements of both the inner and outer walls, surrounding the courtyard. The Green-Eyed Man looks around nervously as he slowly places the lid back on his urn. Before he can dismiss it, Alithyra looses an arrow into his thigh. The Green-Eyed Man cries out in pain and drops his urn as he falls to the side. Alithyra fires another arrow at the urn, but it bounces off harmlessly and knocks it several feet away from the Green-Eyed Man. He wrenches the arrow from his thigh and crawls toward his urn as Eeshlith appears on a nearby tower and turns a ballista to the inside. The Green-Eyed Man nearly reaches his urn when Aldtaw comes through the gate wielding an arbalest, a large metal crossbow with a crank.

He fires off a metal bolt, impaling the Green-Eyed Man through the leg and pinning him to the ground. Roaring in pain, the Green-Eyed Man begins the long process of freeing himself from the bolt.

"Face it, old friend," says Aldtaw bitterly as he cranks to reload. "You've lost. We set a trap and you fell right into it."

Several defenders emerge from the gate and surround the Green-Eyed Man as slowly he rises to his feet.

"It's not over yet, Aldtaw," says the Green-Eyed Man.

"It is for you," says Aldtaw.

Aldtaw raises the arbalest and aims at the Green-Eyed Man. At the last second, he shifts his aim and fires the bolt in a different direction. The Green-Eyed Man watches in horror as the bolt slams into his urn, shattering it in a magical explosion that sends him and several defenders flying into the nearest wall. Magical energy envelops Aldtaw and Eeshlith, and they grasp their heads in pain.

"What have you done?" asks the Green-Eyed Man.

"We're sorry, Mabon," says Eeshlith. "You brought this on yourself."

As the souls flee the remains of the urn, one stays in the courtyard as it hovers above the ground. It takes shape, with several chains forming in the air like tendrils. Morat appears and Garu flees the battle, disappearing through a portal. Fully formed, the malevolent specter shrieks in fury and rips into the surrounding defenders as it slowly walks toward Mabon, who fearfully presses himself to the wall.

"Now you get what you deserve," says Aldtaw venomously.

As Morat closes in on the former soul hunter, it hooks its chains into his shoulders, causing him to cry out in pain. Aldtaw watches coldly while Eeshilth looks on in horror.

"Not like this," says Eeshlith.

Eeshlith aims the ballista in Morat's direction and fires. The massive bolt easily penetrates the chains and slams into Morat's back, sending him flying into the wall and pinning him in place. Mabon limps to the side out of range of Morat's chains as the specter flails in an attempt to free itself.

Eeshlith quickly reloads the ballista and fires another bolt. She scores a direct hit to Morat's head, obliterating it. The chains go slack, and Morat's form evaporates in a cloud of blue mist. As Mabon struggles to his feet, Aldtaw approaches and jams the arbalest into his chest.

"I surrender," says Mabon.

Aldtaw presses the arbalest harder into his chest, vengeance burning in his eyes. "No you don't. Now, you pay for your crimes."

Before Aldtaw can pull the trigger, Pelagius appears and pushes the large crossbow down.

"He will pay for his crimes, but not like that," says Pelagius.

"He stole years of my life from me," says Aldtaw. "And now, I'm old and losing my memories."

"Are you?" asks Mabon. "Now that my urn has been destroyed, think back."

Aldtaw closes his eyes and concentrates for a moment. "I don't understand. I remember everything."

"Your memory loss and rapid aging were part of a contingency spell I placed on you, along with your immortality," says Mabon. "Now that my urn has been destroyed, all spells upon you and Eeshlith have been lifted."

"I still have aged nearly sixty years in a matter of months," says Aldtaw. "I shall be dead within the month."

"Actually, you've only aged forty," says Mabon. "The rapid aging just made it feel like you were reaching the end."

"For a canin, forty is a lot," says Aldtaw. "Will the destruction of the urn reverse the aging?"

"No, but it will halt it," says Mabon. "You could also use the power remaining in the largest shard to reverse some of the aging."

"I'll consider it," says Aldtaw. "But don't think for a moment that I trust you."

As the conversation continues, King Demonicus emerges from the castle. "Well done, Pelagius. Victory is yours. Your sentence is now complete. In a few days, once we have buried the dead, we can send a small contingent to Devil's Den to arrest Alasdar."

Demonicus turns to Mabon. "So, you are the Green-Eyed Man. You will be put on trial for your crimes. Guards, take him away."

Captain Mughan and several guards place Mabon in chains and clasp mage restrainers on his wrists. As they escort him inside, Mabon turns to Kevnan, who had been observing from the doorway.

"I have a request," says Mabon. "When you have the time, please come see me in the dungeon."

Mabon disappears into the castle as Kevnan ponders his request.

Chapter 83

Garu stumbles through the portal just outside of Devil's Den's main gate. He runs up to the door and starts pounding on it.

"Open the gate!" shouts Garu, clearly in a panic.

Charndergh and Yilrig peer over the wall.

"Fetch the master," says Charndergh.

"We will fetch him at once, sir," says Yilrig.

Yilrig vanishes from view as Charndergh looks down upon the panicking Garu. After a few moments, he signals to the guards to open the gate. As the gate opens, Garu rushes through and nearly slams right into Alasdar.

"What happened?" asks Alasdar, already looking angry.

"My Lord, I once again bring ill news," says Garu. "The battle has been lost."

A look of rage crosses Alasdar's face, causing Charndergh and Yilrig to nervously back away.

Alasdar walks right up to Garu "How? The battle was going so well."

"They set a trap, sire," says Garu. "We never stood a chance."

Alasdar begins to seethe with rage before suddenly calming down. "Come with me, Garu. No need to demoralize the remaining troops with the full report."

Garu follows Alasdar to the throne room, with Charndergh closing the doors behind them. Alasdar turns to Garu, enraged. "You and the Green-Eyed Man had that battle won! Tell me exactly what happened after I left!"

Garu recounts the events of the disastrous battle. Alasdar remains silent as the tale concludes.

"So, not only did my army get annihilated in one move, I am now out of soul hunters," says Alasdar.

"Unfortunately, that is the case, sir," says Garu.

"And you fled like a coward," says Alasdar.

"Your orders were for me to report back if something went wrong," says Garu.

"I wasn't expecting you two to completely bungle this!" shouts Alasdar. "You are completely useless, you sniveling worm."

Fear crosses Garu's face as Alasdar aggressively approaches, and he flees to the doors. He slams into the doors and pushes with all his might, but they won't budge, indicating that Charndergh has locked him in. Garu glances back and watches as Alasdar approaches. The soulborn's flesh squirms and roils as he slowly walks toward his terrified minion.

Alasdar grows to about twelve feet in height, but his skin does not grow with him and shreds from his body. His exposed muscles bulk up significantly, becoming twice as large as the muscles of a troll. Razor sharp claws sprout from his hands and feet, and his teeth become jagged and blade-like. Hundreds of tendrils composed of blood vessels and tendons extend in varying lengths from his body. Attached to each tendril is a face, each of which is of a completely different individual. Some are male, some are female, and they are of many different species. Alasdar's own face hovers just above his freshly-flayed head.

Garu drops to his knees. "No, please. Give me one more chance. I can still be useful. I swear."

"That was your last chance," says Alasdar in a deep gravelly voice. "Farewell, Garu."

Several new tendrils sprout from Alasdar's body and shoot forward. They entangle Garu, wrapping around his arms, legs, and feet, and drag him toward Alasdar. As Alasdar draws Garu in, the faces surround him and he screams in terror. Pulling him up against his own body, Alasdar looks into his fear-filled eyes and grins malevolently.

Another tendril wraps around the base of Garu's skull and extends up the back of his head. This tendril rapidly moves back and forth, cutting a deep incision into Garu's flesh as he shrieks in pain. The tendril withdraws and Alasdar laughs as he grabs onto Garu's flesh and pulls the skin off his head, as though removing a mask. The tendril returns and attaches itself to the back of the skin as Alasdar releases his grasp. The skinned face joins the others in the ocean of swirling flesh that surrounds Alasdar's body.

Garu opens his mouth and emits a strangled scream of agony as the tendrils already entangling him saw into his flesh. More tendrils appear and snake their way into the wounds and force themselves into his nose and ear holes. His skin roils with the tendrils moving around underneath, apparently wrapping around his bones.

Then, the tendrils go taut and rapidly pull in all directions. Garu screams as the tendrils rip him to pieces, his shriek ending abruptly as they tear his head into four chunks. The tendrils, including the ones with faces attached, withdraw into Alasdar's body and he shrinks down to his normal size. As his own face slips back onto his head, his skin reappears. Alasdar returns to the throne and takes a seat.

"General Charndergh, enter," says Alasdar.

Charndergh opens the doors and approaches the throne, carefully bypassing the mess on the floor. "What do you wish, My Lord?"

"Mobilize our remaining troops on the battlements," says Alasdar. "After my failed insurrection, we can likely expect some sort of retaliation."

"I will carry out your orders immediately," says Charndergh.

General Charndergh exits the throne room as Alasdar seethes over these recent events.

Chapter 84

Mabon sits in his cell slumped against the wall. The wounds are heavily bandaged, his wrists still bound by the mage restrainers, and his hair has become disheveled. After several minutes, Eeshlith enters the dungeon accompanied by Captain Mughan. He escorts her to a nearby cell and she steps in willingly, the captain closing the door behind her. Mabon watches curiously as Mughan departs.

"Why are you in here?" asks Mabon.

"I have committed the same crimes as you," says Eeshlith. "I turned myself in."

"You could have escaped in the aftermath of the battle," says Mabon. "Instead, you have condemned yourself. They will most likely execute us both."

"Since I helped defend against your attack, I may be shown some leniency," says Eeshlith. "I do not deserve it, considering all the horrible things I have done in your service, but unlike you, I am at least attempting to redeem myself."

"There is no redemption for me," says Mabon. "Despite the destruction of my urn lifting the hold Babu had over me, nothing has changed. My personality has been warped beyond repair."

"So, you're not even going to try?" asks Eeshlith. "You truly regret nothing?"

Mabon thinks for a moment. "What could I possibly do from in here? It is far too late for me. As for regrets, I am beginning to have a few."

"What are you going to do about these few regrets?" asks Eeshlith.

"I don't know," says Mabon. "If Aldtaw is willing to take me up on my offer, I will reverse some of the rapid aging as promised. That is about all I can do."

"There must be something else," says Eeshlith. "You have to do something to make up for some of the atrocities you have committed."

"I don't have to do anything," says Mabon. "There is nothing else I can do. At least not for redemption. Perhaps there is one thing. Something that will allow people to understand my motivations for swearing service to Babu."

"What might that be?" asks Eeshlith.

"That is the reason I asked Kevnan to come down for a visit," says Mabon. "I believe that it is time for the story of the Green-Eyed Man to be revealed to the world."

Chapter 85

Aldtaw sits on the edge of a bed, staring intently at a large shard of Mabon's urn. Pelagius enters followed by a few of the others. Kevnan notices the old canin and sits close by.

"Something on your mind?" asks Kevnan.

"I'm considering Mabon's offer," says Aldtaw. "If it is possible to get back some of the years he stole, then I should probably do it. However, I have no idea if this is just another trick."

"I personally don't trust him," says Kevnan. "However, he seems to have nothing to gain from tricking you."

Aldtaw looks up at Kevnan. "What of his request to you? Why do you think he wants to see you?"

"I'm curious about that myself," says Kevnan.

"I would advise against granting his request unless he can give you a good reason to do so," says Aldtaw. "It's up to you, of course, but I see no reason why you should oblige him."

"Very well," says Kevnan. "For now, I shall not go down there. What about you?"

Aldtaw rises to his feet. "Truthfully, I have nothing to lose. If what he says is true, I can get some of my life back. If he's lying, he likely doesn't have much longer to live either."

Aldtaw leaves the room and walks across the castle grounds. Entering the dungeon, he is stopped by the guards, crossing their halberds in front of him.

Aldtaw peeks through the weapons and sees Mughan inspecting the cells. "Is there a reason I'm not allowed in, Captain?"

Leaving their barrier in place, the guards turn to their commander. Mughan looks at Aldtaw and motions to the guards to admit him. "Let him through."

The guards withdraw their weapons and step aside. Aldtaw enters the dungeon and approaches Mabon's cell. Mabon does not immediately acknowledge him, but Eeshlith glances up, surprised to see him.

"How does this work?" asks Aldtaw.

Mabon looks over at him. "What?"

Aldtaw holds up the shard. "Reversing the aging. You said you could do it with the largest shard of the urn."

Mabon raises his hands, showing Aldtaw the mage restrainers on his wrists. "I can't do anything. These special irons prevent me from performing magic."

Aldtaw turns away. "Then you were lying."

Mabon stands up and grabs the bars. "Wait. I can't do it, but it can still be done. You must be the one to perform the task."

"How?" asks Aldtaw. "I'm not a magic user."

"Place the shard against your chest."

Aldtaw warily follows his instructions.

"Now, close your eyes and concentrate."

Aldtaw shuts his eyes and begins to concentrate. After a few minutes, the shard glows blue. The glow spreads from the shard and envelops Aldtaw's body. As the glow intensifies, Aldtaw's aging reverses and he rapidly grows younger. After a few minutes, the glow fades, and the shard crumbles into dust. Aldtaw opens his eyes and looks himself over.

"I'm not fully back to the age I was when you imprisoned me, but it's a start," says Aldtaw.

"Roughly twenty years of the rapid aging has been undone," says Mabon.

"If I find another large shard, can I undo the rest?" asks Aldtaw.

"I'm afraid not," says Mabon. "That piece held the last of the urn's power. That is all I can do."

"Very well," says Aldtaw. "Goodbye, Mabon."

Aldtaw leaves the dungeon and Mabon sinks back onto his cot.

Chapter 86

Adotiln meditates in her chamber in Grimadert's castle. As she continues, the ghostly image of Bojan appears in her room. Realizing that she is in the middle of something, he simply waits for her to finish. A few minutes later, she opens her eyes and, failing to notice the spectral image, goes to the other side of the room to retrieve a book.

"Adotiln," says Ghost Bojan.

Startled, Adotiln turns around. Her eyes grow wide when she sees who it is. Adotiln drops her book. "Bojan? Why are you here?"

"I am the reaper that has been assigned to you," says Ghost Bojan.

"Why are you a reaper?" asks Adotiln. "You shouldn't have owed Rasthor anything upon your death."

"I obtained my debt after death," says Ghost Bojan. "Something happened that I am going to need your help with."

"What do you need?" asks Adotiln.

"All in good time," says Ghost Bojan. "The task is something that cannot be completed at this time."

"Can't you tell me?" asks Adotiln.

"Not at this time," says Ghost Bojan. "I am under specific orders not to give you that information until the time is right."

"So, why reveal yourself to me?" ask Adotiln.

"I have your first assignment," says Ghost Bojan. "We must be off. I can brief you on the way."

"Very well," says Adotiln. "I'll see if Grimadert will let me leave, and then say goodbye to Iriemorel and Thakszut. You may want to stay out of sight."

"Only you can see me unless I fully manifest," says Ghost Bojan.

Adotiln packs up a few provisions and leaves her room. Traversing through the castle, she finds Grimadert and his assistants in the main laboratory. Thakszut lies on the table, as they appear to be working on him for some reason, and Iriemorel stands close by.

"What are you doing?" inquires Adotiln.

"Implanting a special amulet into his chest," says Grimadert. "Until it runs out of power, it should act as a nullifier that prevents his Demonic Potential from activating. If he needs it, he can turn the knob to lower the nullifier's power. Be silent now. This is a very delicate operation."

Several minutes pass as Grimadert continues to tinker. After a while, he finally finishes and turns to Adotiln.

"Now, what can I help you with?" asks Grimadert.

"I know you wanted me to rest and recover, but something has come up," says Adotiln. "I must go."

"Very well," says Grimadert. "Off you go."

"Really?" asks Adotiln, surprised.

"Your body is now strong enough to withstand life outside these walls," says Grimadert. "You are free to go. These two still need a few more days to recover, though."

Thakszut sits up as Adotiln approaches.

"You can track me down later if you wish," says Adotiln. "But you do not have the debt that I do."

"I think Pelagius is expecting to see me anyway," says Thakszut. "Have safe trip."

Adotiln grins. "No guarantees." She approaches Iriemorel. "Farewell, my friend."

"Farewell, Adotiln," says Iriemorel. "It is good to see you alive again."

"It would probably be best if neither of you mentioned my revival to Pelagius," says Adotiln. "He would likely try to storm the castle."

Iriemorel chuckles. "Agreed. Not a word shall be mentioned."

"Thank you. Good luck with your new body."

Adotiln exits the laboratory and Rogi and Giro escort her to the main gate. As the gates close behind her, she turns to the ghostly image of Bojan.

"Where are we going?" asks Adotiln.

"We're headed to the ruins of Ethor," says Ghost Bojan.

Adotiln's eyes widen, and her mouth opens. "Ruins? What happened to Ethor?"

"I'll explain on the way," says Ghost Bojan. "Suffice to say, a few angry hauntings are hanging around. We must retrieve those souls."

Adotiln and Ghost Bojan begin their trek down the road, heading for the town.

Chapter 87

Several days later, a contingent of thirty guards, led by Captain Mughan, arrives at the gates of Devil's Den. Mughan knocks on the main gate and Commander Yilrig peeks out from the gatehouse.

"What is it?" asks Yilrig.

"I am Captain Mughan, leader of the royal guard. We are here for your master."

Charndergh appears above the gatehouse. "Is that so? This is a very bold move. We still have one thousand troops here and there are only thirty of you."

"We are not here for a battle," says Mughan. "We could easily outnumber your forces if we wanted to lay siege. Tell Alasdar to surrender immediately or we will be forced to attack."

Charndergh looks at Commander Yilrg. "Let's play their game for now. Go get the master."

"We will obey, sir," says Yilrig.

The umbra warlord departs and Charndergh turns back to the guards.

"He'll be out shortly," says Charndergh.

"Very well," says Mughan. "We will wait."

Yilrig walks down the hall and enters the throne room. Alasdar sits on the throne, still seething over his loss. "What do you want, Captain?"

"Sire, Captain Mughan and several guards have just arrived at the gate," says Yilrig. "They have demanded your surrender."

"Oh, have they now?" says Alasdar. "Well, I'm not in the mood to surrender today. Tell them to come back tomorrow and maybe I'll consider it."

"We do not believe that they will take that as an answer," says Yilrig. "They even threatened to lay siege with a larger force if you do not comply."

Alasdar throws his head back and emits an exasperated sigh. "Umbra warlords. Even gaining sentience, they still have no concept of sarcasm."

"My Lord?" inquires Yilrig.

"Never mind," says Alasdar. "Return to the main gate and invite them in. Tell them to come to me if they wish me to surrender."

"As you wish, Master," says Yilrig.

Yilrig exits the throne room and heads back to the gatehouse. He finds Charndergh still arguing with Mughan.

"If you do not open this gate immediately, we will have no choice but to report your noncompliance to the king," threatens Mughan.

Yilrig approaches Charndergh. "The master wishes for them to come to the throne room to discuss terms."

Charndergh nods and turns back to Mughan. "We will open the gates, Captain. Alasdar wishes to negotiate in the throne room."

Mughan snorts in frustration and stamps a hoof as the gates open. The thirty guards enter Devil's Den and Charndergh and Yilrig escort them to the throne room.

Alasdar sits on his throne, waiting for their arrival. "General, Commander, return to your posts and await further orders."

Charndergh and Yilrig bow and exit the throne room. Alasdar turns his attention to Mughan. "Welcome, Captain Mughan. To what do I owe the pleasure?"

"There is no pleasure for you," says Mughan. "We are here to arrest you for treason. Surrender now."

"What are the conditions of my surrender?" asks Alasdar. "Surely we can be civil about this."

"There are no conditions," says Mughan. "Either surrender now or the fortress will be taken back by force. Our forces now outnumber yours, so I do not believe a siege would be in your interests."

Alasdar thinks for a moment and steps down from the throne. "It would seem you have me at a disadvantage. You win, Captain. I surrender."

Alasdar extends his arms forward and the guards immediately clap him in irons, complete with a pair of mage restrainers on his wrists.

"I appreciate the cooperation," says Mughan. "We shall be off."

Aladsar forces back a smile and scowls as the guards lead him away.

Chapter 88

Pelagius sits at a table in the grand hall, munching on a large turkey leg. Kevnan and Alithyra enter the room and sit next to him.

"We've been looking for you," says Kevnan. "I thought you'd be in your chamber getting ready for the journey home."

Pelagius lowers the turkey leg and swallows. "I can't leave yet."

Alithyra grabs a nearby loaf of bread and sniffs it. "Why not? We're not prisoners anymore."

Pelagius nods. "We're not, but I believe that I should remain here and help repair and rebuild. This battle would not have happened if not for me."

Ralkgek enters the room, carrying a sack on his back. "I thought I heard you in here. Is everyone ready to go?"

"As I was telling Kevnan and Alithyra, I'm not leaving yet," says Pelagius. "There is still more I feel obligated to do."

Alithyra looks over at Ralkgek. "I see you're ready to depart."

Ralkgek nods. "Babu is dead, Alasdar's forces have been defeated, and he is soon to be arrested. The threat is over."

"So, you're leaving immediately?" asks Kevnan.

"Yes," says Ralkgek. "If I leave now, I should make it across the border and to the closest town in Necrotia before nightfall."

"Why not stay and help rebuild?" asks Pelagius. "I plan to do so, and so do most of the other defenders."

"I've done my part," says Ralkgek. "This is something I feel I must do, same as your need to stay."

Pelagius sets down his turkey leg, stands, and approaches Ralkgek. He grabs Ralkgek's arm and the two shake hands. "Then good luck to you, Ralkgek."

"Same to you, Pelagius."

Ralkgek turns and leaves the room. Pelagius returns to the table and takes another bite of his snack. "You two can depart for home whenever you wish. Our quest is at an end."

Alithyra shakes her head. "If you're staying, then so am I."

Kevnan nods in agreement. "I'm in no hurry to get back. Helping here will probably improve relations with King Demonicus as well."

Pelagius smiles. "Indeed, it will. I'll be happy to have your help too, my friends."

"Should we start now?" asks Alithyra.

Pelagius finishes his turkey leg. "I believe the castle staff plans to start clearing the rubble tomorrow, but I'm sure the king would appreciate it if we got a head start. Let's start clearing some rubble."

About the Author

Eric Balch was born and raised in Texas and attained a Bachelor's degree from Texas Christian University. He went on to co-own a successful business making and selling dog treats and dog food, but that business was sold years ago.

Eric has been writing for many years now, but it was only recently that he completed his first book. He hopes that the success of it will inspire him to greater efforts and more exciting titles in the future.

In his free time, Eric likes to read, watch movies and play video games. One of his passions is for cooking and he loves spending time creating great food in the kitchen. Halloween is one of his favorite times of the year and he enjoy nothing more than preparing his house for Trick or Treaters. His yard haunt, Deadman Manor, is popular with both the kids and parents alike and many of his neighbors look forward to the annual home horror

Eric married is wife Jenn on Friday November 13, 2020 in a literary themed wedding. He and his wife still live in Texas today with their 2 dogs: a Havanese named Merlin and Jack Russell Terrier, Kerry. He is looking forward to continuing to write stories that will appeal to as many as possible. He primarily writes fantasy novels.

You can follow Eric Balch on

Facebook - https://www.facebook.com/ericbalchauthor/

Website: https://ericbalch.com

Goodreads: https://www.goodreads.com/author/dashboard?ref=nav_profile_authordash

Twitter: @EricBalch4

Instagram: https://www.instagram.com/ericbalchauthor

Tumblr: https://www.tumblr.com/blog/ericbalchauthor

Pintrest: @Halloweenman33

Made in the USA
Coppell, TX
17 March 2022